FALL SE

Christopher Mitchell is the author of the The Magelands and Masters & Makers fantasy series. He studied in Edinburgh before living for several years in the Middle East and Greece, where he taught English. He returned to study classics and Greek tragedy and lives in Fife, Scotland with his wife and their four children.

By Christopher Mitchell

The Magelands Origins

Retreat of the Kell
The Trials of Daphne Holdfast
From the Ashes

The Magelands Epic

The Queen's Executioner
The Severed City
Needs of the Empire
Sacrifice
Fragile Empire
Storm Mage
Soulwitch Rises
Renegade Gods

The Magelands Eternal Siege

The Mortal Blade
The Dragon's Blade
The Prince's Blade
Falls of Iron
Paths of Fire
Gates of Ruin
City of Salve
Red City

City Ascendant
Dragon Eyre Badblood
Dragon Eyre Ashfall
Dragon Eyre Blackrose
Dreams of Kell
God Restrainer
Holdfast Imperium
World's End

The Magelands Dominion

Serpent Dominion
Demon Witch
Death Seer
Blood Burden
Kin Strife
Tempest's Edge
Creator of Worlds

Masters and Makers

Fall Seldom Kings
The Making of Abigone

Brigdomin Books Ltd
First Edition, May 2024
ISBN 978-1-915978-39-4

ACKNOWLEDGEMENTS

I would like to thank the following for all their support during the writing of Masters & Makers - my wife, Lisa Mitchell, who read every chapter as soon as it was drafted and kept me going in the right direction; my parents for their unstinting support; Marilyn Hopwood for reading the books in their early stages; James Aitken for his encouragement; and Grant and Gordon of the Film Club for their support.

Thanks also to my Advance Reader team, for all your help during the last few weeks before publication.

THE WORLD OF THE MASTERS & MAKERS

Upper Down – A small mountain realm between the old Northern Provinces and the old Central Provinces of the Elestian Empire. Historically part of the Duchy of Down, it gained independence with the collapse of the Elestian Empire, splitting away from what became the kingdoms of **Greater Down** and **Lesser Down**. Upper Down sits astride one of only three passes through the mountains, but its most significant attribute is that it remains the last realm still governed by Masters and Makers.

The Elestian Empire – Sometimes referred to as **The First Empire**, the Elestians governed vast tracts of the continent for almost a thousand years. Ruled by an elite aristocracy of Masters and Makers, it eventually collapsed after prolonged rebellions and uprisings. Its collapse led to widespread massacres of Masters and Makers, reducing their numbers until few were left alive. The old calendar system ended upon the death of the last Emperor, and the years are now dated from this momentous event. ***Fall Seldom Kings*** begins in Year 107, i.e. one hundred and seven years since the fall of the Elestian Empire.

The Sanctian Empire – Centred around the island of Sanctos, the Sanctian Empire arose from the ashes of the Elestian Empire. Sometimes referred to as **The Second Empire**, the Sanctians have been re-conquering many of the old provinces, and re-uniting them under its rule. The Sanctian Emperor views Masters and Makers as wicked and blasphemous, and he has pledged to hunt down and execute the last remaining survivors.

The Westlanders – Hailing originally from the great plains to the west of the old Northern Provinces, the Westlanders swept through those provinces following the collapse of the Elestian Empire. Seen as a primitive, violent people by the citizens of the old Central Provinces, the Westlanders are mistrusted and feared. Known for their worship of the three moons as much as for their raiding and brigandage, the Westlanders are unrivalled in warfare.

Masters – Men who possess the ability to transmute elements.

Makers – Women who possess the ability to summon objects.

DRAMATIS PERSONAE

Upper Down

King Alfgang IV the Great, King of Upper Down

Prince Alfgang the Pius, Heir to the throne of Upper Down

Princess Kilbride, Eldest Daughter of King Alfgang IV

Princess Abigone, Youngest Daughter of King Alfgang IV

Princess Frida, Wife of Prince Alfgang the Pius

Prince Alfgang (Alfie), Son of Prince Alfgang the Pius (7)

Duke Hector, Duke of Ridden, Frida's brother

Lord Walter, King's Champion and brother of Hector and Frida

Duchess Perpetua, Wife of Duke Hector

Lothar, Commander in Mountain Rangers

Marie, Lady-in-Waiting to Princess Kilbride

Ireni, Duke Hector's Mistress

Joachim, Captain in the Royal Guard

Towie, Sergeant in the Royal Guard

Princess Nolan, Middle Daughter of King Alfgang IV (in Lesser Down)

Lord Rupert, Son of Duke Hector (8)

Lord Artur, Son of Duke Hector (6)

Westlanders

Stefan, Chief and Ally to King Alfgang IV

Dravid, Chief and Ally to King Alfgang IV

Gorgan, Chief and friend of Stefan

Rymont, Chief and friend of Dravid

Sanctians

Princess Hygilt, Great-Niece of Emperor Antonio

Prince Valentino, Brother of Emperor Antonio

Count Sebastian, Nephew of Emperor Antonio

Others

Amery of Yearl, Duke Hector's Lawyer

The World of Masters & Makers
The Westlands
Northern Provinces
Desert
Upper Down
Klef Mordain
Lesser Down
Esttal
Greater Down
Campsie
Anster
Guran
Central Provinces
Jallin
Yearl
Elestia
Osbruek
Mylos
Anster
Dibain
Aubruk
Subnestia
Nessos
The Thousand Lakes
Sanctos
Geathan
Western Colonies
Ocean
Ocean
Southern Provinces
N
W
E
S
Road
Town
Ocean

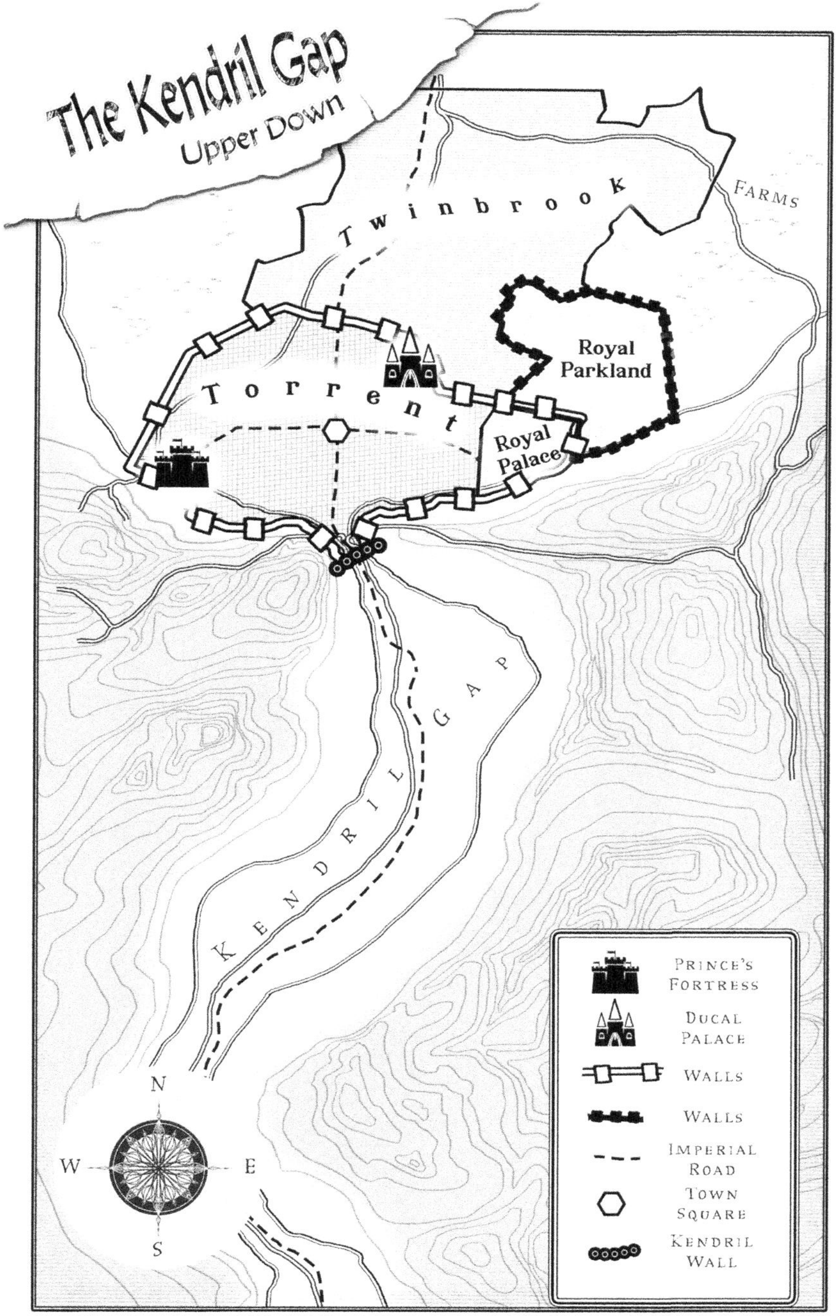

The Kendril Gap
Upper Down
Twinbrook
Farms
Royal Parkland
Torrent
Royal Palace
Kendril Gap
N
W
E
S
Prince's Fortress
Ducal Palace
Walls
Walls
Imperial Road
Town Square
Kendril Wall

CHAPTER 1
THE WIDOW

Torrent, Upper Down – 8th Day of Lamenta 107

'I would rather cut the girl's throat,' said the king, 'than give her to those from whom she fled.'

Princess Kilbride watched her father from the shadows of the colonnaded audience chamber. The sun was streaming through the gaps between the columns, and the two imperial envoys were bathed in the light, their eyes on the old king of Upper Down.

'Your Majesty,' said one of the envoys, 'need we remind you that this girl, as you call her, is Her Highness Princess Hygilt, the grand niece of the Most Exalted Emperor Antonio? We are under orders to demand that you release her from custody.'

King Alfgang laughed. 'Custody? You speak as though you believe Hygilt were my prisoner, when, in truth, she came to my royal court to escape the cruelty of the imperial household.'

'If that is the case, Your Majesty,' said the envoy, 'then we ask that we be allowed to talk to her in private.'

'And if I refuse?'

'Then, Your Majesty, we have been instructed to deliver this warning – that if you do not surrender Princess Hygilt to us, the armed forces under the command of the Most Illustrious Prince Valentino shall invade your lands of Upper Down.'

The tall Westlander chiefs laughed. The old king smiled at his allies, then turned his gaze back to the two envoys.

'Your threats are nought but chaff in the wind,' the king said. 'Upper Down is impregnable. Prince Valentino's army will crash upon the Kendril Wall like waves upon the rocky shore, and I shall observe their destruction from the battlements.'

'We have two further demands, Your Majesty,' said an envoy.

'I am in a generous mood,' said the king. 'Let us hear what else the noble emperor desires.'

'All Westlander brigands are to leave the territory of Upper Down immediately,' said the envoy. 'For too long you have allowed them to raid the lands to the south of your realm, offering them protection and refuge; and secondly, you are to re-open the Kendril Wall to allow merchants and travellers safe passage through the mountains.'

'Now we get to the nub of it,' said the king. 'The presence of Princess Hygilt within this realm was merely the excuse; what you in fact seek is the hobbling of my kingdom. Upper Down is a sovereign nation, and we do not take orders from a foreign empire.'

'Are you formally refusing these demands, Your Majesty?'

The old king said nothing for a moment, as the air in the colonnaded hall stilled. Princess Kilbride kept her silence as she watched the gathered crowd of advisers, mercenary chiefs, and the members of the royal household exchange glances. On her right, Prince Alfgang, the son and heir to the throne of Upper Down, was wearing an expression that bordered on fury; and Kilbride knew that his anger was directed not at the imperial envoys, but at their father the king.

'I have an answer for you,' said the king; 'an answer that even the slow-witted Valentino should be able to understand.' He raised his left hand, and the two envoys cowered back a pace. 'Ever-living and blessed spirits,' the king went on, 'I call upon your power. Take the water from these men, and in its place give them salt.'

The two envoys screamed, but their voices cut short as they fell to the marble floor. They writhed for a moment, then lay still. Salt issued from their eyes, nostrils and mouths, crusting over their features, and a thin white film spread across their exposed skin.

'I must protest, father!' cried Prince Alfgang. 'Those men came here as emissaries.'

'They came here to threaten us, son,' said the king. 'Still your temper.'

'You bring shame upon our kingdom,' said the prince. 'Who will wish to treat with us now? You have indelibly tarnished the reputation of this realm.'

The king glanced around the audience hall. 'Is this appeaser truly my son and heir?' His gaze caught upon Kilbride, the only other child of the king present. 'What say you, daughter? Do you agree with your brother's assessment?'

Kilbride bowed her head. 'You are the king, my lord and father. I obey your commands.'

King Alfgang laughed. 'A wise response. Perhaps you should be my heir.' He turned to the Duke of Ridden, who was standing to the right of the throne. 'Hector, have your men escort the envoys to the battlements of the Kendril Wall. I shall follow shortly, along with the rest of the court.'

Duke Hector bowed his head. 'As you will, Your Majesty.'

He snapped his fingers, and six men-at-arms emerged from the shadows of the colonnade. They crossed the floor of the hall, and lifted the bodies of the envoys. Hector strode forwards, and led them from the audience chamber.

'Everyone is dismissed,' said the king. 'Everyone except my children.'

The mercenary chiefs and court advisors bowed and walked from the hall, along with their guards and retinues. The old king waited until only his son and daughter remained, then he stepped down from the gilt throne.

'Once again,' he said to the prince, 'you air your grievances in public, my son. Is this a game to you?'

'It is certainly not a game, my lord,' said the prince. 'The position of envoy is sacrosanct. Am I to keep my silence when you flout the ancient laws of this land?'

'Yes,' said the king. 'Observe your sister. There is no doubt in my mind that she also disagreed with my actions, and yet she was able to restrain her emotions. Perhaps you are too weak to ever be king. Perhaps I should amend the law of succession to disinherit you. Little Alfie, your son, would make a better monarch, despite having lived for a mere seven summers.' He extended a finger, and jabbed the prince's chest. 'You think with this, instead of using your brain. The good folk of this realm name you Alfgang the Pius, but I prefer Alfgang the Weak, for weak you are, son – weak, and at the mercy of your emotions.'

The prince's eyes radiated contempt. 'You seek to alter my epithet, father? In that case, might I rename you Alfgang the Tyrant? For only a tyrant would so misuse the sacred gifts the spirits have bestowed upon our family line.'

'Call me whatever pleases you,' said the king. 'Your opinions are worthless. Kilbride, arrange for our carriages to collect us from the Courtyard of the Shrines; we shall all be going to the Kendril Wall. We will show the people of Upper Down how we deal with those who threaten this realm.'

Kilbride bowed. 'Yes, Your Majesty.'

She turned, and walked from the colonnaded hall, her heels clacking off the marble floor. She went through an opening, and found a crowd of courtiers and advisers standing outside. Marie, her lady-in-waiting, approached her as Kilbride walked through the busy hallway.

'His Majesty is going to the Wall,' Kilbride said to her lady-in-waiting, 'and he wants the entire court to follow him.'

'Shall I have someone find your sister, my lady?' said Marie.

'Abigone will be enjoying herself somewhere in the Royal Parkland,' said Kilbride. 'Send someone to look for her, but don't linger. If she isn't here in ten minutes, we shall leave without her.'

Marie bowed her head, then she disappeared through a palace doorway. Kilbride eyed the group of courtiers gathered round her.

'Have the king's carriages prepared,' she said. 'His Majesty expects to leave from the Courtyard of the Shrines in a few moments.'

The courtiers lowered their heads, then dispersed.

'Not you,' Kilbride said to one of them.

'Your Highness?' said the old courtier.

'Find Captain Joachim of the Royal Guard,' Kilbride said. 'Tell him the autumn leaves are falling early this year.'

The courtier's eyes flickered with confusion, but he bowed and hurried away. Kilbride savoured the solitude of the empty hallway for a moment, conscious of the events she had just set in motion. One consequence would be the death of the elderly courtier, for Kilbride had little doubt that Captain Joachim would arrange for some accident to befall him before he could tell others of the cryptic message he had been asked to deliver. It was a shame for the old man, but Kilbride forced any pity from her heart. She walked to a doorway that led out into the wide Courtyard of the Shrines, and found several of the palace staff busy hitching the horses to the royal carriages that would take them to the Wall. The high cliffs that bordered the southern edge of the courtyard were reflecting the rays of the morning sun, and the dozens of white-washed little shrines were brilliant in the light. Kilbride walked through the crowd, avoiding the horses, and made her way to her favourite shrine. Like the others, it had been cut out of the rock of the cliff face, but, unlike most, it was at ground level, just a yard and a half above the gravel of the courtyard. Flowers had been arranged next to a warped and grimy glass case edged in gold that sat in the base of the alcove. Within the case was an ancient relic from the early days of the fallen empire – the Crystal Rose of Down, its stem and petals as vibrant and shimmering as they had been on the day the object had been summoned centuries before.

'Mother Maker,' Kilbride whispered, as she touched the glass case; 'guide my hand this day. Forgive what I must do, for it is an act of love.'

'Are you praying for the souls of the envoys, sister?' said a voice.

Kilbride turned, and saw Prince Alfgang the Pius standing close by.

'I was praying for the future, my lord and brother,' she said.

'I doubt the spirits will listen to any prayers uttered by our family,' he said, 'not after Father abused their gifts. Is it any wonder that Masters and Makers are despised and hunted down? The blessings from the spirits should be used to heal and enrich the lives of the people, not to murder innocent envoys.'

'Things will change when you are king, my brother,' Kilbride said.

Alfgang lowered his gaze. 'And when will that be? I am in my forty-second year of life, and our father looks strong and hale enough to reign for another two decades. I will be an old man by the time I ascend the throne, as old as Father is now. Perhaps I should allow the noble king to pass the line of succession on to my son.'

'Do you believe the kingdom will survive another two decades?' said Kilbride. 'Father has not only angered the realms to the south of Upper Down, but he has now challenged the new Empire of Sanctos. Prince Valentino's army is marching north to crush us.'

'They will never breach the Wall of Kendril, sister, and you know it.'

'Do you dismiss the rumours coming from the south?' she said.

'I do. Shame and defeat are the cause of these rumours. The lands conquered by the new empire desire to save face, and so they claim that Valentino is in possession of a miracle weapon. The imperial army is happy for us to believe this, for they wish us to panic and flee; but our father is far too stubborn to yield to mere rumour. Come; our carriage is ready.'

'Are you travelling with me this day, brother?'

'I am. Our father made it clear that I am not welcome to share his carriage.'

'You should have held your tongue. Did you not think of the effect your words would have upon the members of the king's court? The Westlanders already hold you in contempt.'

'Should I care what those vile brigands think of me? The sooner they are expelled from Upper Down, the better.'

'There are too many of them residing here, brother. At this moment in time, the Westlanders could overwhelm the armed forces of Upper Down, if they chose to do so. We must be careful in our dealings with them, and use their bitter rivalries to ensure they turn on each other. That requires patience, not unseemly outbursts in the king's presence.'

The prince raised his eyes, and smiled. 'You scold me, sister.'

'I meant no disrespect.'

'But your words carry weight with me. I shall try to act as you advise.'

He gestured towards the line of carriages. The king and two of his closest ministers were boarding the first, along with an officer from the Royal Guard, and the prince and Kilbride strode to the second. They were joined by a young aide to the prince, and Marie, Kilbride's lady-in-waiting; and they climbed up into the comfortable carriage.

Kilbride and her lady-in-waiting took one bench, and the prince and his aide sat down opposite them.

'Was there any sign of Abigone?' Kilbride said.

'No, my lady,' said Marie.

'She will be in the park with her little animal,' said the prince.

'Better there than in the palace, my lord,' said Marie. 'That thing scares me.'

The prince laughed as the carriage got underway. 'It is a harmless little creature,' he said. 'A small dog would be more than a match for it.'

Princess Kilbride narrowed her eyes. 'I don't care for the way it looks at me. It gazes upon everyone but Abigone with undisguised hostility.'

'You were not here when it first arrived,' said the prince. 'It was very timid back then. And remember, Abigone will be taking it with her when she leaves.'

'How will she be able to leave if the imperial army is camped in the pass?'

'Our sister's wedding might have to be delayed until Valentino decides to give up and go home,' said the prince.

'I would not be upset if that resulted in a long delay. Abigone is too young to marry.'

'She is the same age as Nolan was, and only two years younger than you were. Do you ever think of your husband?'

Kilbride gazed out of the carriage window. 'I am forbidden from wearing any colour other than black, brother. My thoughts turn to my slain husband every morning when I get dressed. At twenty-six, I am deemed too old to remarry, and our father has made it clear that he expects me to care for him in his dotage. A life of widowed servitude lies in store for me. All the same, I fear for Abigone. I had already been acquainted with Roderick before I married him; our sister has never laid eyes upon her betrothed.'

'That is because Lord Henry's domains are so far from Upper Down; three months of travel is required to reach his father's kingdom of Nessos.'

'And why is it so far away, brother; do you ever ask yourself that question? It needs to be remote; otherwise, it would likely be raided by the Westlanders, just as they raided Greater Down to kill my husband.'

'I sense much anger within you, sister.'

Kilbride said nothing, her gaze upon the large gates of the Royal Palace as they were being opened. The line of six carriages was being flanked by men-at-arms from the Royal Guard, and two mounted knights in armour were leading the way. The convoy rolled into the streets of the walled town of Torrent, its neat rows of wood-framed houses lining the roadside. On their left, the high cliffs reared up like a wall, rising for hundreds of feet into the southern sky. The convoy took a left turn at a junction, and the fabled pass of Upper Down came into view – a tear-shaped opening in the heart of the cliffs, that cut through to the narrow ravine on the other side. Waterfalls spilled down either flank of the gap, and the mighty Kendril Wall sat at its base, blocking the pass with a wide sweep of masonry that towered over the houses of the town. An enormous gatehouse-fortress was positioned in the centre of the high wall, and the road through the pass ran under its turrets and battlements. The tall, reinforced gates were closed and barred, shutting off Upper Down from the south. It was through those gates that the Westlander raiding parties would issue, riding their armoured horses through the ravine and into the lowlands of Greater Down; and it was through those gates that they would return, bringing their wagons of plundered goods, along with any captured aristocrats valuable enough to be ransomed back to their wealthy families. Such was the fear engendered by the Westlanders, that many years had elapsed since any merchants had felt safe enough to brave the journey across the mountains through the pass at Upper Down.

'I was with Roderick the morning he was killed,' Kilbride said. 'I tried to persuade him to refrain from attacking the Westlander raiders, but his duty came first. Forty mounted Westlanders slaughtered over a hundred of Roderick's men that day, then they sent my husband's head back to me, wrapped in his bloodstained surcoat. Those responsible for his murder are living in Upper Down, sheltered and honoured by our father; and you wonder if I have anger in my heart, brother?'

The carriages slowed as they reached the open space by the base of the Kendril Wall. Soldiers formed up into lines, and courtiers came forward to open the carriage doors. The prince waited until the king had climbed down from his own carriage, and then he stepped onto the wide flagstones. He extended a hand, and helped his royal sister descend; then his aide and Kilbride's lady-in-waiting joined them.

Duke Hector of Ridden was waiting for the royal party by the main entrance to the gatehouse.

'Your Majesty,' he said, bowing before King Alfgang the Great; 'the bodies of the two imperial envoys have been carried up to the battlements, and the officers of the watch have been assembled.'

The king peered into the duke's face. 'And yet you are troubled by something, no?'

'Nothing of any import, Your Majesty.'

'Out with it, lad.'

'It appears, Your Majesty,' Hector said, 'that my noble brother, the Royal Champion of Upper Down, is... well, he...'

'He is drunk?' said the king.

Hector's cheeks flushed. 'Yes, Your Majesty.'

The king shrugged. 'Tell me – when is Walter not drunk? I would be more surprised were I to find your brother sober.'

'I beg that you do not remove him from his position, Your Majesty.'

'Why would I do that? I care not if he drinks all day; his post is merely honorific. It would be a different matter if I actually relied upon his military acumen.' He glanced around to ensure that the members of his court had assembled behind him, then he gestured to the gatehouse. 'Let us ascend to the battlements.'

Duke Hector led the way, the king by his side, and the royal party entered the gatehouse through an open doorway. Plunged into its gloomy interior, they took a spiral staircase that wound its way up to the battlements, then they emerged into the shadows of the Kendril Gap. Above and to each side, the cliffs were forming an unbreakable barrier; while, to the south, the narrow ravine snaked its way towards the lowlands of Greater Down, and the lands that had once been the Central Provinces of the old empire. A wide, paved road ran downhill, by the banks of a fast-flowing stream. Fifty yards from the base of the Kendril Wall, the road bridged the stream, and, standing on the grass on the far side, a group of four imperial scouts were waiting, the reins of six horses tied to the nearby trees.

Kilbride took up a position by the battlements, as the others from the royal household gathered close to the king. Several yards away, the salt-encrusted bodies of the two envoys were being guarded by Hector's men-at-arms. The king glanced down at them, and a smile touched his lips.

'Are their comrades down in the ravine watching?' he said.

'They are, Your Majesty,' said Hector.

The king's smile deepened. 'Secure ropes to the ankles of the envoys, and then suspend them from the battlements, in clear view of their fellows.'

Hector snapped his fingers, and his men-at-arms got to work. As they fixed the ropes to the battlements, Kilbride caught sight of Captain Joachim among the soldiers up on the wall. Their eyes met for a brief instant, then Kilbride looked away.

The men-at-arms hoisted the two envoys into the air, then they dropped them over the side of the battlements. They each fell six feet, then the ropes went taut, and they swung from their ankles, their bodies brushing off the outer blocks of the Kendril Wall. Small showers of salt fell like soft rain from their skin, as the ropes creaked under the weight. Kilbride's eyes went to the imperial scouts, who were staring up at the battlements.

'Here is my answer!' cried the king. 'The same fate awaits any who threaten my realm; take that message back to Valentino!'

The scouts ran for their horses. They loosened the reins, and mounted. A few gave anxious backward glances at the tall gates in the centre of the wall, as though they expected Westlanders to pour forth at any moment, then they urged the horses on. The two riderless horses were led along with them, as they cantered down the road towards the south.

King Alfgang the Great laughed, his eyes bright with merriment. A few others of his court laughed along with their king, but Kilbride and the prince remained silent.

'This wall was built by the finest Masters and Makers of the old empire,' said the king. 'It has stood for five centuries, and it will be here long after each one of us has crumbled into dust.'

'Pray do not say that, Your Majesty,' said one of the courtiers. 'May your reign last forever!'

The king's smile faded. 'Save your sycophancy for my son,' he said. 'I am an old man of sixty-five, and the spirits will claim me when they are ready.' He turned, as though he was looking for someone, then his smile re-appeared. 'Walter!' he cried. 'My brave Champion. Step forward.'

A handsome but dishevelled-looking man in military uniform edged through the crowd of courtiers. Even at a distance, Kilbride could smell the whisky on the man's breath.

'Yes, Your Majesty?' Walter said.

'In every way,' the king said; 'looks, demeanour, intelligence – you are inferior to your brother the Duke of Ridden, as though you were but a poor imitation. Nevertheless, as the brother of my son's wife, you have attained a position of high rank in my kingdom. Tell me – are you grateful?'

'I, uh, I am very grateful, Your Majesty.'

'As you should be. Have a company of Mountain Rangers sent out after the imperial scouts. I want to know when Valentino will be arriving, and I want to know how many soldiers he is bringing to the pass.'

'Yes, Your Majesty.'

The king arched an eyebrow. 'Why are you still here, Walter? Be gone.'

Walter lowered his gaze and shuffled away, and the king turned to Hector.

'Apologies for my brother's behaviour, Your Majesty,' the duke said.

The king smiled, but said nothing. From the edge of the crowd, Kilbride saw Captain Joachim whispering to a young soldier, and her heart pounded. She turned back to the king, forcing a neutral expression on to her face.

'Since you are all gathered here,' the king said, 'I wish to speak a little about certain rumours that have reached my ears. These rumours tell of a strange and powerful weapon in the hands of the upstart empire of Sanctos. Emperor Antonio and his brother Prince Valentino are supposed to have defeated fleets and conquered realms with these weapons; but I tell you now that this is nothing but mere propaganda. There is no such weapon. The Sanctians are forging their new empire using old-fashioned methods – by fire and the sword; and these methods will not work here. Behind the great Wall of Kendril, the realm of Upper Down is completely safe. Nothing can hurt us here – nothing.'

A crossbow thrummed amid the silence, and a steel bolt struck the king in his left eye. Alfgang the Great staggered, as courtiers screamed and soldiers lifted their weapons; then the king fell, his body crashing onto the stonework of the battlement's walkway. The prince rushed to his father's side, as chaos broke out. Captain Joachim hauled a young soldier from the crowd and threw him to the ground next to the dead body of Alfgang the Great.

'This is the man!' Captain Joachim shouted, as he drew his sword. 'This man killed the king!'

The prince glanced up. 'Arrest him, Captain; he is not to be...'

The captain plunged his sword into the young soldier's chest before the prince could complete the sentence.

The prince rose to his feet, anger filling his eyes, and every man and woman on the battlements got down onto their knees before him.

'Long live the king!' Kilbride cried, as she bowed her head. 'Long live King Alfgang the Pius.'

CHAPTER 2
THE CHAMPION

Torrent, Upper Down – 8th Day of Lamenta 107

The five-hundred-year-old great Wall of Kendril had three gates that led out into the narrow gorge to the south of Torrent. Two of them were part of the gatehouse complex – the main gates, and a small postern; while a second postern was located at the far end of the wall, next to one of the waterfalls that spilled down the steep cliffs. It was by this small gate that Walter stood, surrounded by forty men of the Mountain Rangers. Every one of them knew that the King's Champion had been drinking, but Walter had been their commanding officer for five years, and none mentioned it.

'Don't engage with the enemy,' Walter said, raising his voice over the sound of the waterfall. 'Follow the imperial scouts down the valley until you see their army, then get back here and report to me. Got it? Be careful – I would rather not have to tell your mothers that you were killed on a reconnaissance expedition; that would seriously eat into my drinking time.' He smiled, but none of the elite soldiers responded in kind. 'All right, Commander; lead them out.'

The officer in charge of the detachment saluted, then soldiers from the regular Upper Down Wall Militia removed the thick bars from the postern gate and swung it open. The Mountain Rangers trooped through, taking a track that led down by the side of the cliffs. Walter watched until all forty had passed through the mighty wall, then he gestured to the militia soldiers, and they closed and re-barred the gate.

The Champion's well-built aide emerged from a door in the flank of the gatehouse-fortress – a man whose height and strength was matched only by his capacity for alcohol.

'Have they gone, sir?' he said.

Walter nodded, his head swimming.

The soldier strode forwards. 'I wish I was going with them.'

Walter raised an eyebrow. 'I'm sure I could arrange that for you, Lothar. When's the last time you were on an actual expedition?'

'I've been looking after you for three years, sir,' Lothar said. 'My days of roaming through the mountains with the Rangers are over; well, until you get sick of me.'

Walter placed a hand onto the Kendril Wall to steady himself.

Lothar smiled. 'Feeling rough, sir? I know the cure for that. What say we wander back to the officers' wardroom and continue where we left off? It's unlikely that the king will want to humiliate you twice in the same day, and we still have half a flagon of whisky to get through.'

'You are a bad influence,' said Walter. 'Is whisky all you ever think about?'

'No, sir. I often think about women, too. If the whisky's too much, we could take a walk into Twinbrook and find a nice beer hall. It's not like we have anything planned for the rest of the day.'

Walter felt his stomach turn, and he waited for the sense of nausea to pass. 'Did you hear what the king said to me?'

'Yes, sir. He said you were a poor copy of your brother, the noble Duke of Ridden. Does it bother you?'

'It's no worse than some of the things my father used to say when he was still alive. I think his last words to me were, *Be more like Hector*. It was at that exact moment when I decided to do the opposite of whatever my brother did.'

Lothar laughed. 'And how is that working out for you, sir?'

'Why don't we find one of those beer halls you mentioned, and I'll be happy to tell you all about it. Only; let's not pick anywhere with too many Westlanders, not after what happened last time.'

'That Westlander slipped and fell onto my fist, sir,' said Lothar. 'A terrible accident.'

'That's not the way I remember it.'

'Well, you were rather drunk, sir. I had to carry you all the way back to Torrent.'

'Don't exaggerate,' said Walter. 'You only had to carry me the last few hundred yards. I was still conscious.'

Lothar laughed. 'If you say so, sir.'

Walter pushed himself away from the wall, and they began walking towards the streets of Torrent.

'The walk to Twinbrook should clear our heads,' said Lothar. 'Perhaps we should pick a beer hall that serves food. Too much beer on an empty stomach, sir, and I'll be carrying you home again. I also happen to know that a new brothel has opened up by the fruit market. We should get in there before the Westlanders have a chance to wreck the place.'

They were crossing the cleared space between the wall and the streets of Torrent, when a clamouring broke out behind them. Walter turned, then he grimaced as he raised his gaze to the battlements of the Kendril Wall. Shouts and cries were echoing off the sides of the cliffs – a confusing swirl of sound.

'Sir?' said Lothar.

'Wait a moment,' said Walter. 'What do you think is going on up there?'

'It's hard to tell, sir. Is that cheering?'

'It sounds like cheering and lamenting rolled into one.'

A soldier burst out from a door in the gatehouse.

'The king is dead!' he cried. 'The king has fallen!'

Every soldier in the vicinity stopped what they were doing, and Walter felt his mind steady a little. His stomach was still churning, but his thoughts began to clear, and he walked back towards the wall.

'Remain at your posts,' he said to the soldiers by the base of the wall.

He saw the line of carriages that had ferried the royal court to the Kendril Gap. Their drivers and guards were staring up at the battlements of the wall along with every other soldier in the area. Walter strode past them, with Lothar shadowing his steps. They entered the gloom of the old gatehouse, and Walter hurried for the stairs that led to the battlements. A soldier was running down them, and Walter reached out and gripped the man's shoulder.

'What's happening up there?'

The soldier stared at him, his eyes wide, then he saluted.

'The king is dead, sir,' he gasped.

'How?'

'A crossbow, sir. Accidental discharge. His Majesty took a bolt through the eye. I have been ordered to get the carriages ready to take the members of the royal court back to the palace.'

Walter frowned in confusion, then he released the man, who ran across the floor of the gatehouse's entrance hall. Walter glanced at Lothar, then he sprinted up the spiral staircase, taking two steps at a time. He was dizzy and nauseous by the time he reached the crowded battlements. He caught a glimpse of his brother issuing orders, a confident and calm expression on his face. Walter tried to suppress his feelings of loathing for Duke Hector. What the king had told him had been repeated by many others over the years, not only by his father. Yes, Walter was tall, handsome and intelligent; but his older brother eclipsed him in every regard, and had done so for as long as Walter could remember. On top of that, everyone loved Hector. In a royal court riven with rivalries and petty animosity, Duke Hector of Ridden was one of the very few people respected and admired by all sides.

Walter pushed his way through the crowd of courtiers. The same mixture of grief and elation was apparent on their faces, and most ignored Walter as he barged past them. He came to a tight ring of people, and shoved his way to the front. Lying on the smooth flagstones of the battlements' walkway was the king – Alfgang the Fourth, with a bolt lodged deep in his left eye. The body of a soldier lay next to him, the front of his uniform stained with blood; while Prince Alfgang and Princess Kilbride were kneeling by the corpse of their father, uttering prayers to the spirits of the dead.

'What the fuck?' Walter muttered, before he could stop himself.

Hector turned, and his eyes narrowed at his younger brother. 'Is that all you have to say, Walter?'

Walter stared at Hector. 'How could this happen? Some soldier told me it was an accident.'

'That is our assumption,' said Hector. 'We may never know the truth, as Captain Joachim of the Royal Guard killed the culprit before he could be questioned.'

'One bolt is accidentally discharged,' said Walter, 'and it happens to hit the king in the fucking eye?'

The clamouring from the gathered courtiers fell into silence, and Princess Kilbride turned her gaze to frown up at Walter.

'I will deal with this situation,' said Hector. 'Walter, you will clear the battlements. The members of the royal court are to be escorted back to the palace immediately. But first, brother, you will pay your respects to the new monarch of Upper Down – King Alfgang the Fifth.'

'What?'

'Kneel before the new king, brother.'

Walter frowned, his mind reeling from alcoholic confusion, then he glanced down at Prince Alfgang, who was continuing with his prayers as though no one else was present. Walter lowered himself to his knees, and bowed his head.

'Your Majesty,' he said. 'I am your humble servant.'

The new king ignored him.

'Would every lady and gentleman of the court please make their way to the stairs,' said Hector, as Walter continued to kneel. 'The King's Champion shall lead you back to the Royal Palace. Princess Kilbride shall take custody of the late king's body, and the soldiers of the Royal Guard shall provide an escort. Walter – on your feet.'

Walter pushed himself up, then he staggered, almost toppling into

Princess Kilbride. Hector's hand shot out, and grabbed his brother's arm, preventing him from falling.

'Of all the days to get drunk, brother,' Hector hissed.

Walter smiled as he steadied himself. 'Why would this day be different from any other?'

'You are being called upon to serve the realm. Supervise the transport of the late king down the stairs with Princess Kilbride.'

Walter nodded, then he turned to the crowd of courtiers. 'You all heard the duke – proceed down the stairs. Make your way to your carriages, and then wait for the late king's body to be brought down.'

None of the courtiers moved. Walter gestured to Lothar, who summoned a handful of soldiers, and they began to push the courtiers towards the staircase, clearing the area around the king's body. The courtiers looked unwilling to leave, but the soldiers guided them towards the stairs. Duke Hector extended a hand, and Princess Kilbride took it. He helped her to stand, and she gazed down at the new king, who was still praying by his father's side.

'Your Majesty,' she said. 'Brother.'

Alfgang glanced at her.

'We are going to move the body,' she said. 'Do you wish to accompany us to the palace?'

'Not yet,' said Alfgang. 'Hector – remain here with me. I need some time to digest what has happened.'

The duke bowed. 'I will be at your side, Your Majesty.'

The new king got to his feet and took a few paces back. Walter signalled to the waiting soldiers from the Royal Guard, and they walked forward. Two men took hold of the fallen king's shoulders, and another two lifted his legs.

'Take your time, lads,' said Walter; 'nice and careful.'

'Take them all to the palace, brother,' said Hector; 'and then wait there. His Majesty and I will join you soon.'

Walter glanced at the new king, but Alfgang the Pius looked as though he was in a daze, his eyes on the flagstones where his father had lain.

'What will we do with the dead soldier?' said Walter.

'My men-at-arms will take care of that,' said Hector; 'just as I shall question Captain Joachim.'

'Where is the captain?'

'I ordered him to return to his quarters in the gatehouse.'

'Is he under arrest?'

'Not yet,' said Hector. 'Let us see what he has to say for himself first.'

Walter turned to the soldiers carrying the body of the fallen king. 'Commander Lothar, take the lead. The princess and I will follow on.'

Lothar saluted, then he strode to the stairwell ahead of the others, while Walter and Kilbride lined up behind the soldiers.

'Clear the way for the king!' Lothar bellowed down the stairs, then he began to descend. The soldiers holding the fallen monarch followed after him, easing the body down one step at a time, as Walter walked with the princess in silence. They descended to the entrance hall at the bottom of the stairs, where two lines of soldiers had formed a guard of honour. The king's body was led between them, and Walter kept his gaze on the ground. Part of him felt as though he was dreaming, and he had to force a sombre expression on to his face. A manic urge to start laughing crept through him, and it was with some effort that he managed to stay silent.

They emerged out into the autumnal sunlight to find the line of carriages full and waiting to leave. A crowd of civilians from Torrent was gathering by the edge of the streets, their eyes peering towards the carriages. At the sight of the king's body being carried out from the gatehouse, a roar of voices rose up. By the far side of the crowd, two tall, armoured Westlanders gazed at the body, then they turned and hurried away, pushing the civilians of Torrent aside.

Walter led the procession to the first carriage, which had its side doors open. The soldiers lifted the king's body into the interior, and laid it down onto one of the padded benches. The soldiers withdrew from the carriage, then Walter helped Princess Kilbride climb on board. He followed her up, and sat down next to her.

'Get everyone to the palace,' he said to Lothar, who was standing outside.

'Yes, sir,' said his aide.

The carriage door was closed, and they began to move off, the clatter of hooves and wheels over the cobbles echoing off the cliffs. Walter glanced at the body of the king opposite him, then he looked away. He wiped perspiration from his forehead, and settled into his seat.

Kilbride said nothing, then she removed a shawl of black lace from her shoulders and placed it over the king's head.

Walter glanced at her. 'My commiserations for your loss, Your Highness.'

'Your breath reeks of whisky, Walter,' she said. 'I might become intoxicated by your mere presence.'

'Thank you,' he said. 'I didn't know I was so charismatic.'

'You are a disgrace.'

'I'm a professional drunk. Look at me; I can barely walk, and yet I managed to get us all down here without a hitch. Did you see the king being struck?'

'I did.'

'There's no way that could have been an accident. I can believe that bolts are sometimes discharged by mistake – I've seen it happen maybe twice in five years – but for the bolt to strike the king's eye? Besides, everyone knows that Captain Joachim didn't exactly like the king. How convenient that he killed the soldier, eh?'

'My father has just died, and you are spreading malicious gossip?'

'It's what everyone else will be saying. And now we have a new king. Did you see those two Westlanders scurry away? They will be shitting themselves right about now. The new king fucking hates them.'

'Do you think you can speak to me in that manner because we grew up together?'

Walter shrugged. 'I'm just saying the truth. Whoever killed the king probably hates the Westlanders, too.' He smiled. 'It wasn't you, was it?'

'I will not dignify that question with a response.'

'I was joking, Killie.'

'You are making jokes while the body of my father lies not one yard from us?'

'I doubt he cares.'

'I care.'

'When we arrive at the palace,' Walter went on, 'everyone will have to change into mourning clothes. Well, everyone except you – you came prepared.'

The princess looked away, her eyes red.

'Shit; I'm sorry, Killie,' he said. 'I'm so drunk that I'm saying whatever comes into my head. You won't tell your brother about this, will you? Or my brother, for that matter.'

'Our brothers are set to become the two most powerful men in the kingdom,' Kilbride said.

'I know, which is why I'm hoping you won't tell them that I was making an arse of myself.'

'You owe your entire position,' she said, 'to the fact that your sister is married to my brother.'

'Do you think I don't know that?'

'You have thoroughly abused the great honour that was bestowed upon you, Walter. You are the King's Champion, and you spend your days and nights drinking, whoring and gambling.'

'Thanks. I try my best.'

'My brother will likely command you to sober up,' she said. 'You know his attitude towards this sort of behaviour. My father tolerated it, but my brother won't.'

'Stop nagging me, Killie. You're giving me a headache.'

'The kingdom is in peril, Walter. Upper Down is home to thousands of armed Westlanders, who will be thrown into panic and confusion by the death of the king, and we have Prince Valentino's imperial army approaching from the south. If we are not careful, we will be squeezed between the two. The realm needs its champion, not a drunken idiot.'

'Are you going to advise your brother to replace me?'

Kilbride eyed him, then she shook her head. 'No.'

'You can if you want to. I didn't ask to become the King's bloody

Champion. I'd be happy to fade into obscurity, as long as I had a decent pension.'

'You are brother-in-law to the new king, and brother to the realm's most powerful nobleman. You will never be allowed to fade into obscurity. Your personal happiness is irrelevant.'

'What about you? Your father, no offence, treated you as a servant. Worse, he never listened to your advice, despite you being the most intelligent person in his court. That must have rankled. Will your brother be any different?'

'My brother will be different in a number of ways.'

Walter gazed at the body of the fallen king. 'Forty fucking years. Four decades on the throne, and it's over in a second. Upper Down was poor and insignificant when he became king, but at least nobody hated us. Look at us now – rich, prosperous, and despised by all. Every realm in the Central Provinces will laugh when they hear about this; and the Emperor will throw a party.'

Kilbride kept her gaze upon him. 'No more bullshit, Walter; tell me honestly – where do you stand on the Westlanders and Princess Hygilt?'

'The Hygilt question is easy,' he said; 'we should hand the girl back to the imperial army. We had no business snatching a princess of the new empire.'

'Then you don't believe my father's version of events – that Hygilt ran away from the imperial court?'

'Does anyone believe it? I don't think I've ever heard such an obvious fabrication. We could have got away with years of raiding and suchlike, but taking Hygilt was bound to stir up a wasps' nest. If we give her back, then Valentino might turn round and go home.'

'And the Westlanders?'

Walter bit his lip.

'Do you fear them?' said Kilbride.

'You would have to be insane not to fear those big bastards, Killie,' he said. 'Ten of them could take on an entire company of regular Upper Down militia; and there are thousands of the mad fuckers living here. If they didn't hate each other so much, they could take over the kingdom in a couple of days. Why did your father allow them to settle here?'

'Why do you think? The money, Walter. The tribute and taxes paid by the Westlanders filled the realm's coffers. My father took ten per cent of everything they looted from the southern kingdoms, in exchange for allowing them to use Upper Down as their base. The Wall of Kendril protects them as much as it protects us.'

'Will your brother try to get rid of them?'

Kilbride said nothing.

'Do you think I'm likely to tell the Westlanders your plans, Killie?' he said.

'You have already proved that you have a loose tongue when you have been drinking. You might inadvertently let something slip.'

Walter narrowed his eyes. 'You've been planning this, haven't you? Did you know what was going to happen today? Come on, Killie; I'm not *that* drunk.'

'I am insulted that you would suggest such a thing.'

'All right. For future reference, I fucking hate the Westlanders. There. Will that do? My loyalty is to Upper Down, not those armoured thugs.'

'Will you stay off the drink for the rest of the day?'

'I will be standing guard by the king's body,' he said.

'You didn't answer my question.'

'Yes. I will do my actual job for once.' He glanced out of the window. 'My hangover should commence before sunset. Perhaps people will mistake my suffering for grief.'

The line of carriages rolled through the palace gates and came to a halt in a large courtyard by the front of the Royal Palace. Commander Lothar, who had been marching alongside the lead carriage, opened the side door, and assisted Princess Kilbride to descend to the gravel. Walter climbed down next, then soldiers entered the carriage to retrieve the king's body. All over the courtyard, weeping courtiers were gathering. A few of the older ones rent their robes and beat their chests as they keened out their laments. In the streets outside the palace grounds, more civilians were assembling, and cries rang out as the soldiers carried the body of the king towards the main palace entrance.

One of the Westlander chiefs barged his way through the courtiers, a dozen huge men in plate armour trailing him.

'Is it true?' Chief Dravid cried. 'Is the king dead?'

The Westlanders stopped, and blocked the path of Walter, Kilbride and the soldiers carrying the body. Dravid reached out and pulled back the shawl of black lace covering the king's face, and his features paled. A few of the armoured warriors muttered something in the tongue of the Westlanders, as Dravid stared at the king for several long seconds.

Walter coughed. 'You are in His Majesty's way, Chief Dravid.'

Dravid eyed the King's Champion with contempt. 'How could you allow this to happen, boy?'

'It was an accident,' said Kilbride.

Dravid ignored her.

'I will count to three,' said Walter. 'By the time I finish, you will have moved from our path, Chief Dravid.'

The Westlander chief shot him a look of disgust.

'One...' said Walter. 'Two...'

Dravid snorted a laugh, then strode away, his armoured retinue keeping pace as they crossed the courtyard.

Walter exhaled, then he gestured to the King's Guardsmen to resume their way to the palace.

'What would you have done if he hadn't moved?' whispered Kilbride, as they set off again.

'I hadn't worked that part out,' said Walter.

'Thank you for not contradicting my explanation.'

'We are no longer friends, Killie,' he said, 'but we have known each other since before either of us could walk or talk. It may not mean anything to you, but it means a lot to me.'

They entered the palace, and found the hallway flanked by mourning courtiers. Walter guided the soldiers to the main audience chamber, then he ordered Lothar to set a large table down in front of the gilt throne. The tall soldier did as Walter bade, and the table was moved into position, and a clean cloth was placed over it. The body of the king was laid down onto the table, and then Walter commanded that the hall be cleared. Soldiers pushed the courtiers out, and the doors were closed, leaving only Walter and Kilbride standing by the body of the fallen king.

'What now?' said Walter, as they gazed down at the table.

'I will summon servants to wash and clean the king's body,' she said; 'then we shall dress him in his finest robes. Once that has been done, we shall allow mourners to enter the hall to pay their respects. You should go to your rooms in the palace and change into your dress uniform, and then, you and I shall stand here until the new king arrives.'

Walter pointed at the crossbow bolt embedded into the king's left eye. 'And that?'

'Would you do the honours?'

Walter reached out and gripped the bolt in his right hand. 'Look away,' he said, then he ripped the bolt from the king's face, and set it down onto the table.

'You didn't look away,' he said.

'No, I didn't,' she said. 'Did you know that my father refused to execute or exile the Westlanders who killed my husband, Walter? When I returned to Upper Down after Roderick had been butchered, I expected to see the bodies of his murderers hanging from the gallows' arm. Instead, I found them drinking and laughing in the Royal Palace. My father had fined them an extra ten per cent of their takings for that raid. That's all my husband was worth to him. That's all I was worth. Why would I look away?'

Walter glanced at the princess, but her gaze remained fixed on the body of her father. Saying nothing, Walter turned, and strode from the hall.

CHAPTER 3
THE DUKE

Torrent, Upper Down – 8th Day of Lamenta 107

'May the spirits forgive me, Hector, my dear friend,' said Alfgang the Pius, 'for I have shamed myself this day.'

The Duke of Ridden gazed at the new king. 'How so, Your Majesty?'

'My father has died, and yet my heart is conflicted,' said Alfgang. 'I should be feeling nothing but sorrow, but I am weak.' He closed his eyes. 'Part of me is glad he is dead. What dishonour I bring upon my name. Part of me is already thinking of the future – of the laws I wish to change, and the reforms I intend to enact, when my father has not yet been buried.'

'You are our king, Your Majesty,' said Hector. 'It is natural that your thoughts should turn to the running of the realm. That only proves your sense of duty.'

The king nodded as the two men stood on the empty battlements of the Kendril Wall. Below them, the executed envoys were still swinging from the ropes bound to their ankles, as they dusted the exterior of the wall with salt.

'Look at what my father did, Hector,' said Alfgang; 'and look how swiftly he was punished for his transgressions. He called upon the spirits to kill those two men, and he met his own end not one hour later.

Tell me that this is not the clearest evidence that the spirits desire justice. My father offended them, and he paid the price.'

Hector said nothing.

'Have them cut down and buried with full honours,' said Alfgang.

'I shall, Your Majesty, as soon as you are ready to travel to the Royal Palace.'

'I need a few more moments,' said Alfgang; 'and I shall be travelling to my own palace first, to inform my wife and our son of the evil that has transpired this day. Poor Alfie – to lose his last surviving grandparent at such a young age. My father may have despised me, but he doted upon Alfie. He adored that boy.' He glanced along the battlements, as if to ensure that they were alone. 'I have known you since you were born, Hector, and you have long earned my trust and admiration.'

'Thank you, Your Majesty.'

'I want you to serve as my chancellor; do you accept?'

Hector smiled. 'I would be delighted and greatly honoured to serve the realm in such a role, Your Majesty.'

'That pleases me.' He pulled a ring from a finger of his left hand, and handed it to Hector. 'You are hereby appointed to the role with immediate effect, and you may use the seal upon this ring to issue commands in my name. As you will no doubt be arriving at the Royal Palace before me, I wish you to remove every single one of my father's ministers and advisors from office. Have them arrested and placed under guard.'

'All of them, Your Majesty?'

'Yes. I intend to wield a broom that will sweep aside all remnants of my father's rule.' He gazed out to the horizon. 'This is a new dawn for Upper Down. As my chancellor, I shall confide in you before we go our separate ways this morning. Here are my priorities – firstly, we shall release all of the hostages currently being held within the Royal Palace, including, of course, Princess Hygilt. Tomorrow, at dawn, you and I shall escort the young princess south, and personally deliver her into the custody of her grandfather, the Illustrious Prince Valentino of the Sanctian Empire. I will then concede to the empire's demands, in full.

We shall expel the Westlanders from Upper Down, re-open the Kendril Wall to merchants and travellers, and thereby restore our reputation in the world. The days of foreign bands of armoured men using our realm as a base from which to instil terror in the kingdoms of the Central Provinces are over, my friend. What do you say to that?'

Hector paused, choosing his words carefully. 'It is a plan of great wisdom and courage, Your Majesty; however, it might not be a simple thing to expel every Westlander. They may refuse to leave, or worse, they might attempt some act of violence. One must also consider the impact upon the royal treasury were the Westlanders to cease contributing to the realm's revenue.'

'I would rather Upper Down be poor and honourable, than remain a nest of savage raiders. The Westlanders have slaughtered countless civilians in the southern kingdoms; they have desecrated their womenfolk, abducted their children, and looted their possessions. What manner of king would I be were I to allow them to continue thus?'

'And the mission tomorrow, Your Majesty? Must you go in person?'

'I must, and you shall accompany me. It is imperative that Prince Valentino understands that Upper Down is no longer ruled by Alfgang the Fourth. My father has been so deceitful over the years, that the illustrious prince might not believe the news unless we are there to present it to him.'

'He may try to arrest you, or hold you captive for a ransom.'

'He will not. He will be well aware that I am also a powerful Master, just as my father was. I shall have the power of the spirits to aid me.'

'The Sanctians loathe Masters, Your Majesty; just as they loathe Makers. They perceive those with the powers you possess to be blasphemous – a living sacrilege. Prince Valentino might feel duty bound by his religion to assault you.'

'Not if I return his granddaughter to him,' said Alfgang. He glanced away. 'Do you know if… I, uh, what I mean is, uh…'

'Your Majesty?'

Alfgang's face darkened. 'Did my father ever lay hands upon her, Hector?'

'Not to my knowledge, Your Majesty. Princess Hygilt is a girl of fourteen.'

'I know that, and yet I needed to ask. My father's heart was rotten; do you understand? He has a history of... improper conduct where young women are concerned.'

'I see. In the case of Princess Hygilt, Your Majesty, I assume that she was deemed too valuable a hostage to be abused. As far as I know, she has been kept secluded within well-guarded quarters of the Royal Palace. She has maids to assist her, and no one is allowed to enter her presence without the king's personal authority. When I arrive at the palace, may I have your permission to send someone to check on her current condition?'

'By all means. Ensure that she knows that I intend to deliver her to her grandfather tomorrow.'

'I shall, Your Majesty. Now, if I could please be excused, I wish to speak with Captain Joachim before I leave for the palace.'

'Do you suspect foul play?'

'I am unsure, Your Majesty. However, Walter may have had a point, no matter how crudely he expressed it. It does seem a dreadful coincidence that an accidental crossbow discharge would strike the eye of the monarch. For one thing, it would imply that the soldier responsible happened to be aiming at the king.'

'Do not be too hard on Joachim, Hector,' said Alfgang. 'He has served in the Royal Guards with distinction for many years.'

'That is true, Your Majesty. It is also true that he had a well-known grudge against your royal father, dating back many years. The captain blamed the fallen king for the death of his brother, who was slain in an altercation with a few Westlanders. He claimed that Alfgang the Great allowed the perpetrators to escape justice. The late king denied this, naturally, but the matter was known about in the royal court.'

'I have heard the rumours,' Alfgang said. 'Nevertheless, I require you to question him with dignity and honour. Is that understood?'

'Yes, Your Majesty.'

The two men strode towards the spiral staircase and began to descend, leaving the battlements behind them. Halfway down, the duke paused.

'This is where I leave you, Your Majesty,' he said.

Alfgang eyed Hector. 'Great events are sweeping over the realm, my old friend, and I am placing much trust in you. Of all the men in the kingdom, it is to you that I turn.'

'I will not let you down, Your Majesty.'

Hector watched as the king continued to descend the stairs, then he turned for the passageway that led to the officers' quarters. Standing outside the door of Captain Joachim's rooms were two soldiers from the Wall Militia, and they saluted Hector as he approached.

'Has anyone tried to enter the captain's quarters?' Hector said.

'No, my lord,' said one of the soldiers. 'No one has been on this floor of the gatehouse since Captain Joachim was consigned to his rooms.'

'Open the door, if you please.'

The soldier reached for a set of keys hanging from his belt, then he unlocked the thick wooden door. He pushed it open, then stepped aside, allowing Hector to pass through the doorway. The interior of the chamber was in semi-darkness, and Hector paused for a moment. His nose crinkled from an unpleasant odour as his eyes adjusted to the gloom. He saw a bed, its sheets and blankets neatly made up. The chair next to it was empty. Hector turned, and nearly collided with something heavy that seemed to be hanging from the ceiling rafters.

One of the soldiers cried out. 'My lord! The captain...'

Hector stepped back, his eyes wide as he stared at the body. One end of a belt had been fastened round Captain Joachim's neck, and the other had been fixed to the ceiling. Hector cursed.

'The room was locked the entire time, my lord,' said one of the soldiers.

'And you heard nothing?' said Hector.

'Nothing, my lord. Should we cut him down?'

Hector glanced up at the captain's face. Even in the dim light of the shadows, it was clear that Joachim was dead.

'No,' he said. 'Inform the gatehouse commander of what has transpired, and leave everything exactly as it is.'

The three men left the room, and Hector gestured for the door to be re-locked.

'I am needed at the palace,' he said. 'Ensure that no one enters these quarters until the commander arrives to begin his investigation.'

'Yes, my lord.'

Hector returned to the stairs and hurried down them. By the time he reached the bottom, the new king had already departed the gatehouse, taking several of the courtiers and soldiers with him. Hector's eight men-at-arms were standing by the main entrance, awaiting their lord, and the duke signalled for them to fall in behind him. He said nothing as he strode across the courtyard, where the crowd of civilians had grown. The line of carriages that had brought the royal court to the Kendril Wall had gone, leaving only the open-topped wagon that had transported the two dead imperial envoys from the palace.

'Fetch me a horse,' Hector said, 'then make your way by road to the Royal Palace. I will meet you there.'

The sergeant in charge of the detachment of men-at-arms saluted, then he ran back to the Wall, where a long row of stables sat to the right of the gatehouse. Hector gazed at the gathered civilians as he waited. Some seemed to be experiencing grief at the death of their king, while others looked almost hopeful. Hector kept his feelings to himself, while ensuring that he presented a calm exterior. The lower classes needed to see that the powerful men of the kingdom did not panic during moments of crisis, and the Duke of Ridden was nothing if not powerful.

The sergeant led a grey mare to the duke's side, and Hector mounted. He eyed the civilians, and then the sergeant, anticipating his needs, sent the men-at-arms into the crowd to clear the road. Hector dug his heels into the mare's flanks, and the horse set off, her iron-clad hooves clattering off the cobbles. The civilians on either side of the road stared up at him as he guided the mare north. As soon as he was through the crowds, Hector allowed the mare to break into a gallop, and they raced through the clean, wide streets of Torrent. Within a few minutes, Hector had reached the main town square, where another crowd was forming, all anxious to hear any news. Hector took one of the lanes to the right, ignoring the pleas and questions coming from the civilians, and rode towards the ducal palace, his residence within Torrent. The palace was the smallest of the three within the walled town, but it was possibly the most opulent and comfortable. The Royal Palace to the east covered a large area, more if the parklands were included; while Prince Alfgang the Pius dwelled with his wife and son within an ancient complex built into the side of the cliffs that was more a rough fortress than a luxurious palace. Soldiers by the gates of the ducal palace opened them when they saw the duke appear, and Hector slowed the mare to a walk as they passed through into the walled gardens. Hector dismounted as soon as the gates had been closed, and he passed the reins to a soldier.

'Keep the mare here,' Hector said. 'I will be leaving again in a few minutes.'

'Yes, my lord,' said the soldier.

Hector strode towards the main entrance of the compact palace, passing the trees and rosebushes. Leaves were littering the ground, turned to mush by the rains that had fallen overnight. Hector glanced up as he entered the palace, and found Amery, his lawyer and assistant, waiting for him.

'Is it true, my lord?' said the man.

'Yes,' said Hector, without breaking his stride. 'The king is dead.'

'Long live the king,' said Amery.

Hector glanced at him. 'Indeed.'

He walked into a small but comfortable study, went straight to the desk and produced a bottle of brandy from a drawer. Amery walked in after him, and closed the door. Hector filled two glasses, and slid one over the surface of the desk towards the young man.

'I have heard a few rumours, my lord,' said Amery. 'Was it murder?'

'We may never know,' said Hector. He sat down by the desk. 'This is a fucking catastrophe, Amery. Alfgang the Great ruled Upper Down for forty years, and his idiot son thinks he can snap his fingers and return things to the way they were before.'

'His, uh, *idiot son* is now King Alfgang the Fifth, my lord,' said Amery.

Hector raised a hand and showed Amery the ring the new king had given him. 'And I am now his chancellor.'

'Congratulations, my lord. Should I send word up to the Ridden Estate, to summon your wife and sons here for the coronation?'

'Not yet,' said Hector. 'The new king intends to personally ride out to meet Prince Valentino tomorrow, and he wants me to go with him. He is going to return Hygilt to the custody of her grandfather, and then he will submit to every demand the Sanctians have made. Do you understand me, Amery? *Every* demand. Alfgang the Pius plans to expel the Westlanders from Upper Down.'

'I see, my lord. As you will no doubt be aware, this will have an extremely adverse effect upon the ducal finances. You depend upon the coins spent by the Westlanders in the beer halls, casinos and brothels of Twinbrook. Without that source of income, you will...'

'Spare me your litany of woe, Amery,' said Hector. 'I am familiar with our accounting books.'

'What time will you and the new king be leaving tomorrow?'

'Alfgang the Pius will be departing at dawn.'

Amery frowned. 'I thought you said you were going with His Majesty, my lord?'

'I will not be travelling south,' said Hector. 'There are other matters to which I must attend.' He drained the brandy in his hand. 'I will now leave for the Royal Palace, in order to get there before our new monarch arrives. I will be taking a dozen men-at-arms with me, to go with the eight already on their way to the palace.'

'Should I accompany you, my lord?'

'No. I have another task for you – a task that will require the utmost discretion and tact. As soon as I get to the palace, I will instruct Chief Dravid of the Westlanders to come here, and then you will tell him what I require.'

'I am at your service, my lord. What do you require?'

'Sit down,' said Hector, 'and I will tell you all about it.'

. . .

Ten minutes later, Hector emerged from the palace. The soldiers by the gates were standing next to the grey mare, and the dozen fresh men-at-arms were lined up next to them. As Hector was about to walk down the steps, a voice came from behind him.

'Are you leaving? Is the king really dead?'

Hector frowned at the sight of his young mistress Ireni.

'Yes, and yes,' he said.

Her eyes flashed with worry. 'What shall we do?'

'Stay in your room,' he said.

'If there is to be a coronation,' she said, 'then will your wife be arriving soon? The last time Lady Perpetua was here, you forced me to pretend that I was a kitchen maid, and I...'

'I do not wish to repeat myself, woman,' he said. 'Go to your room and remain there. I will summon you if I need you.'

'But...'

'One more word,' he said, 'and I will throw you onto the streets. You are embarrassing me.'

Ireni lowered her gaze, then she turned and walked back into the palace. Hector strode down the steps and approached the waiting soldiers.

He gazed at the dozen men-at-arms. 'You will make your way on foot to the Royal Palace,' he said. 'When you arrive, join the eight already there, and then await my instructions. I am sure that you understand the seriousness of the situation. You are all proven and loyal men of my duchy, and I know each one of you by name. I know that you will not let me down.'

He gripped the reins harnessed to the mare, placed a foot into the left-hand stirrup, and pulled himself up into the saddle. The soldiers opened the gates, and Hector set off again, the mare bearing him through the streets of Torrent. He turned towards the east of the town, keeping to the middle of the road to avoid the streams of civilians who were also making their way to the Royal Palace. A group of grim-faced and armoured Westlanders were moving in the opposite direction, heading towards the unwalled town of Twinbrook that sat to the north of Torrent. They towered over the civilians, who moved from their path. The gates of the Royal Palace were closed and barred, but they opened for Duke Hector, and he guided the mare through the crowds. Soldiers from the Royal Guard were pushing civilians back with their long, oval shields, and Hector squeezed through the gap. He dismounted in the large courtyard, and passed the reins to a soldier.

'Princess Kilbride and the King's Champion are with the late king's body in the main audience chamber, my lord,' an officer said to him.

'Has the new king arrived yet?' said Hector.

'No, my lord; not yet.'

'And the late king's ministers? Are they present?'

'All officials are waiting for the doors of the audience chamber to be opened, my lord.'

Hector gave the officer a curt nod, then he strode towards the palace. He eyed the sullen group of Westlanders out in the courtyard, then caught sight of Chief Dravid, who was surrounded by over a dozen of his huge, armoured men. They were arguing about something in their own language, and Hector barged into the middle of their group. He was one of the few natives in Torrent whose height matched that of the Westlanders.

'My noble Chief Dravid,' he said, interrupting the conversation.

Dravid eyed him. 'Hector,' he said, 'have you thought of some clever scheme to save our arses from the fire? If not, then you are wasting my time.'

'I suggest that you visit my ducal palace, my noble chief,' said Hector. 'When you get there, speak to my assistant Amery, though I advise that you enter through the back door, alone. Amery will give you the details.'

Dravid's eyes tightened. 'If this is a trap...'

'I have no need for traps,' said Hector. 'If I wished to see the Westlanders expelled from Upper Down, I would simply stand by and allow the new king to do so.'

'And what if I am asked by someone why I am there?' said Dravid. 'It will look suspicious if I arrive at the palace of the Duke of Ridden not two hours after the death of Alfgang the Great.'

Hector thought for a moment. 'Tell them that you are there to collect a slave girl that I have sold you. Her name is Ireni. Amery will deliver her into your hands.'

'Ireni?' said Dravid. 'I thought she was your mistress? She is no slave.'

'She is now. Take her and do as you will with her.'

Dravid and a few of the Westlanders laughed, then Hector tilted his head and strode away. Several courtiers and soldiers glanced at him as he made his way to the main entrance of the palace. An officer of the Royal Guard was keeping watch by the large doors, and Hector approached him.

'Twenty of my men-at-arms will soon be arriving, Lieutenant,' Hector said. 'Have them sent onwards to the audience hall.'

'Yes, my lord,' said the officer.

Hector entered the palace, and heard the low drone of lamentations. Courtiers, officers and officials were lining the wide corridors, and many of the older ones were openly weeping. Hector was careful to present his features as showing the requisite amount of grief, along with some calm assurance.

'My lord!' cried a courtier. 'Where is our new king?'

'His Majesty is on his way to the palace,' said Hector. He caught sight of a group of the dead king's ministers, and he came to a halt before them.

'My noble lords,' Hector said, eyeing the dozen old men. 'Might I join you in commiserating this day's dreadful loss?'

'What does the new king plan to do with us, Hector?' said one.

'That is something I need to discuss with you urgently,' said Hector. 'I would be greatly obliged if you were to meet me in the library in a few minutes. I have been asked to brief the members of King Alfgang the Fourth's government on a few changes.'

'How many changes?' said another.

'Not as many as you might expect,' said Hector. 'The new king desires continuity, and he understands the need for wise advice. I predict a handover of power that will ruffle very few feathers.'

The old men smiled.

'I will speak to my noble brother for a moment,' Hector said, 'then I will join you in the library.'

He strode away, and came to the doors leading to the grand audience chamber. Six soldiers from the Royal Guard were standing outside, blocking the way.

'I'm sorry, sir,' said one, 'but Princess Kilbride and Lord Walter have forbidden access to the audience hall without their permission.'

Hector raised his hand, displaying the ring given to him by the king.

'As the new chancellor of Upper Down,' he said, 'I outrank them both. Open the doors.'

The soldiers glanced at the ring, then at each other.

'His Majesty Alfgang the Pius is only a few minutes behind me, gentlemen,' said Hector. 'I pray that you do not hinder my work.'

The soldiers frowned, then two of them opened the door.

'Keep everyone else out,' said Hector, as he entered the audience hall.

The soldiers closed the door behind him, and Hector strode across the marble floor. At the far end of the hall, a table had been set up in front of the throne, and the fallen king's body was resting upon it, dressed in fine robes of state. A triangular patch of black material was covering his left eye, and the blood had been scrubbed from his face. Behind the table, Kilbride and Walter had been talking, but both were looking at Hector as he approached.

Kilbride frowned. 'I gave orders that...'

'I am afraid I countermanded them, my lady,' said Hector. 'Your royal brother has appointed me as his new chancellor.' He glanced down at the body of the king. 'You have done a good job preparing the body for a public viewing, Your Highness.'

'You're the chancellor?' said Walter.

Hector showed them the ring. 'I am. Does that surprise you, brother?'

'Not in the slightest. There's a group of people in Upper Down that you've fooled into thinking you're not a complete bastard, and Alfgang the Pius is one of them.'

Hector pretended to ignore the comment. 'Where is Princess Abigone? Surely, Her Highness should be here for the public viewing?'

'We have staff out looking for her,' said Kilbride.

Hector nodded. 'Walter – I am appointing you to lead the search for the missing princess. Find her, and make it quick.'

Walter frowned. 'I'm the King's Champion. I'm supposed to stand guard by his body.'

'I will stand in for you,' said Hector. 'Go.'

Walter gave him a look of withering contempt, then he strode from the hall.

'Should we allow the public in now?' said Kilbride.

'Not yet,' said Hector. 'I have one thing to do first. Do not open the doors until I return, my lady. Is that understood?'

Kilbride rolled her eyes.

'Perhaps you might learn to show me a little more respect, Your Highness,' said Hector, 'at least in front of your royal brother. After all, His Majesty trusts me enough to make me his closest and most senior advisor.'

Hector walked away, and left the hall by a side door, which had two soldiers standing on duty in the corridor outside. They saluted the duke as he passed, and he halted for a moment.

'Twenty of my men-at-arms will be arriving shortly,' he said. 'Tell them to wait for me right here, and then knock upon the door of the library.'

'Yes, my lord,' said one.

Hector opened another door and entered the palace library. Inside, all of the fallen king's ministers had assembled, and they got to their feet when Hector strode inside.

'Thank you for coming, gentlemen,' Hector said. 'As I mentioned earlier, the new king, His Majesty King Alfgang the Fifth, the Pius, will be arriving at the palace soon. By the time he gets here, I wish for his new government to be ready to receive their orders.'

'How many of us are losing their jobs?' said one.

'I will get to that in a moment,' said Hector.

'Is that His Majesty's ring I see upon your finger, Duke of Ridden?' said another. 'Are we to assume that you will be a member of the new government?'

'You assume correctly. I...' Hector paused as the door was knocked. 'Please excuse me for a moment.'

He went to the door and stepped outside.

'Your men are here, my lord,' said a soldier.

Hector glanced along the corridor and saw his twenty men-at-arms. He gestured for them to approach, and they came to a halt in front of him.

'The old king's government is inside the palace library,' he said, pointing towards the door, 'and that is the only entrance. Your orders are clear – eliminate them all. The new king wants them gone. Make doubly sure that each one is dead, and then guard the door from the outside until I return. Any questions?'

'Just to be sure, sir,' said one; 'you want us to execute the entire government?'

'I order this as chancellor of Upper Down,' said Hector. 'Be resolute, and ruthless. What you are about to do, you do for the good of the realm. Proceed.'

Hector stood back and watched as the heavily-armed men entered the library. A few cries arose from the startled ministers inside, and then the door was closed. Hector smiled, then he returned to the audience hall, where the soldiers on duty allowed him to pass. He strode up to Princess Kilbride, and took his place by the right hand of the fallen king.

'Are we ready now?' Kilbride said.

'Yes,' said Hector. 'We are ready. It is time to let the public see Alfgang the Great one last time.'

CHAPTER 4
THE MAKER

Torrent, Upper Down – 8th Day of Lamenta 107

'Yes, Tulip,' said Princess Abigone from the branches of the tree; 'I know that they are probably looking for me. However, I have no wish to be found. They will be calling me back to the palace for some boring chore, or another harp lesson, and I much prefer it here.'

She glanced down. In the distance, several servants were roaming the vast parkland to the east of the Royal Palace, checking the benches by the side of the small lake, and all of the other places Abigone liked to visit.

The small furry creature that was draped over her left shoulder mewed into her ear.

'Should I go down, Tulip?' Abigone said.

The creature made another noise, which Abigone interpreted as a *no*. The princess liked to believe that Tulip could comprehend whatever she was saying, though Kilbride and her father often teased her for it. It was true that Tulip recognised his own name; and he certainly knew Abigone's face, as he followed her around wherever she went. She lifted a hand and scratched the creature under his soft chin, and he purred, nuzzling his face into the side of her head.

'I don't want to leave Upper Down,' she whispered. 'In fact, if you weren't coming with me, I would refuse to go. Why would I want to marry some boy I've never met? What if he's a brute, or worse, a cowardly weakling? What if his breath smells? Still, I am grateful to him for one thing – sending you all the way from his kingdom to here, to keep me company.'

She quietened as another group of courtiers walked past the stand of trees where she had taken refuge.

'Princess Abigone!' one of them called out. 'You are needed at the palace, Your Highness!'

The princess lifted her middle finger in the direction of the courtiers, then she sat back against the wide branch. Tulip jumped down from her shoulder and landed on her lap. He circled a few times, then settled down on her dress. For the thousandth time, Abigone wondered what type of animal he was. He was sort of like a dog, though smaller, but he refused to obey any verbal commands. His brown fur had an almost purple tinge to it, though his tummy and limbs were paler; and his gaze could melt her heart. Whatever he was, Abigone was sure that he was the only example of his kind living in Upper Down. While others had boring old horses and dogs as pets and companions, she had Tulip. Abigone had named him when she had first received him, before she had known he was a boy. Her father had tried to force her to change his name, but Abigone hadn't wanted to confuse the creature, as he was already answering to Tulip by then. Other animals kept their distance from him, and so too did many humans, which made Abigone laugh. He was such a sweet and harmless little creature – so why did so many others seem to be wary of him?

Abigone glanced up at the walls surrounding the parkland. To the south were the high cliffs that marked one boundary, while the palace lay to the west. High stone walls followed the rest of the perimeter. The park was large, but Abigone knew that her knowledge of what lay beyond was hazy. Despite being almost eighteen, her father had never once allowed her to leave the palace grounds. Not only that, but she was forbidden from entering certain wings of the palace, and had seldom ever attended any gatherings in her father's audience chamber. The last time she had been there, several of the tall Westlanders had stared at her in a way that had enraged her father, and she had never been allowed back. She knew she wasn't stupid, but she had to admit that she knew little of the outside world. She shook her head in frustration. Her birthday was in nineteen days, and that would mark the beginning of her journey into the far south-west, all the way to the lands of Lord Henry, her betrothed.

She picked up her book on romantic poetry, and leafed through its pages until she reached her favourite sonnets. The slim volume dated from the time of the Elestian Empire, and while Abigone loved the sentiments expressed within the sonnets, she adored the courtly atmosphere conjured up by the poems – all those handsome princes and beautiful princesses risking everything for love, and the grand balls where every noble would gather to dance. Compared to the court of the old empire, that of Upper Down seemed rustic and backward, not to mention filled with all those rough Westlander savages in their filthy plate armour. There was another thing about the book that she liked – it didn't shy away from the existence of the great Masters and Makers who had dominated the old empire. Abigone had learned that there had once been a time when the entire land was ruled by Masters and Makers, a powerful elite who could call upon the sprits to aid them. That era had long passed, and Masters and Makers were feared and loathed everywhere, with Upper Down remaining the sole realm still governed by a family whose ranks contained them. Her father and brother were powerful Masters, and Abigone herself was a Maker, albeit one who had received no training. With no other Makers in the realm, there had been no one to teach her how to use her powers. So bad had it got, that her father had forbidden her from telling anyone about her secret, in case no one would wish to marry her. Would she be able to keep it from Lord Henry after they had become husband and wife? The traits ran in family lines, so there was a chance that any children she conceived would possess the same powers. The thought frightened her a little; would she be cast out from her new family if they discovered the truth?

'Hey!' cried a voice from the base of the tree. Tulip's head darted up, and he hissed.

Abigone glanced down.

'It's only Walter, Tulip,' she said. 'He's probably so drunk that he doesn't know where he is.'

'Abbie,' Walter said, 'you need to come down.'

'Are you lost?' she said. She pointed. 'The palace is that way.'

'Something's happened,' he said. 'You have been summoned.'

'Am I in trouble?'

'No.'

'How did you know where to find me?'

'Killie and I used to play in these trees when we were younger,' he said; 'and I remember her saying that you liked it here, too.'

'My sister and I are princesses. You should use our proper titles.'

'I will if you come down.'

'Tell me what's happened, and I might come down.'

'No,' he said. 'I can't tell you news like this while you are sitting in a damn tree.'

Abigone sighed. She glanced at Tulip, who was regarding Walter with suspicion, then she placed her book into a bag, which she slung over her shoulder. Tulip climbed up onto her other shoulder, and then Abigone clambered down to the ground. Her leather boots touched the soft grass, then she glanced up at her older cousin.

'I'm down now,' she said. 'What's so important?'

'There was an accident,' he said. 'I'm sorry, Abigone, but your father the king is dead.'

She stared at him. 'No.'

'Your brother is now the king,' Walter went on. 'Everyone is going to the palace, and I was sent to find you.'

'What... what happened?'

'Your father was struck by a crossbow bolt while he was standing on the Kendril Wall. I wasn't there, but Killie says it was an accident.'

Abigone felt her body shake, then she burst into tears. 'Father!' she cried. 'Where is he?'

'I will take you to him,' said Walter.

'Can I sit down for a moment first? I'm not sure I can walk.'

Walter glanced around, then nodded. Abigone sat on the grass, and Tulip nuzzled her face, as though he knew she was in pain. Walter sat down next to her, but kept his distance from her furry companion.

'I don't understand,' she said. 'A crossbow bolt?'

Walter nodded. 'It struck him in the eye.'

'That doesn't sound like a fucking accident!' she cried, her tears increasing. 'Who did it?'

Walter raised an eyebrow, as though he had never heard her swear before. 'A soldier. He's dead.'

'Why?'

'Why what?'

'Why did he do it?'

'I don't know, Abbie. It's all a bit of a blur to me.'

'Were you drunk?'

'I was very drunk. My hangover is just commencing.'

'You should have protected him. It was your job to protect the king. You are the most useless champion this kingdom has ever had.'

'Quite possibly.'

'I can't believe it,' she said. 'My father was always so strong. What will we do without him?'

Walter said nothing.

'You and Killie are secretly pleased, aren't you?' she said. 'You always hated my father, and my sister did, too. You acted as though he was cruel and selfish, but he wasn't. He was kind, and generous, and... and he was a better man than you will ever be.'

Abigone continued to cry, as Walter gazed into the distance. She hated her cousin at that moment – why couldn't he be more like his brother, the Duke of Ridden? Hector was every inch the noble knight, a man beloved by the kingdom; while Walter was nothing but a drunken fool. Her father had once told her that Walter spent all of his money on whisky and prostitutes, but, at the time, she hadn't known what the second word had meant. When she had looked it up in a dictionary, she had been appalled and disgusted; firstly, that there were women prepared to degrade themselves in that manner, and secondly, that her weak-willed cousin was the kind of man who paid for their services. It seemed like the opposite vision of what the romantic sonnets had told her about courtly life. How could good men like her father die, while rotten ones like Walter were left alive? Didn't the spirits care?

'I hate you,' she said.

'I know.'

'Everyone hates you. Everyone laughs at you, Walter. That is why you have never found a wife. Your brother and sister married, and my brother and sisters did the same, but no one will ever marry you. No woman wants you, except for the ones you pay, and it serves you right.'

Walter smiled. 'I have some bad points, too, you know.'

'Is that your response? A feeble joke?'

'I thought it was quite good.'

'I shall go to the palace,' she said, getting to her feet, 'but you shall not escort me. You will walk twenty paces behind.'

'Excellent,' he said. 'That way, I won't be too close to your deranged little pet.'

'Ignore him, Tulip,' she said. 'He isn't worth it.'

She strode off down the grassy slope. She knew that Walter would be trailing along at her rear, but she didn't once glance over her shoulder to see if he was there. She crossed a little bridge over a stream that came down from the cliffs, and joined one of the main paths through the vast parklands. Within a minute, several palace courtiers had seen her, and she was soon surrounded by fussing maids and red-faced servants.

'Where have you been, Your Highness?' said one. 'We have been searching for you for over an hour.'

'Have you heard the awful news, Your Highness?' said another. 'May the spirits lead your father's soul to a better place.'

Abigone remained silent on the walk back to the palace, and no one got too close to her, due to the fact that Tulip hissed at any who tried. When they reached the rear entrance to the palace, the courtiers led her through the cool marble corridors to the grand audience chamber, which had soldiers posted outside each door. They were letting the crowds of officials and courtiers in, but only in small numbers, while hundreds of others were waiting their turn. The queue was halted for a moment to allow Abigone into the hall, and the soldiers stopped any of her companions from following her in. Abigone strode past a line of people that stretched all the way to the throne, then she saw Duke Hector and Kilbride standing by a table covered in cloth of gold. Hector looked like the ideal knight at that moment, his uniform immaculate, his handsome features noble and unwavering, while a hand rested upon the hilt of a sword. Even Kilbride looked regal and, for once, her black clothes suited the occasion. Abigone's gaze went to the table as she got closer, then her heart seemed to stop. Her steps faltered, and she thought she was going to faint, then Hector rushed forward, and took her arm.

'It's going to be all right, Your Highness,' he said. 'Be brave for your people.'

She stared at him, then her gaze went back to the body of her father. Hector led her up to the table, then he fetched a chair for her and helped her sit.

'Father!' she sobbed, as the tears began to flow again.

Hector passed her a silk handkerchief, and she pressed it to her face. It smelled of rose blossom, and his act of kindness made her tears spill down her cheeks. Walter appeared in the hall. He walked over to where Hector was standing, but the duke utterly ignored his presence. After a few moments, Walter moved away, and took up a lesser position to the rear of the table, his gaze lowered. The queue began moving again, as the officials of the realm paid their respects to their fallen monarch, but Abigone gave them none of her attention; instead, she stared at the body of her father.

Time passed. The queue seemed to never end, and Abigone began to loathe those who shuffled past the body of the king, and even their tears seemed superficial compared to her own. The main doors of the hall swung open without warning, and a dozen men-at-arms in bright armour strode into the hall.

'The king approaches!' cried one. 'Long live His Majesty King Alfgang the Fifth.'

Abigone looked up, and saw her brother enter the hall, accompanied by his wife Frida, and their seven-year-old son. Alfgang the Pius was wearing black, and Frida's features were veiled, while the young prince was staring at the crowds with wide eyes. The queue hushed, then moved aside, and the new king and his family approached the table by the foot of the gilt throne. Alfgang got down to his knees in front of the table, lowered his head, and began to pray. The men-at-arms flanked them on either side, creating a barrier that sealed off the table from the other mourners, excepting the four who had been keeping watch. Abigone got to her feet, embarrassed that she had been sitting while Hector, Kilbride and Walter had been standing, then she lowered her eyes and pretended to pray.

An old man hurried into the hall, and Abigone recognised him as one of her brother's trusted servants. He approached the kneeling king, and whispered something in his ear. At once, Alfgang's expression changed, and Abigone saw anger in his eyes. He got to his feet, and turned to the officer in charge of his men-at-arms.

'Clear the hall,' he said. 'Family members only shall remain.'

The soldiers got to work, shepherding the officials from the audience chamber, then the doors were sealed. Alfgang gazed in turn at those who were left, then his eyes fell upon Hector.

'Why?' said the king.

Hector looked confused. 'Your Majesty?'

'I told you to place my father's ministers under guard, and yet you had them slaughtered, Hector. Why?'

The others turned, and Abigone almost gasped.

'I did what I felt to be in the best interests of your reign, Your Majesty,' Hector said. 'Had we left any of King Alfgang the Great's closest allies alive, they would have worked to undermine your rule. It was harsh, but necessary, and I wished to spare you from having to make the decision. Let me carry the responsibility, I beg you. Punish me if you see fit to do so, but I did it out of love and admiration for you, my blessed monarch, and in order to give your reign the best possible start.'

'I will punish you, Hector,' said Alfgang, 'of that there is no doubt. However, I have more pressing matters to attend to, and your reprimand shall have to wait until I return from my negotiations with the Illustrious Prince Valentino. Under the circumstances, I cannot allow you to accompany me.' He turned to Walter. 'King's Champion, you shall escort me south at dawn tomorrow.'

Walter bowed. 'As you wish, Your Majesty.'

'Ensure that you remain sober this night,' the king said. 'If you are inebriated at dawn, my wrath will be swift and unforgiving.'

'Yes, Your Majesty.'

'As for you, Hector, for disobeying my very first command as king, I am suspending you from your duties as chancellor, pending my return. You will have no authority to act on my behalf until this mess has been sorted out.'

Hector bowed, but said nothing.

'Did you send word to Princess Hygilt?' said the king.

'Apologies, Your Majesty,' said Hector. 'I had not the time to attend to that duty. Shall I do so now?'

'No,' said Alfgang. 'I want you to clean the library. That is how you will spend the time while I am south with Prince Valentino. Be gone from my sight.'

Hector bowed again, then he strode from the hall.

'My brother did what he thought was right,' said Frida. 'I implore you to show mercy, my husband.'

Alfgang glanced at her. 'I most likely will, my dearest wife, but I wished to give Hector a fright. He did this to show that he will interpret my commands as he sees fit, and I must act to correct this behaviour. If he does it again, I will not be so merciful.'

'So he gets to keep being chancellor, Your Majesty?' said Walter.

'Everyone deserves a second chance, Walter,' said the king. 'You and

Kilbride will remain here with us for the rest of the day, and we shall stand sentinel over the body of my dearly-missed father. Abigone, you can go and rest, and take your little animal with you. In fact, I have a job for you. Enter the quarters of Princess Hygilt, and inform her that she will be leaving Upper Down tomorrow, for I intend to take her with me when Walter and I travel south to meet Prince Valentino. Tell her that her confinement is at an end.'

Abigone bowed her head. 'Yes, Your Majesty.'

She turned and walked from the hall, relieved that she wasn't going to have to stand by the dead body of her father for hours, but confused by what her brother had told her to do. Hadn't Princess Hygilt run away from the imperial court of Sanctos to seek refuge in Upper Down? If that was the case, then why would her brother be sending her back?

She emerged from the hall, and found herself amid a crowd of officials still waiting to queue past the fallen king. They stood back from her as Tulip hissed, and she walked through the gap they had created. It was a novel experience to walk through the palace on her own without any servants or ladies-in-waiting shadowing her every step, but none wanted to miss seeing the old king for the last time, and so none offered to accompany her. Tulip's presence was probably putting them off as well, though Abigone couldn't understand why that would be.

She entered a part of the palace where she had rarely trod, and approached a guarded doorway.

'His Majesty King Alfgang the Fifth has given me express permission to visit Princess Hygilt,' she said to the soldiers on duty. 'Open the door.'

Their eyes narrowed for a split second, then the officer in charge nodded.

'Certainly, Your Highness,' he said. He unlocked the door, and Abigone was allowed through. She smiled to herself, revelling a little in the way that the soldiers had obeyed her orders, then she remembered that her father was lying on a table, and her expression fell again. She came to another door, and knocked.

An old woman opened it and peered out into the corridor.

'Your Highness,' she said.

'I am here to speak to Princess Hygilt,' said Abigone. 'I have news for her.'

The old woman bit her lip for a moment, then stepped aside. 'Please come in, Your Highness.'

Abigone entered a plain apartment, with white walls and very little furniture. There was a large barred window that looked out over the parklands, and sitting next to it was a girl, wearing clothes that made her look like a servant.

'You have a visitor, Your Highness,' said the old woman; 'this is Princess Abigone, sister to the new king. Princess Abigone, this is Princess Hygilt, great-niece of the Sanctian emperor.'

The girl turned, and glanced at Abigone. 'I know who she is,' she said. 'She is always in the park. Every day, I watch her enjoy the freedom I am denied.'

Abigone frowned.

'Princess Abigone says that she has news for you, Your Highness.'

Hygilt shrugged, and turned to gaze out at the park again.

'Would you care for a drink or other refreshment, Your Highness?' the old woman said to Abigone.

'No, thank you.' She walked over to the window and looked out at the park she so dearly loved.

'I like your cat,' said Hygilt, 'though he is a little larger than the ones I am used to.'

Abigone eyed the young princess. 'My what?'

'Your cat,' said Hygilt. 'Did you not know the type of animal that is draped over your shoulders? Does he have a name?'

'He is called Tulip.'

'Tulip?' she said, a smile appearing on her lips. 'That's almost as funny as hearing the news about your father.'

'How dare you?' said Abigone. 'When you ran away from the imperial court, who was it that gave you shelter? My father rescued you from a life of cruelty, and protected you...'

'Is that what he told you?' said Hygilt. 'Honestly – is that what he said?'

'My father was not a liar.'

'Your father was many things, Abigone,' said Hygilt. 'Being a liar was among the least of them. His brutish Westlanders seized me from the castle of the Lord of Camspie, when I was visiting my cousin. They dragged me all the way here, hooded and in chains. I thought your father would execute them for what they did, but... do you know what he did, Abigone? He laughed.' A tear slipped down her cheek. 'He laughed, and said that I would make a good third bride for him in a few years.'

'You disgust me,' said Abigone. 'You lie as easily as breathing. My father would never have behaved in such a reprehensible manner.'

Hygilt shrugged again. 'You don't see it, do you?' she said. 'I bet you were spoiled by him. I bet you never heard him say or do anything that would break the spell he had over you. It will hurt when you finally realise the truth about your father, and I pity you for that.'

'I will not take the bait,' Abigone said. 'I shall retain my dignity and deliver the news, and then, with any luck, I shall never see you again.'

Abigone waited for the girl to ask for the news, but Hygilt remained silent.

'My brother, the new king,' Abigone went on, 'wished me to tell you this. Tomorrow, at dawn, you will be removed from the palace and sent back to your grandfather, Prince Valentino.'

The girl's eyes lit up, and she got to her feet. 'Is this true?'

'It is,' said Abigone. 'Personally, I hope the prince of Sanctos punishes you horribly for running away. I hope he...'

Hygilt ran to the old servant woman, and they embraced, each weeping tears that, to Abigone, looked uncomfortably like tears of relief and joy.

'Praise the new king!' cried the old woman. 'You are going home, my dear girl.'

Abigone watched the girl and the old woman mix tears with laughter, and her temper surged. She glanced at Tulip but, instead of hissing at Hygilt and the servant, he was gently purring on Abigone's shoulder, as if he approved of what had transpired.

Something was wrong, but Abigone couldn't put it into words. It was impossible to believe that her father had laughed when the Westlanders had brought Hygilt before his throne; especially as he had told his daughter that the girl had run away, and that his men had rescued her. But then, why did the girl seem so happy that she was going to be sent to her grandfather?

She turned to gaze out of the window at the park. She would leave the palace again, and find somewhere to be alone with her thoughts. Maybe if she thought about it long enough, the spirits would reveal the truth to her.

'I shall see myself out,' she said, but neither the girl nor the old servant paid her any attention.

Abigone turned her back to them, and walked away.

CHAPTER 5
WITHOUT SLEEP

Torrent, Upper Down – 9th Day of Lamenta 107

It was still dark when Walter arrived at the Kendril Wall, and all three moons were visible in the sky, despite the approach of dawn. Waiting in the shadows of the cliff by the postern gate were forty soldiers from the Mountain Rangers, all standing in silence.

Commander Lothar walked up to meet him. 'You look like shit, sir.'

'And if it's possible,' Walter said, 'I feel worse than I look.'

'I thought you were taking a break from the booze last night, sir.'

'I didn't touch a drop – that was the problem. I couldn't sleep. I lay awake all night, staring at the damn shutters, and begging the spirits to let me drift off.'

Lothar shook his head. 'You should have had a little whisky, sir; that would have done the trick.'

'How could I? I promised the new king that I would stay sober. It didn't occur to me that I needed a drink to get to sleep.'

'Are you going to be fit for today, sir?'

'I'll have to be. I have no choice. Have you seen any sign of our new sovereign?'

'One of his officers was here a few minutes ago, checking that we were ready. His Majesty will be along soon.'

Walter and Lothar approached the Rangers.

'Morning, lads,' said Walter.

'Morning, sir,' muttered a few.

The clack of iron horseshoes on cobbles echoed across the forecourt in front of the great Wall of Kendril. The soldiers turned. The new king was approaching, mounted upon a white stallion. Next to him were ten knights in armour, also mounted, along with a spare horse.

The Mountain Rangers bowed their heads.

'Good morning, Your Majesty,' said Walter, keeping his eyes lowered.

'Good morning, Champion,' said Alfgang. 'Have you briefed your men?'

'I held a briefing yesterday evening, Your Majesty, after I was relieved from duties in the audience chamber. Did you remain there for much longer?'

'I watched over my father's body all night,' said the king.

Another noise arose – that of boots marching, and dozens of soldiers in the uniforms of the Royal Guard emerged from the shadows. In their midst was a single covered wagon, being pulled by four horses.

'How many soldiers are we taking, Your Majesty?' said Walter.

'We shall have your forty from the Mountain Rangers,' said the king, 'and I have brought ten knights and one hundred and twenty men-at-arms. Enough for an escort fit for an imperial princess, but not enough to threaten the army of Prince Valentino.'

'I assume Hygilt is in that wagon, Your Majesty.'

'You assume correctly,' said the king. He gestured to the spare horse. 'You shall ride with me this day, Walter, for I mean to talk with you during our journey south.'

Walter suppressed a groan. He nodded to Lothar. 'Take care of the gate, Commander.'

'Yes, sir,' said his aide.

Walter walked up to the spare horse, a light brown gelding. He ran a hand down its flank, then he gripped the saddle, placed a boot into the stirrup, and pulled himself up, his guts churning. He took hold of the reins, then he noticed the king looking at him.

'You look ill, Walter,' he said.

'I'll be fine, Your Majesty,' he said. 'Commander – open the gate.'

Lothar gestured to the small team of Wall Militia guarding the postern gate, and the men removed the thick bars. The gate was pushed open, and the king urged his stallion on. The postern was wide enough for a wagon or a pair of horses to pass, and the knights lined up as the king rode through the Wall. Walter went next, wishing he was on the ground as the gelding moved under him. He followed the king through the open gate, and down the track that ran by the cliff face. The knights came after him, followed by the Rangers, the wagon, and the men-at-arms from the Royal Guard. The king and Walter rode down the slope for a hundred yards, then Alfgang halted his mount, and they waited for the soldiers to assemble behind them on the slope. Walter watched the gate being closed, then he glanced up at the sky. Somewhere to the east, hidden by the massive cliff face, the sun was starting to rise, and the sky was brightening.

'My knights shall lead the way,' the king said, 'and then Walter and I shall escort the wagon of Princess Hygilt, flanked by the men of the Mountain Rangers. The men-at-arms shall follow.'

An officer in the Royal Guard barked out a few orders, and the soldiers moved into position. The knights rode on ahead, and then the wagon was pulled up to where Walter and the king were stationed. Walter peered through a gap in the fabric covering the back of the wagon, and saw the young princess, wrapped in warm blankets to keep out the autumnal chill. Next to her were three older women, all sitting on the padded benches. Walter wished that he was with them, so that he could stretch out on the blankets and get some sleep. Hygilt saw him looking at her, and the young princess smiled. She looked tired, but her eyes were shining with hope.

'She looks younger than I had imagined, Your Majesty,' Walter said, averting his gaze.

'Is this the first time you have seen Princess Hygilt?' the king said.

'Yes, Your Majesty. She has been locked up in the northern wing of the palace since she... arrived in Upper Down.'

'She was abducted, Walter. It is all right – you can say it. We don't have to pretend that she ran away any more. The time for lies and deceit is over.'

'Yes, Your Majesty.'

'You can temporarily ignore my customary address, Walter. If we are to ride together for many hours, perhaps days, then I do not wish to hear *Your Majesty* every time you open your mouth.'

With everyone in position, the knights at the front of the group began to lead their horses on at a steady walk, and the others followed. Walter's gelding kept pace with the king's stallion as they descended the steep track, and the wagon's wheels trundled along after them.

'What should I call you... Your Majesty?' said Walter.

'Cousin will suffice,' said the king.

Walter chewed his lip.

'Does that not appeal to you, Walter?' said the king. 'We share the same great grandfather – Alfgang the First, the king who founded our realm of Upper Down; therefore, we are cousins.'

'Yes, but you are married to my sister.'

'That is true, of course. Second cousins are permitted to wed. Were that not the case, then the royal lines of these parts would have died out long ago. You may call me *brother* if that makes you feel any better.'

'It doesn't. If people heard me say that, they would assume that I was taking liberties.'

The king smiled. 'You are a hard man to please, Walter.'

They rode on for twenty minutes as they descended through the steep and narrow ravine. They joined the main road that led down from the gatehouse in the Kendril Wall, and their speed picked up a little on the smoother surface. On their right, the stream formed by the waterfalls rushed down the slope, its noise drowning out the cries of the birds awakening for dawn. The high cliffs began to lower a little, and the pass widened and levelled out. Walter glanced over his shoulder. The Kendril Gap was just visible at the summit of the slope to their rear; a semi-circle of sky hemmed in on all sides by rock. It was a sight that Walter had seen many times, but it never failed to impress him. Before the construction of the Kendril Wall, which blocked the lower half, the gap would have been a complete circle, an eye gazing through the otherwise impenetrable cliffs.

'It is a marvel to behold, isn't it, Walter?' said the king.

'Yes, sir.'

Alfgang smiled again. 'No army has ever breached that wall, not in five hundred years. It is not through fear that I have decided to treat with Prince Valentino; rather it is to restore our realm's tattered reputation. My father alienated all of the lands to our south by allying himself with the Westlanders. He abused the security bestowed upon us by the Kendril Wall, and made our name synonymous with banditry, rape and pillage – that is the error I shall correct. Do you agree with this course of action, my champion?'

Walter hesitated. Had the old king asked him such a question, his response would have been automatic. *Yes, Your Majesty, of course I agree.* Alfgang the Pius, on the other hand, seemed to expect honesty. Walter thought through his views.

'Are you thinking, Walter,' said the king, 'or has the lack of sleep befuddled you?'

'How did you know I didn't get any sleep?'

'You are a habitual drinker, Walter, and yet I ordered you to abstain. I am aware of the effects that will have had upon your ability to rest. When was the last time you passed an evening without alcohol?'

'That's harder to answer than your first question, sir. I don't know – three years?'

'Is it any wonder that you are ill? You have become dependent upon whisky, and I have sat back and said nothing while your health and mind deteriorated. I should have intervened. However, you are still young. It is not too late for you, Walter. I recall you in your youth – strong, intelligent, charming. When did you decide that you should attempt to ruin your own life?'

'Try growing up with Hector as your big brother.'

'Come now; do not shift the blame onto another's shoulders. Did your brother force you to drink every night?'

Walter's spirits flagged. Being exhausted and ill was bad enough, without a lecture on sobriety from the new king. He had been expecting it, but that didn't make it any easier to hear.

'Let us return to my earlier question,' said Alfgang.

'All right,' said Walter. 'I think... well, it might not be too late for me, but it might be too late for Upper Down. Your father invited the Westlanders into the realm over twenty years ago, and they have terrorised every kingdom and duchy in the old Central Provinces to our south. They have killed dozens of local nobility, and abducted dozens more; not to mention all of the peasant farmers and townsfolk they carted off or slaughtered. They have burnt countless villages, and several castles, and carried off enough gold to gild a mountain. I admire your intentions, but I fear that those who hate us will require more than a simple apology.'

'Let us focus on the positives,' said Alfgang. 'Why do you admire my intentions?'

'Because, well, I suppose because it's the right thing to do.'

'Exactly, Walter. It is the right thing to do. It will not be easy; I realise this. Delivering Princess Hygilt to her grandfather is a necessary first step. It will not appease all of the kingdoms that we have angered in recent years, but if it prevents the Empire of Sanctos from becoming our foe, then it will have been worth it.'

'The next step will be far harder.'

'I assume you are referring to the fate of the Westlanders resident within Upper Down?' said the king.

'Yes. Dravid, Stefan, and the other chiefs will not cooperate. If you forbid them from raiding, they will ignore you. If you try to expel them, they might overthrow your rule. There are too many of the big bastards and, if I'm being honest, then man-for-man they are superior warriors. Who do we have? The Royal Guard? The Town Militia? The best forces under our control are the Mountain Rangers, and we only have two hundred of them.'

'Those chiefs you mentioned – Dravid and Stefan? They loathe each other, Walter, and therein lies the secret of how we shall defeat them. We shall play each against the other, favouring one, then another, until they rip out each other's throats.'

'Should you be confiding this in me, sir? For all you know, I might be on Stefan's payroll. Or Dravid's. Or any of the other chiefs.'

The king laughed.

'How am I to take that?' said Walter. 'Let's see. Either you think I'm so useless that none of the Westlanders would bother trying to bribe me, or else you see me as a paragon of virtue?'

'What if neither is true?' said the king. 'You are hardly a paragon of virtue, Walter; and yet I believe that the Westlanders would eagerly take you into their payroll if you were willing to join with them. Is it possible that you turned to drink through a sense of despair? You saw what my father was doing to Upper Down, and yet you were powerless to stop it. I have been close to despair for twenty years; forced to watch as my beloved realm was transformed by the Westlanders into a hive of savagery. I, however, turned to prayer rather than alcohol.'

'Less of a hangover,' said Walter, 'but just as futile.'

'I happen to disagree. When I use my abilities as a Master, I can feel the presence of the spirits. I ask them to change one thing into another, and it happens. How could I not pray?'

'I doubt your father prayed much, and he was also a Master.'

'My father was worse than you know, Walter. Some of the things he did would make you weep were I to recite them to you. This world is a far better place without him.'

'Will you have me executed if I agree with you on that point?'

'I would be obliged if you did not repeat my words to another soul, Walter. To go back to your earlier question – I am more than happy to confide in you. There is a place for you in my government, if you can restrict your drinking to once or twice a week, instead of every night.'

'I thought you would insist that I gave it up completely.'

'I require you to be clear-headed, not abstinent. I need loyal and clever allies, people who care about the future of Upper Down; people willing to do the right thing, even if it is painful.'

'Do you think I am one of those people?'

'Yes, Walter; I do. You have been hiding for a long time, but I know the contents of your heart.'

Walter looked away, afraid that his eyes might well up. He was ill and exhausted, he told himself. That was why he was feeling emotional. It had nothing to do with what the king had just said to him.

'Shall we see if our guest is comfortable?' said Alfgang.

The king steered his stallion closer to the flank of the wagon, and Walter followed him.

'Good morning, Your Highness,' Alfgang said. 'Are you enjoying the journey?'

The fabric covering the rear of the wagon opened, and Princess Hygilt smiled up at the king.

'It's a bit bumpy, King Alfgang,' the girl said, 'but that's all right. Do you know how long it will take?'

'Who can say?' said the king. 'We are not certain of the position of your grandfather's army. It is likely that we will first encounter the scouts sent south by Lord Walter. They will be able to tell us how many miles remain. We might even be travelling through the entire day and night, but do not fear – we will find Prince Valentino, and you will be reunited with your kin.'

Hygilt nodded. 'I want to say thank you. I thought... I thought I would be trapped in that palace for the rest of my life, wedded to your father.'

'The king wanted to marry you?' said Walter.

'This is Lord Walter, Your Highness,' said the king. 'He was not involved in any of the decisions taken by my late father.'

'I am glad to hear that,' said Hygilt. 'The king was waiting until I was sixteen, Lord Walter.'

'And that story about you running away?'

'All lies. Did you believe it?'

'No, Your Highness,' said Walter. 'Not for a minute. I... I'm sorry about what happened to you, and I'm sorry that I was too much of a coward to do anything to help you.'

'There was nothing you could have done, Walter,' said the king.

'Princess Abigone believes that I ran away,' said Hygilt. 'She seemed very upset when I contradicted her yesterday.'

'My youngest sister held to her belief that my father could do no wrong,' said the king. 'It will take time for her to realise her mistake.' He smiled. 'Did you happen to see her strange little animal?'

'That thing's a menace,' said Walter. 'I swear it secretly wants to tear out my throat.'

Hygilt laughed. 'It seemed sweet to me. It is a cat. There are many of them on Sanctos, but it seems that Tulip is the only one in Upper Down.'

'A cat?' said the king. 'No one here knew how to classify the creature. It was a gift from Abigone's betrothed, Prince Henry of Nessos. That reminds me, Walter; I intend to call off my sister's wedding. I do not see why she should have to marry a man she has never met. And it might be better to introduce her to a son of the local aristocracy, rather than one who dwells so far away. I shall talk to her regarding this once we have removed the Westlanders from our midst.'

'Are you going to kill those savages?' said Hygilt.

'I rather hope that I can tempt them into killing each other, Your Highness. They may appear united to an outsider, but they are riven into factions. I shall use that against them.'

'You should ask my grandfather to help you.'

The king smiled. 'One step at a time, Your Highness.'

They rode on for another hour, and came to a wider section of the pass, where meadows filled the space between the rocky cliffs of the gorge. They paused for a few minutes to allow the horses to drink from the stream, and Walter dismounted. He knelt by the fast-flowing water, and splashed some on to his face.

'How goes it with the new king, sir?' said Lothar.

'Surprisingly well,' said Walter, as he sat down by the river. 'I was expecting to be soundly berated, but... You know, I may have misjudged him.'

A low rumble echoed across the valley, and the Mountain Rangers were the first to react, their eyes scanning the approaches to the north.

'Hooves,' muttered Lothar.

'Is the imperial army coming?' said a soldier from the Royal Guard.

'Not unless they got round behind us,' said Walter, pulling himself to his feet. 'That sound is coming from the north.' He caught sight of the king, who was also dismounted, and he ran to him, as the sickly feeling in his guts increased. 'Your Majesty,' he cried, 'get back onto your horse, take Hygilt and your knights, and ride south as fast as you can.'

The king raised an eyebrow.

'Do you not hear the horses, Your Majesty?' Walter said. He gestured to Lothar. 'Get the Royal Guard into lines to block the road, and place the Rangers on the flanks. Now, Commander.'

'What is happening?' said Hygilt from the back of the wagon.

Walter felt like throwing up. 'Westlanders.'

'You don't know that, Walter,' said the king. 'It could be messengers bearing word from Torrent.'

'Your Majesty, please,' said Walter. 'Trust me. That sound is being made by dozens of horses. They will sweep through us like a blade reaping wheat.' He approached the king, and leaned in closer. 'Your Majesty,' he said, 'you may need to use your Master abilities.'

'I will be doing no such thing, Walter,' said Alfgang.

'But if the approaching forces are hostile, then...'

'I will not shame the spirits by abusing the blessings they have bestowed upon me,' said Alfgang. 'My Master abilities are to be used to heal, not maim; to help, not kill.'

Walter suppressed a curse, then he turned away from the king. 'Lothar! Get those fucking soldiers moving!'

The Royal Guard were standing around in confusion, waiting for an order from the king, and only the Mountain Rangers were getting into position. Each was armed with a longbow and a long knife, and they were crouching or kneeling on the grass, preparing their bows. Walter ran into the crowd of Royal Guardsmen.

'Shields to the north!' he shouted. 'Defend your king.'

A cry rang out, a terrible cry of fear, and a soldier pointed to the north. Emerging from the shadows of the cliffside were close to a hundred mounted warriors, their plate armour reflecting the rays of the morning sun. The first ranks had their lances lowered, while the others had long swords, war axes or maces gripped in their right hands. The Royal Guard stared in terror as the Westlanders charged down the road towards them. The mounted warriors began to fan out when they reached the wide meadow, forming an arc of steel and thundering horseflesh. Walter turned back to the king, but Alfgang already looked defeated, his eyes wide with despair.

'We are betrayed,' the king whispered. 'Save us, blessed spirits.'

The ten knights formed up round the king and the wagon as the Westlanders grew closer.

'Loose!' Walter cried.

The forty Rangers aimed their longbows into the mass of charging Westlanders and released their arrows. Half a dozen horses went down, throwing their riders, but the rest rolled onwards, unstoppable; invincible.

The Westlanders smashed through the ragged lines of the Royal Guard, their lances piercing flesh, then the second wave drove on, swinging their swords and maces. Soldiers fell, crushed by the weight of the horses, or bloodied by the blades of the Westlanders. Within moments, the first Westlanders reached the ring of knights surrounding Alfgang and the wagon. One of the older women screamed, then an axe split her skull open. The knights tried to rally, but dozens of Westlanders charged them. On the flanks, the Rangers sent out a flurry of arrows, but then the wings of the charging Westlanders closed in on them, and they were cut down. Walter ran to his horse and pulled a sword from the side of the saddle. He threw the scabbard to the ground, as the carnage unfolded before his eyes. Walter tried to reach the wagon, but it was already too late. A Westlander lunged out with a mace, striking the unarmoured king in his chest. Alfgang fell to his knees from the impact of the heavy blow, then the Westlanders speared his body with their lances. Among them, Walter saw Chief Dravid, who was laughing as he drove his lance through the king's back. Walter ran at them, heedless of the danger, then he was struck from behind as a horse collided with him. Walter fell to the grass, then hooves clattered down next to him. He tried to scramble clear, and he was struck by a hoof in the back of the head. He saw a flash, then felt nothing.

When Walter awoke, the back of his head was in agony, and he could barely open his eyes. Something touched his lips, and he felt whisky on his tongue. He spluttered, but that made the pain worse.

'The king...' he gasped.

'Alfgang the Pius is dead, sir.'

Walter squinted in the strong sunlight. 'Where are we?'

'In the mountains, sir,' said Lothar, who was crouching over him. 'We are all that survived. The Westlanders tore us to pieces.'

'Hygilt?'

'Taken, sir. The last I saw of the girl, she was alive. She was screaming, but alive.'

Walter lifted a hand to shield his eyes from the sun, and tried to sit up. Strong hands reached for his shoulders, as two Rangers assisted him. He leaned his back against a boulder and looked at his surroundings. He was in a rocky gully near a mountain track that he didn't recognise. Also in the gully were around two dozen soldiers, the majority Mountain Rangers, although a few from the Royal Guard were dotted here and there.

'Where in the mountains are we?' he said.

'We're south-east of Torrent, sir,' said Lothar.

'How did we get up here?'

'A few of the lads carried you, sir.'

'That's not what I meant. Why aren't we all dead?'

'The Westlanders were concentrating on the king and Hygilt, sir. I ordered the retreat as soon as the king fell. Should we have stayed?'

Walter said nothing.

'We will rest here for an hour, sir,' Lothar went on, 'and then we will trek along the old goat paths. We should be back in Torrent this time tomorrow.'

'Torrent?' said Walter.

'Yes, sir. Where else?'

'The Westlanders might be in control of Torrent by then.'

'I know, sir.'

'It was Dravid. I saw him. How did he know we would be there?'

'Someone betrayed us, sir. Everyone knows that the Westlanders have spies all over Upper Down.'

Walter lowered his gaze. 'The king is dead.'

'Yes, sir.'

'Two kings in two fucking days.'

'Yes, sir.'

Walter sobbed, oblivious to the gazes from the surviving men. It felt as though the world was ending, and he didn't care who saw him weep.

CHAPTER 6
WITHOUT HOPE

Torrent, Upper Down – 9th Day of Lamenta 107

'It's a beautiful morning, my lady,' said Marie. 'Should you not be out on your balcony?'

Kilbride glanced up at her lady-in-waiting, then she returned her attention to the paperwork covering her desk. 'It is too bright outside to read, and I have hundreds of royal documents to study. The new king has asked me to familiarise myself with the inner workings of the late king's government, and I want to complete this task before His Majesty returns to Torrent.'

'Too bright to read, my lady?' said Marie.

'My eyes tire in the sunlight,' Kilbride said. 'You can open one more shutter, and then I would be obliged if you fetched me a flagon of water with ice and lemon.'

The lady-in-waiting curtsied, then she strode up to one of the tall windows in Kilbride's study. She took a pole and reached up with it, unfastening a latch built into the shutters. She put the pole down, and opened the shutters wide, flooding the shadow-filled room with light. Kilbride blinked.

'That's better, my lady,' said Marie. 'I shall return with your water in a few moments.'

Kilbride rolled her eyes as Marie left the room. At times, she wished her lady-in-waiting would keep her distance, but it was as though Marie felt that she had to be seen to be useful. Sitting still and quiet in the corner of the room while Kilbride worked seemed alien to her, and she was continually fussing over the princess.

Kilbride gazed at the sheaf of papers laid out in front of her. They were part of a correspondence between Upper Down and Lesser Down, where Kilbride's sister Nolan lived, married to a prince of that kingdom. The king of Lesser Down was demanding that King Alfgang the Great use his authority to prevent the Westlanders from raiding his territory, and, in his response, the old king had agreed. Lesser Down would be spared, as Alfgang hadn't wished for a repeat of what had occurred in Greater Down, where his eldest daughter's husband had been butchered.

Kilbride stopped reading, her thoughts going to the sight of Roderick's severed head wrapped in his bloody surcoat. Was that why Lesser Down had never been attacked by the Westlanders? She had assumed that it was due to the fact that the small kingdom was relatively impoverished; but no. Her father had felt contrite enough after Roderick's death to insist that the Westlanders left his other daughter's kingdom alone. Or perhaps Alfgang hadn't wanted to lose the friendship of the one realm that didn't actively loathe Upper Down.

Before his departure, Alfgang the Pius had hinted that a place in his government would be found for Kilbride, and he had further hinted that it might be the role of chamberlain, with responsibility for mending the broken relationships with the patchwork of kingdoms to the south. No such mending would be able to take place while the Westlanders remained in Upper Down, but the new king had plans to take care of that matter. Kilbride smiled. For the first time in many years, she felt hopeful about the future. Her brother had his faults, but they were trivial compared to the flaws of their dead father. If anything, the new king was too trusting, too optimistic, too... idealistic. He believed that the spirits would help resolve every difficulty, and so acted accordingly. In many ways, Kilbride loved that aspect of her brother's personality, even if he sometimes appeared naïve. To him, no problem was too big to solve; no obstacle insurmountable. His enthusiasm was infectious, and Kilbride's mood had lifted considerably. She felt not an ounce of guilt for her role in the death of her father, and with Captain Joachim's apparent suicide, there was nothing to link her to that act of base treachery. The old bastard was dead at last, and Kilbride would treasure the sight of the bolt striking his left eye for as long as she lived.

She would never tell her brother the truth, that was obvious. In fact, she would never tell anyone about the conspiracy. An *accidental discharge*. She could laugh out loud at the ridiculousness of the notion, but without any proof to the contrary, she had got away with murder. Vengeance for Roderick had been her primary motive, but it pleased her greatly that her brother had been given a chance to show his mettle. He would make a good king, perhaps even a great king, and he would pull Upper Down back into the light.

The door opened.

'Thank you, Marie,' Kilbride said, without looking up. 'Place the water on the desk.'

'I can get some water for you, my lady; all you have to do is ask.'

Kilbride peered up, and saw Hector standing by the open door. 'Oh, it's you.'

'May I please come in?'

'I don't know,' she said. 'I think you owe us all an explanation about your behaviour yesterday. Right now, you should be riding south with the king. Instead, you are awaiting punishment for what I can only call a wicked and ghastly crime.'

'I made a dreadful, dreadful mistake,' he said. 'I completely misjudged events. I deserve my punishment, and I will accept whatever His Majesty decrees when he returns. I am not here to make excuses, Your Highness; I am here to humbly apologise.'

'Why did you do it, Hector?'

'I did not lie to the king when he asked me the same question,' he said. 'I disposed of the members of the previous government to prevent them conspiring against us. The new king wished to dismiss them all from the service of the crown, and I felt that this would anger and wound them deeply. I honestly believed that I was helping the realm. However, I now understand that I should have obeyed His Majesty's command to the letter. Do you think he will ever forgive me?'

'You know what he's like. He has probably forgiven you already. I, on the other hand, will need a little more proof of your good intentions.'

Hector raised his palms. 'The library is spotless. I toiled through the evening and night, scrubbing and cleaning as though I were a servant. The bodies of the slain ministers have been sent to the mortuary for burial, and their blood wiped from every surface.'

'How many people assisted you?'

'One. I was unable to carry the bodies out on my own. I received many offers of help, from the palace staff, and from a few Royal Guardsmen, but I turned them all down. Well, all but one, as I said. Does that satisfy you?'

'At one stroke, you removed decades of valuable knowledge and experience from the realm.'

'I feared that knowledge and experience would be used against us. I knew that King Alfgang the Pius would never sanction their executions, and I acted to remove a potential threat to his reign. Our new king has a kind and generous heart, and I did not wish anyone to take advantage of that fact. Did you see him leave Torrent this morning?'

'No one was there, except for the soldiers he was taking with him. His trip is to be kept secret, and I did not wish to draw any attention to what he was doing.'

'Do you think Walter managed to remain sober?'

'Yes, I do.'

'I hope you are right. I worry about my brother. One day, he is going to drink himself to death. Now, may I come in?'

Kilbride sighed, and nodded. Hector strode into the room. He walked over to the open window, and gazed out at the parklands.

'If this were my office,' he said, 'I would never get any work done. What a marvellous view.'

'Was there any other reason for your visit?' she said.

'Yes.'

'Well; out with it, Hector.'

'If things turn out well, you and I will soon be members of the new king's government. I shall be chancellor, and you shall be chamberlain – the two highest-ranked offices in the realm. We will need to work closely together on many matters of state.'

'We shall.'

'I propose that we pledge always to be completely honest with each other,' he said. 'After all, our aims are the same – to defend the reign of the king, and to ensure Upper Down prospers in peace.'

Kilbride said nothing.

'I have always admired your keen intelligence,' Hector went on. 'You were under-appreciated by the late king, which, in my opinion, was a tragedy. I trust that the new king will not make the same mistake. For instance, I imagine that His Majesty will call upon your counsel regarding the course of action to be taken against the Westlanders. Do you know of His Majesty's intentions in this matter?'

'Not in any detail.'

'Did you know that he intends to expel them? His Majesty told me this yesterday.'

'Did he?' she said. 'When?'

'When we were alone upon the battlements of the Kendril Wall.'

'Do you disagree?'

'Do you?'

Kilbride said nothing, and Hector turned to gaze at her.

'There are two ways of looking at the situation,' he said. 'On the one hand, we can rightfully condemn the terrible suffering the Westlanders have inflicted upon our neighbours to the south; and on the other, we can clearly see how dependent we have become upon the wealth the Westlanders have brought to Upper Down. While we should applaud the King's principles, we should not lose sight of the fact that they will bring us perilously close to bankruptcy. That seems to be the dilemma we are facing.'

'And you want to know where I stand on this?'

'I do. It would be wise if we did not work at cross-purposes.'

Kilbride considered her response. As for his suggestion of complete honesty, it was utterly out of the question.

'I am willing to keep an open mind,' she said.

Hector smiled. 'That is all I ask. Tell me – do you ever think of the time we spent together?'

'Never.'

'Are you trying to hurt me?'

'No. I was out of my mind with grief and anger when I made that particular... mistake with you, Hector. The death of my husband brought out the worst in me for a time.'

'I seem to recall that it brought out your best, and I certainly don't consider it to have been a mistake. I assume that none of your family is aware that we were once embroiled in passion?'

'You assume correctly.'

'I think about it, sometimes,' he said.

'Do you forget the deal we made? You would never mention our dalliance, and I was never to mention that you have been hiding the fact that you are a Master.'

'I haven't forgotten,' he said. 'I forget nothing. I especially remember the taste of your lips on mine.'

Kilbride narrowed her eyes. 'How is your wife these days? I haven't seen Perpetua in some time.'

He smiled. 'She is fine. She hates it down here in Torrent, as I am sure you know. She insists upon spending all of her time on the Ridden Estate, which is several days' journey away by carriage. Thank you for asking, though; I shall be sure to pass on your best wishes whenever I next happen to see her. As for the other... thing, I want you to know that my door is always open if you ever wish to rekindle what we once had. That is all. No pressure, and no ultimatums. I just wanted you to know.'

'Divorce your wife, and then approach me in the proper manner,' she said. 'Otherwise, my answer remains the same.'

'And if I did so, you might consider it?'

'I might.'

'We would make a formidable team, you and I,' he said. He smiled again, and his eyes pierced her. 'And, at long last, you would be able to wear a colour other than black.'

He strode from the room, and Kilbride bowed her head, unsure of how to feel about his advances towards her. He hadn't mentioned their affair in years, so why had he brought it up? And was he serious about divorcing his wife for her? She knew in an instant that, despite the raw attraction she felt towards him, she would never agree to be his wife. It wasn't just the rumours of countless affairs that cemented her opinion, it was something else. Just as Kilbride had been less than honest with him, she sensed that, behind his handsome features, Hector was hiding something. She got to her feet, all thoughts of work abandoned, and walked out on to her wide balcony.

Hector was clever, she knew, and, like her, he had a ruthless streak. Alone among the members of the royal court, Hector had managed to remain close to both the old king and the new; and with the elimination of the former ministers, he was now the second most powerful figure in the entire kingdom. What would he do with his power? Was it conceivable that he would try to convince the new king to allow the Westlanders to remain within the realm? Alfgang would never agree. If his meeting with Prince Valentino went as planned, then the new king would be committed to the removal of the warlike foreigners, and no amount of persuasion would be able to change his mind.

Kilbride's gaze went over the Royal Parkland. There were a few pine and spruce, but the other trees were in the midst of losing their leaves, and gardeners were out, armed with rakes. If it remained dry, then by nightfall there would be a dozen little bonfires blazing, and the scent of smoke would be drifting over the palace. She wondered if Abigone was somewhere in the park, reading her silly poems. There had been a time when Kilbride had savoured the love sonnets of the old empire, but those days were long past. She chose to think of herself as pragmatic, but it was more likely that her experiences had made her cynical, and part of her was envious of Abigone's innocence.

She walked back into her study, and saw a flagon of water sitting on her desk. There was no sign of Marie, but her lady-in-waiting would have seen Hector come and go. Marie was a little infatuated by the handsome duke, as were many of the women who worked in the Royal Palace, and she was probably gossiping to her friends about his visit. Almost nothing happened in the palace without at least one courtier, soldier or servant witnessing it, and Kilbride wondered what they had made of Hector scrubbing the blood from the library floor. Kilbride walked over to the desk, and glanced down at the piles of documents – the entire written record of her father's reign. Forty years of charters, correspondence, proclamations and writs, and all of it was on her desk. Strictly speaking, as chancellor, the documents should have gone to Hector first, but Alfgang had entrusted them to her. Her appetite for reading them had dissipated since the duke's unseemly advances, but she could not allow herself to become distracted. When the new king returned from the south, she wanted to have a grip on the affairs of the realm.

She sat down, and reached for a document.

'My lady,' said Marie.

Kilbride frowned. 'What is it?'

'An officer from the Town Militia wishes to speak to whoever is in charge,' her lady-in-waiting went on. 'Is that you, my lady?'

'I assume it cannot wait until His Majesty returns?'

'The officer is unaware that King Alfgang departed the palace this morning, my lady.'

'Send him in.'

Marie bowed her head, and hurried through the doorway. Kilbride thought about hiring a secretary. She would need one when she was formally appointed as chamberlain; in fact, she would require several. She tidied some of the documents into piles, then waited. A few moments later, Marie escorted a young captain into her presence.

'How can I help you?' said Kilbride.

The captain took off his cap and lowered his gaze. 'Your Highness,' he said, 'thank you for seeing me. The major in command of the day watch in Torrent sent me here to request assistance, and to alert you to the presence of a large group of armed Westlanders within the town.'

'The Westlanders are in Torrent?' she said.

'Yes, my lady.'

'How many?'

'Perhaps eighty, my lady.'

'And what are they doing?'

'Causing a nuisance in the town square, my lady. They have disrupted the market, set up camp, and are drinking heavily. The Town Militia have asked them to depart Torrent, and to make for their homes in Twinbrook, but they refused to leave. The major would like to request reinforcements to clear them from the streets.'

'Who let them into Torrent? Are the gates leading to Twinbrook lying open?'

'No, my lady. It appears that the Westlanders passed through the Kendril Wall on their way back from a raid, and...'

'A raid? What raid? No raid was authorised.'

'It is possible that they left Upper Down a few days ago, before... before the king was killed.'

'What does the Wall Militia have to say about this?'

'I don't know, my lady.'

'Don't you ever coordinate? Sometimes, it feels as though we have a dozen branches of the armed forces, and none of them speak to each other. Return to your commanding officer, and inform him that I will be sending reinforcements to assist with... persuading the Westlanders to leave Torrent. For now, keep them contained within the town square, and try to protect the lives and property of the civilians.'

'Yes, my lady,' said the captain.

He hurried from the room, and Kilbride got to her feet. 'Marie?'

Her lady-in-waiting appeared at the door. 'Yes, my lady?'

'Is Duke Hector still in the palace?' she said. 'If he is, find him and ask him to join me downstairs. We will need to visit the commander of the Royal Guard.'

The woman bowed and rushed away. Kilbride waited a moment,

then she got to her feet and strode from her study. It was located at the far edge of her sprawling quarters on the second floor of the palace. She would turn it into her official office when she became chamberlain, rather than use the tiny rooms where the previous custodian of that rank had worked; that way, she wouldn't have far to walk each morning. She imagined entertaining ambassadors and emissaries from far flung realms out on her balcony. Her staff would serve them fine wines from the vineyards found on the northern slopes of Upper Down, and they would discuss the important affairs of the world.

Kilbride picked up a few waiting courtiers as she made her way downstairs. The corridors of the palace were quiet, and a sense of mourning was in the air. The body of her father had been moved from the audience hall at dawn, in readiness for the funeral scheduled to take place upon the following morning. After that, there would be a coronation to plan, and that fell squarely under the chamberlain's remit. The role of placing the crown upon her brother's head belonged to the Duke of Ridden, but the chamberlain had a prominent role to play in the ceremony, and she wondered if she should wear something other than black for the occasion.

She found Marie and Hector in a downstairs hallway. The duke glanced at Kilbride, then strode over to greet her.

'What have you heard?' he said.

'A few Westlanders are being drunk and disorderly in the town square of Torrent,' she said. 'We are going to need some mounted soldiers of the Royal Guard to usher them back to Twinbrook.'

The duke nodded.

'The officer I spoke to seemed to be under the impression that they had come through the Kendril Wall,' Kilbride went on. 'Do you know anything about that?'

'No, Your Highness.'

'You look a little anxious, Hector,' she said. 'You must be aware that this is a fairly common occurrence. The Westlanders know fine well that they are not to disturb the peace of Torrent – they have Twinbrook for that – but they like to test our patience now and again. Do you wish to accompany me to the office of the Royal Guard?'

'I think I shall, yes.'

They turned, and began to walk down the long hallway, followed by a large group of officials and courtiers.

'Do you know of any raiding parties that might have gone out over the last few days?' she said.

'No, Your Highness,' said Hector.

'I wonder if they saw the king and Walter riding south,' Kilbride went on. 'Their paths would have intersected. If so, then the Westlanders might be aware that we have removed Princess Hygilt from the palace. She was travelling in a covered wagon, but they might have seen her.'

They reached the office where the commander of the Royal Guard was based, and, within a few minutes, the soldiers on duty that day were being summoned from the palace barracks. Kilbride, Hector and the commander of the Guardsmen walked outside into the autumn sunshine, and watched as horses were brought from the stables. Over two hundred soldiers were given weapons, and they began to mount their horses.

Kilbride glanced up at Hector as the men got ready, but the duke seemed distracted. She wondered if he was regretting his earlier words to her. He had been right about one thing, though – they would indeed make a formidable team if they ever got together. It was never going to happen, but for a brief moment she pictured herself as his wife. That would make her not only a princess of the realm, but the Duchess of Ridden, putting her at the same rank as Queen Frida, her brother's wife. She might even be richer than the new queen, as the Ridden Estate was vast and extremely profitable.

'I think I will lead the foray,' Hector said.

Kilbride frowned, then she and the officer glanced at him.

'With your agreement, of course, Your Highness,' he said.

'And why would you wish to do that?' said Kilbride. 'Things could get a little ugly.'

'I think I will be able to prevent any violence,' said the duke. He eyed the officer. 'Fetch my horse.'

'Yes, my lord,' said the officer.

'Don't get yourself killed now, will you, Hector?' said Kilbride.

The duke smiled, but Kilbride could see that it was false. 'I will try my best, Your Highness.'

Kilbride remained on the palace steps as Hector and the officer descended into the crowd of horses and soldiers. The Duke of Ridden was led to his mount, and he climbed up into the saddle. The palace gates were opened, and the duke led the two hundred mounted Guardsmen out into the streets of Torrent. When they had all departed, soldiers closed the gates, and Kilbride returned to her study.

An hour passed without any news arriving from the town square, and Kilbride became so engrossed in reading the realm's documents that she had almost forgotten about the incident. Shouting from somewhere outside disturbed her concentration. She considered closing the balcony doors, then more cries echoed up from the courtyards, followed by the sound of boots and horses' hooves on the cobbles. Kilbride put down the paper that she had been reading, and listened. Some of the cries sounded like those born of grief, and her first thought was that something terrible had happened to Hector.

Kilbride arose from her chair, just as Marie entered the room.

'Do you know what's happening?' said Kilbride.

'No, my lady. I came here to see if you knew.'

'We shall find out together.'

The noise coming from the courtyard faded as the two women walked along the corridors of the palace. They went down two flights of stairs and found the lower floor deserted. The noise increased again as they strode towards a doorway that led outside. Kilbride reached the door, and looked out. The Courtyard of the Shrines was crammed with horses, soldiers and courtiers, and the air was filled with the sound of weeping and grief. Standing tall in the centre of the crowd was Duke

Hector, and Kilbride exhaled in relief at the sight of him. He turned, and she saw tears streaking down his cheeks. Their eyes met across the courtyard, and the duke slowly shook his head. He was holding something in his arms; something wrapped in a blanket.

Kilbride stepped down to the cobbles and began to push her way through the crowd towards Hector.

'It is over!' wailed an old man. 'Upper Down is finished!'

Marie was shoved by someone trying to get past, and almost fell, then grim-faced soldiers from the Royal Guard caught sight of Kilbride and her lady-in-waiting. They pushed through the crowd, forcing the courtiers back, until a path was opened up between the princess and the Duke of Ridden.

'The Westlanders?' said Kilbride.

'They had gone by the time we reached the town square, my lady,' said Hector, his eyes red.

She pointed at the bundle in his arms. 'What are you holding, Hector?'

'Something the Westlanders left for us,' he said. He took a few paces towards her. 'My lady, I am so sorry.'

Kilbride's heart seemed to stop. Hector pulled back the corner of the blanket, revealing the severed head of the new king.

'Alfgang the Pius is dead,' he said.

Kilbride stared at the head of her brother, as the soldiers and courtiers raised their voices to lament. All of her dreams and plans, and with them, all of her hopes for the future, evaporated into nothing.

Her brother was dead, and Upper Down had lost another king.

CHAPTER 7
WITHOUT FEAR

Torrent, Upper Down – 9th Day of Lamenta 107

Hector struggled to contain his fury. Two yards in front of him, Kilbride looked as though she was about to collapse, and the noise coming from the mourning soldiers and courtiers gathered in the Courtyard of the Shrines was making it hard to think.

'The Westlanders need to pay for this crime!' shouted an officer from the Royal Guard.

'We do not know who was responsible for this wicked act,' said Hector, 'and we must not prejudge anything until we have learned the truth. It may be that the Westlanders discovered the slain body of King Alfgang the Pius; it may be that His Majesty was struck down by Prince Valentino's men.'

Kilbride fell to her knees on the cobbles, and her lady-in-waiting crouched by her. The princess looked too stunned to weep.

Hector took hold of a courtier by her shoulder. 'You there,' he said; 'send word to Queen Frida, informing her of this terrible news. Tell my sister that her husband's death shall be avenged.' The courtier bowed and hurried away, and Hector turned to face the soldiers in the courtyard. 'I shall lead a detachment south to recover the king's body,' he said. 'I need a hundred volunteers and their mounts. Who is with me?'

A roar rose up from the assembled Guardsman, and several began to remount their horses.

'You could be riding into an ambush, my lord,' said an old palace courtier.

Hector raised his chin. 'I will not allow the body of our king to be devoured by wolves and crows.' He stepped forward, and handed the bundle containing Alfgang's head to Kilbride's lady-in-waiting. 'Your Highness,' he said, placing a hand onto Kilbride's shoulder, 'you should go into the palace.'

'The new king…' Kilbride gasped.

'I am sorry, my lady,' Hector said. 'He is dead.'

'No,' said Kilbride. 'Little Alfie – he is our new king.'

Hector blinked. 'Yes. Of course, Your Highness.'

'We must protect him,' Kilbride whispered. 'Hector; listen to me. We must protect Alfie.'

Hector straightened his back. 'I am ordering a full mobilisation of all forces loyal to Upper Down,' he said. He pointed at the commander of the Royal Guard. 'Have word sent out to every branch of the militia, and send a full company of Guardsmen to reinforce the palace residence of Queen Frida and His Majesty King Alfgang the Sixth, the boy-king. Secure the gates along the walls of Torrent, and ensure that all are closed. Her Highness Princess Kilbride is in charge of Upper Down while I retrieve the body of the boy-king's father. Obey her orders. The government of the realm shall see us through this time of trial. I want my hundred volunteers mounted and waiting by the palace gates. Now is not the time to mourn – that will come soon enough – now is the time to take the necessary steps to preserve our realm. Each one of us shall do their duty, from the lowliest servant, to the highest ranked officers of the kingdom; I expect no less.'

He crouched down again. 'I will be back as soon as I can, Your Highness.'

'Walter,' she said.

'I know,' said Hector. 'I will do what I can.'

Hector strode through the crowd, and remounted his horse. He gestured to the palace gates, and they were pushed open for a second time that morning. Hector led the hundred volunteers into the streets of Torrent, where frightened-looking civilians were starting to emerge from their homes. Hector ignored them, and urged his horse into a trot.

Those stupid fucking Westlanders. How could Dravid have been so negligent, so careless? Hector's mind raced, and his rage grew. The idiot chief was supposed to have slipped back into Twinbrook with as little fuss as possible when he returned from the mission assigned to him by the duke. Instead, he had allowed his men to get drunk in the town square of Torrent. Worse, they had brought back the head of the king they had slain, and had left it in the square for all to see. Dravid would have to pay for his arrogance; had he forgotten that he worked for Hector? The townsfolk would put two and two together, despite Hector's protestations that Prince Valentino might have been behind the king's death. Most natives of Upper Down already loathed and feared the Westlanders, and Dravid's indiscretion had sealed their hatred forever.

Too angry to formulate any new plan, Hector led his men towards the mighty Kendril Wall. He had sent Amery to bribe the officers on duty to allow Dravid's raiding party to come and go that morning. Would any mention that little fact to others, or would they be frightened into silence by the terrible consequences their actions had brought about? They would have to die; Hector couldn't afford to take any more risks.

They reached the gatehouse in the centre of the wall, and Hector ordered that the main gates be opened. The soldiers of the Wall Militia looked nervous and scared as they got to work. The huge beams were taken down from the tall, iron-rimmed doors, and the gates were swung open, each creaking on their hinges. Hector dug his heels in, and his horse cantered onto the wide road leading down the steep and narrow ravine. He heard the hooves of a hundred other horses behind him, and then the great gates were closed.

. . .

They rode for over an hour, the smooth surface of the road speeding beneath them. Hector used the time to clear his thoughts. He had to remember that his plan had succeeded. Dravid would be dealt with, but with King Alfgang the Pius no longer a threat, Upper Down was one step closer to belonging to Hector. A new government would have to be formed, and quickly. With all of the old ministers of state dead, Hector would rise to the top, with or without Kilbride by his side. There was always Abigone, if Kilbride remained stubborn enough to refuse his advances. Either princess would suffice as a new bride, once he had rid himself of Perpetua.

He slowed his mount when he saw a wisp of smoke on the horizon. The valley widened at that point – the perfect place for a cavalry ambush. Hector led the hundred volunteers off the road and into a grassy meadow, aiming for a bonfire. Blood was staining the ground in patches, and weapons and armour were lying scattered around. Hector brought his horse to a halt, and dismounted. He stared at the bonfire. Upon it were heaped the bodies of dozens. Almost all of the dead were wearing the charred remains of uniforms belonging to the Royal Guard, but there were also those from the Mountain Rangers, as well as a handful of dead Westlanders on the pile of smouldering bodies. Twenty yards from the base of the bonfire, a single headless corpse was splayed out on the ground, and Hector walked towards it, followed by his volunteers.

The king's body had been stripped of clothes, and had been horribly mutilated. His hands had been hacked off, along with his genitals, and his torso had been punctured by numerous lance blows. Hector fell to his knees, sickened by the sight. He bowed his head. For once, he wasn't feigning grief. He had done this. He had arranged for the Westlanders to butcher the new king, and they had followed his orders. He heard the sound of weeping coming from some of the volunteers, but no tears came from his eyes. He wondered how it was possible to weep false tears in front of Princess Kilbride, and yet not be able to cry when faced with the awful truth of what he had done. He remembered Hygilt, and got to his feet.

Hector had told Amery not to mention the presence of the imperial princess to Chief Dravid, but she had no doubt been discovered by the Westlanders. What had they done with her? His eyes scanned the grass, but he saw no other bodies. An abandoned wagon was resting a little distance away, but it was empty, and its horses had been taken. Hector turned back to the bonfire. The flames were dying away, leaving a mixture of ash, bones and unburnt flesh. Was her body amid the pile? And Walter – was he there, too? Had Hector killed his own brother? That hadn't been his intention; more of a calculated risk.

'We will have to search through the bodies,' he said to the volunteers. 'I want four men to hitch their mounts to the wagon, and to prepare it for the journey back to Torrent. Place the king's remains into the back of the wagon, and make sure the body is fully covered. Everyone else will pull that heap apart. If Princess Hygilt or my brother is in there, I need to know. I will search the perimeter of the meadow, to see if there is anything else to be discovered.'

He strode away from the bonfire, keeping his gaze averted from Alfgang's body. More than anything else, it was imperative that the people of Upper Down never realised the truth about Hector's involvement in the murder of the king. He made a list of those who would have to be eliminated. The three officers of the Wall Militia that Amery had bribed, and Chief Dravid and any of his men who wouldn't or couldn't keep their mouths closed were at the top of the list. If he played it well, he could position himself as the avenger of Alfgang the Pius. He would execute the officers from the Wall Militia on suspicion of allowing Dravid's raiding party to come and go, and he would lead a raid of his own, into the heart of Twinbrook to seek out and punish Dravid. If he could accomplish all that, then the people of Torrent might even see him as their saviour.

He came across more patches of blood, but all of the bodies had been dragged over to the bonfire. He glanced around the meadow, and noticed a heap of discarded weapons. The Westlanders viewed the swords used by the militia as inferior, and had left them on the grass.

Hector made sure no one was watching, then he crouched next to the pile of abandoned swords.

He extended a hand.

'Take this iron,' he whispered, 'and in its place put coins of gold.'

The swords shimmered on the grass, then the metal transformed itself into a heap of small gold coins. Hector reached out and picked one from the ground. Each coin had been stamped with the profile of King Alfgang the Great on the obverse, and an image of the Kendril wall on the reverse. It was strange how his Master powers would sometimes interpret his demands but, in this case, what they had created was perfect for his needs. He gathered up the coins, and filled his pockets with them. Why hadn't Alfgang the Pius used his own powers against the Westlanders? Hector knew that he had been strong enough, but his sense of morality had probably got in the way, costing him his life. A man as weak as that had no right to be king. Alfgang may have had good intentions, but what use were they without an iron will?

Hector got back to his feet. He walked over to his horse, and transferred the gold to the saddle bags while the soldiers continued to work. Despite the gruesome tasks that he had assigned to them, none of the volunteers made any complaint as they pulled the heap of dead apart.

A sergeant approached.

'My lord,' he said, 'there is no sign of your noble brother within the mound of slain. It may be that his body was too badly burned to be recognisable, as there are several charred skeletons at the base of the heap. There is also no sign of the princess, but we found the bodies of three older women, who may have been accompanying her.' He lowered his voice. 'I heard what you said by the palace, my lord, but it seems clear that the Westlanders were indeed responsible for the death of the king. There were a dozen Westlander corpses in the mound, and several had been killed by arrows – arrows fletched in the style used by the Mountain Rangers. From the evidence, I would guess that the Westlanders ambushed the king's party right here.'

'I cannot but agree,' said Hector. 'When we return to Torrent, I intend to bring the Westlanders responsible for this outrage to justice. I will need true and loyal men to assist me, and I shall need to keep my intentions secret for now. Can I rely upon you, sergeant?'

The soldier saluted. 'Yes, my lord.'

'The first thing I want you to do when we reach the Kendril Wall,' said Hector, 'is raid the officers' quarters in the gatehouse. Someone there allowed the Westlanders to pass through the gates this morning, and I want their heads. Is that understood?'

'Yes, my lord.'

'What is your name?'

'Sergeant Towie of the Royal Guard, my lord.'

'I will see that you and your men are handsomely rewarded for the work you carry out this day. Let us prepare to leave this place of slaughter.'

The soldiers were called back from the mound, and they began to climb up into their saddles. The four soldiers by the wagon had transported the remains of the king, and had covered him with uniform jackets taken from the slain. They had also hitched four horses to the front of the wagon. Two soldiers were up on the driver's bench, while the other two were flanking the body of Alfgang in the rear.

A sharp whistle pierced the air, and Hector turned to see a dozen Mountain Rangers hurrying up the road from the south on foot. Hector raised his arm in the air, and the Rangers left the road and ran across the meadow. Their officer saluted the Duke of Ridden, and was about to speak when his gaze fell upon the mound of dead.

'A terrible tragedy for the realm has occurred,' said Hector. 'A band of Westlanders orchestrated an ambush in this place. The king is dead.'

The Mountain Rangers recoiled in shock.

'King Alfgang the Great is dead, my lord?' said the officer.

Hector narrowed his eyes. 'When did you soldiers leave Torrent?'

'Yesterday morning, my lord,' said the officer. 'We were instructed by Lord Walter to scout out the position of the imperial army. Why was the king down here?'

Hector lowered his head. 'King Alfgang the Great died yesterday, and his son King Alfgang the Pius died here this morning.'

The group of Rangers fell silent.

'I know this news is hard to hear,' Hector went on, 'but I require you to perform your duty. Upper Down will survive these awful events because, when called upon, its brave men and women rose to the challenge. Now, do you have news of your own to deliver?'

The officer wiped a tear from his face and stood to attention. 'Yes, my lord. The imperial army has been seen to the south, under the personal command of Prince Valentino. His forces number somewhere in the region of twenty thousand, and they have a baggage train that stretches for several miles. At their current pace, I would estimate that they will arrive before the Kendril Wall the day after tomorrow.'

'Twenty thousand?' said an officer from the Royal Guard.

'This is my best guess,' said the Ranger, 'and that number includes servants, baggage handlers, and everyone else required by an army on the move.'

'Leaving a fighting force of around ten to twelve thousand?' said Hector.

'I would assume so, my lord.'

'And was there any sign of a so-called miracle weapon?'

'None that we could see, my lord. However, the contents of the baggage train could not be discerned.'

'Are you the only unit of Rangers out here?'

'No, my lord. I left over half of our company a little further south, to monitor the advance of the imperial army. They will be withdrawing to the Kendril Wall this evening.'

'I see. I have some bad news regarding your commander, my noble brother Lord Walter,' said Hector. 'The Champion was accompanying King Alfgang the Pius this morning, and is missing, presumed dead. I shall be assuming command of the Mountain Rangers until further notice.'

The officer saluted again. 'Understood, sir.'

'We shall be travelling north now,' said Hector, 'to bear the body of the fallen king to Torrent.'

'Are we leaving the mound of dead where it is, my lord? Might I volunteer my men to dig a mass grave for the fallen?'

Hector placed a hand onto the Ranger's shoulder. 'You are a credit to Upper Down. I accept your offer, and I thank you for it. Do not imperil yourselves. If the imperial army arrives before you have completed this deed, withdraw to the north with all haste.'

'Yes, my lord.'

Hector signalled to the wagon. 'Move back to the road, and head north. We are returning to Torrent.'

He mounted his horse, and the large group of soldiers separated, the Rangers remaining where they were, while Hector's volunteers rode across the meadow, flanking the wagon as it made its way to the road. The journey north was slower, and the sun had dipped behind the cliffs to the west before Hector and his men reached the summit of the ravine where the Kendril Wall stood. The tall gates opened, and the soldiers passed through the gatehouse. Hector gestured to Sergeant Towie as he dismounted. The sergeant nodded to several of his colleagues, and they joined the duke on the cobbles.

'Remember what I told you, sergeant,' Hector said. 'Be swift, and without fear or mercy. Bring me the heads of the officers who were on duty by the wall this morning. Kill any who try to stop you.'

The soldiers drew their swords, and ran into the gatehouse. Hector and the others waited by the wagon, and the duke quelled his anxiety. Would any of the officers have the opportunity to tell Sergeant Towie who it was that had paid the bribe? More importantly, would the soldiers believe them?

Ten minutes elapsed before Towie and the others returned. The sergeant was carrying a large hessian sack, and several of his men had blood on their swords. The sergeant approached Hector, and opened the sack. The duke glanced down, and saw four heads lying at the bottom. Amery had only bribed three men, but he could hardly fault the efficiency of the soldiers.

'These were the officers in charge of the gates this morning, my lord,' said Towie. 'We caught them whispering together in the officers' wardroom.'

Hector nodded. 'Good work, sergeant. There are now four fewer traitors in Torrent.'

'And the raid on the Westlanders, my lord? Me and the lads are keen to take part, if you will permit it.'

'It will take place tomorrow evening,' said the duke. 'I will come to the palace for you at sunset, but no word of warning must reach Twinbrook before then. Might I be assured of your silence?'

'Yes, my lord.'

'Come this way.'

The duke strode to his horse, and the rest of the volunteers gathered around him. He reached into his saddle bags and began distributing the gold he had made in the meadow.

'This is for you to share,' he said, as he handed the coins out to the soldiers. 'Loyalty and service should be rewarded, and I am grateful for all that you have done for Upper Down on this most terrible of days.'

The soldiers looked on with wide eyes as each was given the equivalent of several months' pay.

'This is incredibly generous, my lord,' said an officer. 'Thank you.'

'It is my pleasure,' said Hector. 'Now, let us complete the last leg of our journey, and transport the body of the king to the palace. The eyes of the townsfolk will be upon us, and I require that your behaviour be above reproach.'

'Of course, my lord,' said the officer.

They remounted, and the procession got underway again. The light was failing by the time they reached the front of the palace. As the duke had predicted, the roads had been lined with citizens of Torrent, each out to discover if the awful rumours had any substance to them. The volunteers behaved perfectly, each respectful and sombre as they escorted the fallen king home through the crowds of weeping and bewildered townsfolk.

The palace gates were being protected by a full company of Royal Guardsmen, and the convoy passed through as the first lamps were being lit. The stars were coming out, and the Little Red Moon was close to full. To the east, the Silver Moon was rising, and, though it was a mere crescent, its light was stronger than anything coming from the Little Red Moon. Only the Big Red Moon was absent from the evening sky. In a matter of days, something that only occurred once every few years would happen – all three moons would be full and visible in the sky at the same time. To the superstitious, it was a portent; to the Westlanders, a significant religious occasion, but to Hector, it was merely the workings of inanimate rocks in the sky that cared nothing for the fate of Upper Down.

Hector dismounted, and a servant led his horse to the stables. He ordered four soldiers to carry the body of the fallen king into the palace, and dismissed the rest. Hector led the way through the crowds of soldiers in the front courtyard, the four behind him bearing Alfgang the Pius in their arms. The crowd parted as a hush descended, and Hector kept his features mournful but serene as he entered the palace.

A group of courtiers approached.

'Shall we take the king to the audience hall, my lord?' said one. 'The people will want to pay their respects one last time to His Majesty.'

'No,' said Hector. 'His Majesty's remains are not in a fit state to be seen by the citizenry; the savages who slew him made sure of that. There will be no public viewing. Where are the princesses?'

'They are in their quarters, my lord.'

'Summon them. I will take the body to the private chapel and meet them there. Ensure that they bring the late king's head.'

The courtier lowered his gaze. 'Yes, my lord.'

Hector strode onwards, and led the men carrying the body down a single flight of stairs to the palace crypt. They passed the stone chambers where the previous kings of Upper Down had been interred, and entered the royal family's private chapel to the great spirits. Candles were already lit, and Hector instructed the soldiers to place the remains of the king onto a wooden table.

'Stand outside, and guard this chapel,' Hector said.

The four soldiers bowed their heads, and left the room.

Hector sat in a wooden chair next to the covered body. A surge of regret and guilt passed through him like a wave, and he began to weep. He put his head in his hands. What had he done? Alfgang the Pius had trusted him, had called him a friend, had appointed him to be chancellor of the realm, and Hector had repaid him with betrayal. What kind of man could do that? He tried to tell himself that it was all for the best, that Alfgang was too weak and self-righteous to be king, that he would have destroyed Upper Down, but they were nothing more than excuses. He had murdered his own king, one day after the previous king had died. It was too late for regret, far too late, but the tears did not cease.

He felt a hand upon his shoulder, and glanced up to see Kilbride standing in the chamber next to him, along with a lady-in-waiting, who was holding the same bundle that Hector had given her hours before. He got to his feet, and Kilbride embraced him. He put his arms around her as he wept, then he pulled away. He glanced at the lady-in-waiting, who was also crying, and took the bundle from her, and then he laid it down by the dead king's shoulders.

'Don't look at the body,' Hector whispered. 'I don't want you to remember your brother as he is now. But know this, I will kill those responsible. I will kill them all.'

'I know you will,' said Kilbride.

'Where is Abigone?'

'She was too hysterical to leave her quarters,' said Kilbride. She nodded to the lady-in-waiting, who curtsied and left the room.

'What did you discover?' Kilbride went on.

'It was Westlanders, no doubt about it,' Hector said. 'Tomorrow night, the men who did this will suffer.'

She leaned closer. 'It was Dravid,' she whispered in his ear. 'Dravid did it. He's been boasting about it openly in the beer halls of Twinbrook.'

Hector nodded. 'Did he say why he did it?'

'To stop my brother from driving the Westlanders out of Upper

Down. What about the Kendril Wall? Who allowed Dravid and his men to pass?'

'I have dealt with them,' said Hector. 'Four officers were on the payroll of the Westlanders. They will trouble us no more.'

'How did Dravid find out about my brother's plans? Only a handful of people knew that he was heading south to meet Prince Valentino.'

'That I have yet to discover,' said Hector.

'And Walter?'

'We saw no sign of him.'

'So Walter might be alive?'

'Many of the bodies were too badly burned to identify. I fear that we have lost him, Your Highness. We also saw no sign of Princess Hygilt.

'Dravid has her,' said Kilbride. 'He has been boasting about that, too.'

Hector said nothing.

'You were right before,' she said. 'We will have to work together. We must put our differences aside if we are to save this kingdom.'

'Valentino is bringing twenty thousand men with him.'

'But they will never breach the Wall. Do not despair, Hector. If you give up, then I will, too. I need you to be strong. We have a boy-king to protect.'

'Where is he?'

'Safe, with his mother. Tomorrow, when they arrive for the two funerals, I will insist that they remain in the Royal Palace. Our two families must stay united.'

Hector nodded. 'Your courage and strength gives me hope, Your Highness.'

'If I could get through the death of my husband, I can get through this.'

He gazed at the steely determination in her eyes. If only she knew, he thought. If only she knew.

CHAPTER 8
WITHOUT SOLACE

Torrent, Upper Down – 10th Day of Lamenta 107

Abigone awoke to find Tulip licking her face. Her room was in darkness, but the shutters by her window were edged in light. Abigone pushed Tulip away, and the small creature mewed.

'I'm not in the mood,' she said. 'Leave me alone.'

Tulip sat on the bed sheet and gazed into her eyes.

'Don't you understand?' Abigone said. 'We've lost everything. My father. My brother...'

She waited for the tears to come, but none did. Perhaps she had run out. She wondered what time it had been when she had finally drifted off to sleep; it had been the longest night she could remember. Hour after hour of misery and grief. She had listened to the sound of courtiers wailing and weeping in the corridors outside her suite of rooms, and she had been awake when the soldiers had changed shifts. When she had heard their boots thumping through the palace, she had imagined that they were coming to take her away, or perhaps to kill her, and she had never been more terrified. The loss of Alfgang the Great had been more than she could bear, but her father had been an old man. The death of Alfgang the Pius, on the other hand, seemed unreal to Abigone, and she had been unable to believe it, even though she had seen the bundle that had been carried around by Kilbride's lady-in-waiting. When her sister had then told her of Hector's arrival with the rest of their brother's body, Abigone had refused to go to the chapel with her, for if she had, then she would have been forced to face the truth – he was gone.

Her beloved brother, too good to live in such a cruel world. Alfgang the Pius had never hurt anyone. If someone wronged him, he would respond with kindness and understanding, choosing mercy over retribution, as though revenge was an alien concept. Too good for the world, and so the world had devoured him.

Tulip raised a paw and touched her face. Abigone stared into his eyes, and he blinked at her.

'You know I am sad, don't you?' she said. 'You are all I have now, my sweet boy; please don't leave me.'

As if to reply, Tulip snuggled in against her face, pressing his fur into her nose. A knock sounded at her door, and Tulip glanced up, his body tensing a little.

'It's all right,' Abigone said. 'I won't let anyone hurt you.'

'May I come in?' said a voice. 'It's Kilbride; can I come in, Abbie?'

Abigone closed her eyes.

The door opened, despite her lack of response, and the floorboards creaked under her sister's footsteps. The door closed again.

'Abbie, how are you?' Kilbride said.

Abigone pulled the blanket over her head, covering Tulip at the same time. She felt her sister sit down on the edge of the bed.

'I know this is a terrible time,' Kilbride went on; 'the worst time, but I am here to ask that you get up. Frida and little Alfie are due to arrive soon, and then the funerals will take place. It will only be us there. There will be no crowds, just us; just the family. But, we should greet Frida and Alfie by the doors of the palace when they get here, and people will see us, but only for a minute or two. I need you to be there by my side, Abbie. The poor people of Torrent need to see us both. We have to be strong for them, just for a little while.'

'How can there be a funeral, when there hasn't been a viewing?' said

Abigone, then she immediately regretted her words. Speaking to her sister was the last thing she had wanted to do; it would only encourage Kilbride to keep talking, when Abigone was desperate for her to leave.

'We have decided against a public viewing,' Kilbride said. 'The... body of our brother has been cleaned and dressed in a fine uniform, but... a viewing would not be a good idea. It would only upset people. It's better that we get the funeral over with as soon as possible. The coffins are here; they arrived at dawn. Our father has already been placed into one, and the staff are about to do the same for our dear brother.'

'Don't I get to see him first?'

'I asked you to come with me to the chapel last night, Abbie. But, if you really want to see him, then if you get up now, I will take you downstairs.'

'Do you think I should?'

'I want you to get up, but... no, Abbie. It might be better if you don't look at what is left of our brother.'

'Did you look?'

'I helped to prepare the body, just as I did with Father, so, yes. I saw him.'

'Then I want to see him, too.'

'How quickly can you get ready? I can send in a few servants to assist you.'

Kilbride pulled the blanket from her sister's face, and Tulip hissed at her.

'Why did you do that?' said Abigone.

'To help you get up.'

'I don't want to get up. I will stay here. I can't face the world, not today.'

'You are a princess of Upper Down,' said Kilbride. 'You have duties that outweigh your personal feelings.'

'I want my father and brother back,' said Abigone. 'Fuck duty.'

'Should that be our message to the people – that we don't care what happens any more? If we give up, then the soldiers may as well go home, and the servants, too. Do you think the Westlanders will sit in Twinbrook and do nothing if we are too overcome by grief to protect ourselves? We are under threat, Abbie; I am not going to lie to you. The situation we are facing is grave. The Westlanders killed our brother, because he wanted to throw them all out of Upper Down; and an imperial army is marching north, to punish us for kidnapping Princess Hygilt.'

'Hygilt ran away,' Abigone said.

Kilbride stared at her. 'Do you still believe that?'

'It's true.'

'It's not true. If it was true, then why was she locked in her quarters? Why wasn't she allowed to go into the park? Why weren't we allowed to speak to her? Think, Abbie.'

'You're saying this because you hated Father.'

'You are the only person in the palace who believes the story that Father told us about Hygilt. Everyone else just pretended to believe it, because... well, because that's the way things were when Father was king. People were too afraid to speak the truth in front of him, in case he lost his temper. You didn't see it, because Father never lost his temper with you. You were his favourite child, but you must understand that he didn't treat the rest of us in the same manner. He was cruel and awful to our brother when he was growing up, and he thought very little of me or Nolan. When I married Roderick, and when Nolan married Wolfgang, we were glad to leave Torrent; glad to be free of Father's control. Coming back here almost broke me. No, it did break me, for a while. I had to learn how to be strong all over again.'

'You are exaggerating,' Abigone said. 'You talk as though Father was a beast, but the truth is that he didn't love you as much as he loved me; and that's not my fault.'

Kilbride glanced away. 'We are wasting time. I want you to get up. You need to act like a princess for a few painful hours, and then you can go back to bed.'

'What's the point?'

'Little Alfie is the point,' said Kilbride. 'Our seven-year-old nephew is the new king, and he has just lost his father. When he arrives at the palace, I want him to be able to look up and see that we are there for him.' She got to her feet. 'Will you do it for Alfie? I am going to give you two minutes, and then I shall send the servants in.'

Kilbride walked over the shutters, unlatched them, and threw them open. The morning sunlight flooded the room, hurting Abigone's eyes.

'Two minutes. Abbie,' Kilbride said, then she strode from the chamber, closing the door behind her.

'Bitch,' Abigone muttered.

She pulled back the blanket and swung her legs over the side of the bed, so that her bare feet were touching the varnished floorboards. She felt hollow, as though there was nothing inside of her, and she shivered in the chill autumnal air. Tulip tried to manoeuvre his way onto her lap, but she pushed him off.

'Sorry, Tulip, but you heard what my stupid sister said. She didn't look very sad, did she? I don't think she even cares that my father and brother are dead.'

She stood, and Tulip's gaze followed her as she went over to a wash-basin. She poured in some freezing cold water from a jug, and splashed some on her face, then she walked to her dresser and sat down, waiting. Tulip jumped down from the bed and rubbed his flank against her ankles, so Abigone picked him up and set him down onto her lap. She rubbed his ears, and glanced into the large silvered mirror that sat atop the dresser. She looked a mess. Her eyes were red, her skin pale, and her brown hair resembled a bird's nest.

The door opened, and three old women walked into the chamber.

'Your Highness,' said one, as they bowed low, 'we are here to help you get ready.'

'Then get on with it,' said Abigone.

'Yes, Your Highness.'

One of the old women held up a selection of clothes that she had brought with her.

'I have my own clothes,' said Abigone.

'These belong to Princess Kilbride,' said the woman. 'She picked them out for you.'

'Why would I wish to wear my sister's clothes?'

The old woman smiled sadly. 'Because, Your Highness, you have nothing in black.'

One hour later, Abigone descended the stairs of the palace, the three old women trailing along behind her. Abigone's hair had been tied up in a severe manner, and her forehead felt as though it was being pulled upwards. The clothes chosen for her were unflattering, and the shoes were uncomfortable. The back of her heels would be blistered by the end of the day, the skin rubbed raw, not that anyone seemed to care. She felt like a theatre prop – there to be viewed and then ignored. A large group of courtiers and soldiers were standing by the bottom of the stairs, and they fell into silence as Abigone approached, each bowing their heads. Among them, Duke Hector detached himself from those with whom he had been speaking, and strode towards the princess.

'Your Highness,' he said, inclining his head. 'May I please be allowed to express my deep sorrow, and to offer you my most sincere condolences?'

Abigone gazed up at him, but not even the duke's handsome bearing could disturb her melancholy.

'The carriage of His Majesty King Alfgang the Sixth shall be arriving shortly,' the duke went on. 'Might I escort you to the palace entrance?'

'I want to see my brother.'

'There will be time for that, Your Highness,' Hector said, 'but first we will welcome our new monarch.'

He held out an arm, and she placed a hand onto it. He covered it with his own hand, then he led her along the palace corridor, as the crowd parted.

'Your presence this morning is greatly appreciated, Your Highness,' Hector said.

They passed through the tall entrance, and stood on the steps that led down to the courtyard at the front of the palace. Kilbride was already there, along with a handful of officials and officers from the Royal Guard. Hector excused himself, then he strode down the steps towards the gates, where hundreds of soldiers were guarding the palace perimeter.

Abigone frowned. 'Where's Walter? Is our idiot cousin too drunk to attend?'

Kilbride caught her glance. 'Walter was with our brother yesterday, Abbie,' she said. 'Did you not know?'

'What? Why did no one tell me? Is he dead?'

'We don't know for sure,' said Kilbride, her eyes welling a little; 'but yes; probably.'

'You can cry for him, but not for our father or brother?'

'You have not seen my tears, but that does not mean I have shed none. Please, Abbie; let us try to be civil to one another.' Her gaze went to Abigone's shoulder, where Tulip was draped like a scarf, but she said nothing more.

'I had to bring Tulip,' Abigone said. 'I couldn't leave him alone in my room.'

'I don't mind,' said Kilbride.

'If you say so.'

Down in the courtyard, Hector was marshalling the soldiers, forming them into thick ranks that flanked the driveway leading from the gates to the palace entrance.

'Hector is the only man left,' said Abigone. 'What will we do if he gets killed?'

'Let us pray that does not happen,' said Kilbride.

Abigone snorted. 'Don't pretend that you like him.'

'Hector and I have had our differences, that is true; but we have agreed to stand united in this crisis.'

'I'm not stupid. I know what went on between you.'

Kilbride's eyes narrowed. 'You shouldn't concern yourself with silly rumours.'

'How did you manage to lure him into your bed?' Abigone said. 'And how are you able to look Perpetua in the eye? I don't think I would be able to do it. Poor Hector.'

Kilbride said nothing.

'Are you angry with him because he put a stop to the affair?' Abigone went on.

'It was years ago, and I'm not angry with him.'

'But you aren't denying the affair. What a wicked thing to do. Your husband had only been dead for a few months before you seduced Hector. Men can be weak like that, sometimes; but you knew exactly what you were doing.'

'You know nothing about what happened.'

'Maybe I should ask Hector.'

'Why do you hate me, Abbie?'

'I don't have time to go into every reason.'

Kilbride fell silent, and a small pang of guilt passed through Abigone. She hadn't intended to be cruel, but sometimes the words just came out before she could stop them. She thought about her sister's question. Why did she hate Kilbride? Was it because she had loathed their kindly old father? Or maybe it was because she had tainted the image of Hector that Abigone had once treasured. Kilbride had clearly tricked the Duke of Ridden into conducting a sordid little relationship, and he had lost the lustre of perfection in Abigone's eyes. She still admired him greatly, but he would never be the man she had once thought he was.

At that moment, the palace gates opened, and a carriage approached, along with a large escort of heavily-armed soldiers. Four horses pulled the carriage through the gates, and across the courtyard. The gates were closed, and the carriage came to a halt at the bottom of the steps. Hector strode past the horses, and opened the carriage's side door. He reached up with a gloved hand, and helped his sister descend to the cobbles. Hector and Frida embraced in front of the massed ranks of soldiers, then the boy king made his first appearance. He peered out from the side of the carriage, his young eyes taking in the sight of the soldiers and the palace.

'A cheer for His Majesty!' cried an officer of the Royal Guard.

The soldiers raised their swords. 'Long live the king!' they roared.

Alfie jumped in fright, and his chin quivered. His mother broke away from Hector, then she reached up and lifted the boy down to the cobbles. She held him close, and whispered something into his ear. The child nodded, then he took his mother's hand as they turned for the stairs. Hector flanked them as they ascended towards Abigone and Kilbride.

'Welcome to the Royal Palace, Your Majesty,' said Kilbride, a forced smile on her lips. She bowed her head, and Abigone did the same.

'Say hello to your aunties, Alfie,' said Frida.

'Hello,' said the boy, his voice a whisper.

'Hello,' said Abigone.

The boy gave her a shy smile. They reached the top of the step, and Hector turned them gently, so that the entire party were facing the ranks of soldiers. Beyond, a huge crowd had gathered on the far side of the palace walls. Abigone felt sick just looking at all of the faces turned towards them, then she remembered what Kilbride had said about duty.

'I will say a few words,' whispered Hector.

He took a small step forward, and raised a hand in the air.

'Citizens of Upper Down,' he said, his voice strong and clear; 'on this saddest of days, I wish to thank you all for your messages of sympathy. Our hearts have been touched by the kindness that you have shown. Amid the mourning and the grief, I also wish to say this – the future of Upper Down is standing before you. His Majesty King Alfgang the Sixth begins his reign today. For the next eleven years, the new king shall be supported by the senior members of his family. We shall guide him into maturity, and then we shall stand aside when he comes of age. For the moment, however, we shall pay our deepest respects to His Majesty's two predecessors, at the funerals to be held in the private family chapel. I regret to announce that there shall be no public viewing for King Alfgang the Pius, and I ask that you respect this decision. Tomorrow, we shall make further announcements regarding the formation of His Majesty's new government, and the life of our realm will go on as normal. The markets will open, the walls will be guarded, and stability will return to Upper Down. Long live the king!'

'Long live the king!' the soldiers cried.

Hector lowered his arm, and turned. 'Shall we?'

The rest of the royal party moved to face the palace entrance, and they filed into the building. Hector led the way, and they descended into the crypt. The chapel was bright with the light of a hundred candles, and the two coffins had been placed just under the family shrine, which sat in a shallow alcove along one wall. Two old priests were waiting for them, and they guided the family members to a row of wooden seats. The new king was placed in the centre, with Hector and Kilbride to his right, while Frida and Abigone sat down to Alfie's left.

'Let us begin,' said one of the priests. 'The great spirits have...'

'Wait,' said Abigone. 'I want to see my brother first. Kilbride said that I could.'

The priests glanced at her.

'Would that be wise, Your Highness?' said Hector. 'I would recommend that the coffin remain closed.'

'It's not up to you,' said Abigone. 'Alfgang was my brother, and I want to see him.'

Kilbride got to her feet. 'I did say that she could. Perhaps everyone could wait outside for a moment?'

'If Abigone can bear it, then so shall I,' said Frida. 'I, too, wish to see him one last time.'

Kilbride's composure wavered, then she bowed her head. She gestured to the priests. 'Please leave us.'

'Yes, Your Highness,' said one. 'We shall remain outside until you are ready to commence with the ceremony.'

'I shall take little Alfie out, too,' said Hector. 'He is far too young for this, and I, to my lasting grief, have already seen the late king.'

The three men and the boy left the chapel, and Abigone closed the door. She glanced at Kilbride and Frida, then they made their way to the coffins. Each had been emblazoned with a coat of arms. Alfgang the Great's was depicted with a sword, while his son's insignia had a quill in its centre.

'I will need some help,' said Kilbride, 'but first I must ask you both – are you sure?'

Frida choked back a sob. 'Just get it over with, Killie.'

'Abbie,' said Kilbride, 'please take hold of the left side of the coffin lid, and I will take the right.'

The two women moved into position, then they lifted the lid clear of the coffin, and set it down onto the floor of the chapel. Abigone straightened, and gazed inside. Her brother's body was dressed in a smart uniform, but his hands were missing. She suppressed a wave of nausea, and glanced at his face. Make-up had been thickly applied, but there was no disguising the disfigurement. Coins had been placed to cover the eyes that had been gouged out, and a scarf had been draped over his neck.

Frida sobbed, then she leaned over and kissed her husband's cheek, and the head rolled away to the side, the scarf slipping. Abigone put a hand to her mouth, as bile reached her tongue. Kilbride reached into the coffin and placed the king's head back into position, using the scarf to prop it up. Frida turned away, her complexion greying, then she collapsed to her knees, weeping and shaking.

'I feel sick,' Frida gasped. 'Who could do such a thing to my beautiful husband? He never hurt anyone in his life. He was a good man. Why is this happening to us?'

Kilbride glanced at her, then she picked up the coffin lid. Abigone took the other end, and they placed it back on to the coffin. When it was secure, Kilbride crouched down next to Frida and embraced her. Abigone looked at them for a moment, then she walked to her chair and sat down, putting her head in her hands. Tulip appeared on her lap, and pressed himself against her arm, and Abigone wondered why she hadn't noticed his presence while the coffin had been open.

Kilbride ushered Frida to her seat, then she walked to the door and opened it.

'We are ready,' she said. 'Thank you for waiting.'

It was almost midday by the time the twin funerals were completed, and the two coffins interred into a temporary sarcophagus in the family crypt. The priests were thanked, and then the royal family went back upstairs. Hector had arranged for a private lunch to be served in a small dining room, and the servants were told to wait outside as the family entered and took their places.

No one said anything for a while, as Hector served out food to each person sitting round the table.

Kilbride lifted her gaze when the duke placed a plate in front of her. 'Thank you,' she said, 'though I don't have much of an appetite.'

'We should all try to eat something,' said Hector. He turned to Alfie. 'Your Majesty, might I say how brave you have been? We are all very proud of you.'

The boy nodded, his gaze lowered.

'Will you be living here now?' said Abigone. 'You, too, Frida, of course. I know that you already have a home, but shouldn't the king live in the Royal Palace?'

'I was going to get to that, thank you, Abbie,' said Kilbride. 'What do you think, Frida?'

'I don't know,' she said. 'I think I want to lie down.'

'We don't need to decide everything all at once,' said Hector, 'but I believe the two princesses have a good point. Stay here tonight, at least, sister, and then we can discuss it again tomorrow.'

'Do you think everything will be fine tomorrow, brother?' said Frida. 'My world has collapsed.'

'You are stronger than you think,' said Kilbride.

'No,' said Frida. 'I'm not. I often watched you, Killie, when you returned from Greater Down after the death of your husband. You... I am not like you. I cannot force myself to be strong. You could, but I can't. I wish I was dead.'

'Don't say that,' said Abigone. 'You have a son.'

Frida got to her feet. 'I need to be alone.'

'Where are you going, mama?' said the boy.

Frida glanced at Kilbride. 'May I use your rooms to rest, Killie?'

Kilbride narrowed her eyes. 'I... uh...'

'Don't worry,' Frida said. 'I'm not going to kill myself.' She gazed at her son. 'I would never abandon my boy; but I can't sit here and pretend everything is going to be all right. Let me go; let me rest.'

'Ask for Marie,' said Kilbride. 'My lady-in-waiting will escort you to my quarters, and she will see to anything you need.'

Frida nodded, then she kissed Alfie on the cheek and walked from the dining room.

'My poor sister,' said Hector. 'She will need a long time to get over this calamity. For we three, however, I am afraid that we do not have the luxury of an extended period of time in which to grieve. I hate to sound heartless, but we have much work to do.'

'I agree,' said Kilbride. 'The first thing we need to do is establish a regency council, and promulgate a law to that effect.'

'Then we shall need good lawyers,' said Hector. 'My assistant Amery is highly literate in the workings of the law. I shall have him summoned from the ducal palace. When he gets here, I will instruct him to prepare the necessary documents.'

Abigone frowned. 'When you said *we three*, Hector, were you including me or Alfie?'

'I was talking about you, Your Highness,' said the duke. 'Alfie is too young to take on any responsibilities; whereas you are almost eighteen. As a princess of the realm, your place upon the regency council is assured. The new king connects us – he is my nephew, and he is also your nephew.'

'Are you saying that the three of us should rule Upper Down until Alfie is eighteen?'

'That is exactly what I am saying,' said Hector.

'Are you forgetting that I am supposed to be leaving soon? Lord Henry awaits me in Nessos.'

'We have been meaning to talk to you about this,' said Kilbride. 'Under the circumstances, it might be prudent to indefinitely postpone your marriage to Henry.'

'No,' said Abigone. 'You can't do this to me.'

'But I thought you weren't keen to be wed, sister? I thought you would be happy to hear this.'

'A whole new life is waiting for me,' Abigone said.

'But you have never met the man.'

'Your sister is correct, Abigone,' said Hector. 'Even if we wished to proceed with the wedding, the pass is currently being blocked by twenty thousand imperial troops. There is no way through.'

'We could send Valentino a message. If he is a gentleman, he will allow me to pass.'

'Or he will take you prisoner, just as we took his granddaughter into captivity.'

Abigone got to her feet, and Tulip dug his claws into her waist to cling on.

'Hygilt ran away,' she said, masking the pain.

Hector and Kilbride glanced at each other.

'Princess Hygilt is in the custody of the Westlanders, Abbie,' said Kilbride. 'Whether you believe Father's story or not, there is no doubt that she is most certainly a captive now.'

'I intend to rescue her this evening,' said Hector. 'Please sit down, Your Highness.'

Abigone pulled Tulip from her waist and winced. She retook her seat, and the animal settled down on her lap again. Alfie reached out with a hand to pet him, and Tulip hissed at the boy.

'Must that infernal animal be here?' said Hector.

'If you want me as part of your stupid regency council, then Tulip stays,' said Abigone. 'All right; I'm sure you and my sister have already concocted a plan. Let's hear it.'

CHAPTER 9
UNTOUCHED

South of Torrent, Upper Down – 10th Day of Lamenta 107

Walter stumbled down the steep track, his boots slipping on the loose rocks. Two Mountain Rangers grabbed his shoulders and pulled him back. Walter swayed, the pain in the back of his head pounding.

'Perhaps we should take a short break, sir?' said one of the militia soldiers.

'Very well,' said Lothar.

The two Rangers helped Walter to sit, and he groaned. 'My fucking head.'

'The next time a horse tries to kick you, sir,' said Lothar, 'I recommend that you get out of the way.'

'Sound advice, though a little late,' said Walter. He glanced around as the other soldiers crouched or sat by the side of the mountain track. 'How far is it to go?'

'Another hour, perhaps, sir,' said Lothar, 'then we should come to the base of the cliffs. Do you know the waterfall in the Royal Parkland? That's where we should emerge. There is a guarded turret blocking the route, and then we will be five minutes from the palace.'

'The Westlanders must never learn of this route through the mountains,' Walter said.

'No one who is not a member of the Mountain Rangers knows of it, sir; and we keep our secrets.'

He produced a flask and passed it to Walter.

Walter pulled the stopper out, and took a sip of whisky. It burned his throat and warmed his chest, dulling the pain in his head a fraction. He passed it back to Lothar, and closed his eyes. They had been walking on and off for a day and night, crossing the treacherous ridges and clambering up and down gullies. No wagons or horses could take the pass they had traversed, and it was difficult enough for experienced Mountain Rangers.

'We will be home soon, sir,' said Lothar.

'And what awaits us there?' said Walter. 'The first thing we shall have to do is give everyone the bad news, that's if the Westlanders aren't already living in the Royal Palace. Even if they aren't, what kind of welcome do you think we'll get? I had one task – to protect the king.'

'No one could have protected him, sir,' said Lothar. 'The Westlanders carried out their ambush with perfection. We can hate them, but we cannot deny that they are good at what they do. Their timing was immaculate. Only the king could have protected himself, sir, and yet he chose not to.'

'And now Upper Down has no Masters left to defend the realm. Well, I guess little Alfie might be one, but it will be years before he will be able to use any of his abilities. And who will train him? It feels as though an era is ending. Upper Down was the last realm ruled by Masters and Makers, and now it's over. The Sanctians will hunt down any that remain in the south, and the Westlanders will take care of the rest. If I believed in the spirits, then I would accuse them of betraying us.'

A few of the Rangers eyed him.

'All right, then,' said Walter. 'Would a believer like to explain to me why the Masters and Makers are almost extinct? I'm all ears.'

'Faith is hard,' said one of the Rangers.

'No fucking kidding,' said Walter. 'I'll tell you why it's hard. It's hard because all the evidence points to the contrary. Once you accept that there are no spirits out there listening to our prayers, everything else starts to make sense.'

'The spirits answered my prayers yesterday, sir,' said the Ranger.

'Did they? What the fuck were you praying for?'

'That you be spared, sir.'

Walter closed his mouth.

Lothar smiled. 'So ends today's theological dispute. Tomorrow, we shall be discussing portents and the role of the priesthood.'

'You can be a right smartarse, Lothar.'

'Thank you, sir. Shall we get back underway?'

Walter and the Rangers got to their feet and began to move off down the steep slope. As they descended, Walter noticed that no one had mentioned food for several hours. They were all hungry, but with their rations being left behind after the ambush, there was little point in complaining about it. Walter began to daydream about food, picturing plates and bowls filled to overflowing; then he felt selfish for forgetting what had happened to Alfgang the Pius. The awful events of the previous day were never far from his thoughts, and anger towards the Westlanders burned within him.

They trudged down the winding track for an hour, then it levelled out, and they followed the banks of a stream through a narrow gully. Ahead of them, the gully opened up, and the Rangers hurried forwards. The cliffs came to an end, and the stream transformed into a waterfall. Walter and the Rangers stood at its top, and gazed out over Upper Down. Torrent lay immediately before them and to the left, while the unwalled town of Twinbrook sprawled away to the north. Beyond that, the fields and meadows of the small kingdom were laid out in a neat patchwork of farms and vineyards, with a few villages dotted across the landscape. The parkland next to the palace was directly below them, and Walter could make out the stand of trees where he had found Abigone two days before. No one spoke for a few long minutes, as a mixture of relief and apprehension spread over the men. They had made it home, but that had been the easy part.

Lothar led them all to the left, where a rough track continued on through the ravine. After trekking for another hundred yards, they found their path barred by a high stone wall, with a closed gate in its centre. Looming up behind the wall was a slim turret, where several soldiers from the Royal Guard were stationed to guard the entrance of the narrow pass.

'Hey there!' Lothar called out. 'Open the gate – the King's Champion is returning to Upper Down.'

A face appeared in a turret window, then there was a flurry of activity on the other side of the wall. Soldiers emerged from a cave, and others from the turret, and the gates in the wall were pushed open.

'It's been a long time since anyone arrived in Torrent this way,' said a sergeant from the Royal Guard. He eyed Walter, and sprang to attention. 'My lord; you're back.'

'I am,' said Walter. 'How are things in Torrent?'

'Well, my lord, you are supposed to be dead, for a start. As for Torrent, I believe that a double funeral took place in the Royal Palace earlier today. Two kings were laid to rest in a single morning.'

'A double funeral?' said Walter. 'How is that possible?'

'Lord Hector rode south and retrieved the body of Alfgang the Pius yesterday, my lord,' said the sergeant. 'The whole town is talking about it. He managed to bring the body of His Majesty back before twenty thousand imperial soldiers arrived. He's some man, your brother. With all due respect, it seems as though he did a better job of protecting the king than you did, my lord.'

A few Rangers tensed at the sergeant's words.

'My brother is indeed a marvel,' said Walter. 'Women blush whenever he passes, and even his shit smells sweet.'

The sergeant smiled. 'I'm sure they do, my lord.'

Walter gestured to the Rangers, and they passed through the wall. The men from the Royal Guard watched them, but none spoke. Walter led the Rangers down another steep path, which emerged from the side of the cliffs next to the base of the waterfall. They strode through the Royal Parkland in silence, and reached the rear of the palace, where more soldiers were posted. Walter turned.

'My fellow Rangers,' he said. 'Thank you for leading me over the mountains. I want you all to return to your barracks to get some food and rest. I will deal with this next part on my own. In many ways, it would have been far better for my somewhat tarnished reputation if I had been killed defending the king yesterday, so maybe you should have left me to die, eh? Still, I won't hold it against you. Dismissed.'

Walter turned, and ascended the steps leading to the rear entrance of the palace. Moments later, Lothar appeared by his side.

'You weren't including me in that, were you, sir?' he said.

'I was, but you can come along, if you have a taste for seeing me being humiliated again.'

'I will be there for you, sir, when it is over.'

They reached the doors of the palace, and the soldiers on duty stared at Walter.

'Yes, I'm back,' said Walter. 'Did you miss me?'

The soldiers said nothing.

'I am looking for Princess Kilbride,' said Walter. 'Do you know where I might find her?'

'Her Highness is having a private lunch with Princess Abigone, Lord Hector, and the new king, my lord,' said one of the soldiers.

'Excellent,' said Walter. 'I wouldn't want to miss that.'

'They left instructions that they were not to be interrupted, my lord.'

Walter shrugged and entered the palace, with Lothar by his side.

'Do you know where they will be, sir?' Lothar whispered.

'I can take a guess.'

They ascended a flight of stairs, and came to a corridor filled with soldiers and courtiers, all standing close to a doorway.

'Something tells me they might be in there,' Walter said.

'It's the King's Champion!' someone cried. 'Lord Walter has returned!'

The small crowd surrounded Walter as he tried to get to the door. Several courtiers were talking at the same time, asking Walter questions, while others were clearly trying to block his way to the dining room. Amid the clamour, the door opened, and Kilbride peered out.

'What is causing this noise?' she said. 'Could we not please have a little quiet out here? I...'

Her face froze when she saw Walter, then she pushed a few courtiers out of the way and threw her arms around him.

'You're alive,' she whispered.

Walter narrowed his eyes. 'This is not the welcome I was expecting.'

Kilbride pulled away, looking a little embarrassed. 'Come in,' she said.

'Wait out here, Lothar,' Walter said, then he followed the princess into the small dining room.

Hector got to his feet, his eyes wide. His mouth opened, but no words came out.

'Well, look who it is,' said Abigone, remaining seated. 'We thought you were dead, Walter.'

'Sit,' said Kilbride.

Walter noticed the presence of little Alfie sitting round the table. He bowed his head, then he crouched by the boy-king.

'Your Majesty,' he said. 'I was with your father when he died. I am sorry. We were ambushed by a hundred mounted Westlanders just a few hours south of Torrent.'

Alfie stared at him, his eyes red with tears.

'I have visited the scene, brother,' said Hector. 'How did you escape with your life?'

'My head was kicked by a horse,' said Walter, 'and I was dragged away unconscious by the surviving Mountain Rangers.' He got back to his feet. 'I told them that they should have left me to die, but you know what the Rangers are like. They never listen to a damn word I say.'

'Did you come through the Kendril Wall?' said Hector.

Walter sat down, ignoring the question. 'I hear there were two funerals this morning.'

'That's right,' said Abigone. 'You missed them.'

'Sorry about that,' said Walter.

'Are you hungry?' said Kilbride.

'Ravenous,' he said. 'I haven't eaten since... uh, two days ago. Can I start on the food, while you keep talking?'

'I am not altogether sure that you should be present for this meeting,' said Hector. 'We were discussing serious matters of state. Eat, by all means, but take the food to your quarters. I would imagine that you require some rest after all that you have been through. I can debrief you later.'

'Why the fuck would I give you a debriefing?' said Walter. 'You aren't my commanding officer.'

'Watch your language in front of His Majesty,' said Kilbride.

Walter laughed. 'The realm is on its knees, but some things never change. A few minutes ago, you all thought I was dead; and yet here is my brother, who is trying to exclude me from the conversation; Kilbride, who is scolding me about my language; and Abigone, whose weird little animal is looking at me as if it wants to take a shit on my face.'

The others glared at him.

'Walter is my uncle,' said the boy king.

'That is so, Your Majesty,' said Hector, 'but...'

'You said that you were going to be my regents because I am your nephew,' the boy went on. 'I am Walter's nephew, too.'

'Thank you, Alfie,' said Walter, 'but I have no desire to sit on any regency council.'

'And we have no intention of inviting you on to it,' said Hector. 'There are several full bottles of whisky in a cupboard just behind you, brother. Why don't you take them, and disappear somewhere for a few days?'

'Hold on a moment,' said Abigone. 'I don't want to be on the council, either. I am supposed to be travelling south. If I have to do it, then why shouldn't Walter?'

'Because you are not a useless drunk, Your Highness,' said Hector.

'What happened to my father?' said the boy king.

Walter put down his fork. 'It was all over very quickly, Your Majesty,' he said. 'When the Westlanders charged, your father was defending the wagon where Princess Hygilt was hiding. He had ten brave knights with him, but the Westlanders surrounded them. I… I asked the king to use his abilities as a Master, but…' He lowered his gaze. 'Your father believed that the spirits would never forgive him if he used his Master powers to kill. He preferred to die rather than abuse the gifts he had been given. The Westlanders cut him down where he stood. That's all I remember. A horse ran into me. I was knocked over, and then the horse kicked the back of my head.'

'And then?' said Kilbride.

'I woke up several hours later with a pounding headache.'

'How exactly did you return to Torrent?' said Hector.

Walter ignored the question for a second time, as Kilbride rose from her seat and walked round to the other side of the table. She crouched down behind Walter, and parted the hair at the back of his head. Walter grimaced from the pain, but said nothing.

'You were very lucky,' she said. 'You have a large bump, but there is no fresh blood, and your skull appears to be intact. You should rest for a day or two, but I would advise against drinking any alcohol.'

Walter glanced at her. 'I couldn't help but notice that you are the only person in the room who hasn't given an opinion about my suitability to sit on the regency council, Killie.'

'I prefer to think things over before opening my mouth,' she said, as she returned to her seat. 'Rest assured,' she went on, 'that we will find an appropriate role for you, Walter. There is a mountain of work to be done, and very few people I trust to do it.'

Walter smiled. 'That almost sounds as though you trust me, Killie. I thought those days had long gone.'

'You will lose that trust if you go back to drinking,' she said.

'I see. So, if I don't want to be burdened with a ton of responsibilities, I should follow my brother's advice and take the whisky to my quarters? You're making this too easy for me, Killie.' He stood. 'Well, this was fun. We should do lunch again some time.' He bowed his head before Alfie. 'Your Majesty; may your reign be long and prosperous.'

The others watched as Walter opened the cupboard and removed two bottles of whisky. He pushed them into the deep pockets of his Ranger's overcoat, then he picked up a tray of food.

'You know where to find me,' he said, then he opened the door and left the dining room.

Outside, the corridor was still crowded with soldiers and officials. Walter barged past them, and found Lothar leaning against a wall, waiting for him.

The Mountain Ranger eyed the whisky. 'You seem to have emerged from that situation rather well, sir. What now?'

'My quarters,' Walter said, passing him the tray of food.

'Which ones, sir?'

'Well, seeing as how we are in the Royal Palace, perhaps those ones? Unless you fancy walking halfway across Torrent to my quarters in the ducal palace; or perhaps you meant my little apartment in town?'

'Sarcasm is an awful trait, sir.'

'So is asking stupid questions.'

They walked along the corridor, then took a spiral staircase to an upper floor. There was an old tower in the north-western corner of the palace, and they ascended again when they reached it. Walter had the entire upper level to himself, but as the tower was draughty and cramped, it sounded grander than it was. Walter unlocked the door, and used a box of matches to light a few oil lamps and a couple of candles.

'Why don't you open a window, sir?' said Lothar. 'The sun is shining outside.'

'The shutters have been jammed shut for years,' Walter said. 'Ignore the mess.'

'That would be an impossibility, sir,' said Lothar, as he walked in. 'I would have to close my eyes. Perhaps you should get a maid.'

'Maybe I should get ten, and we could have a party.'

Walter closed the door, and pulled off his coat. They sat, with the tray resting on Lothar's knees.

'I would put it down, sir,' he said, 'but I see no space for it amid the piles of clothes and heaps of empty bottles.'

Walter swept the clothes from a chair and pulled it over. 'Set it down there.'

They ate for a few minutes, and Walter started to feel a little better with something in his stomach.

'How did it go with your brother, sir? Did he humiliate you?'

'Not particularly,' said Walter. 'If anything, he seemed a little disappointed that I was still alive.'

Lothar smiled at him. 'Princess Kilbride, on the other hand, seemed positively delighted to see you, sir. I have never witnessed her act like that before; she is usually so reserved.'

'Yes, well, her father and brother have just died. I wouldn't read too much into it.'

'I saw pure relief on her face, sir.'

Walter poked the contents of a plate with a fork. 'Kilbride and I go back a long way. We fight, a lot, but we've known each other since we were born. Did you know that I am only two days older than her? Her mother and my mother were friends, and they were pregnant at the same time. Killie and I were inseparable for years. We played together every day, mostly in the parkland, where we must have climbed every damn tree. We fell from quite a few as well. We fished in the stream; we climbed the cliffs; we rode ponies across the grass. Oh, and we had our school lessons together, too.' He laughed. 'I proposed to her when we were nine.'

Lothar grinned. 'What did she say, sir?'

'She said yes, naturally. We were nine; what else was she going to say? And then, a few years later, she dropped me, as if she were scraping dogshit off her shoe.'

'She dropped you, sir?'

'Yes. It happened very quickly. One day, everything was normal, and then... nothing. She completely lost interest in being my friend. It hurt;

I cannot lie. I was devastated. I mean, she wasn't just a friend; we were best friends.'

'Did she ever say why, sir?'

'She didn't need to; it was blindingly obvious. My brother returned from the Ridden Estate, where he had undergone cavalry and military training for several years. I remember him walking into a room when he first got back. He was in his full dress uniform, and he was tall and had broadened out. He looked... like a king. He was twenty-one; we were thirteen, and Kilbride was utterly smitten with him. She worshipped the ground he walked on, and followed him everywhere he went. Do you see? Even back then, I couldn't compete with my brother.' He leaned forward in his chair. 'Do you want to know the worst part? Hector was completely aware of what was happening. He knew that Killie and I were best friends, and he also knew that she was infatuated with him. So, what does he do? He flirts with her, leading her on; telling her that she's the one for him. And, of course, Killie lapped it all up. It was disgusting – a grown man acting like that towards a child. Still, he didn't mean any of it. He was doing it to fuck with me. He thought it was hilarious.'

Lothar said nothing.

'That's what I don't get,' Walter went on. 'Everyone thinks Hector is some kind of hero, a noble paragon of knightly virtue; when the truth is that he's a mean-spirited shit. He's the most two-faced bastard I've ever met. Why does no one see it but me?' He reached for his coat and withdrew the two bottles of whisky, setting them down on the floor by his feet. 'He told me to take these and then disappear for a few days. Then he called me a useless drunk.'

'Shall we open them, sir?'

Walter stared at the two bottles for a moment. He was desperate for a drink, but he knew he would be playing into his brother's hands.

'I don't know if I'm in the mood for whisky,' he said.

'I could go downstairs and get some beer, sir,' said Lothar. 'Or, we could go out. We still haven't visited that new brothel I was telling you about.'

'My head is too sore. I wouldn't be able to concentrate.'

Lothar laughed. 'You would hardly need much concentration for what I have in mind, sir.'

'You know what I mean. I don't want to go out. And it would look bad, visiting Twinbrook when two kings have just died.'

'I could bring a couple of girls up here, sir. We could pay them extra to tidy the place first.'

'You know, Lothar, I am grateful that you saved my life yesterday, but I have to say that you are a bad influence. Your suggestions always revolve around us drinking ourselves to oblivion, and seeking out prostitutes. I think I'm a little too tired for either activity today.'

'But the afternoon has barely begun, sir.' He picked up one of the bottles of whisky. 'This is excellent quality. Are you sure you don't want any?'

Walter nodded. 'Quite sure.'

'I'll tell you what, sir,' said Lothar, as he got to his feet. 'I'll take the tray downstairs, and load it up with a few cold beers. We can put the whisky aside until later.'

'All right,' said Walter. 'You do that.'

Lothar picked up the tray and walked from the room. Walter's eyes drooped as soon as his aide had gone, and he yawned. He glanced at the whisky, and thought about what his brother had said. For a moment, he was filled with loathing for Hector, and that made his mind up. If Hector wanted him to drink the whisky, then he wouldn't. He stood, and felt a rush of dizziness wash over him. He sat back down again, closed his eyes, and within seconds, he had fallen into a deep and dreamless sleep.

CHAPTER 10
UNPREPARED

Torrent, Upper Down – 10th Day of Lamenta 107

'Where's Mama?' said the boy-king.

'She is sleeping in my bed, Your Majesty,' said Kilbride.

Alfie looked around the study, as though he was confused. 'Where's Grandfather?'

'Grandfather isn't here any more.'

'But this is Grandfather's house. It's time for my reading lesson and I want to go home. Is my father at home?'

Kilbride sat down next to the boy. She took his hand, but he pulled it away. After two nights of very little sleep, she could feel her energy fading, and she stifled a yawn. With Frida resting in her bed, and the young king sitting in her quarters, she knew she had to stay awake, but it was becoming a struggle.

'When is Father coming to take me home?' said the boy.

'I'm sorry, Alfie, but your father is dead,' she said. 'He won't be coming home again.'

The boy started to cry.

'Do you remember what your Uncle Walter told you?' she went on. 'Your father was very brave, but he died yesterday. We had a funeral for him this morning, and you were there. Do you remember being in the chapel?'

'Uncle Walter was dead,' the boy said, 'but he came back.'

'We only thought Uncle Walter was dead. We were wrong.'

'Are you wrong about my father?'

'No.'

'What if you are wrong?'

Kilbride said nothing.

'I want to look for Father. Is he in the same place as Uncle Walter was?'

Kilbride put her head in her hands. She could feel the despair start to eat into her, as exhaustion sapped her strength. She needed to focus on the future, or risk Upper Down being swept aside by forces beyond her control. To the south, imperial soldiers under the command of Prince Valentino were advancing; and to the north, the Westlanders were effectively in control of Twinbrook. One wrong decision, and Torrent would be crushed between the two. The responsibility seemed too much to bear, and she cursed Walter for the way he had preferred to take the whisky rather than shoulder any part of the burden. While he was off getting drunk, Kilbride was left with the seven-year-old king of Upper Down, and his grief-stricken mother. True, Walter had been through a terrible experience, but hadn't they all suffered? How dare he act as though the realm meant nothing to him? It was typical of Walter. Every time Kilbride sensed that he was ready to act responsibly, he would do something stupid and selfish. Hector's cold welcome hadn't helped. Kilbride had expected at least a glimmer of brotherly affection from the Duke of Ridden upon discovering that Walter was alive; but no. Instead, Hector had been rude, and Walter had reciprocated. Kilbride could have slapped Hector when he had brought up the whisky, and she had almost slapped Walter when he had taken it.

Alfie stood up. 'I am going to look for Father,' he said. 'I will find him and bring him back, and then I can go home for my reading lesson.'

'You must stay here, Your Majesty,' Kilbride said. 'This is your new home. Do you like it? The Royal Palace is much bigger than that draughty old fortress where you used to live, and we can bring all of your things here. Your mother will also be living here, of course; and me, and your Aunty Abigone.'

'Does Uncle Walter live here, too?'

'Sometimes,' she said. 'Uncle Walter has three different houses. That's a lot, isn't it?'

Alfie narrowed his eyes. 'Which room is mine?'

Kilbride stood. 'Why don't we have a look around, and you can choose one?' She glanced over to the doorway, where her lady-in-waiting was sitting, her eyes half-closed. 'Marie,' she said, 'please stay here, in case Queen Frida requires anything. I am going to show His Majesty around.'

'Yes, my lady,' said Marie.

'I know I have been asking a lot of you recently,' Kilbride said. 'I shall find the queen a lady-in-waiting of her own as soon as I am able. For now, you will have to do the work of two.'

Marie frowned, and Kilbride felt like grabbing her by the throat and shaking her.

She turned to the boy king. 'Wait here for a moment, Alfie.'

The boy eyed her with suspicion. 'Where are you going?'

'To the bathroom,' said Kilbride.

'Are you coming back?'

'Of course. I'll just be a minute.'

Kilbride strode away. She entered the small bathroom, went inside, closed the door, and sat down on the edge of the bath. She burst into tears, unable to suppress them any longer. Let it all come out, she said to herself, fighting a desire to curl up into a ball on the bathroom floor. She felt as though she was standing at the bottom of a mountain, watching as an avalanche rumbled its way down the slope towards her, devouring everything in its path. Everyone was expecting her to be resolute and strong, but she was barely able to accept the loss of her brother. Worse, his death was her fault. If she hadn't conspired to have Alfgang the Great murdered, then his son would still be alive.

She stood, and wiped her face with a towel. She closed her eyes and breathed, until her face wore a more neutral expression. One hour at a time, that's how she would deal with things. One hour at a time, and one thing at a time. Little Alfie was expecting to be given a tour of the palace, in order to select new quarters for him and his mother, so that is what Kilbride would do.

She opened the door and stepped out of the bathroom, to find two officers standing in her study, one from the Town Militia, and the other from the Royal Guard.

'Can I help you?' said Kilbride.

The captain from the Town Militia bowed. 'My lady,' he said, 'Westlander forces have broken through one of the gates in the walls of Torrent, and are rampaging through the streets. We need reinforcements immediately.'

'Which gate?' she said.

'The one by the wine merchants' district, my lady. I estimate that at least two hundred mounted warriors under the command of Chief Dravid have entered Torrent, and more may follow. We need the Royal Guard sent out to assist with pushing them back into Twinbrook.'

'What is Dravid trying to achieve?'

'We are unsure of his motives, my lady. Some of his followers are looting the houses and marketplaces close to where they entered the town.'

'Are they moving towards the Royal Palace?'

'We are unable to say, my lady. They might be in Torrent purely to raid, or it might be an attempt at seizing power.'

Kilbride lowered her gaze. 'Has it come to this? The Westlanders are raiding us this time?' She turned to the officer from the Royal Guard. 'How many soldiers can you spare, Major?'

'None, my lady,' said the officer.

'We can surely send a few detachments to assist the Town Militia, no?'

'Lord Hector has requisitioned all spare soldiers from the Royal

Guard, my lady,' said the major. 'We would be leaving the Royal Palace undefended if we sent reinforcements out into Torrent.'

The boy king glanced up. 'Are the Westlanders coming?'

'Stay here with Marie,' said Kilbride. 'I have to find your Uncle Hector.'

'Don't leave me!' cried the boy.

Kilbride hurried to the door leading from the study and looked out. Several courtiers were standing in the corridor, and they bowed in Kilbride's direction.

'Summon Princess Abigone at once,' she said. 'I need her here.'

'Her Highness gave instructions that she wasn't to be disturbed, my lady,' said one.

'Why? What is she doing?'

'Her Highness is sleeping, my lady.'

'Then wake her up; that's an order. The Westlanders have infiltrated Torrent, and I need her here to look after the boy king. Go.'

The courtier bowed again, then he rushed off. Kilbride re-entered the study and went up to Alfie. She crouched by him, and took his hand.

'I have to leave for a while, Your Majesty,' she said. 'Aunty Abigone will be here in a few minutes, and she will take care of you. All right? She will be bringing Tulip with her. You like Tulip, don't you?'

'No,' said the boy. 'It tried to scratch my hand.'

'Then keep your hands away from him. I will be back as soon as I can.'

She stood, and glanced at Marie, who bowed her head.

Kilbride gestured to the officers. 'Take me to Lord Hector.'

The three of them left the room, and squeezed past the remaining courtiers. A few broke away, and began to follow Princess Kilbride and the two officers as they made their way down a flight of stairs. The officers led Kilbride to the rear of the palace, and they emerged into the autumnal sunshine in front of the Royal Parkland. Hector was standing on the grass by the base of the steps, talking to a group of men from the Royal Guard.

Kilbride hurried down the steps. 'Hector, may I have a moment?'

The duke turned. 'I thought you were looking after the boy king,' he said.

'I was,' she said. 'I need Guardsmen to be sent out into Torrent – Chief Dravid has broken through the gate by the wine merchants' district, and…'

'Yes, I know,' he said.

'But I was told that you have requisitioned every spare soldier in the palace.'

'That is correct.'

'What the fuck is going on?' Kilbride cried.

Hector glanced at the officers standing close by. 'Perhaps, Your Highness, we should be having this little chat in private.'

Hector placed a hand onto Kilbride's arm, but she shrugged it off. They walked ten yards to the left, and Hector lowered his voice.

'Did you forget that I am leading a large force into Twinbrook this evening, Your Highness?'

'You are leading them into Twinbrook to fight Dravid. There is no need; he is in Torrent.'

'But my force isn't ready. I will need several hours to make my preparations. Besides, I am relying upon the cover of darkness.'

'Dravid is rampaging through Torrent with two hundred men.'

'That is extremely unfortunate, but there is nothing I can do.'

Kilbride took a step back, her eyes wide as she tried to comprehend what he was saying to her.

'People are going to die,' she whispered. 'Our people.'

'That is regrettable, Your Highness, but we must keep our nerve,' said Hector. 'Chief Dravid will be punished, of that there is no doubt. By dawn tomorrow, I will have removed the threat he poses to Upper Down, and I will have retrieved Princess Hygilt from his custody.'

'By dawn tomorrow, half of Torrent might be ablaze.'

'That is a risk we shall have to take. Look – I shall be taking six hundred of the Royal Guard with me this evening, which leaves you some six hundred here to defend the palace. You will be safe. On top of that, you have a couple of hundred men of the Mountain Rangers; and there are the soldiers of the Wall Militia also, so the Kendril Gap should remain secure.'

'What about your men in the ducal palace?' she said. 'Can you spare any of those?'

Hector shook his head. 'Unfortunately, I will be needing them for tonight; and they will be arriving here just before I set off for Twinbrook. Hold tight, Your Highness, and do not panic. Dravid is just trying to scare us, I think. He is revelling in the death of King Alfgang the Pius, and wants to show off in front of the other chiefs. He and his men will most likely spend the rest of the afternoon robbing and pillaging, and then, this night, I shall teach him a lesson he will never forget.'

'This is unacceptable. I don't think I will be able to stand back and do nothing while Dravid's men trample over Torrent.'

'You must try to see the bigger picture, Your Highness. We have to focus on keeping the Westlanders divided. With Dravid in Torrent, there will be other opportunities to exploit in Twinbrook. Trust me.'

Kilbride felt the weight upon her shoulders increase. 'This is too much to ask.'

'Do you wish to excuse yourself from the decision-making apparatus, Your Highness? I am prepared to act as sole regent, if that becomes necessary. Amery, my lawyer, has been summoned from the ducal palace. When he arrives, he is to start drafting the legal documents needed to confirm the legitimacy of the regency council. If you no longer want to be a part of it, let me know, and I shall make the necessary amendments. I do not want you to overburden yourself.'

'Are you trying to push me out?'

'Not at all,' Hector said. 'I am merely offering you the choice. The responsibilities of leadership are not for everyone.'

'I will be on that damn council,' she said.

Hector smiled. 'One more thing before I get back to work. I spoke to my contacts in the Wall Militia after lunch, and it appears that Walter did not return to Torrent through the Kendril Gap. I don't suppose you happen to know of any other routes through the mountains?'

She shook her head.

'That is a pity,' he said. 'If another route exists, then it would seem to be a matter of the utmost importance, as we wouldn't want Prince Valentino's forces discovering it. If the imperial army is able to bypass the Wall of Kendril, then our position will be grave indeed. If you happen to hear anything, you will let me know, won't you?'

'Yes,' she said.

'I would ask my brother, of course,' he said, 'but I imagine that Walter is thoroughly intoxicated by now. He is such a disappointment to me, but I suppose that his behaviour shouldn't surprise me any more. Good day, Your Highness.'

Kilbride watched as Hector turned away and strode back to the officers of the Royal Guard. She glanced to her left, and saw the captain from the Town Militia waiting for her.

She walked over to him. 'Duke Hector cannot spare any men. The best I can offer you is a small detachment of Mountain Rangers.'

'Then what are our orders, my lady?'

'How many of the Town Militia are currently out on the streets?'

'All of them, my lady. We are occupying the main junctions leading to the Royal Palace and the Kendril Wall, but we cannot be everywhere at once. At best, we might be able to contain Dravid's men, and keep them penned up in the northern districts of the town.'

'But your forces must outnumber his several times over, Captain.'

'That is true, my lady, but our men are part-time soldiers, and they are poorly armed and equipped compared to the Westlanders. If we knew their intentions, we might be able to concentrate our forces, but we have no idea where Dravid will strike next. Even with the addition of the Mountain Rangers, a defensive posture is the best we can do.'

'This is my command,' she said: 'set up roadblocks, form a perimeter to seal off the northern districts, and evacuate every civilian you can reach. I will send the Mountain Rangers to the town square as soon as they are ready to leave the palace, and you can redeploy them from there. We will limit the extent of the damage caused by Dravid, but you will not attack his position. Contain the Westlanders, if you can. If they break through your lines, regroup and form a new perimeter.'

'And if they strike out towards the Royal Palace, my lady?'

'I hope they do, Captain. If Dravid is stupid enough to assault the palace defences, we will tear his men to pieces. If he advances in this direction, fall back and let him pass, then cut off his lines of retreat. I know that I am asking much of you and your men this day, but relief is coming.'

'Relief, my lady? When?'

'At some point during the night, but I can give you no details.'

The captain bowed his head. 'Do you wish to hear the current estimate of casualties, my lady?'

'No. Return to your men and pass on my orders. Dismissed.'

The captain saluted, then he turned and hurried away.

Kilbride made her way up the steps and into the rear of the palace. A few courtiers began to follow her, but she kept her gaze averted from them. She strode towards the small office on the ground floor where the commander of the Mountain Rangers worked, and knocked on the door. She pushed it open without waiting for a response, and entered the room. Three men from the Rangers were gazing up at a large map of the mountains to the south of Torrent, and they saluted when they saw Kilbride.

'How many men can you spare?' she said. 'Chief Dravid has broken through the wall protecting Torrent, and is ravaging the northern neighbourhoods.'

The three officers glanced at each other.

'Lord Walter is our commanding officer, ma'am,' said one. 'We take our orders from him.'

'This is an emergency,' she said. 'Lord Walter was injured south of the Wall, and is resting. How many can you spare?'

'Around eighty, ma'am.'

'Thank you. Send them to the main square of Torrent to assist the Town Militia. You will be taking your orders from them for the rest of the day, but I imagine your men will be used to reinforce the roadblocks being set up.'

'Yes, ma'am.'

She glanced up at the large map on the wall. The position of the Kendril Wall was clearly marked, as were the contours of the ravine to its south, but she could see no sign of any alternative routes through the mountains.

'Was there something else, ma'am?' said the officer.

'Have you debriefed the Rangers who escaped the slaughter with Walter?'

'Yes, ma'am.'

'I have been told that they did not return via the Kendril Wall.'

The officers said nothing.

'The Duke of Ridden has been making enquiries,' Kilbride went on.

'Certain operational matters are kept confidential, ma'am,' said one of the officers. 'Perhaps you should speak to Lord Walter regarding this.'

'And if the Duke of Ridden asks you directly?'

'We shall give him the same response, ma'am.'

Kilbride nodded. 'Thank you once again for your assistance, gentlemen. Please ensure that the eighty Rangers depart the palace as soon as possible.'

The three men bowed their heads and Kilbride left the room. She took a flight of stairs to an upper level, and walked back to her quarters. Inside, a sullen-faced Abigone was sitting close to the boy king, while Marie had dozed off in her chair.

'At last,' said Abigone, getting to her feet as she cradled Tulip in her arms. 'I am not a babysitter, sister, and I am not at your beck and call. As for your useless lady-in-waiting; well, just take a look at her. The servants are sleeping while we do all the work.'

'Have you finished?' said Kilbride. 'We are all exhausted, Abbie.'

'Yes, but some of us get to sleep, while others are allowed to get drunk. Where's Hector?'

'He's with the Royal Guard.'

'Is this what it means to be on the regency council? We three do everything while others relax? It's not fair. Perhaps I should go along to Walter's quarters and help him drink the whisky.'

'Oh shut up, Abbie. I asked you to look after Alfie for twenty minutes, and you're acting as if you have the weight of the world on your shoulders.'

'Don't you dare tell me to shut up!'

Kilbride walked past her sister and went out on to the balcony.

'I hadn't finished,' Abigone yelled. She walked out next to Kilbride, and pushed her sister in the shoulder. 'Are you listening to me? I am going crazy from lack of sleep; look at the bags under my eyes. If I don't get some rest, I think I will go mad.'

Abigone pushed her again, and Kilbride slapped her across the face.

'Get a grip of yourself,' Kilbride cried. 'Do you think you are the only one suffering? Right now, Westlanders are looting and pillaging homes in the northern districts of Torrent. I want to sleep, too. I'm so tired I might collapse at any moment, and yet I can't risk it. We are the only ones left, Abbie. Me, you, Hector and Walter. There is no one else. Frida is too sick with grief to help us, and Alfie is just a boy. I need you. Upper Down needs you. If we don't stick together, we shall be destroyed.'

Abigone took a few paces back, a hand on her cheek. Tulip was squirming in her embrace, and his eyes were casting evil glances in Kilbride's direction.

'Please don't fight,' said Alfie.

Kilbride and Abigone turned. The boy king was standing by the balcony door, his face wet with tears.

'Go to your rooms, Abbie,' said Kilbride. 'Get some rest.'

Abigone stared at her, then she strode from the balcony without another word.

'Shall we see if your mother is feeling any better, Your Majesty?' said Kilbride.

Alfie nodded, and Kilbride took his hand. They walked back into the study, then they went through another door.

'These are my quarters,' Kilbride said. 'I have a sitting room, a bathroom, and your mother is resting in my bedroom.' She pointed to a door. 'She's in there. Let's knock first.'

Kilbride rapped her fist against the door, then she pushed it open. Inside, Frida was sitting fully clothed on Kilbride's bed, her eyes open but unfocussed.

'How are you feeling, Frida?' said Kilbride.

The woman did not respond.

'Mama?' said Alfie.

Kilbride and Alfie walked closer to the woman.

'Can you hear me, Frida?' said Kilbride.

Frida's eyes flickered over to where her sister-in-law and son were standing.

'Do you need anything?' said Kilbride.

'I heard shouting,' she said.

'That was just me and Abigone. Sorry. Did we disturb your rest?'

'I wasn't resting. Leave me alone.'

'But your son is here, Frida, and he...'

'I said leave me alone!' Frida cried. She burst into tears. 'Why did you make me look at the body, Killie? Why?' She turned to the boy king. 'Those savages ripped your father to pieces! Our family is cursed. The spirits have abandoned us. Hide, Alfie. The Westlanders are coming for us, and I can't protect you. Run into the mountains and hide, before they tear you limb from limb.'

The boy started to cry, and Kilbride retreated, dragging Alfie back by the hand.

'Your mother is not herself at the moment, Alfie,' said Kilbride. 'We should let her rest.'

'Damn you!' Frida shouted. 'Damn both our families – yours and mine. We let the Westlanders into our homes, and now we are paying the price. They will kill us all!'

Kilbride pulled Alfie from the room, and shut the door. The shouting went on for a few moments, then it ceased, replaced by the low sound of sobbing.

Kilbride crouched down by Alfie, who was shaking and crying. 'Your mother is sick. She needs time to get better.'

'Will I run away to the mountains? Are the Westlanders coming to get me?'

'You will be safe in the palace, Alfie. I promise.'

She led him through to the sitting room, and they sat on a long couch.

'Will you cuddle me, Aunty?' the boy said.

'Of course,' she said.

She put her arms around him, and they lay back on the couch. The boy's trembling stopped, and within moments, he was asleep in her embrace. She tried to free her arm, but he almost awoke, so she remained where she was. She felt her eyes start to close, and forced them back open.

She had to remain awake, she told herself. She had to be ready to face the next emergency. Upper Down was relying on her. She tried to picture what was happening in the northern half of Torrent, but it was useless – the pull of sleep was irresistible.

Her eyes closed again, and she slipped into a deep slumber.

CHAPTER 11
UNDONE

Torrent, Upper Down – 10th Day of Lamenta 107

Hector gazed into the west. The sun was setting over Torrent, its dying rays lending a dark red glow to the tendrils of smoke rising from the northern districts. He wondered how many innocent civilians had been assaulted, robbed or murdered by Dravid's raiding party since they had broken through the gate of the walled town. Whatever the final tally, Hector would be able to use it to justify the strike against Dravid's base in Twinbrook. The Westlander chief had been a useful ally over the years, but he had gone too far, and it was time he paid the price.

Hector turned, and looked out over the Royal Parkland, where six hundred men-at-arms from the Royal Guard were lined up on the grass. To their left were a further hundred that had arrived from the ducal palace, along with twenty of Hector's personal knights, all mounted. The Duke of Ridden raised a hand, and every soldier focussed their attention upon him.

'Men of Upper Down,' he cried. 'Do you see the smoke rising over Torrent? Can you see what those Westlander renegades are doing to your fellow citizens? Not only was Chief Dravid responsible for the ghastly murder of King Alfgang the Pius, he is now allowing his men to rape and pillage the decent folk of Torrent. We shall not stand for this. This night, we shall take the fight to him, and sow terror in the hearts of our enemies. We shall not strike his forces head on, for that is what he will be expecting; instead, we shall outflank Chief Dravid, and strike at his base in the town of Twinbrook. We will travel light, and we will move with silence and haste. We will march through the Royal Parkland, and then we shall enter Twinbrook. We know where Chief Dravid lives. Let us slake our swords in the blood of vengeance this night – vengeance for our fallen king, and vengeance for the horrors Dravid has unleashed upon the men, women and children of Torrent!'

The men cheered, and then Hector strode down the steps at the rear of the palace. He joined the officers and knights, who had gathered in front of the seven hundred men-at-arms.

'I will lead from the front this evening, gentlemen,' he said.

Sergeant Towie led a spare horse over the grass and stopped next to the duke.

'Your mount, my lord.'

'Thank you, sergeant.'

Hector gripped the reins, placed a foot into a stirrup, and pulled himself up onto the saddle. The duke cast a glance over his shoulder, but there was no sign of either of the princesses. He had been expecting Kilbride to watch their departure, and he was a little disappointed that the rear of the palace was deserted.

Hector glanced at the officers and knights of his force. 'Follow me.'

He selected a path through the parkland, and the mounted knights moved off with him, followed by the soldiers, their boots tramping over the grass. Hector had ordered that no lamps be lit in the parkland that evening, and the force moved through the evening darkness, each man having been ordered to remain as quiet as possible. The Silver Moon came out from behind a cloud, and the parkland was bathed in its white light, while the Little Red Moon was close to setting. Hector had been hoping that the cloud cover would remain in place all night, but none of that would matter when they were under the streetlamps of Twinbrook.

They marched for thirty minutes, until they approached the high stone wall that surrounded the parkland. A slim tower was guarding a small postern gate in the wall, and both were almost hidden by dense undergrowth. The duke dismounted, then he led his mount towards the tower, and approached the postern gate. A door in the tower was lying open, and four soldiers emerged from the gloom of the interior. They saluted the duke.

'Prepare to open the gate,' said Hector, then he turned and gazed at his force of over seven hundred men.

'Beyond that gate,' he said, 'lies the town of Twinbrook. Before we enter, you all need to remember something. The civilians who dwell in Twinbrook are our fellow citizens – they are not to be harmed in any way. They, too, have suffered at the hands of Dravid's men, and we are coming as their liberators. Remember this, also – our quarrel this night is not with every Westlander. We shall target only those who are members of Chief Dravid's warband; the other Westlanders are not to be touched. We shall make straight for the neighbourhood under Dravid's control. Once there, we shall surround it, and move in, killing any who stand in our way. It is likely that Dravid's home will contain some of the hostages he has cruelly abducted from their homes in the south. One of those captives might be Princess Hygilt. If any such hostages are found, they are to be freed, and treated with tenderness and compassion. We shall escort them safely back to the Royal Palace, along with any stolen plunder we happen to find.'

He gestured to the soldiers by the postern gate, and they pushed it open, revealing a narrow and deserted alleyway in the back streets of Twinbrook. The twenty knights dismounted, and each gripped the reins of their horses. Hector led his mount through the gate, and onto the cobbles of the lane. It ran between terraced rows of brick houses, but each window and front door was closed and barred. The twenty knights came after him and, when they were all through, they remounted their horses, and walked them to the end of the lane. The seven hundred men-at-arms came next, marching two abreast through the gate, and filling the alleyway from end to end. Hector signalled the advance, and the mounted knights emerged into another quiet residential street by the edge of Twinbrook. Hector kept his pace slow enough so that those on foot could keep up, as they made their way towards the centre of the town. A few streetlamps had been lit, and Hector saw several faces peer out of the windows on either side of the road. They reached a busier street, lined with several brothels and taverns, and a few screams rose into the air as dozens of civilians scattered. A small group of Westlanders stared up at the Duke of Ridden, then they fled down a back alley. Hector reached a major intersection, where five roads met, and another group of loitering Westlanders glanced up at the approaching force. A few edged away, but a gigantic man remained in the middle of the road, and folded his arms across his chest.

'What are you doing here, Duke?' he called out. 'Twinbrook is our town; that was the deal.'

A few of his comrades laughed.

'My fight is not with you this night, Chief Gorgan of the Far Lakes,' Hector said to the Westlander.

'No? Who are you here for?'

Hector smiled. 'Oh, I think you can guess. It is time to bring Dravid down a peg or two.'

'Dravid upset you, did he, Duke?'

'His men are currently pillaging Torrent,' Hector said. 'He broke the rules. You can come and watch if you like, but I would be obliged if you stood aside to allow my men to pass.'

'And if I don't?'

'Then I will grind your skull into the cobbles, Gorgan. The choice is yours.'

The Westlander chief laughed, then he gestured to his men. 'Move aside for the Duke of Ridden. He's here for that filthy dog Dravid, and about damn time.'

Hector inclined his head slightly towards the Westlander chief, as Gorgan's men moved to the side of the road.

'I think me and my boys will accompany you, Duke,' Gorgan said.

'I've been waiting a long time to see Dravid shamed. If you happen to bump into his brother, I want you to give him to me.'

'That depends upon your intentions,' said Hector. 'I will not be handing him over if you wish to spare his life.'

The Westlander chief laughed. 'He insulted one of my men, Duke. I will not be showing him any kindness this night.'

Hector urged his horse back into motion. He took the first road leading away to their right, and his force followed him into the heart of Twinbrook, while Gorgan and his men walked by the side of the knights. They passed enormous beer halls, from where the sounds of riotous drinking were coming. Several Westlanders were throwing up into the street, while a few others were fighting each other outside a brothel. Of the local inhabitants, there was little sign. A few natives of Upper Down were working in the taverns, but most were locked up tight within their homes. It was well known that Twinbrook transformed into a different town as soon as night fell. During the day, locals would be out and about, getting on with their business while the Westlanders slept off their hangovers; but the nights belonged to the tall foreign warriors and their entourages.

Hector reached another junction. By that time, several dozen drunken Westlanders had joined Gorgan's men in trailing along beside his force, curious to discover what the Duke of Ridden was doing in Twinbrook with so many soldiers. A few of them were hurling insults at the Royal Guardsmen, who were ignoring them as ordered. Hector gestured to his officers.

'I want the beer hall ahead of us surrounded and cut off,' he said, 'along with all of the buildings at its rear. This is Dravid's base of operations, but the chief is not at home. While he ravages Torrent, we shall do the same to him. As soon as the entire block has been sealed off, order your men in. There will be wagons and horses by the rear, and I want them brought here. I shall lead the knights and my ducal men-at-arms directly into the beer hall.'

The officers saluted, then they began to issue orders to their men. The soldiers from the Royal Guard began to move off, with two hundred going down the streets to either side of the huge beer hall, while a further two hundred secured the area in front of the building. A few staggering Westlanders emerged from the main doors of the beer hall, and their eyes widened at the sight of the knights and soldiers.

Hector drew his sword, and raised it above his head. 'For Alfgang the Pius!'

The knights and the hundred ducal men-at-arms let out a roar, and charged towards the beer hall. Sword blades flashed out, and the Westlanders by the wide doors fell screaming. Hector's horse entered the cavernous beer hall, followed by the knights and the men-at-arms. With so many of Dravid's men off raiding Torrent, the building was almost deserted, and the men-at-arms slaughtered those inside within a few minutes, leaving their bodies lying in their own blood on the sticky floor of the beer hall.

'Take out all the plunder you find,' Hector cried, 'and guard it by the front of the beer hall.'

He dismounted, and handed the reins to a soldier, as the men-at-arms began to strip the interior of the building of its valuables. Chests of gold were removed, along with tapestries, paintings, silver plate and boxes of jewellery. Hector strode to the rear of the hall, a dozen men-at-arms by his side. They broke through a door, and found a few older Westlanders cowering in the corner of a room. Hector raised his sword, and drove it through a man's chest, then his men-at-arms dispatched the rest. Hector pointed to the crates and sacks stacked up by the walls.

'Leave nothing,' he said; 'take it all.'

Hector walked out of a side door, and emerged back into the street. A large crowd of Westlanders had gathered to watch the proceedings, but none were interfering. He gestured to a sergeant of the Royal Guard. 'Spread the word – if Dravid's' brother is found, bring him to me alive.'

'Yes, my lord.'

Hector walked round to the front of the beer hall, and watched as the pile of recovered loot grew. Soldiers were ferrying the contents of Dravid's home base out from the buildings, and stacking it all up, while others kept guard. A line of wagons approached down one of the streets that flanked the beer hall, each pulled by two horses, and being driven by Royal Guardsmen. They came to a halt by the mound of plunder, and soldiers began loading the backs of the wagons. A man was dragged out from the side of the beer hall, kicking and screaming as four men-at-arms gripped his arms and legs. They hauled him over to where the duke was standing and pinned him to the ground.

'This is Dravid's brother, my lord,' said one. 'He refused to come quietly.'

Hector smiled, then he glanced over at the crowd of Westlanders, and saw Gorgan and his men among them. He gestured to the chief, and the man approached, a wide grin on his face. Gorgan shouted something down at Dravid's brother in their own language, then the chief leaned over and pulled a long knife from his belt. He reached out, and slit the throat of Dravid's brother, letting the blood pool on the cobbles.

'Thank you for that, Duke,' Gorgan said. 'Much obliged.'

'Then perhaps you could tell me where I could find Chief Stefan of Saltmere this fine night?'

'And why would you be looking for him, Duke? I have no quarrel with Stefan.'

'Neither do I. I merely wish to speak to him.'

'Do I have your word that you won't try anything untoward?'

'I swear it.'

Gorgan nodded. 'All right, Duke. Stefan has recently taken possession of the beer hall down Fleshmarket Close.'

'I know the one,' said Hector. He turned, and watched as more plunder was removed from Dravid's home. A squad of men-at-arms emerged from one of the buildings to the rear of the hall, leading five bedraggled civilians. Among them was a young girl, her gaze lowered as she stumbled over the cobbles. Hector strode towards them, and bowed his head.

'Your Imperial Highness,' he said to the girl. 'My heart is filled with relief that you are alive.'

Hygilt glanced up at him. She looked terrified, and her hands were shaking.

'Are you hurt, my lady?' said Hector.

The girl stared at him for a moment, then she shook her head. Hector escorted the princess and the other four freed hostages to the wagons at the front of the beer hall, then he summoned his officers.

'Pull your soldiers back from the building,' he said. 'Ensure that Princess Hygilt and the other released captives are adequately protected, then transport them and everything we have taken back to Torrent.'

'Yes, my lord,' said the senior officer from the Royal Guards.

'Avoid the gate by the wine merchants' district,' Hector went on, 'as Dravid's forces may still be in control of that area. When you enter Torrent, wait for me by the clock tower in the butchers' district, and I will rejoin you as soon as I have finished my business in Twinbrook.'

'Are you not coming with us, my lord?'

'Not yet.' He gestured to his twenty knights. 'You shall be my personal escort for the remainder of my time in Twinbrook. Hand your mounts over to my men-at-arms, and come with me.'

The duke strode away from the front of the beer hall, and the twenty knights followed him on foot. They passed through the crowd of watching Westlanders, who parted for them. Gorgan fell in with them, and escorted them along the streets of Twinbrook. The disturbance had brought hundreds of Westlanders out onto the roads, and they stared at the duke and his entourage as they passed. They reached Fleshmarket Close, and were confronted by another enormous beer hall. Sixty armoured men were standing outside the main entrance, their weapons drawn.

'Come no further,' shouted one of them. 'This is Chief Stefan's territory.'

Hector raised a hand to halt his knights, then he stepped forward.

'I am the Duke of Ridden,' he said.

'We know who you are,' said the Westlander. 'What is your business here?'

'I wish to speak to your chief. I am prepared to walk into the beer hall alone.'

The Westlanders by the entrance eyed each other.

'I can vouch for the duke,' said Gorgan. 'He has given me his oath that his intentions are peaceful.'

'All right,' said one of the Westlanders by the door, 'but he must come alone. His knights must remain out here.'

Hector walked forwards, and the Westlanders led him into the packed beer hall. A band was playing music in the middle of the hall, and crowds of Westlanders were drinking beer and singing. The noise rose as many saw the Duke of Ridden walk into their midst, and Hector kept his head held high. His escort led him up a set of stairs to a balcony that overlooked the main hall, and they passed through another cordon of heavily-armed men. Chief Stefan was sitting in a wide booth with a dozen of his closest allies, and their conversation ceased as Hector neared their table.

Stefan laughed. 'I thought my eyes were playing tricks on me,' he said; 'but no – the fucking Duke of Ridden has decided to pay us a visit.'

'Good evening, Chief,' said Hector. 'May we speak?'

'We're speaking now,' said Stefan. He nodded to the man on his left. 'Get the duke a beer.' He turned back to Hector. 'So, you have finally tired of Dravid? That surprises me, especially after he killed Alfgang the Pius for you. There's no need to deny it – I know the truth.'

'Dravid acted like a child,' said Hector. 'He was supposed to slip back into Twinbrook quietly, not boast to all and sundry about what he had done. I had it all worked out. The blame for the king's death was intended to fall upon the imperial army, not the Westlanders. Dravid placed me into an impossible position, and he forced my hand. Hence, I am here, to speak to you.'

Stefan said nothing, his eyes appraising the duke, then he gestured to the wooden benches in the alcove.

'Sit.'

Hector strode forward, then he sat down on the bench as a beer was placed in front of him. Hector took a long drink as the Westlanders watched, then he placed the tankard back onto the table.

'I wish to propose an alliance,' he said. 'Together, we shall destroy Dravid's forces, leaving you as the undisputed master of Twinbrook.'

'I assume you know our traditions, Duke?' said Stefan. 'Among the Westlanders, the one who comes begging for an alliance brings with him a gift to sweeten the deal. What gift do you have for me?'

'I will give you Princess Hygilt,' Hector said. 'My men have removed her from Dravid's captivity.'

Stefan laughed. 'Was that a joke? Why the fuck would I want to be saddled with an imperial princess? Do you think I wish to live out my life as a sworn enemy of the Sanctian Empire? No, Duke, if you want my advice, you should hand the girl over to the imperial army. If you give her to Prince Valentino, he might decide to take his army home.'

'Valentino's army does not concern me,' said Hector. 'The Kendril Wall is impregnable.'

'Let us hope you are right. What else do you have to offer?'

'What do you want?'

Stefan smiled. 'For a while now, I have been considering making Upper Down my permanent home,' he said. 'I want to put down some roots here, and what would accomplish that better than a marriage into the Royal Family? My price for this alliance is Abigone. I want her for my wife, so that my sons are bound to the line of kings. You give her to me, and I will be your true and loyal ally for all time.'

'A princess cannot marry a chief,' said Hector.

Stefan's eyes flickered with rage. 'Are you refusing my request?'

'No,' said Hector, 'I am merely pointing out that for this wedding to go ahead, you would first need to be elevated in rank. The position of Duke of Torrent has been vacant for over a decade – would that suffice?'

'Are you offering me a dukedom?'

'Yes, if you are serious about wishing to settle here. You would become an integral part of the realm, with all of the benefits and responsibilities that brings. It is all or nothing, Stefan. You cannot be half in and half out. If you want Abigone, you must commit yourself and your men to the defence of Upper Down.'

Stefan slapped his thigh. 'Did you hear that, men? I am to be a duke, married to a fucking princess!'

The Westlanders on the balcony cheered and raised their tankards.

'I have a price,' said Hector.

'I thought you might,' said Stefan.

'Firstly, you will help me destroy Dravid's forces. I will harry them this night, but I will require your assistance to eradicate them completely. And secondly, before any duchy or marriage can be considered, you must swear allegiance to the King of Upper Down.'

'Who, that boy?'

'Indeed. King Alfgang the Sixth is our lawful monarch. Naturally, he is too young to rule unaided. A regency council is to be established – a council that will include the highest ranked men of the realm. At the moment, Princess Abigone is due to have a place upon this council; but if you were her husband, then that place would fall to you.'

Stefan frowned, as though he was trying to find some flaw in Hector's proposal. 'This seems too good to be true, Duke.'

'I require strong allies, Stefan,' said Hector, 'and you are the strongest chief among the Westlanders. Think of what we could achieve together. All talk of evicting the Westlanders would cease; instead, our families would be bound together.'

'Would you allow us to continue raiding the south?'

'Of course,' said Hector. 'As soon as the imperial army has departed, the raids can resume. My priority is to enforce law and order onto the streets of Torrent and Twinbrook, and to re-establish stability. Your men will help to uphold the law in Upper Down, while being free to ravage the south. Do you accept this offer?'

'How can I refuse?' he said. 'When do I get to see Abigone? I wish to inspect my bride.'

'I would suggest that you move into the Royal Palace as soon as it is convenient,' said Hector, 'and I will introduce you to the princess after you have sworn allegiance to King Alfgang the Sixth. There will be no physical contact between you and Abigone, however; not until the exchange of wedding vows. We are not savages.'

Stefan laughed, then he gazed at his men, as though he were trying to gauge their reactions.

'I do not wish to rush you,' said Hector, 'but Dravid's men are still in Torrent, and my forces are itching to confront him.'

'My men cannot assist you this night,' Stefan said.

'I know. Can your forces be ready two nights from now? If you agree to the alliance, then that is when we shall next strike.'

Stefan extended a hand. 'I accept your terms, Duke.'

The two men shook hands, and the Westlanders cheered again. Hector drained his beer, then he got to his feet.

'The Duke of Ridden is now my friend and ally,' said Stefan. 'Spread the word, boys. We're moving up in the world.'

Hector inclined his head slightly, smiled, then strode from the balcony.

An hour later, Hector and his twenty knights passed through the town wall of Torrent. They made their way to the tall clock tower in the butchers' district, where the seven hundred men-at-arms were waiting, along with dozens of loaded wagons. Hector summoned the officers, and they assembled by the base of the tower.

'The final part of this night's proceedings is upon us,' the duke said. 'Dravid's forces are still within the walls of Torrent, and they must be removed. By now, many will be drunk; but, more importantly, they will be complacent, thinking us too fearful to attack. They have no idea that we slipped past them, and they will not be expecting an assault from the west. Two hundred of the Royal Guard will escort the wagons to the Royal Palace via the Kendril Wall; while the remainder strike the rear of Dravid's forces, and funnel them towards the narrow streets that lead to the gate in the wine merchants' district. Our objective is to push them back into Twinbrook, but we shall be taking no prisoners. Ensure that every soldier has a loaded crossbow. We shall loose one volley into the enemy, and then we shall charge.'

Sergeant Towie led Hector's horse over to where he stood, while the twenty knights remounted.

'Thank you, sergeant,' said Hector.

'It has been an honour to serve you this night, my lord,' said the sergeant.

Hector pulled himself up into the saddle, and rode out to the head of his men as they split into two groups. The smaller of the two factions began to lead the wagons away to the south, while the rest loaded their crossbows. Hector set off with his twenty knights, and five hundred men-at-arms followed them. A few locals opened their front doors to watch Hector ride past, and several clapped or raised their arms in salute.

They reached an area that had been pillaged. Windows were smashed, and a few houses were ablaze. Debris lay scattered over the road, along with the bodies of murdered civilians; and then the sound coming from Dravid's forces rose up. The duke rounded a corner, and gazed upon Dravid's small army. As Hector had predicted, many of the Westlanders were drunk, and they were staggering north towards the gate in the wine merchants' district, hauling carts and wagons filled with whatever they had plundered from the homes in the northern neighbourhoods of Torrent.

Hector drew his knights to the side of the road, and the men-at-arms formed up into lines across the street. The first few ranks crouched down, their crossbows aiming at the retreating Westlanders, and the others moved up behind them. A few Westlanders turned and saw the threat, and cries broke out.

'We are undone!' a Westlander shouted. 'Flee! Flee to Twinbrook!'

Hector drew his sword, and raised it above his head. 'Loose!'

CHAPTER 12
UNFATHOMABLE

Torrent, Upper Down – 11th Day of Lamenta 107

A great tumult of noise pulled Abigone from her slumber. She panicked for a moment, imagining that Dravid's Westlanders were assaulting the Royal Palace. Tulip licked her face, and she opened her eyes. The dawn light was edging her shutters, and she jumped out of bed, Tulip held in her arms. She ran to the window and flung it open. Down in the main forecourt, hundreds of soldiers were cheering as a man on horseback entered the palace grounds. Behind him were hundreds more soldiers, escorting a long convoy of loaded wagons. Thousands of civilians were lining the streets, adding their voices to the cacophony.

'Long live Duke Hector!' an officer cried, and the noise grew so intense that Abigone put her hands to her ears. Tulip scrambled onto her shoulder as she gazed down. The wagons were pulled into the forecourt, and the returning soldiers mingled with the garrison who had remained. Most of the wagons were loaded with all manner of valuable goods, but Abigone noticed that the last four wagons were piled high with bodies. The crowd surged around the figure of Duke Hector upon his horse, cheering him as though he had returned from conquering the world.

The duke raised his sword, and the crowd hushed.

'Chief Dravid's forces have been vanquished!' he cried. 'Torrent has been liberated. This night, we have struck deep into Twinbrook, and our brave soldiers have rescued the imperial princess from captivity. On the way back to Torrent, we routed the rabble under Dravid's command, slaying more than sixty Westlanders! Not one wagon of looted goods passed through the gates into Twinbrook, and Dravid fled empty-handed, scuttling back to his lair, where a surprise is awaiting him – a surprise that will make him weep in despair. He will find his home looted, and his closest allies dead, including his wicked brother. This is but a taste of the punishment that shall be meted out to those who dare to insult the honour of Upper Down; for I shall not allow Dravid to linger in peace – no, he will be hunted down like a dog, and made to pay for what he did to our beloved king, Alfgang the Pius.'

The crowd roared again, raising their voices in acclamation of their hero. Abigone walked back to her bed and sat down. She smiled. At last, Upper Down had a powerful defender, someone who not only understood how to administer justice to the Westlander barbarians, but who was strong enough to carry it through.

'Hector is so brave,' she said.

Tulip hissed in her ear.

'You disagree?' said Abigone. 'Come now; the duke is a real man. Who else could have defeated Dravid? Walter? The so-called champion was probably drunk all night, while Hector was doing what needed to be done.' She pulled a dressing gown over her long nightshirt, and walked to the door of her apartment. She opened it and saw two guards standing outside, but no courtiers.

'I wish to get dressed,' she said. 'Where are my maids?'

'The staff have gone downstairs, ma'am,' said one of the soldiers. 'They wanted to greet Duke Hector.'

Abigone narrowed her eyes, then she closed the door. Was a princess supposed to get ready by herself? She hadn't done her own make-up or hair in many a month, and she felt irritated at the prospect of having to do so. She walked over to her dresser, sat, and placed Tulip onto her lap. She stared at her reflection for a few minutes, as the noise coming from the forecourt continued unabated. She picked up a brush, and began to pull it through her long brown hair. It needed a thorough clean, but that seemed like too much effort.

She glanced down at Tulip. 'Perhaps I should go back to bed. I'm not in the mood for this. What's the point of having a palace full of servants if they aren't there when you need them?'

Someone knocked on her door, and she smiled.

'That will be them,' she said, as she got to her feet, Tulip cradled in her arms like a baby. 'I hope they are suitably apologetic.'

She walked to her front door and opened it. Standing outside were more soldiers. They looked tired but jubilant, and several smiled at the sight of the princess in her dressing gown.

'What do you want?' she said.

'Lord Hector has asked us to deliver Princess Hygilt into your keeping, Your Highness,' said a lieutenant.

'What?'

The soldiers parted, and Abigone saw the girl standing amid the tall men.

'What am I supposed to do with her?' Abigone said.

'For security reasons, she will be sharing your quarters, Your Highness,' said the officer. 'This wing of the palace is the safest place for a hostage of her value. If you disagree, you can take it up with the duke.'

The officer ushered Hygilt forward a few paces, but Abigone was blocking the doorway.

'Ma'am?' he said.

Abigone cursed under her breath. 'Fine,' she said, 'but I will be making my protests to the Duke of Ridden regarding this. These are my personal quarters, and I do not wish to share them with anyone, not even an imperial princess.'

She moved out of the way, and Hygilt entered the apartment.

'Send me some maids at once,' Abigone said to the soldiers; 'and some breakfast.'

She slammed the door, and eyed the young princess standing next to her. The girl was shivering, and looked exhausted.

'This is temporary,' Abigone said, wagging a finger in the girl's face. 'I want you out of here by sunset.'

The girl said nothing.

Abigone strode away, then she noticed that something was different. She glanced at her shoulder, but Tulip had gone. She gazed around, looking for her beloved companion, then she saw him nestled in Hygilt's arms. The creature was nuzzling the young princess's face, and the girl started to cry.

Abigone put her hands on her hips, ready to unleash a barrage of verbal abuse at Hygilt. She hesitated, as pity for the girl's plight moved through her.

'You were captured by Dravid's men, weren't you?' she said.

Hygilt nodded.

'Did they hurt you?'

Hygilt nodded again.

'Those beasts,' Abigone said. She sighed. 'Come and sit down.'

She led Hygilt into her small but comfortable living room, and pushed the girl down onto a couch.

'I will let you cuddle Tulip,' she said, 'but only because you have had a rough time.'

Abigone examined the girl as she sobbed into Tulip's soft fur. She had bruises and scratches on her bare legs, arms and face, and her feet had no shoes. Abigone crouched down next to her.

'Do you want to talk about it?' she said.

'No,' whispered Hygilt.

'By my reckoning,' Abigone said, 'Dravid held you in captivity for a little over a day. It can't have been that bad. Did they... take advantage of you in any way?'

The girl looked confused.

'Is your honour intact?'

'They didn't rape me, if that's what you mean,' said Hygilt. 'They pushed me around, and hit me, but they didn't do that. Dravid said I was more valuable untouched.'

'Well, that's something,' said Abigone.

'I was so alone, and so scared,' said the girl.

'You're safe now, thanks to Hector. Did you see him fight the Westlanders?'

'Not really. I was being kept in a small room. I heard the soldiers attack Dravid's beer hall, and then some of them took me outside. I saw Hector for a moment, and then I was put onto a wagon. Do you want to know what I did see? I saw what Dravid's men did to King Alfgang the Pius.' She shuddered. 'They killed my servants, and then they made me watch as they cut the king into pieces. They were laughing. It was the worst thing I have ever seen.'

Abigone nodded. 'I saw what they left of my brother.'

'Why did they do that? Your brother was going to hand me over to my uncle.'

'You have just answered your own question. Dravid didn't want you returned to Prince Valentino.'

'I heard them talking on the journey back to Torrent,' Hygilt said, her voice lowering to a whisper.

'Oh yes? What did they say?'

Hygilt looked into Abigone's eyes. 'Nothing. It doesn't matter.'

'Then why did you bring it up?'

'Do you love Hector?'

'Of course I do. He is the best man in the kingdom, by far. But, before you get any funny ideas, he is also my cousin, and I don't love him in that way – I am not Kilbride. I see him more as a brother. He is kind, and strong. Everyone loves him. Well, everyone except Walter, but he is just bitter, and twisted by jealousy.'

Hygilt said nothing.

The front door was knocked again.

'That had better be the maids,' said Abigone. 'There is no room in my quarters for any more waifs or strays.' She turned to the door. 'Come in.'

Several courtiers entered the apartment. From their smiles and manner, it was clear that they had been gossiping about Hector and his brave feats, and they gathered round the two princesses. One of them had wheeled in a trolley laden with food and drinks, while others were carrying clothes in Hygilt's size.

'Might I please eat?' said the girl.

'Don't you want to get dressed first?' said Abigone.

'I am very hungry. Dravid's men didn't give me any food.'

'All right. You eat, and I'll get ready; then we can swap places.'

Abigone stood, and led the courtiers into her bedroom, leaving Tulip in Hygilt's embrace. She sat down by her dresser, and the courtiers got to work, styling her hair and applying her make-up as she sat motionless. By far the most disturbing aspect of Hygilt's arrival was the behaviour of Tulip. Not once in all the time Abigone had known the creature had it ever shown any interest in making friends with anyone else. He usually glared or hissed at other people, and yet he had looked content in Hygilt's arms. Perhaps he sensed that the girl was distressed. Abigone was always telling everyone how clever he was, and maybe this was proof of that claim. Abigone stood once her hair and make-up were finished, and her courtiers dressed her in the same uncomfortable black garments that she had worn the day before.

'I don't know how Kilbride tolerates these horrible clothes,' she muttered. 'Surely we can devise something in black that doesn't make me look like a frumpy old woman?'

'A seamstress is adjusting a few dresses for you, Your Highness,' said one of the courtiers. 'They should be ready by tomorrow.'

'Ah, some good news at last. I assume you were late this morning because you went down to the forecourt?'

'Yes, Your Highness. Apologies that we weren't here for you when you awoke. Did you hear what happened? The duke raided Dravid's home in Twinbrook, and carted off everything that the Westlander chief had plundered from the south. As if that wasn't enough, he then attacked Dravid's men, and sent them fleeing north. All of the things Dravid stole from the townsfolk are going to be returned to them. And he killed sixty Westlanders! Can you believe it? Sixty. What a man.'

'Stop drooling,' said Abigone. 'It is quite unbecoming for a woman of your age and station.'

The courtiers fell into silence. Abigone slipped on a pair of shoes, and one of the women crouched down and fastened the metal buckles. She strode through to the living room, where Hygilt was eating breakfast on her own, while Tulip sat on the couch next to her.

'It's your turn to get dressed,' said Abigone.

'I can do it myself, later,' Hygilt said. 'I don't want any help.'

Abigone shrugged, then she turned to the courtiers. 'I presume you heard that? You are dismissed for now.'

'The imperial princess has cuts and bruises that should be looked at, Your Highness.'

'They will have to wait,' said Abigone. 'Go.'

The courtiers bowed low, then they trooped out of the apartment and closed the door. Abigone sat down, and eyed the plates of food.

'Feeling any better?' she said to the girl.

'When can I go home?'

'This is your home, for now.'

'Please take me to my uncle. Upper Down isn't safe.'

'How dare you say that after Duke Hector rescued you? You ungrateful little brat.'

'Duke Hector is... not a nice man.'

Abigone raised a hand to slap Hygilt, and Tulip sprang onto the girl's lap. He hissed loudly, his claws extended toward Abigone.

'Are you siding with *her*, Tulip?' Abigone cried. 'Fine. If that is how you feel, then you can stay with her today. I am going downstairs, to hear all about what the duke has just done for this realm. I hope this teaches you a lesson.'

She turned and walked away, before her temper got the better of her. She opened her front door, and found the courtiers waiting outside, along with a few soldiers. Abigone ignored their presence and set off, knowing that most of the courtiers would trail along behind her like faithful dogs. She went down a flight of stairs and found the corridor below crowded with soldiers and officials. Many were smiling, and most stopped to bow as the princess passed. She halted in front of a senior officer from the Royal Guard.

'How can I be of service, ma'am?' he said.

'Is my sister awake?'

'Yes, ma'am. She is currently discussing last night's events with Lord Hector.'

Abigone's eyes narrowed. 'Where?'

The officer led her back up the stairs, and took her to the small dining room where they had met the day before. The officer knocked, and opened the door. He was about to introduce the princess to those inside, but Abigone brushed past him and walked into the room. Hector and Kilbride were at the dining table, eating breakfast.

Abigone closed the door. 'Are you having a secret meeting without me? I thought I was supposed to be on this regency council. Well? Am I?'

'You are,' said Hector, who, despite his overnight exertions, seemed fresh and relaxed. 'Please sit, Your Highness.'

Abigone took a seat, and simmered in silence.

'Perhaps some congratulations are in order?' said Kilbride.

'Congratulations, Hector,' said Abigone. 'Why wasn't I invited to this meeting?'

'You are rarely out of bed at this hour of the day,' said Kilbride. 'Hector wanted to eat, and so I thought I would hear about last night while he had breakfast.'

'I also thought that you might be making Princes Hygilt welcome, Your Highness,' said Hector.

'About that,' said Abigone; 'why do I have to share my rooms with her?'

'I am sharing my quarters with Frida and Alfie,' said Kilbride. 'It's not permanent. We shall find better accommodation for everyone soon.'

'But Hygilt already has her own quarters.'

'They were more like a prison, sister. We cannot put her there. She is our guest, not a captive.'

'Are we handing her back to Valentino? That's what our brother wanted to do.'

'We have a multitude of decisions before us,' said Hector. 'Right now, it might be a good idea to bring up a little proposal that Princess Kilbride and I have just been discussing.'

'Is that wise?' said Kilbride. 'You know what Abigone is like. She will not take this news well.'

'I trust that Abigone will understand what we are trying to achieve,' said Hector. He placed his knife and fork onto the table and poured out three glasses of wine. 'Have a drink, Abigone.'

Kilbride smiled. 'You are going to need it.'

'Why?' she said.

'Do you recall any part of your late brother's strategy regarding the Westlanders?' said Hector. 'King Alfgang the Pius planned on defeating them by keeping them divided. Last night, I met with Chief Stefan, and pretended to make an alliance with him. By these means, we can use Stefan against the other Westlanders, sapping their strength piece by piece. In order to convince Stefan that I was acting in good faith, I had to make certain concessions.'

'What concessions?' said Abigone, taking a sip from her glass.

'Stefan had but one demand,' said Hector. 'He desires your hand in marriage.'

Abigone almost choked on the wine, and most of it ran down her chin.

'It is merely a ruse, Abbie,' said Kilbride. 'We would never actually allow that savage to touch you.'

'Listen to your sister,' said Hector. 'You are, for want of a better word, bait. And Stefan has been thoroughly hooked. Two nights from now, he will be leading an assault upon Dravid himself. Hundreds, if not thousands, of Westlanders will die violent deaths on the streets of Twinbrook. Offering you to Stefan was the only way to win his agreement.'

Abigone stared at them.

'We are too weak to defeat the Westlanders on our own,' said Kilbride.

'Do you agree with this?' said Abigone.

Kilbride lowered her gaze. 'I... have my reservations. I also have conditions, conditions designed to protect you, Abbie. First of all, I have insisted that Stefan gets nowhere near you, and Hector has agreed.'

'I told Stefan that there would be no physical contact until several conditions are met,' said Hector. 'I have placed many obstacles in his path. He will need to swear allegiance to King Alfgang the Sixth, for a start. He will need to place his men at our disposal, and he will need to keep the peace on the streets of Twinbrook. Look – we cannot lose. If Stefan abides by this agreement, then many of the other Westlanders will turn on him, and his position will be fatally undermined. And, if he breaks the agreements, then the whole thing will be called off.'

'Is this all I am to you both?' said Abigone. 'A piece of meat to be bartered to a gang of savages from the Westlands? Will this... betrothal become public knowledge?'

'Unfortunately, yes,' said Hector; 'for I cannot prevent Stefan's men from boasting about it.'

Abigone lowered her head as a tear slipped down her cheek. 'I will be utterly humiliated. I am a princess of a realm – fated to be wed to a barbarian chieftain. My reputation will be in tatters, even if what you say is true, and there will be no marriage.'

'Not so, Your Highness,' said Hector. 'The royalty of Upper Down cannot be seen to be intermarrying with a mere chieftain. That is why I also offered Stefan the Duchy of Torrent.'

'You did what?' cried Kilbride, her eyes wide.

Hector raised his palms. 'Like you, I am trying to protect Princess Abigone. When word filters out that she is betrothed, it will be to a duke, not a chieftain. I thought you would be pleased.'

'Are you out of your mind?' Kilbride went on. 'We cannot elevate a Westlander to the rank of duke; and the duchy was not yours to give away. Technically speaking, young Alfie is the current Duke of Torrent; you can't just take that from him.'

'His Majesty holds the duchy because the last duke died leaving no heirs,' said Hector. 'Can you not see what I am trying to do? I shall pull Stefan towards us, and isolate him from the other Westlanders.'

Kilbride stared at Hector, and Abigone could see her sister trying to separate the duke's words from his motives.

'Do you promise that I shall never be wed to him?' said Abigone. 'Do you swear it?'

'I swear it,' said Hector. 'That day shall never come. However, in order to maintain the ruse, Stefan will have to visit the palace to pledge his allegiance to the new king. I think that a short introduction at that time might be prudent, to keep Stefan's hopes alive. That will necessitate a face to face meeting. You will not be left alone in a room with him, though. I shall be there, along with Princess Kilbride. We shall pack the room with soldiers and courtiers, to give Stefan no opportunity to get too close to you. For this occasion, you will have to put on a brave face, and pretend that you are a willing participant. If you scream and shout at him, then he may be tempted to go back on his word. Can you do this, Your Highness? Can you pretend that you do not loathe him for a few minutes, for the good of the realm?'

'If I ever see him in the palace,' Abigone said, 'then I will tell him what I am about to tell you.'

'And what might that be?'

Abigone got to her feet. 'It will be easy to remember, as it only consists of two words – fuck off.'

She turned and strode from the room before she could start crying. How dare they? She could believe that her selfish sister could have devised such a scheme, but she was heartbroken that Hector had gone along with it. She hurried along the palace corridors towards her apartment, and ran inside, slamming the door behind her.

She staggered into the living room and collapsed onto the couch, where Hygilt was curled up with Tulip. Abigone put her head in her hands and wept, then she felt a hand on her arm.

'What's wrong?' said Hygilt.

'Nothing. Leave me alone.'

'Has someone else died?' said the girl.

'No. My sister and Hector are planning to sell me to Chief Stefan. They promised that I wouldn't have to marry him, but the shame is too much to bear. I hate Kilbride; I hate her so much.'

'Why are you angry with your sister?' said Hygilt. 'This sounds like Hector's plan.'

'Don't be stupid. Only my sister could have devised such a scheme.'

'Are you sure about that? Hector... I...'

'What?' cried Abigone. 'What do you have to say about the man who has just saved this realm from Dravid?'

Hygilt averted her gaze. Tulip wriggled free of her embrace, and hopped onto Abigone's knee.

'Oh, now you're back,' sobbed Abigone; 'little traitor.'

'Maybe you don't know Hector as well as you think you do,' said Hygilt.

'Out with it,' said Abigone. 'Say whatever it is you have to say, or never speak to me again.'

'Well,' the girl said, 'when Dravid's men were bringing me back from... from the place where they killed Alfgang the Pius, they talked. They talked a lot. I think they forgot I was there. Dravid was telling his men how he had known where the king would be. Someone told him, Abigone. Someone betrayed the king, and paid Dravid to kill him. It was Hector, that's what he said. It was Hector who had Alfgang the Pius murdered.'

Abigone's tears dried up, her anguish replaced by anger. She straightened her back, and looked at the girl with as much contempt as she could muster.

'You pathetic little wretch,' Abigone said. 'You have done nothing but lie since you arrived in Upper Down. First, you made up ridiculous stories about my father, and now you are doing the same thing about Hector. Do you always lie about the men who help you?'

Hygilt seemed to shrink a little. 'I'm not lying.'

'I will have to tell Hector about this.'

'No! Please, Abigone, please don't tell him! If he knows that I told you, then you will be in as much danger as me.'

Abigone shook her head. 'You can't stop yourself, can you? Would you rather still be in Dravid's clutches? Hector saved you, Hygilt. Why would he do that if he had murdered my brother?'

'He was trying to kill Dravid; he didn't care about me. He wanted to stop Dravid from telling everyone the truth. Everyone in the beer hall knew that Hector was paying Dravid to work for him. It's not a secret to the Westlanders; they all know.'

Abigone got to her feet, then she reached out and picked up Tulip. 'I have heard enough of this nonsense,' she said.

'Please be careful,' said Hygilt. 'Don't trust Hector.'

Abigone left the room and sat down on her unmade bed. She stroked Tulip for a few minutes, her thoughts whirling in confusion and fury. Had it not been for Hector's words in the dining room, when he had outlined his plan for her to marry Stefan, she would have thrown Hygilt out of her apartment. It couldn't possibly be true. She wondered if the Westlanders had been playing a game with Hygilt – lying to her in order to undermine her faith in the duke. It was either that, or the imperial princess was a compulsive and unrepentant liar. Her thoughts went to her father. She had been told by several people that Alfgang the Great's story about Hygilt running away was nothing but a fabrication, but she had refused to accept it.

Was there a chance that she had been wrong about her father? And, if so, then could she be wrong about Hector?

No. Perhaps Hector was indeed a little more ruthless than she had previously imagined, but that didn't mean he had arranged for the murder of her brother.

No. If she was wrong about that, then almost everything else she believed in would also be wrong.

No.

She lay down on the bed, feeling more alone than ever before.

'Do you still love me, Tulip?'

The creature nuzzled her face, and settled down by her head.

Abigone closed her eyes. 'You are all I have.'

CHAPTER 13
SOBRIETY

Torrent, Upper Down – 11th Day of Lamenta 107

Walter stretched and opened his eyes. For a moment, he couldn't remember when he had gone to bed, then it all came back. He had fallen asleep in a chair in the other room, exhausted by his journey over the mountains. The pain in the back of his head returned, but it had lessened.

Something else was different, then he realised that, for the third morning in a row, he had awoken without a hangover. Three evenings without alcohol – how had he managed it? He felt a little queasy, but refreshed.

He sat up, and pulled the sheet from his body. Someone must have undressed him, for he was only wearing a pair of cotton shorts. He walked over to the bedroom window and peered through the shutters. The sun was high in the sky, which meant that he had slept for the entire afternoon, all night, and then most of the following morning. He retreated from the window, and saw his clothes neatly folded on a chair. He dressed quickly, and opened the door to the other room. Lothar was reclining in a chair, snoring, a large tray of empty beer jugs sitting on the floor by his legs. Walter smiled and walked in. He was about to wake Lothar, when he noticed the two bottles of whisky that he had taken from the dining room. He picked up one of them, and read the label. As Lothar had stated, the quality was impeccable. He hesitated as a craving slowly began to grip him. A small measure of whisky wouldn't make him drunk, but it might quell the queasiness in his stomach. He noticed that his hands were trembling a little. Some whisky would sort that out, too. He needed to shave, and it would be irresponsible to do so if his hands were unsteady. He sat down with the bottle, and opened it. He inhaled the scent of the whisky, then took a swig. At first, it made him feel even sicker, so he took another long swig, and his guts calmed. He held out a hand. Steady. He took a third swig to make sure, then he got up and went over to his wash-stand. The jug of water had probably been sitting there for several days, but as he was only intending to use it to wash and shave, it made no difference.

He poured some of the tepid water into a basin, then splashed some on his face. He reached for the soap, rubbed his hands together, and spread the lather over his cheeks and chin; then he took the razor blade and began to shear off three days' worth of stubble from his face.

Lothar groaned from his chair, and Walter flicked some water at him, making him jump.

Walter laughed as Lothar gazed around.

'What time is it?' said the Mountain Ranger.

'Almost noon.'

'Shit. We slept in.'

'For what?' said Walter. 'I wasn't aware that we had anywhere to be.'

'You fell asleep not long after lunch, sir,' Lothar said, 'and you missed Dravid's raid into Torrent.'

Walter almost cut himself with the razor blade. 'Dravid raided Torrent?'

'Yes, sir. Then, later in the evening, Duke Hector led out a major expeditionary force. They should be back by now; in fact, they should have arrived back hours ago.'

'My brother attacked Dravid's forces?'

'I'm not entirely sure, sir. I watched him lead hundreds of men-at-arms east through the Royal Parkland. I don't know what he was planning.'

'And you didn't think to wake me?'

Lothar laughed. 'I tried, sir. You were dead to the world. After that, I put you to bed, and got stuck into the beer. I thought I would wake up around dawn, but perhaps I ended up having one beer too many.'

'So it was you who undressed me?'

'Yes, sir. I never did get around to organising those girls I was talking about. We could always do it tonight, if you're in the mood.'

Walter finished shaving, and rinsed the blade in the hand basin. 'Maybe.' He patted his face with a towel. 'We should probably go downstairs and find out what's been happening.'

Lothar smiled. 'Or, sir, we could open that whisky, and...' His eyes went to the bottle. 'You cheeky sod, sir! You've already had some.'

'I was feeling a bit shaky when I got up, and I didn't want to shave in that condition. I might have cut my own throat.'

'Is it any good? I've never had whisky that expensive before.'

Walter walked over and sat down opposite his aide. 'Try it.'

Lothar raked about on the tray for a clean glass, then he poured himself a measure from the open whisky bottle. He sniffed it, then took a sip.

'Blessed spirits, take me now,' he cried. 'It tastes as sweet as sweat from a whore's cleavage.'

Walter raised an eyebrow. 'That's not the comparison I would make, but each to their own.'

Lothar filled another glass and passed it to Walter.

Walter took it. 'Just the one, and then we'll be off.'

'If you say so, sir.'

They sat back, sipped from their glasses, and Lothar launched into a story about when he had been drinking with the Rangers after getting lost in the mountains. Walter listened in silence, and laughed at the right moments, but his attention was drifting. If Dravid was still in Torrent, then shouldn't the King's Champion be doing something about it? Wasn't that his job? They finished their first glasses, and Lothar picked up the bottle to refill them.

'Lord Walter?' came a shout from the door.

'Just pretend we're not in,' Lothar whispered.

Walter eyed him, then got to his feet and walked to the door. He opened it, to find a young courtier standing outside.

'Yes?' said Walter.

'I have a message from Her Highness Princess Kilbride, sir,' the courtier said, 'inviting you to join her in a carriage that is waiting for you in the palace forecourt. Scouts have reported that the first units of the imperial army have arrived in front of the Kendril Wall, and Her Highness is travelling there to see them for herself. The princess says that she will wait ten minutes for you, and then she will leave on her own if you aren't there.'

'I'll be there,' Walter said. He turned to Lothar. 'Get your boots on; we're leaving.'

Walter and Lothar ran along the palace corridors and down several flights of stairs, dodging the crowds of officials and courtiers that were going about their business. They emerged into the sunlight at the front of the palace, and saw a carriage preparing to set off.

'Wait!' Walter cried.

Kilbride peered out of the side window, then told the driver to stop. Walter and Lothar raced across the cobbles. Lothar climbed up onto the railing at the rear of the carriage, and Walter opened the side door. He took a seat opposite her and closed the door.

'I was just about to leave,' said Kilbride.

'We came as fast as we could,' Walter said. 'What do we know about the imperial army?'

'Nothing, as yet; hence the journey to the Kendril Wall.'

The carriage set off, its wheels trundling through the open gates.

'Dravid?' said Walter.

'What about him?'

'I heard he raided Torrent.'

'You heard correctly. Your brother defeated him last night.'

'Is Dravid dead?'

'Unfortunately not.'

'So Hector messed it up?'

Kilbride eyed him. 'No, Walter, your brother did not *mess it up*. He led seven hundred men-at-arms deep into the heart of Twinbrook, destroyed Dravid's base of operations, and then, on the way back to Torrent, he caught Dravid's forces as they were approaching a gate in the town wall, and routed them. He retrieved twenty-seven wagons of plunder, freed five hostages, including Princess Hygilt, and his men slaughtered sixty Westlanders, including Dravid's brother. Does that sound as though he messed it up?'

Walter frowned. 'No. But Dravid got away.'

'Hector has a plan for that.'

'Of course he does.'

'You know, Walter, your constant sniping at your brother makes you sound petty and weak. It is a very unattractive trait.'

Walter said nothing.

'So, how was your night?' she said. 'I'm guessing it must have been good, because you look as though you haven't been awake for long. How much did you have to drink?'

'Nothing,' said Walter.

Kilbride gave him a look of frustrated annoyance. 'Why are you lying to me, Walter? I can smell the whisky from here.'

'That's because I've just had a glass. On the evening in question, I had nothing. I was too tired, and my head hurt. I fell asleep after lunch, and woke up an hour ago.'

'And you immediately started drinking?'

'My, uh, hands were shaking.'

'Are you trying to kill yourself?'

'Not particularly.'

'Upper Down is in the midst of its worst crisis in a century, and you're drinking whisky at noon? Walter, please, tell me why you are doing this.'

'I'm not sure I understand the question. Has my role changed? Did I wake up to find myself weighed down with responsibilities? Under Alfgang the Great, it was made clear to me – crystal clear – that my job was purely honorary. I had nothing to do except occasionally turn up for a ceremony or two, and no one cared what I got up to in my free time.'

Kilbride looked away. 'I cared.'

Walter laughed. 'Really? I'm touched.'

'Hector's assistant turned up this morning.'

'Is that supposed to mean something to me?'

'Amery is also a lawyer, and Hector has asked him to draw up legal papers for the establishment of a regency council. The regents will then sign the completed documents, which will legitimise the authority of the council.'

'Hector made it quite clear that he doesn't want me on the council,' said Walter. 'And I have to say that I'm not particularly keen on the idea, either.' He smiled. 'For once, my brother and I are in agreement.'

'What about duty?'

Walter rolled his eyes.

'As it stands,' Kilbride went on, 'the members of the regency council will be Hector, Abigone and myself. It's not enough. There should be a fourth member.'

'Have you asked Frida?'

'There are two problems with that idea. Firstly, many of the court officials and militia officers will baulk at the notion of three women and one man on the council. Many will assume that we are merely window dressing, and that Hector is the one in charge. Either that, or they will complain about damn women running the realm. The second reason is that Frida is... incapable of being a member of any authoritative body at present. She is lost in grief, and it might be a long time before she recovers to any extent. I would prefer that she focuses on looking after

Alfie. In my opinion, that is her surest route back to good health. The boy will restore some purpose to her life.'

'Your first reason is bullshit,' said Walter. 'Everyone in Upper Down knows that you are the best candidate to lead the realm during the regency.'

'I'm flattered, Walter, but I doubt many share your opinion. There are those in Upper Down who think women are fit only to be wives and mothers, and I am neither. Regardless, you cannot argue against my second point.'

'True.'

'Well? Will you please consider it? Hector...'

She paused, and glanced out of the carriage window, as though she had almost said too much.

'Go on,' he said.

'I worry that you will take it the wrong way.'

'Were you going to sing a song of praise about my noble and perfect brother? Were you going to tell me how wonderful he is; about how his beautiful eyes sparkle like the stars in the night sky? That doesn't bother me; I've heard you say things like that countless times before. I lost you to Hector over a decade ago; believe me – I'm over it.'

For a moment, Kilbride looked as though she was about to start crying.

'You are an idiot,' she said.

'Well, what were you going to say?'

'It doesn't matter.'

'Do you want me on this council or not?'

Kilbride shrugged. 'It is clear to me that you don't care about Upper Down, or what happens here. Forget I spoke; forget all of it.'

'For fuck's sake, Killie; you are impossible at times.'

'And what does that make you? I was trying to have a serious conversation with you, but you can't help dredging up the past. I have told you this before – I am sorry about the way I treated you when we were teenagers. I was young, and I had a crush on your brother. I wish I had held on to what the two of us shared, but I threw it all away in a moment of silly infatuation. Do you think I was still daydreaming about your brother when I got married? I hadn't thought about Hector for a long time by that point, but you never knew, because you refused to speak to me for years. And then, when my husband died, and I came back to Upper Down, I tried to talk to you, but you shut me out. Is it any wonder that Hector and I...'

She froze, her features paling.

Walter narrowed his eyes. 'Is it any wonder that you and Hector... what?'

'Nothing.'

'What are you hiding from me, Killie?'

'Oh shit, I... Look, Walter; I didn't mean to mention this.'

'You and Hector?' he said. 'After you got back from Greater Down? Were you together? You and my utter bastard of a brother?' He put a hand to his face and sobbed. 'You and Hector? This is a fucking nightmare.'

'It was a mistake,' she said, 'an awful mistake. I'm sorry. I was deranged by grief, guilt and anger, and I needed to be close to someone; and you weren't there for me.'

'So you slept with Hector? How long, Killie? How long were you together?'

'Less than a month.'

'Who else knows?'

'Just Abigone. Maybe a few servants, too. I don't know who Hector told about it.'

Walter turned to the driver. 'Stop the carriage.'

The driver turned, and opened the little slat that sealed off the carriage interior. 'What was that, sir?'

'I said stop the fucking carriage.'

The driver closed the slat, and pulled on the reins. The carriage slowed, and ground to a halt on the road. Walter opened the side door and jumped down to the ground. He tried not to look at Kilbride, but he saw that she was crying as he turned away. His hand went to the door to close it, but his mind was stricken by doubts. The right thing to do would be to get back into the carriage, and tell Kilbride what he truly felt about her – that she would always be his best friend, no matter what, and that he still... No. It was too much.

He closed the door, and gestured to Lothar.

'We're walking the rest of the way,' he said.

Lothar stepped down from the rear railing. 'Sir?'

They stood on the road and watched as the carriage pulled away.

'What happened, sir?' said Lothar.

'I don't want to talk about it.'

Another carriage trundled towards them, and they walked to the side of the road.

'Are we still going to the Wall, sir?'

Walter glanced at their surroundings. 'We might as well. We're almost there.'

They set off, and Walter kept his mouth closed for the rest of the journey. How could he have been so stupid? He remembered when Kilbride had returned from Greater Down – it had been the first time he had ever seen her wearing black. He also remembered how badly he had acted towards her. He had expressed his condolences for her loss in a cold and perfunctory manner, and had then gone off drinking with his friends from the Mountain Rangers. After that, he had avoided her. It was his fault that she had ended up in Hector's arms. If only he had acted differently; if only he hadn't allowed his inflated sense of grievance to govern his decisions.

'I am the most stupid bastard living in Upper Down,' he said, as they approached the cleared area in front of the Kendril Wall.

'Am I to comment on that, sir?' said Lothar. 'My natural response would be to make a joke, but you look... well, sir, you look terrible.'

Kilbride's carriage was parked alongside several others, but, apart from their drivers, there was no one in the forecourt. Walter and Lothar entered the gatehouse in the centre of the Kendril Wall, and ascended the spiral staircase to the battlements, where a large crowd had gathered. Soldiers from the Wall Militia were pointing down into the ravine that lay on the far side of the Kendril Gap, and an assortment of officials and officers from the other branches of the armed forces were listening to what they were saying. Walter saw Kilbride standing with her lady-in-waiting amid the crowd, but her face was expressionless. A few yards to her right, Duke Hector was talking to several officers, a smile on his lips. Walter edged closer to the centre of the crowd, then he glanced down into the ravine.

Around three hundred soldiers were gathered out of bow range by the bridge that crossed the stream. They were wearing uniforms of pale grey that Walter had never seen before, and they were digging ditches and dragging timber up the road to construct a rudimentary palisade wall.

'What time did they get here?' said an officer from the Royal Guard.

'At dawn, sir,' said a sergeant in the Wall Militia. 'We think they are imperial scouts, sent ahead by the main army to map the location, and to construct some basic defences.'

'We could easily push them back,' said the officer. 'Why don't we send out some soldiers of our own?'

Hector strode forwards. 'There is no need to send anyone out,' he said. 'The imperial army can sit in the ravine for as long as it likes. Upper Down does not depend upon any goods reaching us from the south; whereas the supply line for the imperial army will extend for over two hundred miles. It is as it has always been. Armies arrive at the Kendril Wall, they camp there until their supplies run out, and then they withdraw. I see no reason to think that it will be any different this time.'

'My lord,' said the officer, 'I bow to your wisdom. However, might it be sensible to deliver Princess Hygilt to her illustrious grandfather? That was, after all, King Alfgang the Pius's intention before he was so brutally cut down.'

'We are going to keep our choices open at the moment,' said Hector. 'Perhaps a deal can be struck with Prince Valentino – one that guarantees the security of Upper Down – but I'm not sure if divesting ourselves of our prime negotiating asset would be the prudent course of action.'

'She is not an asset,' said Walter, 'she is a fourteen-year-old girl.'

Hector glanced at his brother, and smiled. 'I was unaware that you were here, Walter.' He narrowed his eyes. 'I would have thought it was a little early for whisky, brother; and have you been crying? A drunk's tears come easily, but they seldom mean much.'

A few of the officials and officers laughed.

'You are nothing without an audience,' said Walter.

'Did I require an audience to rescue Princess Hygilt, or to vanquish Dravid's forces? In my humble opinion, all I required was a little fortitude, and some brave men under my command. Tell me – what was the King's Champion doing while I was leading a force into Twinbrook?'

Walter said nothing.

'Well?' said Hector. 'No sarcastic response, Walter? You disappoint me. I suppose that you have no reply to make, because everyone on the battlements can smell the whisky on your breath. Perhaps you should return to the palace, and cease embarrassing yourself. This is adults' business, and you are behaving like a child.'

'That's enough, Hector,' said Kilbride. 'There is no need to humiliate him in front of everyone.'

Hector raised an eyebrow. 'You are quite correct, Your Highness, and I apologise unreservedly. I try to hold my tongue whenever I see my brother squander his potential, but I am only a man, and like all men, I sometimes stumble.'

'Fuck you, you pompous prick,' said Walter.

Hector shook his head as though saddened, and a low murmuring against Walter arose among the crowd.

'Maybe we should go, sir,' said Lothar.

Walter eyed his aide. 'I'll decide when it's time to go.'

'I do not envy your position, Commander Lothar,' said Hector, 'although I must say that you are doing a wonderful job.'

A strange expression passed over Lothar's features, then he bowed his head. 'Thank you, my lord.'

'That's quite all right. Now, as I was saying, I feel it would be best to allow the imperial army all the time it likes down in the ravine. They need to learn that they will never break through the Wall of Kendril, no matter how hard they try. We shall see how long it takes before they are ready to negotiate; and then, we might be willing to hand over our imperial hostage, in exchange for a treaty of some kind. You should all know that Princess Hygilt is being well looked after in the Royal Palace, and she is recovering from her ordeal as Dravid's captive.'

Walter turned away while Hector was still speaking, and began to make his way to the stairs. Several hostile glances were aimed at him by a few of the officers on the battlements, but he ignored them. What did any of it matter? Hector was right about one thing – no army had ever come close to breaking through the Kendril Wall. It was too high for ladders or siege engines, its surface was too smooth to climb, and it was situated at the top of a steep and narrow ravine. The Wall itself was eight yards thick, and no battering rams or stone throwing machines could conceivably make much of a dent in it, not while the defenders rained stones, arrows and boiling oil down upon them.

Walter reached the stairs and descended to the ground floor of the gatehouse, then he and Lothar walked out into the large forecourt separating the Wall from the streets of the town.

'Did you really have to say *Fuck you* to Duke Hector, sir?' said Lothar. 'Everyone knows what he did last night; the entire town will be talking about it. And soon, they will all be talking about you.'

Walter shrugged.

'You could have just stood there and said nothing, sir.'

'Do you think I don't know that?' He glanced at his aide. 'What did he mean when he said you were doing an excellent job? How would he even know who you are? And what was that weird look on your face?

'Duke Hector must have seen me in your company many times, sir. I assume he guessed that I am your aide.'

'And the look?'

'What look, sir? I don't know what you mean.'

Walter frowned.

'I was surprised, sir, that's all,' said Lothar. 'I wasn't expecting your brother to address me.'

Walter came to a halt. 'And now we'll have to walk all the way back to the Royal Palace.'

'Not necessarily, sir. Your apartment in town is only a few streets away. If I recall correctly, it's well-stocked with whisky and beer; although the whisky isn't as good as the stuff in the palace.'

'Is that your recommendation, Lothar? Should we just call it a day and get drunk?'

'Can you think of anything better to do, sir?'

Walter stared out at the town of Torrent. 'No. I can't.'

Lothar smiled. 'Then I'm your man, sir.'

CHAPTER 14
LEGALITY

Torrent, Upper Down – 12th Day of Lamenta 107

Kilbride tried to read the document again. Her eyes had already scanned the text three times, but she had taken none of it in. It was a statement detailing the assets held by the crown of Upper Down – the land, property, businesses and gold that had come into the possession of little Alfie, following the death of his father and grandfather. It made the boy the richest person in the realm, but Kilbride could not keep her thoughts focussed on the words and numbers on the page in front of her. She placed the document back onto her desk, got up, and walked on to her balcony.

A cold wind was gusting over Torrent from the north, but the sky was clear, and the sun was shining above the mountains to the east. Kilbride inhaled the fresh air, and tried to clear her thoughts as she gazed down at the Royal Parkland. Everything looked tranquil, as though the Imperial army wasn't building a large camp in the ravine just south of the Kendril Wall, mere miles from where Kilbride was standing. Twinbrook also looked to be at peace, though she had no doubt that Dravid would be plotting his revenge. The hostile forces threatening Torrent seemed illusory from Kilbride's balcony, and it hadn't been their proximity that had been distracting her all morning.

It was Hector who was dominating her thoughts. She had attempted to voice her concerns to Walter in the carriage during the ride to the Kendril Wall on the previous day, but he had jumped to the wrong conclusion, and had assumed that she had been about to praise the Duke of Torrent. And then she had got angry, and had hurt him by blurting out the truth about a stupid affair that she had barely given any thought to in years.

Everyone loved Hector. He was brave, noble, handsome, and valiant. These were held to be indisputable facts within the realm of Upper Down, and Walter was one of the few to question them, which was why she had tried to raise the topic with him. Kilbride felt herself to be a good judge of character, and there was something about Hector that had been troubling her for days. Something nebulous and undefined, as though his words and actions didn't align with his motives. Yes, he had defeated Dravid; and yes, he had recovered the body of Alfgang the Pius. If she examined what she knew of his actions, then they would seem to prove that his reputation was well-earned; but her newly-arisen doubts remained. She had tried to find a flaw in his logic regarding his proposal to have Abigone betrothed to Chief Stefan, but his words had made sense, if he had been telling the truth. She recalled the discussion she had shared with Hector on the morning before they had learned of Alfgang the Pius's death. He had been hinting that he would be happy to see the Westlanders remain in Upper Down, and he had been attempting to cajole Kilbride into revealing her opinion; and yet, if his words regarding Stefan were to be believed, he now desired their destruction. As for the way he treated Walter, it sickened Kilbride to the core. In order to work with Hector, Kilbride had been doing what she had always done – putting the realm first. She had quashed her personal reservations for the good of Upper Down, but she couldn't shake the feeling that there was something inherently untrustworthy about the Duke of Ridden.

What did he want? Kilbride couldn't fathom it, and that small seed of doubt had grown and blossomed into a tangle of thorns that had entwined itself round her mind. There was no point in asking Abigone for her opinion. Like countless others, her admiration for the duke had blinded her to his mistakes, such as the inexplicable murder of the old king's ministers; while Walter's view of his brother was the entire opposite – he saw only arrogance and ill-intent in Hector, and ignored the good he had done for the realm. Was Kilbride alone in seeing both the good and the bad that seemed to exist side-by-side in the duke's character? He was clever, but sly; plain-speaking, but duplicitous. He was also the most powerful man in the realm, with the wealth and might bestowed upon him by the Duchy of Ridden. The faith shown in him by the armed forces and citizenry of Upper Down acted as a shield, protecting him from criticism. That was the worst part – that even if Kilbride found any evidence that damned Hector, few would believe it.

She had no choice. If she wished to have any say in the future of the realm, she needed to remain close to the duke, and she needed him to believe that she trusted him. If he discovered her doubts, then he had the strength and influence to remove her from any position of authority. If he ordered the militia to arrest her, for whatever reason, they would obey him. She felt nauseated that she would have to continue to pretend that she liked and admired the duke, but she could see no other path she could take.

If only Walter... She stopped herself. Walter had proved his unreliability time and again. She remembered the long years when he had refused to speak to her, and she would never forget the way he had acted when she had returned from Greater Down. That had hurt her almost as much as the death of her husband. Roderick had been a decent-enough man, but she knew that, given the choice, she would never have elected to become his wife. Their marriage had been political, and she had gone along with it, as always, for the good of the realm. No, that wasn't entirely true. She had also agreed to the wedding to be free of her father's control; and to leave behind the confusing web of emotions engendered by Hector and Walter. She had loved them both at various points of her life, though not at the same time; and she had also loathed them. Since the death of the two kings, she could feel the pendulum inexorably swinging back towards Walter. Despite his flaws, or perhaps because of them, she always knew where she stood with Walter, and she trusted him more than she had ever trusted his brother. At that moment, she could trust that he was hurt and angry. The way his face had crumpled upon learning of her years-old affair with the duke had proved that he still possessed feelings towards her, despite his protestations that he was *over it*.

'My lady?'

Kilbride turned, and saw Marie standing by the balcony door.

'A message has arrived from the Duke of Ridden,' her lady-in-waiting went on, 'requesting your presence in the palace library.'

'Did he say why?'

'No, my lady, but I know that a similar summons has gone out to Princess Abigone.'

Kilbride nodded, and re-entered her apartment. 'Where is Alfie?'

'His Majesty is with his mother, my lady. They went for a walk.'

'A walk? That... surprises me. Did they take plenty of guards with them?'

'Yes, my lady.'

'Where did they go?'

'The Queen Mother would not say, my lady.'

Kilbride walked over to a mirror to give her appearance a cursory glance, then Marie accompanied her as they made their way out of the apartment. They passed through a crowd of courtiers and soldiers in the corridor, and descended to the ground floor of the palace. The doorway of the library was being heavily-guarded, and the soldiers parted to allow Kilbride and Marie to enter. She glanced at the floor, but could see no sign of the blood that Hector's men had spilled when they had slaughtered the ministers; then she caught sight of Hector, Abigone and a few others gathered around a long table.

Kilbride strode over to the table, with Marie in tow, and the duke smiled at her approach.

'Thank you for coming at such short notice, Your Highness,' he said. 'I know how busy you are.'

'Is there news from the Wall?' she said.

Hector shook his head. 'Nothing has changed in the Kendril Gap, Your Highness; and, before you ask, the situation in Twinbrook remains calm, for now.'

Kilbride turned to her sister. 'Where's Tulip? I can't recall the last time I saw you without him.'

'He's with Princess Hygilt,' she said. 'They have taken a liking to each other. I don't mind, honestly.'

Hector gestured to a man who looked to be the same age as Kilbride and Walter. 'This is Amery, my assistant.'

Kilbride glanced at the man. 'I thought he would be older.'

Hector laughed. 'Don't let his age fool, you, Your Highness. Amery has the best legal mind in Upper Down. I recruited him from the finest school of law in the old Central Provinces. This very morning, he has completed the first draft of the regency agreement. Shall we sit?'

Hector took the place at the head of the table, and Amery sat down at his right-hand side. Abigone and Kilbride selected chairs opposite the young lawyer, while the assembled aides and courtiers remained standing.

'Amery, if you please?' said the duke.

'Thank you, my lord,' said Amery. He placed a few pages of handwritten text onto the table. 'This is the basic agreement, which, if signed by the prospective regents, will become a legally-binding document. It temporarily removes all organs of state from His Majesty King Alfgang the Sixth, and places them into the collective hands of the regency council. Acts taken by the council shall therefore have the force of law behind them. All that remains is to fill in the details of the persons who will sit upon said council.'

'Have you added an expiry clause?' said Kilbride.

'I have, Your Highness,' said Amery. 'The agreement shall automatically expire upon His Majesty's eighteenth birthday, when all authority shall revert to the king.' He glanced at Abigone. 'Do you have any questions, Your Highness?'

Abigone shook her head, and Kilbride noticed that she was eyeing the Duke of Ridden warily. Presumably, Kilbride reasoned, she was still upset about the sham betrothal to Stefan; still, it was unusual for her to gaze upon Hector with anything other than blind devotion.

'Are we all in agreement?' said the duke. 'I propose that we three waste no more time. We should sign here and now, to ensure that our government is on a firm and legal footing.'

'I am not signing anything until I have read it,' said Kilbride.

'I wouldn't expect anything less, Your Highness,' said Hector. 'Amery, please give the agreement to the princess.'

The lawyer inclined his head, and passed the papers to Kilbride.

'Let's read it together, Abbie,' she said, holding out the pages so that her sister could see them.

Abigone said nothing, but her eyes went to the document. Kilbride began to read, sifting through the text for any flaws, or clauses that she didn't understand. She came across a line halfway down the first page, and narrowed her eyes.

'It says here that all regents must be aged eighteen years or older,' she said.

'That is correct, Your Highness,' said Amery. 'It would make little sense to deprive the king of any authority until he reaches that age, while at the same time giving authority to someone who has not attained adulthood.'

'Have you forgotten that Abigone is still only seventeen?'

'No, Your Highness. Princess Abigone is free to sign the agreement, but her position on the council will remain in abeyance until her birthday.'

'That's only fifteen days from now,' said Hector.

'So, you are proposing that for the next fifteen days, there shall be only two regents – you and I?'

'Can you see a legal way around this, Your Highness?' said the duke.

'Never mind that part,' said Abigone, her finger pointing to a paragraph on the second page. 'It says here that we shall all have a vote on the council, but that Hector will get two.'

Kilbride squinted at the page. 'She's right. This is unacceptable, Hector; in fact, it's outrageous. Why should you receive two votes? That means you will effectively be the sole leader of Upper Down for the next fifteen days. Legally, you could do anything you wished.'

'There is a very good reason for this discrepancy, Your Highness,' he said, 'one based upon knowledge and experience. I...'

Hector closed his mouth as the library door opened, then he got to his feet as Frida entered the room with Walter.

'Frida?' Hector said. 'I had not expected to see you this day. And I see you have brought our brother along with you. If you wish to make a complaint about his behaviour, then I am afraid that we are rather busy at present. Perhaps we can talk alone after...'

Frida gave him a cold stare. 'Shut up, Hector,' she said. 'I came here to prevent an injustice.'

'What injustice, sister?'

'I demand that Walter is allowed to take his place on this council,' Frida said. 'Is he not Alfie's uncle, just as you are? Is he not the King's Champion?'

Hector turned to look at his brother. Walter looked ill, and his clothes were dishevelled.

'I think Walter might be about to vomit all over the floor,' said Hector. 'I presume that he is, yet again, suffering from the after-effects of too much alcohol?'

'I don't care,' said Frida. 'I want him on the council and, more importantly, King Alfgang the Sixth has insisted upon it.'

'Where is His Majesty?' said Kilbride.

'I left him with the senior officers of the Mountain Rangers,' said Frida. 'Frankly, Killie, I am disappointed in you. I expected Hector to try to exclude Walter, but you? I thought better of you.'

'I tried to speak to Walter about this yesterday, Frida,' said Kilbride. 'He wasn't interested.'

'That is irrelevant. My son wants both of his uncles to be regents, along with his two aunts.'

'Unfortunately,' said Hector, 'His Majesty has no say in the matter. If he was mature enough to be making decisions affecting the realm, there would be no need for a regency council. You, I would accept, but I cannot contemplate allowing our reckless brother to become a regent of the realm.'

'I told you he would say that,' said Walter.

Frida scowled at him. 'And I told you to keep your mouth shut.'

Walter swayed on his feet. 'I can't believe you got me out of bed for this.'

'For once, we are in agreement, brother,' said Hector. 'Perhaps our sister's mind has been tainted by the obvious sorrow she feels towards the passing of her dear husband.'

Frida's drawn features hardened. 'Don't you dare patronise me, Hector. I am in no mood to hear anything other than your agreement.'

'I'm going back to my quarters,' said Walter.

Frida moved to block him, and pushed her hands against his chest, as tears ran down her cheeks.

'No,' she cried. 'You will not leave this room until you have signed that damn document, Walter.'

'Look at me, Frida – I'm in no fit state to take on any responsibilities.'

'Do it for Alfie, brother. That boy adores you. Do it for my son.'

Walter gazed at her, then his back straightened a little, and he glanced at Kilbride.

'Do you want me to join the council, Killie?' he said.

'You know I do, Walter. That's what I was trying to say to you yesterday. We are stronger with four regents.'

'Thank you,' he said. His glance turned to Abigone. 'I think I already know what you will say, Abbie.'

'Then you'd be wrong, Walter,' said Abigone. 'I... I also think you should be a member of the council.'

'What?' said Hector. 'Has everyone in this damn family lost their senses? Walter is a drunk, and he cannot be trusted.'

'I trust him,' said Kilbride.

'No,' said Hector, his eyes flashing with rage. 'I refuse. Without my agreement, there will be no regency council. What none of you seem to understand is that I don't need you. I am in control of ninety per cent of the armed forces of Upper Down, and I am the only person in this room that the citizens would willingly follow. If I were to appoint myself as sole regent, then there is nothing that any of you would be able to do about it. And yet, here I am, trying to build a consensus.'

Kilbride lifted the documents. 'This is not a damn consensus. We have already discovered that it will grant you sole authority over Upper Down.'

'For fifteen days!' cried Hector. 'We are only talking about fifteen days.'

'Yes,' said Kilbride, 'and in those fifteen days, you would be free to amend the agreement to suit you. Is that not true, Amery?'

The lawyer glanced up, his eyes tight. 'Uh, yes, Your Highness. Legally speaking, the duke would be able to alter the terms of the agreement unilaterally during those fifteen days.'

Hector cast his assistant a withering glance, and Amery shrunk into his seat.

Walter took a step towards the table. 'Am I hearing this right? You are pretending to establish a council when, in reality, you are going to usurp power?'

'Don't exaggerate,' said Hector.

'All right,' said Walter, as he took a seat next to Amery. 'I want on this council. I assumed that Killie and Abbie would have a say in the running of Upper Down. Now that I see I was mistaken, I will not stand back and allow my brother to become a tyrant.'

Frida smiled, though her eyes remained sorrowful. 'Thank you, Walter. Alfie will be very pleased. I will collect the young king, and we will return to Killie's quarters.'

She walked from the room, and the door was closed behind her.

'Poor Frida,' said Walter. 'I hate to see her in such pain.'

'As do I,' said Hector, 'but this changes nothing. I will not allow you to join the council, brother. Perhaps, if you were to remain sober for a few months, I might be willing to reconsider.' He glanced at Kilbride. 'Are you willing to sign the agreement as it stands, Your Highness?'

'I mean no offence, Hector,' she said, 'but I cannot append my name to a document that grants one person free rein to rule as an autocrat, even if it is only for fifteen days. My place on the council would be meaningless.'

Hector nodded. 'Very well. Without a consensus on the matter, I fear this meeting is at an end. Sadly, I will have no choice but to continue issuing orders from the Royal Palace without an official agreement in place.'

'I will sign it,' said Abigone.

Hector smiled. 'My dear princess,' he said, 'I thank you from the bottom of my heart. A council consisting of only two members is not what we hoped for, but, under the circumstances, I will accept your kind offer. Amery, amend the papers to show that...'

'Wait,' said Abigone. 'I will sign it, but only if you allow Walter onto the council as well.'

Kilbride stared at her sister. 'I will also sign, if that condition is met.'

Hector said nothing.

'Can I read the document?' said Walter.

Kilbride picked up the pages and passed them across the table.

Hector snorted, as Walter began to read. 'Let us be under no illusions about my brother's motives,' he said. 'He is doing this to irritate me, not because he has any intention of transforming himself into a responsible regent of the realm. It would be childish to imagine otherwise. If I agree to this condition, then do you seriously believe that Walter will change?'

No one responded, and Kilbride watched Walter as he scanned the text on the three pages. He looked barely able to keep his eyes open, and she knew that there was some truth to Hector's words. Walter had not changed his mind because of anything she had said – he had done so to spite his brother, and to prevent him from becoming the sole authority in Upper Down. Did it matter? With Walter's additional vote, Hector would lose his freedom to issue decrees and orders without the agreement of the council.

'Abigone isn't eighteen,' Walter muttered.

'We have covered that, brother,' said Hector. 'Why do you think the topic of *fifteen days* keeps coming up?'

'We should amend that section to give her a vote immediately.'

'That cannot be done,' said Hector. 'By law, all regents must be eighteen.'

'Then we should amend Abbie's birth certificate, and create the legal fiction that she turned eighteen today.'

Hector smiled. 'Are you still intoxicated?'

'Were you present at her birth?' said Walter. 'I certainly wasn't. In fact, I cannot clearly remember the date upon which she was born. Her birthday might be today.' He glanced at Abigone. 'Happy birthday, Your Highness.'

Abigone laughed. 'Thank you, Walter.'

'Are you suggesting that we falsify a legal document, brother?' said Hector.

'Not in the slightest. All we need to do is agree to act as though Abbie was eighteen, and agree that her vote shall count as of today.'

Hector drummed his fingers on the table, his fury evident in his eyes.

'If you don't agree, then there will be no regency council,' Walter went on. 'You can try to rule illegally, brother, you should know that I will oppose you every step of the way. I will inform the commanders and officials of the realm that you have usurped power.'

'No one will listen to the words of a drunkard,' said Hector.

'Are you willing to take the risk?' said Walter. 'If you were, then none of us would be sitting here right now. You would have acted, and you would have seized power. You need the legitimacy of this council to cover your arse, and you know it.'

Kilbride smothered a smile. Walter was saying the things that she, in an attempt not to alienate Hector, had been too afraid to say. She felt the pendulum swing a little further in Walter's direction.

Walter pointed at the second page. 'And what's this about you having two votes?'

'I have already explained that,' said Hector.

'Not very well,' said Abigone. 'Would you please explain it again?'

Hector sighed. 'Out of the... four of us, I clearly possess the most experience of government. I served under King Alfgang the Fourth, and I was appointed to the position of chancellor under his son King Alfgang the Fifth. Without any trace of arrogance, I can humbly claim to be by far the most senior of the proposed regents. Walter's position as King's Champion was a title with no substance, while, with the greatest of respect, neither Princess Kilbride nor Princess Abigone have any experience of governing.'

'I can accept the voting structure,' said Kilbride.

Abigone frowned. 'Why?'

'There would be three of us to counter Duke Hector, Abbie, were he to propose anything we all opposed.'

'And would the three of us stick together?' said Walter.

'We should try our best not to see it like that,' said Kilbride. 'We should take each decision as it comes, and evaluate it based upon rational argument.' She took a breath, knowing that Walter would likely be angered by her next words. She would be lying, but he didn't know that. 'Personally,' she went on, 'I trust Hector. I do not believe that he would abuse his position in a council of four under the terms laid out in this agreement.'

Walter narrowed his eyes at her, while Hector beamed.

'Well, Hector?' said Kilbride. 'The decision is yours. Accept Walter onto the council, and I shall sign the agreement as it stands. Abbie?'

Abigone chewed her lip. 'All right. I will sign.'

Kilbride turned to Walter. At that moment, she longed to be alone with him, to explain her reasoning without the others being present. She would tell him all about her doubts regarding the duke, and about how she valued Walter over anyone else in the realm. *Blessed spirits*, she implored; *please make him understand*.

'Walter?' she said. 'Will you sign?'

Walter gazed back down at the document. His eyes went over the third and final page, then he passed the papers to Amery.

'We are waiting, brother,' said Hector.

'Will Abigone's vote count from today?' he said.

Hector nodded. 'For the sake of the realm, I shall accept this condition.'

Walter rubbed his forehead. 'Fuck it. I'll do it.'

'Then,' said Hector, 'with a heavy heart, I accept Walter's place on the council. Amery, fetch me a quill and some ink.'

Amery snapped his fingers, and a courtier approached with a silver tray, upon which lay a long quill, a small pot of black ink, and a sand shaker. He placed it onto the table, and Amery set the items next to the document. He dipped the quill into the pot, then handed it to Hector.

Amery pointed at the papers. 'Sign all three pages, my lord.'

Hector scrawled his name in spindly letters over the bottom of each page, then he passed the quill to Kilbride. The princess hesitated for a moment, then she dipped the quill into the ink, and signed the agreement, her signature small and wiry next to Hector's flowery script. Abigone went next, and she affixed her own name to each sheet in neat letters, as though she was performing a school exercise, then the quill was given to Walter.

'I can hardly believe I am about to do this,' he said.

'Then why are you doing it?' said Hector.

'For Alfie,' said Walter. 'He is our nephew. I owe him this much, at least.'

He lowered the quill and appended his signature to each of the three pages, his hands shaking slightly, and the ink blotching.

Amery took the pages. He inspected the signatures, and then he sprinkled sand onto them from the shaker to dry the ink. After a few moments, he lifted each page, and tipped the loose sand onto the silver tray.

'The agreement is now legally binding,' he said. 'The regency council is in effect, as of this moment.'

'Thank you, Amery,' said Hector. 'Place the document into the safe located in the palace treasury, where it shall remain.'

'As you will, my lord.'

Hector got to his feet and strode from the room. Several courtiers rushed out after him, then Amery stood and bowed his head. He collected the papers, and walked from the library, leaving only Kilbride, Walter, Abigone and Marie left in the room.

'Walter,' said Kilbride, 'you have just saved the realm.'

Walter narrowed his eyes. 'From whom? Hector?' He shook his head. 'You both trust him, don't you?' He got to his feet. 'I'm going back to my quarters to sleep for a few hours. I'll need some rest if I'm going to be out-voted on every decision.'

Kilbride watched him stagger from the room, then she glanced at Abigone. 'And you, Abbie, you surprised me today. I never thought I would ever see you questioning Hector like that. Has something happened to change your mind about him?'

'No,' said Abigone. 'Don't be ridiculous. What could change my mind about Hector?' She stood. 'Do you trust him, sister? You told him you did. Is it true?'

Kilbride hesitated. She wanted to tell her sister about her doubts, but she was afraid that Abigone would inform all and sundry, and word would inevitably get back to Hector.

'Yes,' she said.

Abigone nodded, then she walked away.

'Are you ready to return to your quarters, my lady?' said Marie.

Kilbride said nothing. She had lied to those she loved the most, and she had lied to Hector. There was nothing else she could have done, she told herself. Hector's authority had been restrained, and that was all that mattered.

She got to her feet. 'Yes. I'm ready.'

CHAPTER 15
DUPLICITY

Twinbrook, Upper Down – 12th Day of Lamenta 107

The beer hall on Fleshmarket Close was subdued as Hector climbed the stairs to the balcony. Hundreds of Westlanders were present, but they were sober, and heavily armed. Chief Stefan got to his feet as Hector approached his alcove, and the two men shook hands.

'It pleases me to see you again, my friend,' said Hector.

Stefan laughed. 'You don't look very pleased, Duke. You look as though someone farted in your face.'

'Yes, well, I had a particularly difficult meeting this morning, and I am feeling a little aggrieved.'

The Westlander chief gestured to the bench. 'Sit, and we shall have one drink before we leave.'

Hector joined the chief around the table in the alcove, and then Stefan shooed everyone else away.

'Has the regency been established?' Stefan said, as he filled two tankards from a jug.

'It has,' said Hector. 'That was the meeting I was referring to. It did not go as planned.'

'Is there anything I should be worried about?'

'That is yet to be determined. I was strong-armed into accepting my drunken brother onto the council as a fourth member. To put it plainly, if the other three vote against me, then any motion I propose will be defeated.'

'Is your brother a threat?'

Hector pondered for a moment. 'He is a nuisance, but not a threat. It is likely that he will be too drunk or hungover to attend many sessions of the regency council, especially if I schedule them for the early morning.'

'I see. Your brother is overly-fond of wine, is he?'

'He doesn't touch the stuff. He drinks beer and whisky, as though he was a Westlander.'

'I approve.'

'I thought you might.'

'What about the others on the council? The two princesses?'

'We needn't concern ourselves with Abigone,' Hector said. 'She is too immature to bear the responsibilities of being a regent, but that matters not, as you will soon be taking her place on the council.'

'How soon?'

'I cannot give you an exact date, but I would imagine that the two of you will be wed within the month.'

Stefan nodded. 'And Kilbride?'

'She is my biggest concern. I used to believe that she trusted me, that she admired me; but now, I'm not so sure. I wish I knew what she was thinking, but she is extremely difficult to read. One thing I can say with certainty is that she has a misplaced affection for my drunken brother. I would rather win her over, but if she decides to oppose me, then I have an idea that will permanently resolve the situation.'

'Are you going to kill her?'

Hector laughed. 'Of course not. Well, not unless it becomes absolutely necessary. She is quite popular among the citizens of Upper Down. They see her as reliable, intelligent, and loyal to the realm. The Widow, that's what many call her. She was angry that I offered you the Duchy of Torrent. She told me that it was not mine to give, and she was right, from a legal point of view.'

'Then why did you tell her?'

'I spun her a tale about how I was trying to isolate you from the other Westlanders. You should also know that I told her that the offer of marriage to Abigone was a sham. It was the only way to make her agree to my plan. She is rather protective of her sister.'

'You admit that you are lying to your family, and yet you believe that I should trust you?'

'Here is the simple truth, my friend,' said Hector. 'I need the Westlanders to remain in Upper Down. Without the income you and your kinsmen bring in from your raids in the south, both the realm and my personal wealth would be adversely affected. I cannot allow that to happen. You can trust me, because it is in my financial interests to help you.'

'Is it all about the money?'

'No. It's about power, too. Did you know that the current Royal Family have been resident in Upper Down for less than a hundred years? The old empire settled them here, so they could govern us on their behalf. My family, on the other hand, has dwelt here for countless centuries. The Duchy of Ridden used to be the Kingdom of Ridden, and my forebears were kings. When the old empire conquered this land, they stripped my family of their royal titles, and appointed us dukes instead. We were then merged into the County of Down, one of the empire's largest provinces. By all rights, when the old empire disintegrated, the lands should have passed back to my family. That did not happen. Alfgang the First assumed power for himself, and proclaimed himself king of Upper Down.'

'You talk as though you long to be king.'

Hector smiled. 'The thought has crossed my mind from time to time. However, first things first. There are three things we need to achieve in the coming days, my friend. First, we must rid ourselves of Dravid. Second, you must swear allegiance to King Alfgang the Sixth. And third, we must ensure that the regency council confirms your elevation to Duke of Torrent. That will clear the way for your marriage to Princess Abigone.'

'When do I get to see her?'

'Does tomorrow suit you?'

Stefan laughed, then he took a long swig from his tankard.

'What has Dravid been doing these past few days?' said Hector.

'Licking his wounds,' said Stefan. 'His men have barely left their beer hall. You shamed him deeply, Duke, and the death of his brother has reportedly sent him mad with grief.'

'How many warriors remain loyal to him?'

'Several dozen have slipped away and joined other war bands,' said Stefan, 'but I would say he has close to four hundred men left in Twinbrook. Much blood will be spilled this night.' He glanced down at the Westlanders crammed into the beer hall. 'Some of my men are going to die.'

'Some of mine, also.'

'How many have you brought?'

'Three hundred.'

'That is not as large as the force you had with you two nights ago. Did the regency council forbid you from taking more?'

'I didn't bring it to the council. If I had, they might have prevented the entire operation. Three hundred is as many as I could muster from my own duchy. Every soldier I have brought owes their loyalty to me, and not to the realm of Upper Down. There is nothing the council could say or do to prevent me from using my own forces.'

'I struggle to understand why you even need the council. Why not just seize power? There is no one strong enough to stop you.'

'The native population of Upper Down is rather conservative, my friend. They do not like change, they mistrust foreigners, and they abhor the thought of revolution. Hence, I am proceeding step by step, in the hope that I can bring the people along with me. Do you recall my desire to keep the money flowing? Above all else, I crave stability. I need the markets to remain open, so that merchants are free to conduct their business. Seizing power in a bloody coup would be detrimental to my aims. I know I could do it if I wished, but the cost would be tremendous. This way is better, even if it takes a little longer. The outcome will remain the same. Shall we depart?'

'One last thing, Duke,' said Stefan. 'I heard that the imperial army has arrived at the Kendril Wall. What are you doing to ensure they don't break through?'

'Nothing,' said Hector. 'The Wall is well-manned with trained militia, but even they will be idle. The imperial army can throw itself at the wall for as long as it likes.'

Stefan leaned in closer. 'And the rumours of a great and terrible weapon? Some of my men are getting a little nervous.'

'You can assure your men that these rumours have no substance to them. There is no secret weapon. The Sanctians are merely trying to frighten us.'

'You seem very confident about that.'

'When one immerses oneself in politics as much as I do, one starts to better discern the truth of rumours. This tale of secret weapons sounds like something I would fabricate, in order to instil fear in my enemies.'

The two men finished their beers and got to their feet. Stefan walked to the front of the interior balcony, and gazed down at the hundreds of warriors packing the hall. He raised a hand, and the assembled Westlanders fell into silence for their chief.

'Two nights ago,' Stefan said, 'the Duke of Ridden gave Dravid a good kick up the arse, but he didn't finish the job; and now Dravid sits in his beer hall like a wounded dog, weeping over his losses. This night, we shall put an end to his suffering!'

The warriors cheered and raised their weapons in the air.

'You all know the Westlander code,' Stefan went on. 'Dravid's men have a choice – if they surrender to us, we will allow them to join our band; if they refuse, then we will cut them down without mercy. We have waited a long time to bring down our hated foe, for Dravid has been nothing but a pestilence, acting as though he were the ruler of Twinbrook. Everyone knows he has taken more than his fair share of the profits from our raids south of the Wall; he has insulted us with impunity, and he has strutted around this town as though he owned it. He is wrong. I own Twinbrook! This town is ours!'

The Westlanders in the hall roared out their approval.

'I have but one rule,' Stefan said: 'Dravid must be taken alive and brought before me. Now raise your tankards, my kin, and drink to victory!'

The warriors lifted their beers and downed them, then, at a signal from one of Stefan's officers, the main doors at the front of the hall were opened, and the Westlanders streamed out on to the street outside.

Hector strode to where Stefan was standing, and they watched as the hall began to empty.

'What is your plan of attack, my friend?' he said.

'My plan is to attack, Duke, nothing more. This is not an open battlefield; my men will be engaged in street-fighting, and any detailed plan would be devoured by chaos. Trust my warriors. They will know what to do.'

A small group of Westlanders approached from the left, carrying armour and weapons. Stefan extended his arms to either side, and a long coat of mail was placed over his shoulders. It fell down as far as the chief's knees, and then plates of burnished steel were strapped to his huge frame, until most of his body was covered. Stefan took a helmet from one of his men, and a long sword from another, then the chief glanced at Hector.

'If you want some armour, Duke, all you have to do is ask.'

'Thank you, but no,' said Hector.

'Do you intend to remain in the rear?'

'I will lead my Ducal Guard from the front, as always, my friend, and they need to be able to recognise me.'

Stefan laughed. 'You are many things, Duke, but you are no coward.'

'If we are victorious this night, then...'

'*When* we are victorious,' said Stefan. 'There is no *if*.'

Hector smiled. 'When we are victorious this night, my friend, I propose that we make our way to the Royal Palace.'

'Tonight?'

'Yes, tonight. Leave loyal men in charge of Twinbrook, and then my soldiers will escort us into Torrent. It is time that the people knew of our alliance. We will openly walk through the streets, side by side, and we shall take in the acclaim of the citizens. I will announce that you are the hero who has brought Dravid low, and then we shall enter the Royal Palace in triumph. How else did you imagine that you would be meeting Princess Abigone tomorrow?'

Stefan smiled, then his eyes darkened.

'Do you fear that I will betray you?' said Hector.

'I fear nothing, Duke.'

'Remember what I said about the need to win over the people. If I walk by your side through the streets of Torrent, proclaiming to all that you are my trusted friend and ally, and then I stab you in the back, I will have lost the affection of the good folk of Upper Down for all time. Why would I do such a thing? My reputation, which I have been carefully cultivating for decades, would be destroyed in an instant.'

'How many of my own men will be accompanying us?'

'It cannot be too many, or the citizens of Torrent will think they are being occupied by a foreign force. Is two dozen acceptable? A guard of honour, consisting of your best. Pick tall and handsome warriors, to impress the people, without terrifying them at the same time.'

Stefan nodded at the small group of Westlanders on the balcony. 'Let us depart.'

They strode down the stairs into the deserted beer hall, and made their way to the main entrance. When they emerged into Fleshmarket Close, the hundreds of warriors gathered outside cheered and roared, and banged their weapons off their shields. Stefan smiled amid the cacophony, then he glanced up to check the positions of the moons. The crowd hushed as he did so, and Hector maintained a respectful silence.

In the eastern sky, the Big Red Moon was rising, five nights from being full; while in the south, the Silver Moon was bright and pure, its white light filling the heavens. It, too, was five nights from full. Only the Little Red Moon was absent, lost somewhere in the clouds to the north.

'King Aloth is watching us,' Stefan cried, a finger pointed at the Big Red Moon; 'and Queen Ninia is giving us her silver light to guide our steps. We shall honour them this night, and offer them our thanks once the battle is won!'

The warriors roared again, and the host began to move off, spreading out through the side streets of Twinbrook towards Dravid's beer hall. Hector strode to a large junction, where his three hundred men-at-arms from the Ducal Guard were waiting for him. Each was armed with a loaded crossbow, and each had an oval shield, and a short sword strapped to their belts.

Hector gestured to them, and they marched along the road in good formation, while Stefan's Westlanders raced past them, laughing and singing as they charged ahead. Hector marched next to a captain from his personal Guard, and they followed the Westlanders through the streets towards the centre of Twinbrook. To their left and right, every house was locked up, with bars and shutters over the windows, and Hector wondered how often the native population of the town sat in their homes at night, huddled in terror at the sounds of the Westlanders outside.

When Hector and the men of his Guard reached Dravid's beer hall, the battle had commenced. Large groups of Westlanders were fighting in the streets around the complex of buildings, but, in the confusion, it was impossible to tell the two sides apart. Hector signalled for his men to halt, then he ordered his officers to block off the main roads leading to the front of the beer hall.

'Loose only at those who charge your lines,' he said to the men, 'and let none of Dravid's men escape.'

The men-at-arms raced off to get into position, and Hector gestured to the twenty knights he had brought with him. They were dismounted, and though each was wearing steel breastplates, they looked almost unarmoured compared to the Westlanders battling in the streets ahead of them.

'We are going in,' Hector said to the knights. 'We did not come here to stand aside, and we shall not allow Stefan to fight this battle on his own.'

'My lord,' said one of the knights; 'how shall we tell the difference between Stefan's men and Dravid's men?'

'Stefan's warriors have been told that we are with them this night,' Hector said. 'We shall make for the side door of the beer hall and break into the interior, to avoid the battles going on in the street. Once inside, assume that everyone is your enemy. Follow me, and stay close together.'

They drew their swords, and gathered round the duke in a tight formation, then Hector raised his sword, and the small body of knights charged into the maelstrom. Westlanders were lying dead or injured on the bloody cobbles, while more than a dozen individual battles were going on. One of the knights was struck in the face by a back swing, the battle axe shearing off the top of his head.

'Do not engage!' Hector cried. 'Make for the door!'

The knights kept together, and forced their way through to the large side door leading into the beer hall. Several of Dravid's Westlanders were guarding the entrance, and the knights ran into them. Two more knights fell, hewn by the swords and axes of the Westlanders. One of the warriors was pulled to the ground, and a knight stabbed his sword down through the helmet visor. Hector slashed his sword across the back of a warrior's unprotected legs, and the warrior fell screaming, to be dispatched by another knight. Hector kicked the door open, and they charged into the building. They burst into a large chamber, where over a dozen unarmed Westlanders were hiding, and the knights slaughtered them, their steel blades hacking them to pieces as they screamed and begged for their lives. They moved into the main beer hall, where numerous battles were taking place among the alcoves and long tables. Hector led the knights to a quieter spot by a side wall, and took a moment to gaze around. Dravid was up on the hall's interior balcony, where he was surrounded by loyal warriors. They had barricaded both of the stairs leading up onto the balcony with wooden benches, and Stefan's men were being cut down as they tried to reach the chief.

'Fight to the end!' Dravid called out from the balcony, a battle axe raised in his right hand. 'Defend our home!'

'What are our orders, my lord?' said a knight.

Hector said nothing. On the ground floor of the beer hall, Stefan's men were winning, but Dravid's position on the balcony seemed impregnable.

'We should withdraw, my lord,' said another knight, 'and torch the building.'

Hector shook his head. He wanted Dravid dead, but he knew Stefan would be furious if he saw the knights set fire to the beer hall. Something needed to be done; something that would not bring the wrath of Stefan down upon Hector.

'Stay away from the stairs,' Hector said. 'Secure the side route out of the building. Go.'

His knights dispersed, but Hector did not follow them. Instead, he moved into a side alcove, and gazed up at the balcony. Several oil lamps were illuminating Dravid's position, and their light was flickering off the besieged chief's steel armour.

Hector raised his hand. 'Take the iron from the balcony,' Hector whispered, 'and replace it with fire.'

The balcony exploded with flames. The tall windows shattered, and Dravid's men screamed amid the fierce flames.

'Take the wood from the roof above the balcony,' Hector went on, 'and replace it with stone.'

A sound like thunder ripped through the air as the roof collapsed, showering the raging fires on the balcony below with tons of rubble. The balcony strained under the weight, then it also collapsed, the timber supports twisting and breaking as the far end of the beer hall disintegrated. Several of Stefan's warriors were flattened by the destruction, and the others pulled back as a cloud of dust rushed past them like a wave. Hector crouched down in the alcove, and debris flew through the air in a deafening roar.

He glanced up. It was hard to see anything through the darkness and the dust, but no noise was coming from the end of the beer hall where the balcony had been. He slipped out of the alcove, and joined the knights by the side door next to the street. Outside, the Westlanders had stopped fighting. Dravid's men were on their knees, surrendering, as Stefan's warriors stared at the destruction. Over a quarter of the beer hall was in ruins, and men coated in dust were staggering out, blood streaming from their ears.

'What happened, my lord?' said one of the knights.

'The balcony collapsed,' said Hector. 'There must have been too much weight for the beams to support it.'

Stefan strode past, his armour covered in dust, and his eyes lit with fury. He gazed at the surrendering warriors, then summoned his captains.

'Dig through the rubble,' he said. 'I want Dravid, and I want him now.'

An hour later, Hector and the surviving knights were back with the men-at-arms of the Ducal Guard. The foot soldiers had experienced no casualties, and barely any had loosed their crossbows during the struggle. They had watched as dozens of warriors had sifted through the ruins at the far end of the beer hall. Two dozen crushed and burned bodies had been dragged out, and Stefan had inspected each one. A few survivors had also been retrieved from the wreckage, and they were kneeling on the cobbles with their hands on their heads. At length, the warriors stirred as a lone figure was carried from the rubble and set down before Stefan. Hector strode across the road, and joined the Westlander chief; then, together, they gazed down at Dravid lying on the cobbles. The chief was dressed in ragged and charred underclothes, and his skin was burnt in several places.

'He is alive, Chief,' said a warrior. 'We found him hiding under a table.'

Hector's heart sank, but he maintained an even expression on his face.

'Where is his armour?' said Stefan.

'He was like this when we found him, Chief,' said the warrior.

Stefan frowned.

Dravid coughed and groaned, then he opened his eyes. 'You dog, Stefan,' he said. 'Too cowardly to face me like a man; instead, you use witchcraft to defeat me.'

'I don't know what you are talking about,' said Stefan. 'There was no witchcraft.'

Dravid laughed. 'You shame yourself further with your lies. Did you not see the flames that devoured my armour and my axe blade? Did you not see the roof collapse upon the heads of my men?'

'It was you who brought down the balcony,' said Hector. 'You overloaded it, and I watched it fall. There is no need to invoke the supernatural to explain your failure, Dravid.'

The injured chief laughed. 'Is this your new friend, Stefan? Be careful, for Duke Hector works only for himself. I was once his friend. It was I who slew Alfgang the Pius, on his orders, and look at me now.'

'Your loose tongue endangered all I have worked for, Dravid,' said Hector. 'The death of the king was to be blamed on Prince Valentino, and yet you left Alfgang's head in the main square of Torrent for all to see. I had to punish you for the murder; I had no choice. If you had done as I had requested, you would still be my friend.' He turned to Stefan. 'We should kill him now.'

Stefan said nothing. He turned his head to gaze at the ruins of the beer hall, then he glanced at the hundreds of watching warriors.

'Do it,' cried Dravid. 'I do not fear death. If you kill me, my soul will be transported to Prince Logar's side, where I shall drink with him for all eternity. Where is he this night, Stefan? Where is the Little Red Moon? Prince Logar knew you were planning treachery, and so he remained hidden, so that he would not have to witness your shame.'

'You will not die tonight,' said Stefan. 'There will be no place for you at Logar's unending feast.' He gestured to a few of his men. 'Shackle Dravid, and escort him to Fleshmarket Close. He is now my prisoner.'

'Damn you!' cried Dravid. 'Let me die like a Westlander!'

Hector stood back, and kept his mouth closed as Dravid was dragged away screaming and shouting by six huge warriors.

Stefan turned to the duke. 'Was there any truth to his words?'

'Regarding what, my friend?'

'Regarding his allegations of witchcraft. My gaze was not upon the balcony when it collapsed.'

Hector shook his head. 'I saw no evidence of foul play.'

'Then what happened to his armour?'

'Perhaps one of your men stripped it from his body?' said Hector. 'It would make a fine prize.'

Stefan eyed him for a moment. 'Gather your men-at-arms, Duke. It is time to see this Royal Palace of yours.'

CHAPTER 16
MODESTY

Torrent, Upper Down – 13th Day of Lamenta 107

'You have it all wrong,' said Hygilt. 'The Masters and Makers corrupt the power of the spirits for their own purposes. They are an aberration. A blasphemous sacrilege.'

'What would you know?' said Abigone. 'Have you ever actually met a Master or a Maker?'

'I met your father and your brother,' said the girl, 'but, apart from them, not that I know of. Fortunately, very few Masters and Makers remain. Upper Down was the last kingdom to be ruled by them. King Alfgang the Great is dead, and so too is his son Alfgang the Pius.'

Abigone glared at her. 'My brother was going to hand you over to Prince Valentino, and you mock his death?'

'I'm not mocking it. Perhaps your brother was a good man, but he was also a Master.'

'He could have killed the Westlanders that ambushed him,' said Abigone. 'He should have killed them.'

'Why didn't he?'

'Because he believed that his abilities should only be used to help others.'

Hygilt glanced away. 'Is that right?'

'Do you admit that not all Masters are evil?'

'I suppose so,' Hygilt said. 'Nevertheless, they are loathed by the spirits. Emperor Antonio wants to wipe them out. There hasn't been a single Master or Maker on Sanctos for decades.' She looked up at Abigone. 'Do you know of any others in your family who possess these abilities?'

'No,' said Abigone, 'and I wouldn't tell you if I did know.'

'What about the boy king? Does Alfgang the Sixth have the same abilities as his father?'

'How would I know that? People don't realise that they're Masters or Makers at his age.'

'Oh. At what age do they realise?'

Abigone shrugged. 'It depends. Around twelve or thirteen, maybe? In the olden days, priests would regularly examine every thirteen-year-old, to see if they could summon the power of the spirits. If they could, then the boy Masters and the girl Makers would be taken away by the priests to be trained.'

Hygilt pulled a face. 'That sounds a bit... creepy.'

'It wasn't. The old empire was practically run by Masters and Makers. Do you think the priests would have mistreated those destined to rule over them? It doesn't matter now, though; all of that has disappeared. When the Elestian Empire fell, mobs of ignorant peasants butchered every Master and Maker they could get their hands on.'

'They deserved to die,' said Hygilt. 'They had oppressed their people for centuries.'

Abigone rolled her eyes. 'What rubbish.'

'Sanctos was the first place to rebel against the Elestians; did you know that? It was easier for us, because Sanctos is an island.'

'I knew that.'

'Did you? The people in Upper Down don't seem to know very much about what lies beyond their borders. I have travelled all over Sanctos, and I have visited many realms in the Central Provinces. My grandfather says that, one day, the whole empire will be reunited; only this time it will be ruled by Sanctians, not Elestians.'

'Upper Down will never be part of your stupid empire.'

Hygilt smiled. 'We shall see about that.'

'Your uncle will never get through the Wall of Kendril.'

'Are you sure, Abigone?'

The two princesses eyed each other as they sat on the long couch with Tulip between them.

'I am looking forward to you being assigned your own quarters,' said Abigone.

'I would rather stay here with you,' said Hygilt. She rubbed Tulip behind the ears, and kissed him. 'And I would miss your cat if I left.'

Abigone simmered with rage, then she scratched her shoulder, the rough fabric of the mourning clothes irritating her skin.

'A princess shouldn't scratch herself like that,' said Hygilt. 'I know you don't suit black, Abigone, but scratching only draws attention to the fact that your dress doesn't fit you properly.'

'Shut up,' muttered Abigone. 'My servants were supposed to be delivering a new wardrobe to me; it's not my fault that I have to wear my sister's clothes.'

'You could always adjust that dress yourself. Don't you know how?'

'As you said, I am a princess. I don't concern myself with such matters.'

Hygilt smiled again. 'I was taught how to sew, among many other things. I had lessons in history, poetry, dancing and mathematics; and I can speak and write in four different languages. I also know how to ride a horse, pilot a sailing boat, and start a fire; and they even taught me how to load a crossbow. What did you learn at school, Abigone?'

'Many things.'

'Such as?'

Abigone turned away, embarrassed by her lack of skills and knowledge. Her father hadn't spent much time focussing on his children's education, seeing his daughters more as beautiful trophies to be fought over by rival princes, each keen to win their hands. And what was the point of learning how to start a fire, when there were dozens of servants around for that sort of thing?

'Do you know how to read and write?' said Hygilt.

'Of course I do!' Abigone cried.

'I was only asking. How many languages do you speak?'

'One.'

'Oh. Where are all your books? I thought you might have a little library.'

'The palace has a library. I was in it yesterday when I signed the regency documents. I read the agreement first, of course.'

'But where are *your* books?'

Abigone got to her feet and walked over to a large cupboard. She opened it, and withdrew the four slim volumes of Elestian poetry that she treasured. She gazed at the damaged spines, then took them over to the couch and set them down next to Tulip. Hygilt picked them up one at a time, and flicked through a few pages.

'I used to love these,' the girl said. 'I remember reading them a few years ago.'

'Do you not love them any more?'

'Not really. My grandfather told me that, under the Elestian Empire, poets were only allowed to write about certain topics. For example, they were forbidden from mentioning poverty or oppression, and they weren't permitted to criticise the Emperor or his family. That led the poets to focus on a romantic past that didn't actually exist. Courtly love was one of the few things they were allowed to write about. I went off them when I realised that.'

'But the sonnets are beautiful.'

'They are very well written; I will grant you that. But imagine what the poets could have achieved without those restrictions. Imagine if they had used their skills to help and inspire people, rather than merely distract them with flowery tales of knights and fair maidens.'

Abigone stared at her. 'But...' Her voice tailed away. What was the point of arguing with the little know-it-all? She glanced down, angry with herself for spending so much of her time daydreaming, when she should have been studying. Kilbride had used her youth far more profitably, reading widely, and seeking out knowledge, and Abigone had always mocked her for it. She wondered if everyone in the palace thought she was stupid. For years, her beauty had allowed her to sail through life, and now she was a member of a regency council, expected to vote on important decisions that affected the realm. She wanted to cry. What did she know about governing a kingdom? Worse, she had utterly neglected her Maker abilities, never once bothering to read a book on the subject, of which there were several in the palace library.

'I'm sorry,' said Hygilt. 'I didn't mean to upset you. With your permission, might we go down to the library and pick out a few books?'

'Why, so you can make fun of my ignorance?'

The girl widened her eyes. 'No, Abigone. Out of everyone in Upper Down, you have been the nicest to me. I don't want to fall out with you.'

Abigone frowned. 'I have been the nicest to you?'

'Yes. Everyone else ignores me, and the Westlanders are brutes. As for your father, he... Sorry. I know you loved him. Sorry.'

'And Hector?'

'You know what I think of that man,' Hygilt said. 'Have you spoken to your sister about what I told you?'

'No. I wanted to yesterday, when I was in the library with her. I wanted to, but she told me that she trusts Hector, and so I kept my mouth shut. The only person who would believe me is Walter, but that's only because he already hates his brother.'

'Do you believe me?'

'I don't know. Hector... I saw him in a different light when we were discussing the regency council. He seemed so ruthless, and he did not behave as a gentleman should. He was trying to twist everything, so that he had the sole authority in the realm, and... I don't know if I should be saying this to you.'

'I understand. All I ask is that you are careful.'

A loud knock thumped on the front door of the apartment.

'I hope that's my new clothes,' said Abigone, as she got to her feet. 'I would do anything to get out of these wretched garments.'

She walked to the door and opened it. Several courtiers and soldiers had gathered in the corridor outside, and one was clutching a large stack of papers.

'Yes?' said Abigone.

'Princess Kilbride sent us here, Your Highness,' said a soldier, 'to deliver these documents to you.'

Abigone eyed the papers. 'What are they?'

'The princess wrote a note that should explain matters, Your Highness,' said a courtier.

A soldier extended a hand, upon which was a folded piece of paper. Abigone took it, and read.

Sister,

As a member of the regency council, I felt it incumbent upon me to share some of the documents of state with you, to further your knowledge, and to prepare you for the decisions we face. Please read them thoroughly.

Yours,

HRH Kilbride.

Abigone sighed.

'Might I bring the papers into your apartment, ma'am?' said the soldier who was carrying them.

Abigone moved to the side and nodded, and the soldier strode into her living room.

'Where shall I put them, ma'am?' he said.

'Place them onto the table in front of the couch.'

'Yes, ma'am.'

The soldier walked over to the table, then he inclined his head before Princess Hygilt. As he did so, his arm brushed against a mug of water, spilling it over the rug.

'You useless fool,' Abigone cried, as she walked over to inspect the damage.

'Sorry, ma'am,' the soldier said. He leaned in close. 'Your sister had another message, Your Highness,' he whispered, as he placed the papers onto the table. 'Hector has returned from Twinbrook, and he has brought Chief Stefan along with him. The duke intends for the two of you to meet today.'

The soldier straightened his back. 'My apologies once again for the little mishap, Your Highness.'

Abigone stared at him. 'That's all right. Dismissed.'

The soldier strode back to the open doorway, and rejoined the crowd of courtiers and other soldiers standing there. The door was closed, but Abigone remained where she was, her feet frozen to the floor.

'These look interesting,' said Hygilt, as she gazed at the pile of documents. 'Might I read some?'

'Stefan is here,' Abigone said. 'Stefan is in the palace.'

'Your betrothed is here?' said the girl.

'Don't call him that.'

'Is that what the soldier was whispering about?'

'Yes. Kilbride sent him. The papers... they were probably just an excuse, so that she could deliver the message to me. Hector wants us to meet.'

'What are you going to do?'

Abigone felt like screaming. 'What can I do? If I ran away and hid in the parkland, they would find me.' She sat down on the couch. 'I have nowhere to go.'

Hygilt released Tulip, and the creature jumped up onto Abigone's lap.

'Wear a veil,' Hygilt said. 'It will shield your face, and no one will be able to tell what you are thinking. A veil would be appropriate, as you are mourning your father and brother; no one will be able to say a thing about it. And do not speak when you see Stefan; instead, listen to what everyone else says. Will others be present at this meeting?'

'There had better be.'

'If Kilbride is there, watch her reactions,' said Hygilt. 'That way, you might be able to tell if they are serious about the wedding, or if, as they have told you, it is merely a ruse. The fact that your sister has passed on this warning is a good sign. I think you might be wrong about her. What if she mistrusts Hector, too, but she is too scared to say anything about it?'

Abigone gazed at the wet patch on the rug. 'I don't have a veil.'

Hygilt got to her feet and strode to the door. She opened it, and smiled at the gathered courtiers.

'Hello,' she said. 'Would one of you please fetch a black veil for Princess Abigone? Her Highness remains very upset about the misfortunes that have beset her family, and she does not wish to walk the corridors of the palace with her tears on view for everyone to see. Please ensure that the veil is thick enough, so that no prying eyes can pierce its privacy.'

One of the older courtiers bowed. 'I shall see to it at once, Your Highness.'

'Thank you very much,' said Hygilt. 'Her Highness would greatly appreciate some haste in this matter.'

The courtier hurried off, and Hygilt closed the door. She walked back to the couch and sat down close to Abigone. She took her hand, and gazed up at her.

'Thank you,' said Abigone.

'That's all right.'

'Why are you being kind to me? I... have not treated you well.'

'You are three years older than me,' Hygilt said; 'almost four, but you have lived a very sheltered life, Abigone. I want to help you. I like you. I wasn't lying when I said that you have been the nicest to me.'

Tulip climbed up onto Abigone, and placed his front paws on her chest as he licked her face.

'Tulip likes you, too,' said Hygilt. 'You are not alone.'

Two hours later, there was another knock at the door. Abigone was sitting at her dresser, gazing at her veiled reflection. She picked Tulip up off her knee and walked to the front door of the apartment, while Hygilt remained in the bedroom.

Abigone opened the door. Standing in the corridor was Hector, along with several of his soldiers, while the usual crowd of courtiers had been pushed to either side.

The Duke of Ridden smiled at Abigone, then he raised an eyebrow. 'A veil, Your Highness?'

'Yes,' said Abigone. 'I refuse to leave my quarters without it. I do not want anyone to see me cry.'

Hector raised his palms, though his eyes remained confused. 'As you wish, Your Highness. Might I come in for a moment?'

'By all means,' she said.

Hector walked in the room, and closed the door.

'Are you here for regency business?' Abigone said.

'No,' he said. 'I have a little surprise for you. I had a very successful night in Twinbrook. My own ducal forces formed an alliance with those loyal to Chief Stefan and, between us, we destroyed Chief Dravid's lair. His men were routed, once again, but this time we finished the job, and Dravid is now in our custody.' He glanced over her shoulder. 'Is Princess Hygilt well?'

'She is.'

'Excellent. Now, about that surprise I mentioned; I did not return from Twinbrook alone. Chief Stefan is here, so that he can swear allegiance to King Alfgang the Sixth. He would also very much like to see you, Your Highness. He believes that you are destined to be his bride. Do you remember we talked about that?'

'I remember I told you to fuck off.'

Hector laughed. 'Yes. I recall that, too. Your reaction did not particularly surprise me or your sister. We had expected you to harbour some concerns regarding our little scheme. What you have to remember is this – there will be no wedding without your consent.'

Abigone narrowed her eyes behind the veil, almost unable to believe what the duke had said. She wanted to scream at him, to tell him that when they had discussed it before, there had been no hint that the wedding was dependent upon her giving her consent. It had been presented to her as a trick, a ruse; something that Hector had sworn was never going to happen. Instead of screaming, she nodded.

'Thank you,' she said.

Hector smiled. 'Are you ready to come downstairs? The rest of the

Royal Court is gathering in the throne room, in order to witness Chief Stefan pledge his oath to His Majesty. Little Alfie is nervous about the occasion, and he would no doubt be delighted to see his aunt there.'

'I will attend.'

'That pleases me. Do you need time to change your clothes?'

'I shall not be changing my clothes,' she said. 'Anything other than black would be inappropriate.'

'It's not the colour,' he said; 'it's that... well, that dress hardly flatters your figure, Your Highness, especially if you are insisting upon covering your face with a veil. I thought a set of fitted outfits was being prepared for you.'

'My new clothes have yet to arrive.'

Hector frowned. 'I see. One last thing – no animals are permitted within the throne room.'

Abigone glanced down at Tulip, who was nestled in her arms.

'Apologies, Your Highness,' said Hector, 'but those are the rules.'

Abigone set Tulip down onto the floor, and the creature gazed up at her.

'Go and see Hygilt,' Abigone said.

Tulip lingered for a few more seconds, then he sauntered off towards the bedroom, where Hygilt was reading the documents Kilbride had delivered. Hector gestured to the front door, and they left the apartment. A small crowd of courtiers and soldiers accompanied them as they descended to the ground floor of the palace, then they strode into a packed hall. The gilt throne of the realm was positioned upon a low platform at one end of the hall, and Hector led Abigone up onto the platform, while the courtiers remained close to the entrance. Kilbride was standing to the right of the throne, along with the most senior officials and militia commanders stationed in Torrent. She glanced at Abigone, and her eyes widened a little.

'Was the veil your idea, Hector?' she said.

Hector rolled his eyes. 'Abigone insisted that she wear it. Perhaps she is feeling a little shy about her imminent encounter with Chief Stefan. Or modest. Yes – that is how we shall describe her... choice of garb.' He glanced at the empty throne. 'Please excuse me, Your Highnesses. It is time to escort His Majesty into the hall.'

Hector left the room through a back door, and Abigone got into position next to her sister, and they both gazed out over the growing crowd.

'Are you going to give me a telling off?' said Abigone.

'No, sister,' said Kilbride. 'I was about to congratulate you. I don't know why I didn't think of putting you in a veil. Your idea was inspired.'

Walter strode in from a side door, and stepped up onto the platform next to Abigone. He swayed slightly, then looked down at the floor.

'Are you drunk?' whispered Abigone.

'I might be,' said Walter. 'How long will this take?' He glanced at her, then blinked, and laughed.

'Does my appearance amuse you?' said Abigone.

'Yes,' he said. 'Is it really you under all that, Abbie? You look...'

'Don't say it. I don't want Stefan to see my face.'

'That sounds a little paranoid. I know he's a Westlander, but he's here to swear allegiance, not to stare at you.'

Abigone frowned. 'You don't know, do you?'

'Know what?'

A trumpet sounded, and the hall fell into silence.

'Be upstanding for His Majesty King Alfgang the Sixth!' cried a courtier.

Everyone turned as a rear door opened. Duke Hector emerged first, carrying a sword aloft. Behind him, little Alfie was wearing heavy regal robes that were edged in gold and bedecked with jewels; while his mother walked behind him, her face also veiled. Hector led the boy king onto the platform, and over to the throne. He glanced up at Walter and his two aunts, then sat in the throne, his hands fidgeting as he stared at the huge crowd before him.

'Long live the king!' Hector cried.

'Long live the king!' the audience shouted, then they bowed their heads in silence.

'The petitioner may approach His Majesty,' Hector said.

Chief Stefan emerged from the thick crowds, with four of his warriors flanking him. They stood head and shoulders over many of the native inhabitants of Upper Down, who parted before them. Stefan's gaze roved over the people standing up on the platform, and he looked past Abigone as though he didn't recognise her. A flash of aggrieved disappointment moved over his features as he came to a halt a few yards in front of the throne.

'On behalf of His Majesty and the regency council,' said Hector, 'I am honoured to welcome you to Torrent, Chief Stefan of Saltmere. Will you please state the reason for your visit?'

Stefan's expression hardened a little, and there was an uncomfortable pause. He looked at Abigone again, as though at last realising who she was.

'I am here, Duke,' Stefan said, 'to pledge my allegiance to the boy king of Upper Down.'

Hector smiled, his eyes betraying his relief. 'Kneel before King Alfgang the Sixth, and recite your oath.'

Stefan muttered something under his breath, then he got down onto one knee before the boy on the throne.

'I swear to loyally serve His Majesty King Alfgang the Sixth as his faithful subject,' he said, 'from this day forth, until my dying breath.'

Hector glanced at Alfie on the throne.

'Thank you,' the boy king whispered.

Stefan stood. 'Now that we've got that over with,' he said, 'I have a few announcements I need to make.'

Hector opened his mouth to say something, but Stefan gave the duke a cold stare.

'Firstly,' Stefan went on, his gaze roaming over the crowd, 'I am moving into the Royal Palace. Now that I am here, I do not wish to leave. Secondly, you should all know that I have ordered the release of Chief Dravid. He has been commanded to depart the lands of Upper Down, and to never return. I judged that he has been punished enough. The loss of his brother will pain him to the end of his days. By now, he will be on a horse, fleeing for the lands to the north. And finally, I wish to make public my betrothal to Princess Abigone, who is soon to be my wife.'

Hector let out an audible groan as many in the crowd gasped.

Abigone kept her features still, then she heard Walter start to laugh.

'Is this a joke?' said the King's Champion. 'You aren't marrying Abigone.'

'Hold your tongue, brother,' said Hector.

Stefan took a step forward. 'Why is my bride wearing a veil? Let me see her face.'

'Her Highness is in mourning,' said Kilbride. 'I ask that you please respect her privacy.'

Stefan snorted. 'Then where is your veil, princess? Or perhaps you do not care about the loss of your father and brother.' He turned to Hector. 'Duke, you promised that I would be able to gaze upon my betrothed, and yet she is dressed like an old widow, and her face is shielded.'

Hector returned the chief's stare. 'Perhaps this is not the time or the place for...'

'No, Duke,' said Stefan. 'This is the time and the place. If you do not remove Abigone's veil, then I shall.'

'Go fuck yourself,' said Walter. 'Who else knew about this? Why am I only learning about this now?'

Stefan clenched his fists and strode up to the edge of the platform. 'What did you say to me, you pathetic coward? Did you dare to insult me? If you weren't drunk, I would make you suffer for your words.' He turned his gaze to Abigone, and reached out to take hold of her veil.

Walter swung his left fist and punched Stefan in the face. The chief cried out as blood streamed from his nose, then the four Westlanders who had been flanking him charged forward, and the hall erupted into chaos. Abigone shrieked as two of the Westlanders lunged out at Walter, then Kilbride pulled her back by the arm. Abigone saw Walter being struck in the stomach, and the champion fell to the floor, his head cracking off the edge of the platform. Soldiers from the Royal Guard moved in, barging through the crowds. Several of them formed a perimeter around the boy king, then they ushered Alfie and his mother towards the rear door. Other soldiers dived into the melee to rescue Walter, and then Abigone was dragged and shoved from the hall by Guardsmen, as Kilbride clung onto her arm. They were ushered into a nearby anteroom, and soldiers blocked the entrance.

Kilbride stared at her sister. 'Go back to your quarters, Abbie.'

'What about Walter?' said Abigone.

'My brother has failed me for the last time,' said Hector, who was standing by Frida and the boy king.

'Are you going to allow the Westlanders to kill him?' Frida cried.

'Of course not,' said the duke. 'The Royal Guard will preserve his life. He deserved a beating, however; the calamity we have just witnessed was entirely his fault. Do you see why I wanted him excluded from the regency council?'

'At least he stood up for me,' said Abigone. 'Where were you when Stefan tried to grab my veil?'

'The veil was a foolish idea,' said Hector. 'You should have guessed that Stefan would not be satisfied. He wanted to see the face of the woman he wishes to wed; was that so difficult? Part of the blame for this debacle falls upon your shoulders. You are selfish and immature. Are you trying to destroy this realm, you stupid girl?'

'That's enough,' said Kilbride, stepping between them. 'Hector, you should ensure that His Majesty and the Queen Mother are safely escorted back to my quarters. Abbie, you should also return to your quarters.'

'What are you going to do?' said Abigone.

Kilbride walked towards the door. 'I am going to ensure that Walter is still alive.' She pushed the soldiers out of the way, opened the door, and disappeared.

Alfie looked up at Abigone. 'Are you going to marry that Westlander, Aunty?'

'She most certainly is not,' said the boy's mother.

'It will be up to the regency council,' said Hector, 'and you, Frida, do not have a vote; therefore, your opinion on this matter is irrelevant. We shall do as Princess Kilbride has suggested.' He gestured to a door, and escorted the boy king and Frida from the room.

Abigone remained silent, then she left by another entrance, surrounded by soldiers. They escorted the princess through the noisy crowds of bewildered courtiers, and led her up the stairs to her rooms. Abigone strode through her front door, and ripped the veil from her face.

Hygilt peered out from the bedroom door, and Tulip ran across the floor and brushed up against Abigone's legs.

'Did you meet him?' the girl said. 'What is he like?'

Abigone picked up Tulip and cradled him in her arms.

'Well?' said Hygilt.

'I believe you,' she said. 'I believe what you told me about Hector.'

Hygilt walked out from the bedroom. 'You do?'

'Yes. I am nothing to him but property to be sold or given away.'

'What are you going to do?'

'I don't know. He is too powerful to overthrow, and now he has an alliance with the Westlanders. Kilbride is too frightened to do anything; I can see that now. And Walter...' A tear slipped down her cheek. 'I thought he was a drunken idiot, but he was the only one who stood up for me. He punched Stefan when he tried to remove my veil, and the Westlanders attacked him.'

'Oh no,' said Hygilt. 'That sounds awful.'

'It was awful. And poor little Alfie saw it all. We have lost.'

'Don't say that.'

'It's true,' she said. 'Hector is in charge of Upper Down, and there is nothing we can do about it.'

'You are wrong, Abigone,' said Hygilt. 'There is always something we can do.' She frowned. 'We just need to work out what that is.'

CHAPTER 17
PRETENCE

Torrent, Upper Down – 13th Day of Lamenta 107

'You are exceedingly fortunate, my lord,' said the doctor, as he washed his hands in a basin of warm water.

Walter gingerly touched his bruised chin, and felt the clusters of dried blood on his jaw line. 'I don't feel particularly lucky.'

'Your arms and chin took the brunt of your fall, my lord,' the doctor said. 'Had your teeth or nose struck the edge of the platform, you would most likely be disfigured. And, if it had been the back of your skull? If that had been the case, then the outcome could have been fatal.'

Walter said nothing.

The doctor looked into his eyes. 'As you are here, my lord, I am duty bound to recommend that you cut back on your drinking. You are damaging your health in numerous ways, and increasing the risk of a serious accident.'

'This wasn't an accident,' said Walter. 'I was attacked by four Westlanders.'

'And who struck the first blow, my lord?'

'Uh, that might have been me. I was trying to protect Princess Abigone.'

'Regardless of your motives, my lord, I would like you to abstain from alcohol for the next few days. Can you do that? There is still a risk that you have received a concussion.'

Walter frowned. 'How many days are we talking about?'

'Four, to be sure.'

Walter shook his head. 'How about I promise to remain sober for the rest of today? That's the best I can do.'

The doctor frowned.

'Can I go now?' said Walter.

'You are not my prisoner, my lord.'

Walter got to his feet. Blood from his wound had spattered down the front of his tunic, and some was staining the leather of his boots. On a table in front of him, several bloody bandages and swabs were lying in a bowl.

'Who knew so much blood could come from my chin?' he said.

'Please be careful, my lord,' said the doctor.

Walter opened the door and stepped out into a corridor on the ground floor of the palace. A small crowd of courtiers turned, and each stared at the blood covering Walter's clothes.

Lothar pushed through the crowd. He cleared a path for the King's Champion, then he narrowed his eyes.

'It looks worse than it is,' Walter said.

'The next time you are in the same room as Chief Stefan, sir,' he said, 'I should be there. I heard you nearly broke his nose.'

'I would have, had I used my other fist,' said Walter, as they strode along the corridor, 'but the angle wasn't right, so I led with my left.'

'And then?'

'Then four Westlanders jumped on me.'

'You were lucky you weren't beaten to a pulp.'

'Soldiers from the Royal Guard pulled me away before that could happen. Or, so I am told. I might have blacked out for a few minutes when I went down.'

Walter and Lothar slowed as six huge Westlanders came into view at the end of the corridor. They were gathered around a doorway, and each was in full armour.

'We should probably take a different route to your quarters, sir,' said Lothar. 'That is where Chief Stefan has taken up residence within the palace.'

'I refuse to divert for those bastards,' said Walter. 'They've seen us. If we turn back, they will take it as a sign of weakness.'

Lothar sighed, as Walter continued walking towards the Westlanders.

'Good afternoon, wankers,' said Walter, as he approached the six men. 'How's Stefan's face? Is he still as ugly?'

One of the Westlanders clenched his fists and took a step forward.

'The chief ordered us to cause no trouble,' said another, pulling him back. 'Walter will get what's coming to him.'

Walter laughed as he passed the doorway, then he and Lothar ascended a flight of stairs to an upper floor. They crossed over to the northern wing of the palace, and ascended again. Walter unlocked the door to his quarters in the tower, and they went inside.

Lothar cleared the clothes from two chairs, and they sat. Walter exhaled, and he felt a hangover crushing his spirits. His stomach churned, and his chin throbbed, exacerbating the headache that was pounding behind his temples. He lowered his gaze, and tried to remember all that he had heard in the throne room.

'Stefan thinks he's marrying Abigone,' he said.

'Is that right, sir?'

'What am I to make of it, Lothar? I can believe that Hector could dream up something like this, but Kilbride? I couldn't see Abigone's face, but she didn't exactly seem enthusiastic.'

'Perhaps she was just shy.'

'Abigone, shy? No. And Stefan has released Dravid. I doubt Hector was very pleased by that news, not after all the effort that went into capturing him. Fucking Westlanders; they always stick together, even when they're fighting each other.'

Lothar picked up a bottle of whisky from the floor, and looked around for glasses.

'The doctor told me not to drink today,' said Walter.

'Since when did you ever listen to the advice of doctors, sir?'

'Well, I did thump my head pretty hard.'

Lothar lifted a tunic from the floor, and found several glasses under it. He picked up two, and wiped them with his sleeve.

'You should get changed, sir,' he said. 'Your clothes are covered in blood.'

'I will, in a while.'

Lothar filled the two glasses with whisky, and held one out for Walter.

'Did you not hear what I said, Lothar?'

'I heard you, sir; I just didn't believe it. One whisky won't hurt you.'

'Why are you always trying to get me drunk?' said Walter.

'I, uh... well, sir...'

'I'm joking, Lothar; but I think I might stay clear of whisky today. I need to think about what I should do.'

'Regarding what, sir?'

'Regarding Stefan. If Hector is trying to force Abbie into marrying him, then I cannot allow it to happen. Abbie is like a little sister to me – an annoying little sister; don't get me wrong – but a sister nonetheless. I will not allow her to be sold like a piece of meat.'

'Isn't it just the way of things, sir? Royal brides are used to create alliances between houses; this has been happening for centuries. King Alfgang the Great arranged many marriages for the members of his family, and for other aristocrats in Upper Down. Did any of them have a say in the matter?'

'I know that Kilbride could have refused to marry Roderick,' said Walter; 'and I refused to...' He fell silent.

'You refused what, sir?'

'I've never told you this, but Alfgang the Great once tried to arrange a marriage for me. The daughter of a duke from... shit, where was it? Anyway, I refused, because the girl clearly didn't want anything to do with me.'

'Do you know that for sure, sir?'

'She was one of the hostages abducted by the Westlanders,

Lothar. I was pretty fucking sure. After I refused to marry her, she was ransomed back to her family for a ton of gold, and then, after that, the king didn't speak to me for about two years. I suspect that's why I was given the position of champion, and then isolated. I had let the king down, by refusing to become complicit in his crimes. Abigone is different. She's mouthy, but I don't know if she's strong enough to say no to Hector. She could easily be bullied into marrying Stefan.'

The two men fell into silence. Lothar offered Walter the glass of whisky again, but Walter shook his head.

'Walter, are you in there?' came a powerful voice from outside.

'Shit,' muttered Walter, as he got to his feet. He opened the door. 'Yes, brother?'

Hector glared at him. 'You disgraced yourself today,' he said. 'You brought the entire Royal Court into disrepute. Not once during the forty-year reign of Alfgang the Great did any violence break out in the throne room. Worse, you terrified little Alfie, embarrassed Princess Abigone, and insulted Chief Stefan. I hope you are pleased with yourself, because...'

'Shut up, Hector,' said Walter. 'You didn't come all this way simply to berate me. Tell me what you want, and then you can piss off.'

Hector took a document from one of the soldiers standing behind him, and handed it to Walter.

'These are your orders,' he said.

Walter unfolded the paper and glanced at its contents.

'As commander of Upper Down's armed forces,' Hector went on, 'I have decided to deploy the Mountain Rangers in an offensive capacity. You are to lead them in an assault upon the imperial army. Your objective is to cause as much destruction as possible, and inflict heavy casualties upon our foe. You leave tomorrow afternoon.'

Walter said nothing.

'No murmurs of complaint, brother?' said Hector. 'I am almost disappointed. I had expected a small tantrum, at the very least.'

'These orders make no tactical or strategic sense,' said Walter. 'I understand why you want me dead, but do you need to throw away the lives of the Mountain Rangers? They are the best soldiers we have.'

'There is a way that I might be willing to rescind these orders, brother,' said Hector. 'If you were to reveal to me the exact location of the route you used to return to Torrent after the death of King Alfgang the Pius, then I would be able to instruct another branch of the armed forces to carry out the attack. As this knowledge is being kept from me by the Mountain Rangers, I have no alternative, other than to order you to lead them in the assault. If you travel by your secretive route, you will be able to surprise the imperial army, will you not? You can see my dilemma.'

Walter laughed. 'Is that why you're here? If you wanted to know the location of the route I took, all you needed to do was ask.'

'Then I am asking you, brother.'

'And I am telling you to go and fuck yourself.'

'In that case, my orders stand. Personally, I think I am treating you rather generously, brother. In some ways, you cannot lose. If this assault is successful, you will be the toast of Torrent; and if you fall in battle, then you will have gone some way to redeeming your reputation. I will insist upon a full state funeral, and I will weep before your coffin; oh, how I will weep. I imagine that Princess Kilbride may even shed a tear for your demise; but fear not, for I will be there to comfort her.'

'Keep your filthy hands away from Kilbride.'

Hector smiled. 'Did that strike a nerve? Did you perhaps hear a few rumours regarding myself and the widowed princess? Do you have any idea how passionate Kilbride can be? No, I wouldn't imagine that you have the slightest notion. It was so easy to take her from you when you were teenagers, and it was just as easy when she returned from Greater Down. She practically threw herself into my bed. What was I to do? I am just a man, and I succumbed to her charms.' He laughed in Walter's face. 'Do you want to strike me, brother? I can feel your fury. Do it, and those soldiers standing behind me will drag you off to the palace jail before you can blink. Assemble the Mountain Rangers at noon tomorrow, and then lead them over the mountains; is that understood?'

Walter said nothing, his hands shaking with anger.

'I need to hear your reply, King's Champion,' said Hector. 'Shall you obey this order, or are you refusing to do so?'

'I will obey,' Walter said.

'Excellent. My business here is done. Fight bravely.'

Hector turned and strode away, leading the soldiers back down the stairs of the tower.

Walter closed the door and returned to his seat.

'Did you hear all that?' he said to Lothar, who was still holding the two glasses of whisky.

'Yes, sir.'

'The stupid prick doesn't realise that I was only conscious for the latter half of the route we took through the mountains. I have no idea how that path connects to the ravine south of Torrent.'

'That wasn't the part that seemed to upset you, sir.'

Walter shook his head in disgust. 'What did Killie ever see in him? The thought of her in his arms makes me want to scream. Compared to that, a trip through the mountains means very little to me.'

'Even if it results in our deaths, sir?'

'At least I would die fighting. Shit, I sound like a damn Westlander.'

'We have until tomorrow at noon, sir. Are you sure you don't want that whisky?'

Walter reached out and took the offered glass, then he hesitated. He knew the whisky would ease the various pains in his head, and it would quell the disturbance in his stomach, but he felt almost sick at the thought of drinking.

'I'd better not,' he said, placing the glass onto the floor. 'We should go down to the Rangers' barracks and let them know about tomorrow. They will need time to plan, and to get ready.'

Lothar nodded. 'We will have plenty of time to enjoy a drink after that, sir.'

'I suppose.'

Walter lowered his gaze. His anger had lessened, and he was annoyed with himself for almost rising to Hector's bait. That was the sole reason he had brought up Kilbride, to try to provoke him into a reaction. As for Lothar, why did the man think that alcohol was the answer to everything? No matter what they were doing, Lothar would forever be encouraging him to take another drink. He liked the soldier, but didn't he have any other interests?

Someone knocked on the door, and Walter got up, mumbling curses under his breath. He opened the door, and saw a young courtier standing outside his rooms.

'I bear a note from Princess Abigone, my lord,' she said.

Walter took the note, and then the courtier curtsied and hurried down the stairs. Walter closed the door and retook his seat, then he cracked open Abigone's wax seal with a thumb, and unfolded the piece of paper.

Dear Walter,

Thank you for what you did this morning, my cousin. If you hadn't intervened, then Stefan would have humiliated me in front of the entire throne room.

I know we have not always been the best of friends, but you are among the few in the palace that I trust, and I am sorry you were hurt for defending my honour.

Can we put aside our old quarrels and be friends? I would like that.

HRH Abigone.

Walter felt his eyes well, so surprised was he by what Abigone had written. He had convinced himself that he was universally loathed, and that Abigone had considered him to be nothing more than a drunken fool. And she trusted him? She wanted to be friends? It occurred to him that Abigone might not have been the only native of Upper Down who had interpreted his actions in a different light from the way Hector had reacted. What had all the palace courtiers and soldiers thought when they had watched Stefan raise his hand to rip away Abigone's mourning veil? Had any of them secretly cheered when they had seen Walter strike the Westlander chief?

'Perhaps I am not as alone as I thought,' he said.

'Sir?' said Lothar.

Walter considered showing him the note, but decided against it. Instead, he folded it up and placed it into an inside pocket. The words had been for him alone, and he would not betray Abigone's trust so quickly.

He stood. 'On your feet, soldier,' he said to Lothar. 'Let's visit the Mountain Rangers; they deserve to know what they will be doing this time tomorrow.'

Walter and Lothar spent the next two hours with the men from the Mountain Rangers, going over the plan for the following day. Large maps were unfurled, and Walter was shown the narrow valley where they would emerge into the ravine south of the Kendril Wall. Their secret route through the mountains was not marked on any map, and none of the soldiers went into any detail regarding its location with Walter, and he did not press them on the subject.

What all of them did agree on, was that the planned assault was a wasteful exercise in futility. Even if they were successful, they would barely make a dent in the imperial army gathering in the ravine, and they had the additional worry of being followed if they tried to retrace their steps through the mountains on the way home. If it came to a choice between dying, or revealing the location of the secret pass to the imperial army, then they knew they would have to do their duty to the realm.

With the overall plan in place, Walter and Lothar left the officers and sergeants of the Rangers discussing the finer details, and they returned to his quarters in the tower.

Lothar reached for the bottle of whisky as soon as they had entered Walter's room.

'You have a mind like a homing pigeon, my friend,' said Walter; 'always returning to the same place.'

'Well, sir, we're free now, aren't we? We have nothing to do until tomorrow morning, and we don't have to get up until close to noon. That sounds like the perfect opportunity for a few little whiskies, eh?'

'There is something I have to do first,' said Walter. 'Amuse yourself for a few minutes, Lothar; this won't take long.'

Walter walked through into his bedroom, opened the shutters to let in some light, and sat down by a side table. He moved the piles of clothes and unwashed glasses onto the bed, then rummaged around in a drawer for paper. He found a few sheets, then picked up a charcoal pencil. The tip was still sharp, and he began to write.

Cousin Abigone,

The doctor said I was very lucky; and he told me that I possess an extremely hard chin, which I have decided to take as a compliment.

Thank you for thinking of me. I would be honoured to be considered your friend.

Pass on my regards to Tulip, and please ask him not to try to eat me next time we meet.

Yours,

KC Walter

He folded up the note, then he lit a candle. His seal was dangling from a chain around his neck, and he held it over the flame for a few moments to heat the metal, then he tipped the candle over, and a few drops of wax dripped onto the folded edge of the note. He pressed the seal into the hot wax, his fingers smarting from the heat, then he waited for it to dry. He stood, blew out the candle, and walked through his living room to the front door, as Lothar eyed him from a chair. Walter left the apartment, leaned over the stairwell, and pulled on a rope. A bell sounded in the hallway on the floor below, and within a minute, a courtier was hurrying up the stairs.

Walter held out the note. 'See that Princess Abigone receives this.'

The courtier bowed, then took the slip of paper. 'Yes, my lord.'

Walter watched the courtier run down the stairs, then he went back into his apartment and closed the door. Lothar smiled, and held up the bottle of whisky.

'I'm not sure I should be drinking,' Walter said. 'What about the doctor's advice?'

'Pah. What do they know, sir?'

'More than you or I.'

'They say these things just to make themselves feel important.'

Walter sat down opposite him. 'Maybe, but this time, I think I'll do as he recommended.'

'Come on, sir. I guarantee that you will feel better after a few drinks; you always do.'

'What is this obsession with getting me drunk?' said Walter, growing a little exasperated. 'Could you not give it a rest for one night?'

'It's not an obsession, sir.'

'Then what is it? Go on; explain it to me. I hit my head off the floor this morning; shouldn't you be making sure I'm not concussed? Is my health less important to you than alcohol?'

Lothar seemed at a loss for words.

'You are my friend, aren't you?' Walter said.

'I think of myself as your friend, sir, as well as your aide.'

'Then please respect my wishes. I have come to rely on you these past few years, Lothar. In fact, you are the only real friend I have in Torrent, or anywhere else for that matter. I mean, apart from Kilbride, and Abigone, I suppose, but they're family. You are the only male friend I have. You have kept me going through some rough times, and I am grateful; but please, just this once, don't try to get me drunk.'

'But...'

'No, Lothar. When I lead the Mountain Rangers over the pass tomorrow, I want to do it without a hangover. I'm sick of feeling this way. For once, I want to actually do my duty and act like the King's Champion. If you can't accept that, then perhaps you should take the night off.'

Lothar stared at him, then he got to his feet and walked over to the jammed window. Enough light was still filtering through the wooden slats to dimly illuminate the room, but it was almost time to light a few lamps. Walter watched his friend, then he heard the man swear under his breath.

'What was that?' said Walter.

'I can't do this any more.'

'What are you going on about now, Lothar? What can't you do? You can have a drink if you want. I'm not asking you to abstain.'

'May the spirits forgive me, sir. I... I am not your friend. If you knew what I was doing, then you would hate me, and rightly so.'

'I somehow doubt that.'

Lothar turned, but he wouldn't meet Walter's gaze. 'Getting you drunk is not my obsession, sir; it's what I am being paid to do.'

'Eh? I'm not paying you for that.'

'No, sir. It's Duke Hector who's been paying me to ply you with drink. I have been working for your brother ever since I got the job as your aide.'

Walter narrowed his eyes. 'Why the fuck would he do that?'

'The duke never shared his reasons with me, sir, but isn't it obvious? Look at the effect your drinking has had on your performance, and the damage it has done to your reputation.'

Walter knew he should be angry, but all he felt was crushing disappointment.

'I'm sorry, sir,' said Lothar. 'I resign my position as your aide.'

He walked towards the front door of the apartment, his gaze lowered.

'Wait,' said Walter. 'Is that it? You were never my friend? I trusted you.'

Lothar paused by the door, then he gripped the handle and walked from the room. Walter watched the door close behind him, then he sat motionless as a barrage of emotions surged through him. For three years, he and Lothar had been inseparable. They had drunk in every beer hall in Twinbrook, and every tavern in Torrent. Walter had made a fool of himself on many occasions; had his brother been laughing at him the entire time? Walter knew the answer to that. Of course Hector had been laughing.

The pain in his head faded away next to the hurt of betrayal. He didn't care that Hector saw him as an object of ridicule; losing a friend was far worse. And Lothar had never been a friend. He had been pretending.

Walter bowed his head. He had never felt so stupid. He wondered if any of the Mountain Rangers had suspected the truth, or perhaps they all knew. Perhaps everyone knew.

He glanced down at the open bottle of whisky. He was alone, and he would always be alone; there was no reason to pretend otherwise. He picked up the bottle and filled a glass. He knew it was a mistake, but he also knew that nothing else would assuage the pain in his heart.

He lifted the glass to his lips, and drank.

CHAPTER 18
PRECEDENT

Kendril Wall, Upper Down – 14th Day of Lamenta 107

When Kilbride had last stood upon the battlements of the Wall of Kendril, only a few hundred scouts from the imperial army had been down in the ravine. Three days later, the narrow valley was filled from end to end, and for as far as the eye could see. Long lines of tents had been erected on either side of the road that wound down the steep slope, and engineers had constructed a timber palisade across the width of the ravine, just beyond bow range. Multiple flags and banners were flying from some of the larger tents, and Kilbride could see soldiers wherever she looked. Thousands of soldiers.

Hector emitted a soft laugh. 'Look at them all, Your Highness,' he said; 'they are scurrying about like ants down there. They must realise that they will never be able to breach the Wall; I just wonder how long it will take for the Illustrious Prince Valentino to admit the truth to himself.'

Kilbride glanced at the duke. She hadn't seen him since the brawl that had broken out in the throne room on the day before, and he was acting as though nothing had happened.

'What are you going to do about Chief Dravid?' she said.

'I don't think there is anything I can do,' he said. 'By now, he could be anywhere.'

'Have you asked Stefan why he let him go? Have you voiced your anger to him regarding this?'

Hector smiled. 'You're not attempting to drive a wedge between myself and Chief Stefan, are you? My alliance with him is purely tactical. Already, I am hearing that several groups of Westlanders have deserted Twinbrook, so disgusted are they by Stefan swearing allegiance to His Majesty. Our plan is working, and if that means I need to continue humouring Stefan for a while, then so be it.'

'When are you going to inform him that he will not be marrying Abigone?'

'Oh, not for quite a while yet. She is the main reason he agreed to the alliance. I would be obliged if you focussed a little more on winning Abigone round to our way of thinking. If she were to flirt with Stefan, it might do wonders for our cause.'

Kilbride tightened her eyes. 'What is your cause, cousin?'

'Everything I do is to benefit the realm of Upper Down, Your Highness.'

They glanced at the top of the stairs as Abigone emerged from the shadows, wearing the thick veil again. The princess looked around at the battlements, then she removed it from her face.

'Were you expecting Stefan to be here, Your Highness?' said Hector.

'One never knows,' she said. Her eyes fell on Kilbride, then she strode forward and joined them by the battlements. 'Why was I summoned?'

'At dawn this morning,' Hector said, 'I received an indication from the imperial army that they wish to meet with the rulers of Upper Down. I imagine that they have another ultimatum they want to deliver. Hence, I sent out word to all members of the regency council.'

Abigone eyed the stairs. 'Is Walter coming?'

'My brother loathes this time of day,' said Hector. 'If I had to guess, he will be unconscious in his quarters. And, when he finally wakes up, it will no doubt be time for him to lead the Mountain Rangers on a small expedition.'

'What expedition?' said Kilbride.

'Walter and his Rangers will be crossing the mountains to take part in a diversionary attack. He seemed quite keen when I told him about it yesterday.'

'Why wasn't this brought before the regency council?'

'Do I need to refer every military decision to the council, Your Highness? Operational matters concerning the defence of the realm are my responsibility. It would be highly impractical to summon the council to vote upon every matter.'

'But Walter is a member of the council.'

'He is also in command of the Mountain Rangers, and as they are the only ones who know the location of the secret pass through the mountains, there was no one else I could send.'

Kilbride bit her tongue. It seemed clear to her that Hector had ordered Walter away to prevent him from voting, or worse, that he was hoping Walter would be slain in battle.

'How were his injuries?' said Abigone.

'Slight,' said Hector. 'A mere bump on the chin. Certainly not enough to excuse him from duty. To his credit, he accepted his orders with good grace.'

Abigone pointed down into the valley. 'What are those?'

Kilbride and Hector followed the line of Abigone's finger.

'Wagons?' said Hector.

'They are not shaped like wagons,' said Abigone. 'They are being pulled by horses, and they have wheels, but that is all they have in common with wagons.'

Kilbride frowned. Several dozen of the two-wheeled vehicles Abigone had seen were being hauled up the steep slope towards the Kendril Wall. Each was draped with heavy tarpaulin sheets, and they were longer than normal wagons. A few imperial engineers were standing close to the head of the convoy, discussing where to position them, then a few tents were pulled up and folded away to make room for the arrivals.

'Catapults, perhaps?' said Hector. 'If that is the case, then they are far too small to inflict any damage upon the Wall. They would need enormous trebuchets to have the slightest chance of making a dent. The Wall, if I need remind you, is eight yards thick. Still, one must admire their enthusiasm, if not their intellect.'

A small group peeled away from the main imperial camp, and soldiers saluted them as they strode through the rudimentary palisade wall.

'Here come the emissaries,' said Hector. 'I have instructed the Wall Militia to allow them through. Shall we descend to the gatehouse? I have a meeting room prepared.'

'Shouldn't we wait for Walter?' said Abigone.

'I'm afraid Walter is now officially late, and we shall have to proceed without him.'

Hector walked towards the stairs, leaving the two sisters by the battlements.

'You seem awfully concerned about Walter this morning,' said Kilbride.

'He got hurt yesterday, because of me,' Abigone said. She looked as though she wanted to say more, but, instead, she glanced away.

'Sister,' Kilbride said, 'in case you have any doubt about the matter, let me be clear – I will never allow Stefan to marry you.'

Abigone half-smiled. 'Not without my consent?'

'What?'

'That's what Hector said to me. He said there would be no wedding without my consent.'

'He said what? No, Abigone, there will be no wedding. Unless... do you like him?'

'What do you think?'

'I think that you would gouge your own eyes out rather than marry that brute. Am I wrong?'

'No.'

'Praise the spirits for that. I thought for a minute... Never mind. The betrothal is a trick. We are trying to lure Stefan away from the other Westlanders, so that they are divided and weak. That's all there is to it.'

'Are you sure Hector agrees?'

'Can we talk about this later? We should go downstairs, before...'

'Before what? Before Hector gets suspicious?'

Kilbride walked away. She glanced along the battlements, to make sure that no one had heard the exchange, then her nerves jangled, and she realised that she was scared of Hector. The Duke of Ridden was a Master, and he could kill her with a hand gesture and a few muttered words, replacing her blood with fire, or her bones with air. For years, she had kept his secret, and had acted as though the knowledge gave her a tactical advantage, but she wished she had told everyone. Did Walter know about his brother's abilities?

She went down the stairs, hearing Abigone's shoes on the steps behind her. Halfway down, Kilbride stopped. She glanced up at her sister.

'You must be careful, Abbie,' she said. 'There are things about Hector that you don't know.'

'I know enough,' Abigone said.

'That is all the more reason for you to be discreet. Why don't I come round to your apartment later tonight, and we can talk privately?'

'Will you be honest with me – completely honest?'

'I will, Abbie, if you are honest with me.'

'Very well. I will be waiting for you.'

The two sisters carried on, and they reached the bottom of the stairs, where two soldiers were ready to escort them.

'This way, Your Highnesses,' said one.

They followed the soldiers to a large room, where Hector was sitting by a table between Amery and Stefan.

The Westlander chief got to his feet as the princesses entered. His nose looked broken, and he had bruises under both eyes.

'You were right, Duke,' he said. 'This girl's reputation for beauty is well-deserved.'

Abigone froze for a moment, her eyes flashing with anger and fear.

'How is your face, Chief Stefan?' said Kilbride.

'Fucking sore,' said the Westlander. 'Walter is lucky not to be here. The next time I see him, I am going to snap the bastard's neck.' He gazed at Abigone, and tried to smile, though the effort seemed to pain him. 'Good morning, my betrothed. From the look of you, our children will be strong and handsome.'

Abigone inclined her head slightly, then she and Kilbride took their places by the table, and Stefan sat down again.

'Before the imperial emissaries arrive,' said Hector, 'I would like to bring up the elevation of Chief Stefan to the Duchy of Torrent. As you correctly pointed out, Kilbride, I was not legally permitted to dispense such titles on my own initiative, but the regency council has the power to do so. Does anyone have any objections?'

Kilbride glanced at Abigone, but she seemed too cowed by Stefan's presence to speak.

'I would like some time to consider the proposal,' Kilbride said.

'Why?' said Hector. 'It seems quite clear cut to me. It would cement the alliance between Chief Stefan and the regency council; and it would be a necessary step before any wedding could be contemplated.'

'No duchy has ever been given to a... foreigner before.'

Hector laughed. 'That isn't true, and I suspect you know it, Your Highness. Were your family not foreigners when they arrived in Upper Down a century ago? Weren't members of your family given titles? I see no difference in this case; unless your objection is based purely upon the fact that Chief Stefan is a Westlander. Do you harbour any ill feeling towards the folk of the Westlands?'

'I try to treat all peoples fairly.'

'Excellent. Shall we put it to a vote? Amery, prepare to record the proceedings.' He smiled. 'Amery makes a fine secretary, don't you think?'

Amery dipped a quill into a pot of ink. 'I am ready, my lord. I have already prepared your proposal. I need only the votes to complete the document.' He glanced up. 'Those in favour of awarding the Duchy of Torrent to Chief Stefan of Saltmere, please raise your hands.'

Hector raised his right hand.

'I abstain,' said Abigone, her eyes on the table.

'Then there is no need to count any further votes,' said Hector, lowering his hand. 'Let the record show that the proposal was carried by two votes to none, with one abstention. Congratulations, Stefan, you are now the Duke of Torrent. When we get back to the palace, Amery will give you the appropriate seal that you can use for official documents and so on, and he will provide you with a few papers detailing the income you can expect to receive from your duchy. I believe you are now the owner of some valuable property within the town of Torrent, along with a few farm estates up north.'

'Will there be a ceremony?' said Stefan.

'If you want one, then we shall have one,' said Hector.

Stefan smiled. 'And will people have to refer to me as duke from now on?'

'They most certainly will.'

The door opened, and a soldier gazed into the room. 'The imperial delegates have arrived, my lords and ladies.'

'Please show them in,' said Hector.

Four men entered the meeting room, their surcoats emblazoned with the insignia of the Sanctian Empire. Hector stood, and gestured to a few chairs, but the men remained standing.

'Before we begin,' said one, 'you should know that we are aware that the last two emissaries who were sent to negotiate with Upper Down were brutally murdered. Can we have your solemn word that this will not occur again?'

'You can,' said Kilbride, before anyone else could speak. 'You shall be treated with the respect your position has earned, and will come to no harm.'

'Thank you, my lady.'

The four men sat.

'Who would like to start?' said Hector.

'We have a new proposal from His Illustrious Highness Prince Valentino of Sanctos,' said the chief emissary. He gestured to a colleague, who handed him a document. 'Upper Down faces a choice,' he went on; 'either you submit to these proposals, or we shall force entry into this realm and lay it to waste. All men of fighting age shall be exiled to the south as slaves, all moveable property will be systematically removed, and the kingdom of Upper Down shall be abolished, and its lands ceded to Greater Down.'

'Was that their price?' said Hector.

'Excuse me?'

'I assume that you had to seek Greater Down's acquiescence in order to move your army through its territory. Did they demand that they be given Upper Down as a reward for their cooperation?'

The emissary smiled. 'Here are the proposals. First, you will deliver Her Imperial Highness Princess Hygilt into our keeping; second, you will dismantle the Kendril Wall and open the pass to all traffic; third, you will allow a peace-keeping force of six thousand soldiers from the imperial army to occupy certain strategic locations within the realm of Upper Down, in order to facilitate the expulsion of all Westlanders from its territory. Do you accept?'

'These conditions have changed,' said Kilbride. 'The previous emissaries did not demand as much.'

'That is correct, my lady. However, that was before your father murdered those emissaries. Did you expect this realm to go unpunished for such a treacherous act of bad faith? Do you accept?'

'How long do we have to consider these proposals?' said Kilbride.

'His Illustrious Highness Prince Valentino has ordained that if we do not return to the imperial camp with a positive response within the hour, it will be assumed that you have refused these terms.'

'We needn't wait that long,' said Hector. 'You can tell him our response now – we refuse.'

The chief emissary nodded, and the four men got to their feet.

'Wait,' said Kilbride. 'There must be more that we can discuss. What if we deliver Princess Hygilt over to you by sunset? Would the illustrious prince be prepared to make any concessions if we did that?'

'No, my lady. The terms must be accepted as a whole, or rejected in their entirety.'

'But you are asking us to surrender our autonomy. With six thousand imperial soldiers garrisoning Upper Down, and the Wall gone, we would be at the empire's mercy.'

The chief emissary smiled. 'Perhaps you should have thought of that before you allowed the Westlanders to rampage over the Central Provinces. It is too late to expect any generosity from the Sanctian Empire, my lady; much too late. These terms are the best you will be offered.'

Hector waved a hand as though dismissing them. 'Do your worst. I will enjoy watching you attempt to breach the Kendril Wall. Tell me – how long is your supply route? How many wagons must arrive each day to feed twenty thousand mouths? And do you think that stream will fulfil your need for fresh water? The illustrious prince is deluded if he thinks he can win this confrontation. Please deliver this counter-proposal to His Imperial Highness: inform him that if he turns his army around and marches home, then we shall release Princess Hygilt. And those are the best terms you will be offered. Good day.'

The emissaries strode from the room.

'I thought we'd be here for hours,' said Stefan. 'They can't possibly have expected you to accept those terms. They have either lost their minds, or they know something that we don't.'

'Are we finished here?' said Abigone, her eyes still lowered.

'Yes,' said Hector. 'You may return to the palace, Your Highnesses. Thank you for attending this session of the regency council. I will remain here, I think, to keep an eye on the activities of our imperial foe.'

Kilbride and Abigone got to their feet and strode from the room.

'Why did you abstain?' said Kilbride, as they descended another flight of stairs.

'What difference does it make?' said Abigone. 'If I had opposed Hector, then he would know...'

'Stop,' said Kilbride. 'I shouldn't have asked. We will save it for tonight when I visit.'

They reached the ground floor of the gatehouse and walked out into the chill autumnal air. Their carriages were lined up in the paved area between the Wall and the streets of Torrent, and a small cluster of courtiers and soldiers were waiting to accompany them back to the palace. Kilbride nodded at Abigone, then she strode to her carriage, where Marie was waiting. The lady-in-waiting opened the carriage door, and they climbed up and sat down on the padded benches of the interior. A soldier closed the door, and the carriage got underway. Kilbride glanced out of the window, and saw Abigone assisted up into her carriage, then she closed her eyes, so that Marie wouldn't be tempted to speak to her.

An hour later, Kilbride was walking through the palace on her own, having left Marie with Frida and the boy-king, as they inspected potential new quarters for them to occupy. Kilbride passed a few courtiers, who bowed in her direction. Only one member of the Royal Court resided in that particular corner of the palace, and the courtiers would be able to guess her destination, but there was no getting around that. Kilbride entered the tower and climbed the stairs. She stopped at a door, and knocked.

There was no response, so Kilbride knocked again, and waited. After a few minutes had passed, she tried the handle, and the door opened.

'Walter?' she said, as she peered into the gloom.

She entered the chamber, then nearly tripped over a pile of unwashed clothes on the floor. She walked up to the window, and pulled on the shutters, but they refused to budge.

'Are you in here, Walter?'

She stepped over a mound of empty bottles, and opened the bedroom door. Inside, Walter was lying on his front, fully clothed.

Kilbride listened to the sound of him snoring, then she crept over and shook his shoulder.

He groaned, then she noticed the dried blood on his chin.

'Walter, wake up.'

He rolled onto his back and opened his eyes. 'Lothar?'

Kilbride smiled. 'No, Walter; it's me.'

He eyed her. 'What are you doing in my bedroom?'

'You missed this morning's meeting of the regency council,' she said. 'I was checking that you were still alive. You stink of whisky. Should you be drinking after hitting your head?'

'No,' he said. 'I should have left the whisky on the floor, along with my self-respect. My head is pounding like a Westlander's drum.'

'And your tunic is covered in blood. Is the wound still bleeding?'

'That's yesterday's blood. Is it noon yet?'

'No. We have an hour or so before the noon bell rings.' She sat on the side of the bed. 'I heard that you are leading the Rangers over the mountains later today.'

'My brother's latest scheme to get rid of me.'

'I need you to stay alive, Walter. Abigone and I cannot defeat Hector on our own.'

'What the fuck are you talking about?'

'I'm scared, Walter. Hector is... well, that's just it – I don't know what he's planning, and it's driving me crazy. I have reached the point where I no longer believe a word that comes out of his mouth.'

Walter sat up, and touched his chin. 'It took you long enough.'

'I know. Under Alfgang the Great, Hector seemed... honourable, I suppose. Maybe not to you, but he was always respectful and frank with me. But now? And something's changed with Abigone. I used to believe that she adored the duke; the same way that she adored our father, but she was too terrified to speak at today's meeting. That was mostly because Stefan was there, but even before that, I could sense a change in her demeanour.'

'What was Stefan doing at a meeting of the regency council?'

'Hector must have invited him. Stefan is now the Duke of Torrent.'

'What?'

'This is what happens if you miss the meetings, Walter. If you had been there, then the three of us could have blocked Hector's proposal. But no, you got drunk instead.'

'It was a mistake.'

'How many more mistakes are you going to make? It breaks my heart to see you like this.'

Walter turned his gaze away from her. 'I am responsible for my own actions; I accept that. What I am going to say next doesn't alter that fact, and I'm not trying to make excuses for my behaviour. I'm telling you this because there is no one else who will understand.'

'I'm listening.'

'Hector paid Lothar to keep me drunk.'

She narrowed her eyes. 'What?'

'I don't know how else to say it, Killie. For three years, Hector has been slipping extra money to Lothar. In return, Lothar had to do his best to encourage me to keep drinking. I'm so stupid. I actually thought he was my friend. He was my only friend. All those times we spent together, and he was working for Hector all along. I found out last night, and that's why I got drunk, even though I knew I shouldn't.'

'I don't know what to say.'

'There is nothing you can say that will make me feel any better.'

'Walter, this might sound mean, but I want you to start acting like the King's Champion. Abigone and I need you. The realm needs you. If we don't stop Hector, then only the spirits know what he will do to Upper Down. If the three of us are united, then we stand a chance, but if we stay divided, then we are finished. Wash, shave, and put on a clean uniform. Do you want me to fetch some food for you?'

He shook his head.

Kilbride stood. 'Get up, Walter.'

'Tell me something first,' he said. 'If I hadn't acted like a cold-hearted prick when you returned from Greater Down, would you have slept with Hector?'

'I think you know the answer to that.'

'I still want to hear you say it.'

'No, Walter, I wouldn't have slept with him. It was you I wanted. Hector has never been my friend; whereas you...? You meant the world to me. And then... then you decided that you would drink yourself to death rather than be in my company. You hurt me, Walter, you hurt me deeply.' She wiped her eyes. 'I know that I've made mistakes that hurt you, too, but we have the chance for a fresh start; we have the chance to be friends again. Can we put the past behind us?'

'Not all of the past,' he said. 'I want to remember the years when we did everything together.'

'That was a long time ago. We have both changed since then.'

'Not everything has changed,' he said. He got to his feet, then he leaned a hand against a wall to steady himself. For a moment, Kilbride thought he was going to throw up over the floor, then he staggered through to the other room. She stood by the bedroom door, and watched as he poured water into a basin, his back to her. He pulled off his bloody tunic, and washed himself; then he began to shave.

'You should get your shutters fixed,' she said, her eyes on his bare skin.

'I know.'

'I told Abigone that I would never let Stefan marry her.'

'You and me both.'

'I know that you and Abigone have never had much time for each other; in fact, I was surprised when you punched Stefan. Why did you do it? Was it because you were drunk?'

'Abigone is family,' he said, 'and Stefan was about to humiliate her in public. I know you don't approve of violence, but I would do it again.'

'I wouldn't say that I completely disapproved of what you did. Stefan, on the other hand, has sworn to revenge himself upon you.'

Walter shrugged as he continued to shave the stubble from his face. 'I couldn't give a shit what he thinks. Ow! Fuck.'

'What is it?'

'I must have nicked the wound on my chin. It's bleeding again.'

She walked over to him and picked up a towel. She gazed up at his chin, then pressed the towel to the wound.

'Maybe you shouldn't shave that bit for a while,' she said. 'You might suit a beard.'

He looked down at her, and their gazes met. Kilbride tried to smile. She was standing too close to him, she realised, their bodies only inches apart.

'I should get ready to meet the Mountain Rangers,' he said, taking the towel from her hand.

'Of course,' she said, taking a step back, and keeping her gaze away from his bare skin.

'I will be gone for a couple of days,' he went on, 'and there's no guarantee that I will return alive. I think my brother hopes I will fall to the imperial army.'

'Then make sure he doesn't get what he wants,' she said. 'You are no good to me dead.'

He smiled. 'That's nice to hear.'

'You know what I mean.' She leaned up and kissed him on the cheek. 'Good luck, Walter.'

She turned, and walked out of his apartment. She paused by the top of the stairs for a moment, all too aware of the feelings she had been suppressing in Walter's proximity. Was she falling in love with him; or, more truthfully, *back* in love with him – for she had adored Walter when they had been teenagers, before Hector had returned from years of military training to steal her from him. Were her feelings for Walter being rekindled? No. She would not allow that to happen. Walter had let her down so many times in the past, and there was no reason to believe that he wouldn't do so again. She took a slow breath, and hardened her heart. She would trust Walter, and she would be his friend, but nothing more. The boy she had loved in her youth had gone forever, replaced by a bitter and cynical man who turned to drink to solve his problems. The last thing she needed in the middle of a crisis was for her feelings to get in the way of what needed to be done.

And if the crisis passed?

She left the question unanswered, and hurried down the stairs.

CHAPTER 19
PREDICTIONS

Kendril Wall, Upper Down – 14th Day of Lamenta 107

'They could be bolt-throwing machines,' said Stefan, as he and Hector stood by the battlements of the Kendril Wall. 'I have seen them used over by the eastern coast. One steel bolt could pierce three men.'

'But they would be unlikely to pierce this wall,' said Hector.

The two men watched as more of the strange wagons were hauled into position towards the front of the imperial camp. The engineers and soldiers clustered round them were staying out of bow range, which meant that they were also out of the range of Hector's Master abilities. Around some of the wagons, wooden wedges were being hammered into place behind each wheel, to stop them from rolling back down the steep slope; while soldiers were attempting to level the ground beneath others, by packing earth into a stable platform.

'I don't think the imperial army realised the pass would be so steep,' said Hector. 'Whatever the purpose of those machines, perhaps they only operate correctly when level.'

Several wagons loaded with timber beams were pulled up the slope, and the imperial engineers gathered round them. Soldiers with shovels were digging into the earth, and then a dozen timber beams were laid out over the flattened ground. One of the strange wagons was pulled onto the new platform, and its tarpaulin cover was removed.

'There it is,' said Stefan. 'What do you make of that, Duke?'

Hector narrowed his eyes. The object that had been revealed seemed to consist of a long metal tube, painted black, and reinforced by several iron bands that ringed its circumference. The tube was closed at the end nearest the wheels, and the open end was aiming upwards at an angle.

'They intend to shoot something at us,' said Stefan, 'but what?'

'I see no levers or tension ropes,' said Hector. 'How would any projectile be propelled through the air? Perhaps flames issue from the hole?'

'I doubt they will try to burn the Wall, Duke,' said Stefan.

Hector shook his head. 'There is little use in speculating. We should discuss matters of which we are knowledgeable.'

'Such as?'

'I hear that more Westlanders have fled Twinbrook.'

Stefan shrugged. 'Only a few dozen.'

'Might more leave when they discover that you have been elevated to Duke of Torrent?'

'That is likely, but what of it? Those choosing to leave are jealous of what I have achieved. Last night, Chief Rymont withdrew from his beer hall, claiming that I had gone soft. He ordered his warriors to depart Twinbrook with him, but more than half stayed. Every one of them joined my war band. I am not the only Westlander who wishes to put down roots in Upper Down, Duke. Here is my prediction – I was the first Westlander to pledge allegiance to the boy-king, but I will not be the last. When the others see how successful I have become; when they hear tales of how rich my men have grown, they will return. By that time, my forces will be in complete control of Twinbrook.' He glanced down at the imperial army. 'Tell me – is Abigone usually so quiet? She barely said a word during our meeting.'

'I think she might have been a little intimidated by your presence.'

'Intimidated? Why? I have never harmed her. I have never even raised my voice in her company.'

'Many Westlanders seem like giants to the local population, and you are no exception, my friend. Also, did you not try to forcibly remove her veil?'

'I see. She thinks I am a savage. Does she not understand that I wish to settle here? By tying myself to the Royal Family, I am giving up my old life; does she not appreciate this?'

'Give her a little time. She is young, and her father ensured that she led a quiet, undisturbed life in the palace. She has never been intimate with a man; do not expect too much too soon.'

'I will expect nothing until our wedding night,' said Stefan. 'Now that I am a duke, there is little to prevent my marriage to Abigone from going ahead.'

'The ceremony itself requires some preparation. I want the entire population of Torrent and Twinbrook to see you and your bride be wed. Huge quantities of wine, food and beer need to be ordered, so that the citizens enjoy the occasion. There is also the wedding dress to consider. Shoemakers, tailors, seamstresses, florists – the list is practically endless. I want this to be an event that lives long in the memories of our people – the uniting of the Westlanders with the royalty of Upper Down. It cannot be rushed.'

Stefan frowned.

Hector saw soldiers approach from the stairs leading up to the battlements, and he noticed Lothar in their midst.

'Excuse me for a few moments, my friend,' he said to Stefan, then he strode up to the soldiers.

'This Mountain Ranger wishes to speak with you, my lord,' said one of the soldiers.

Hector inclined his head. 'Leave us.'

The soldiers saluted, then they made their way back down the stairs, leaving Lothar alone with the duke.

'What are you doing here?' said Hector. 'You were under explicit instructions not to be seen with me. What if word gets back to Walter?'

Lothar kept his gaze lowered. 'Apologies, my lord,' he said, 'but I have been forced to resign my position as aide to the King's Champion. That is why I am here.'

'You resigned? Why?'

'Lord Walter has discovered the truth, my lord.'

Hector shook his head. 'Well, I suppose three years was a good run. What made him suspicious?'

'Perhaps I was too persistent, my lord. Lord Walter grew angry at my behaviour.'

'Does he know that I was paying you?'

Lothar glanced away.

'You will answer my question,' said Hector. 'Is my brother aware that I was paying you to keep him inebriated?'

Lothar kept his head down, unable to meet the duke's glare. 'Yes, my lord.'

'How?'

'Because... I told him, my lord. I had no choice.'

Anger flared in Hector's mind. 'There is always a choice, you fool. You could have denied it. Damn it – what if he tells the other regents about this? You told him?'

'I have been doing this for three years, my lord, but never in the midst of a serious crisis, such as the one Upper Down is currently facing. Shouldn't the King's Champion be sober at a time like this?'

'You dare to second guess my orders? When I chose you for this role, you swore to me that you would not allow any personal feelings to get in the way of your duty. Is that what happened? Did you start to pity my useless brother? Or worse, did you become his friend?'

Lothar said nothing.

'I should have you thrown from the battlements for this act of betrayal,' said Hector. 'If you were married, I would have your wife and children sold into slavery. I know where your parents dwell, Lothar; perhaps I should punish them for your disobedience.'

'I did what I thought was right, my lord.'

'You disregarded my orders! I gave you clear instructions, and you did the opposite. Should I give you one last opportunity to redeem yourself, Commander Lothar? Do you deserve a second chance?'

'I am at your mercy, my lord.'

'You shall undertake one last task for me, or I will be forced to evict your elderly parents from their home. Do you understand?'

'What task do you wish me to perform, my lord?'

Hector clasped his hands behind his back, and gazed out over the battlements. 'The Mountain Rangers are departing this afternoon.'

'Yes, my lord.'

'You are a Mountain Ranger, are you not? You didn't resign from them also, did you?'

'No, my lord.'

'Accompany them on their operation,' said Hector.

'But, my lord, the King's Champion may object to my presence. He...'

'Are you refusing to even try?'

'No, my lord.'

'Join the Rangers, and cross the mountains with them. When you engage with the enemy, ensure that Walter does not return to Torrent.'

Lothar's face paled. 'You want me to assassinate the King's Champion, my lord?'

'Did I use that word? I don't care how it is done. It may be that Walter dies heroically fighting the imperial army, in which case you need do nothing. He might be captured, or he might lose his footing and fall from a cliff. There is only one thing you need to know – if my brother returns to Torrent, I will hold you responsible. In the meantime, I will send soldiers to keep watch upon your parents' home. If Walter reappears, your mother and father will be dragged into the street, and their house will be razed to the ground; and you, Commander Lothar, shall hang. If, on the other hand, Walter falls in battle, I will see that you are handsomely rewarded. I will take you into my ducal guard, and promote you. This is the choice I am offering you; what is your reply?'

'I will do it, my lord.'

Hector smiled. 'Perhaps my investment in you has not been wasted. Dismissed.'

Lothar saluted, then he turned and strode away. Hector walked back to where Stefan was standing, and they gazed down at the work going on around the wagons, which had been manoeuvred into several rows, all facing the Wall. More level platforms were being constructed from timber and packed earth, and hundreds of imperial soldiers were labouring with shovels and pickaxes. The road to the rear of the wagons was clogged with more supplies trying to move forward, while several dozen tents had been removed and sent back down the lines, to clear space.

'I count sixty-four of the machines,' said the Westlander chief. 'They have only removed the tarpaulin from one, but I assume that the others contain the same metal device. You were wrong, Duke.'

'How so?'

'You told me that the rumours of a secret weapon were unfounded.'

'I still believe that to be the case. You made a prediction earlier, and here is mine – those machines will roar with fire and noise, as though Prince Valentino has brought a dozen dragons with him out of the pages of legend, but they will inflict no actual damage upon the Wall. They are designed to terrify us.'

'If that were so, then a mere handful of such wagons would suffice. Would Valentino have gone to such trouble and expense to drag sixty-four machines up here, simply to scare us?'

'I wouldn't like to guess what passes through the mind of the illustrious prince.'

Another wagon was dragged onto a finished platform. Its tarpaulin covering was removed, revealing a second metal tube, identical to the first. All along the battlements of the Kendril Wall, soldiers from the militia were watching the bustling activity by the front of the imperial camp, but Hector did not perceive any signs of fear or panic on their faces. A large group of engineers gathered around the two finished platforms, and there was much pointing and debate among them. The angle of one of the tubes was adjusted several times, as two more platforms were completed. A whistle blew, and many of the soldiers withdrew a few dozen paces, leaving only the engineers. A cart was dragged up the slope, and the engineers got to work, some kneeling by the base of the first tube, while others carried something to its open end. A hush descended as the engineers talked again, and then most stepped down from the platform, leaving only a handful standing by the metal tube. A red flag was raised, and the engineers covered their ears with their hands.

Nothing happened for a few moments, then a loud crack echoed off the sides of the cliffs. The metal tube recoiled, as smoke belched from the open end, then it rolled off the platform and down the hill, crushing several engineers. The metal by the open end had split, and two of the bands ringing it had burst open.

Several of the militia soldiers up on the battlements had cowered back a step or two from the noise of the explosion, but many started to laugh as they gazed at the wreckage of the first tube.

A green flag was raised, and hundreds of imperial soldiers got back to work. The damaged metal tube was dragged towards the camp, while more progress was made on several other platforms. Hector counted the bodies of four dead engineers carried away on stretchers, while others had been injured and were also taken away. Within ten minutes, another metal tube had been hauled up to replace the first one, its platform reinforced with more timber beams. The red flag was raised again, and the workers retreated, leaving engineers gathered round two of the tubes. Their angles were adjusted, and thick beams were hammered into the ground behind each wheel. The engineers covered their ears, and both tubes were activated. The twin roars of noise sent clusters of birds wheeling into the sky, and Hector stared down into the valley to see if any projectiles had issued from the open ends.

Stefan pointed. 'Look there, Duke. Something gouged its way through the grass by the stream.'

'Did you see what it was?' he said.

'No. I saw smoke come from the tubes, and then I saw the soil being ripped asunder. Perhaps it is time to consider our options.'

Hector laughed. 'A bit of earth gets torn up, and you are panicking, my friend? The Kendril Wall is impregnable.'

'I am not panicking, Duke. What we are witnessing is the process of trial and error. The imperial army will continue to make adjustments until one of those... things hits the Wall. At that point, we will know the truth of the matter.'

'My lord?' said a voice.

Hector turned his head, and saw Amery waiting for him. 'Yes?'

'May we speak in private, my lord?'

Hector sighed, then he accompanied Amery out of earshot of Stefan.

'What is it?' said Hector.

'I am uncomfortable in my new role, my lord,' said Amery. 'I was trained as a lawyer, not a spy, and I feel that some of your latest requests have crossed the line into the realms of illegality.'

Hector rolled his eyes. 'Save me your moralising; what have you discovered?'

Amery frowned. 'Princess Kilbride was seen entering and leaving Lord Walter's quarters an hour ago, my lord.'

'Ah, so Her Highness did as I suspected? She visited my brother, eh? Have the Mountain Rangers assembled?'

'Yes, my lord. They were gathering in the Royal Parkland just as I left the palace. I asked them where they were going, but they told me that it was none of my business.'

Amery's gaze strayed down to where the imperial engineers were working on the metal tubes, and his eyes widened. 'Sweet spirits,' he muttered.

'Have you seen these devices before, Amery?' said Hector.

'Never, my lord, but... but I saw drawings when I was in the city of Klef Mordain, and I heard the many rumours that were circulating.'

'You have seen drawings of these tubes?'

'They are named cannon, my lord,' he said. 'The artist who drew them claimed to have seen them employed in the siege of Osbruck, though few believed his tale. He also claimed that they used fire to shoot metal balls at great velocity. The balls ripped holes in the defences of Osbruck, allowing the imperial army to enter the city.'

'Don't get over-excited, Amery,' said Hector. 'I have seen the defences of Osbruck, and they were flimsy compared to the Kendril Wall. Even if what this artist claimed is true, a few little metal balls will not inflict much damage. Besides, one of these devices has already exploded, killing several engineers. They are clearly unreliable; more of a hazard to the enemy than to us.'

'All the same, my lord, it would be prudent to devise a plan to evacuate Torrent.'

'Don't be ridiculous. It would not matter if Valentino had brought a thousand cannon to this ravine; the Wall of Kendril can withstand anything.'

At that moment, another twin roar emerged from the two working devices, and Amery flinched. Hector gazed out, and saw splintered rocks tumble down from a location high up on the side of the cliffs, showering the ground below in rubble.

Amery pointed. 'That's what one of those balls did to the cliff, my lord. It is only a matter of time before the imperial army calculate the correct angle and range to strike the Wall. And then, then they will fire with every cannon at once.'

'Go back to the Royal Palace, Amery,' said Hector. 'I will not have you stand here if all you are going to do is talk like a defeatist. Send me a message when the Mountain Rangers have departed.'

Amery bowed, then he rushed away, racing down the steps of the staircase. Hector shook his head, and went back to Stefan.

'Did you see what happened to the cliff?' said the chief. 'Something tore out over a ton of rock.'

'It was a metal ball, apparently,' said Hector. 'Amery has heard some wild rumours from the east.'

'What I am looking at is not a rumour, Duke.'

Hector smiled. 'Are the engineers having to repair the cannon on the left?'

'The what?'

'They are called cannon, my friend. Look – the reinforcing bands around one have split. Dear, oh dear. They have been firing for less than thirty minutes, and already two have been damaged. At this rate, they will have ruined them all by sunset.'

The sole operational cannon fired again. Something flew over Hector's head, and went clean through the gap above the Wall. He strode to the other side, and gazed down at Torrent, along with several dozen others from the militia. Hector cursed under his breath. The ball had struck the cobbles fifty yards from the Wall, tearing out a long gouge; then it had passed through a wagon, ripping it in half, before smashing into the side of a house, leaving a hole in the timber wall a yard wide. Citizens began to emerge from their homes to see what had caused the noise, while members of the Wall Militia were gazing at the damage. The cannon cracked again, and Hector caught a glimpse of the projectile before it crashed into the front of a tavern over a hundred yards from the Wall. Smoke emerged from the hole in the tavern wall, followed by flames, and the town bells began to ring.

A cold chill seized Hector's heart, but he kept his features calm and confident as he strode back to rejoin Stefan.

'There's nothing to worry about,' he said. 'They might hit a few houses, but that does not mean they will breach the Wall.'

Stefan said nothing, his gaze on the rows of cannon. Ten of the metal devices were being hauled up onto newly-finished platforms of earth and timber beams, and their tarpaulin covers were removed. With work complete on the first row, the soldiers moved back a few yards, and began to repeat the process, digging out earth to fashion level platforms for the second line of cannon. Over by the damaged device, engineers were fitting new metal reinforcement bands to the tube. A forge had been set up between the second and third rows of cannon, and blacksmiths were hard at work, hammering out a supply of new bands. A long line of wagons appeared, and soldiers began to unload their cargo of smooth metal balls. Each took one man to carry, and soon there were small heaps of the balls lying behind every cannon in the front row. The engineers moved to the newly-uncovered cannon, and began to make adjustments to their angles and positions, while the militia on the battlements watched in silence. Metal balls were rammed down each tube, then the engineers covered their ears.

One of the new cannon fired, and its ball struck the Kendril Wall with a loud smack, raising a sustained cheer from the imperial soldiers. Stefan and Hector glanced down. Twenty feet below them, a chunk of the Wall had been gouged out, and several large stone blocks were cracked. Hector stared in disbelief.

'It is a harbinger,' whispered Stefan. 'If one cannon ball can do that, what will sixty do, if they fire all day?'

Hector remained silent, too shocked to put his feelings into words.

'We should order a swift counter-attack,' Stefan went on. 'If we open the gates and send out everything we have, we can destroy those weapons before they destroy us.'

Ten more cannon roared out before Hector could respond, and the battlements shook under his feet as the balls struck the Wall. One of them ripped through a turret, smashing it to pieces, and killing two militia soldiers who had been leaning against its stonework; while others peppered the front of the Wall. A gatehouse tower was hit twice, and the area above the tall wooden gates was pounded. Hector cowered behind the battlements for a moment, then he leaned over and looked down. The gates were still standing, but if they were targeted by the cannon, they would be smashed into pieces.

'Reinforce the gatehouse!' Hector cried. 'Fill the hall behind the gates with rubble and block it. Call out every member of the Town Militia and the Royal Guard, and put them to work - the gates must stand!'

The militia soldiers on the battlements stared at him, their eyes betraying the onset of panic, then an officer saluted, and the men raced off for the stairs. Eleven cannon roared out, and Hector ducked his head below the parapet as the balls slammed into the Kendril Wall. The gatehouse tower was hit again, and it toppled over, falling backwards into the courtyard between the Wall and the edge of Torrent, showering the soldiers on the ground with fragments of masonry. Of all the men on the battlements, only Stefan was still standing tall, his eyes never leaving the rows of cannon arrayed against them.

Hector hurried to the chief's side as the militia rushed down the stairs.

'We should pull back, my friend,' Hector said.

'What about the counter-attack?'

'It is already too late for that. I have ordered the gates to be filled in with rubble.'

Stefan shook his head. 'Look – the cannon are overheating. The engineers keep pouring buckets of water over the metal tubes. Do you see the steam rise? Each one needs to cool down after firing. The end is coming, but we still have time.'

Hector took a breath, embarrassed by the chief's calm demeanour. He gazed down at the imperial camp, and saw engineers working on the first row of cannon, while soldiers continued to construct the platforms for the rear rows. An officer arrived by the first row, surrounded by imperial officials, and the engineers bowed their heads as they answered the officer's questions.

'Perhaps your brother can do something,' Stefan went on. 'When will his Mountain Rangers be arriving in the ravine?'

'If they are setting off now,' Hector said, 'then they will appear somewhere in the valley later tonight, or perhaps early tomorrow.'

'The Wall will still be standing by then,' said Stefan. 'Calm yourself, Duke. I can see the fear in your eyes; if your men also see it, they will despair. I hear your castle up on the Ridden estate is reputed to be unassailable; is that correct?'

'Castle Ridden was designed to withstand any attack from the Westlanders; its walls cannot repel cannon fire. However, you may be right. The castle stands upon a high promontory of rock, with only one path leading up to its gates. The imperial army would find it very difficult to deploy its cannon.'

'Then you know what to do, Duke. Make no public announcements, but get ready to leave Torrent if the worst happens. I am entrusting you with the safety of my bride-to-be; and, as fellow dukes of this realm, we must look to the safety of the boy-king.'

'Of course,' said Hector. 'Will you be joining me in Castle Ridden, if I decide to leave Torrent?'

'I will not be confined within a castle, Duke. If the Wall is breached, my men and I will take to our horses, and conduct the war in the manner to which we are accustomed. I do not fear cannon upon the open plains of Upper Down. The imperial army will chase you all the way to your estate, and we shall strike them from the rear.' Stefan smiled. 'You see? Trust in me, Duke, and we shall prevail. This is not over.'

Hector turned away. Fleeing from Torrent would be the most shameful action he had ever undertaken, and the thought appalled him. He was over-reacting, as was Stefan. So, the imperial army had been able to damage the great Wall of Kendril? They had eight yards of stone to break through before any panic was justified. He gazed down at the cannon. The engineers were still engaged in a discussion with the officer, and the twelve unveiled machines were sitting idle. Behind them, the first three platforms of the second row had been completed, and devices were being dragged up onto them. Hector glanced at the position of the sun, which was hovering over the horizon to the west. At their current rate, the soldiers and engineers would have over sixty cannon in position to fire by the time the sun rose again, and then the true bombardment would commence.

No, he wasn't over-reacting. His mind raced as he thought through amendments to his plan. He would have to bring forward certain aspects, and he would have to work quickly.

'I am going to the ducal palace,' he said.

'A wise idea, Duke,' said Stefan. 'You will need to think of a good excuse to go there, so that no one thinks you are intending to abandon Torrent.'

'I already have a good excuse,' he said. 'My wife is due to arrive in Torrent tomorrow.'

'You summoned your wife here in the midst of a crisis?'

'I have my reasons,' he said.

The two men stared out over the battlements, then Hector strode away.

CHAPTER 20
PRESAGE

Torrent, Upper Down – 14th Day of Lamenta 107

Abigone quickened her pace as she walked along a palace corridor towards Kilbride's quarters. She was being trailed by over a dozen courtiers, and soldiers from the Royal Guard, all of whom were as keen as the princess to find out what was happening at the Kendril Wall. The town bells had been ringing for over an hour, and rumours were spreading throughout the palace. Some were saying that Duke Hector had been slain, while others maintained that imperial soldiers had already entered Torrent. All of it seemed like nonsense to Abigone's ears, but without hard facts, the palace staff were believing whatever they heard.

Abigone turned a corner, and almost ran into Kilbride, who was leading a similar number of courtiers through the palace.

'I was coming to find you, sister,' said Kilbride.

'And I, you,' said Abigone. 'Do you know what's going on?'

'The Royal Guard has been summoned to the Kendril Wall,' Kilbride said, 'along with the Town Militia.' She eyed the large group of courtiers, who were hanging on to her every word. 'Perhaps we should speak privately,' she went on. 'Your quarters are much closer than mine; shall we go there?'

'Princess Hygilt is in my rooms,' said Abigone. 'Is she permitted to hear what you have to say?'

'Her presence might turn out to be rather informative,' said Kilbride. 'Shall we?'

The two princesses got underway again, with Abigone retracing her steps to her quarters.

'Did Walter leave on time?' Abigone said.

'I assume so,' said Kilbride.

'One of my courtiers informed me that you were seen lurking at his end of the palace.'

'I don't lurk, sister.'

'Did you visit him?' said Abigone.

'I did.'

'And?'

'And what? He was well, if that's what you mean. A bump on his chin.'

'That's good. I was worried he might have been seriously hurt.'

They reached her quarters and entered, leaving the crowd of courtiers behind. Hygilt was sitting on a rug playing with Tulip, who ran over to Abigone and rubbed his flanks against her legs. Abigone picked him up, and led Kilbride over to her couch.

'We have a visitor,' she said to Hygilt.

The imperial princess stood, then curtsied before Kilbride. 'Ma'am.'

Kilbride tried to smile, but her eyes seemed distant. She glanced down, then took a breath. 'The rumours regarding a secret weapon appear to be true.'

Abigone stared at her sister, while a strange expression passed over Hygilt's features.

'What kind of weapon?' said Abigone.

'I have heard mixed reports,' said Kilbride, 'but the situation is serious enough for Duke Hector to summon every member of the various militias to the Kendril Wall.'

'But he can't order the Royal Guard to leave the palace,' said Abigone. 'Who will protect us?'

'I negotiated with the commanders of the Guards, sister. They are leaving two hundred soldiers here to defend the palace. We will be fine. I am rather more concerned about the Wall. Do you remember those odd-looking carriages we saw this morning, before the emissaries from Prince Valentino arrived?'

'Yes.'

'Each wagon is actually a long metal tube on wheels; and each tube is capable of launching a projectile with more force than any catapult. I have it on good authority from a member of the Royal Artificers that the Wall cannot withstand a large and sustained bombardment from these devices. He estimated that we have four or five days before the Kendril Wall is breached, though perhaps reduced to rubble would be a more apt description.'

'No,' said Abigone. 'The Kendril Wall cannot be breached. For five hundred years...'

'I know the history, Abbie. Unfortunately, no army has ever brought these... metal tubes to the Wall until now.'

'They are called cannon,' said Hygilt, 'and your artificer is quite correct.'

'Have you heard of these machines?' said Abigone.

'This is why I thought her presence might be useful, sister,' said Kilbride. 'Sit, Princess Hygilt, and tell us what you know.'

Kilbride and Hygilt joined Abigone on the couch.

'We have been using cannon for decades,' said Hygilt, 'but the people of Upper Down don't seem interested in what happens beyond their frontiers. If you had travelled in the south, you would have heard about cannon for yourself.'

'You have been using them for decades?' said Kilbride.

'Yes,' said Hygilt, 'although we have known the secret of black powder for much longer than that.'

'Black powder?' said Kilbride.

'That's what we call the substance that causes the explosions,' said Hygilt. 'When Sanctos was a province of the Elestian Empire, we weren't allowed to use black powder to make weapons. The Elestians burned hundreds of old books that contained information about building cannon, and other devices; but when we rebelled against them, we started studying it again, in secret. It has taken us a hundred years to produce cannon capable of destroying a town wall. Ships were easier.'

'Ships?' said Abigone.

Hygilt smiled. 'How else do you think the Sanctian fleet was able to defeat the navies of every other kingdom along the coast? We had warships fitted with cannon. Nowadays, some of our bigger ships have dozens of them.'

'The nearest coastline is over a thousand miles from here,' said Kilbride. 'We heard a few stories that Sanctos ruled the ocean, but we never discovered why.'

'Well, now you know,' said Hygilt. 'How many cannon has my grandfather brought to the Kendril Wall?'

'Over sixty.'

'Then the Wall is doomed. It will take a few days, as the artificer said; but the outcome is inevitable.'

'You knew about this,' said Abigone, 'but yet you never told me?'

'I like you, Abigone, but I am a prisoner here. And, if I had told you about cannon, would you have believed me?'

'Probably not.'

'What are their weaknesses?' said Kilbride.

Hygilt shrugged. 'I said I knew about them; I didn't say I was an expert. I have seen a few firing during tests. They can overheat, and if they get too hot, they can explode.'

'One has already exploded,' said Kilbride. 'Or, at least, that's what a rather panicky soldier told me.'

'Several might explode or get damaged over the next few days,' Hygilt said. 'That won't alter the outcome. Wherever the cannon go, forges and workshops always follow. There will be teams of engineers working day and night to repair any damaged machines.'

Kilbride closed her eyes, and Abigone studied her sister's face. Kilbride looked tired, and close to despair.

'What is black powder made from?' said Abigone.

'I'm not really sure what goes into it,' said Hygilt. 'In the old days, we used it to make bright and colourful explosions in the sky; we still use it for that – they are very pretty, if a little noisy. Tulip wouldn't like them; most animals get scared by the sound.'

'I presume it burns brightly,' said Kilbride.

Hygilt nodded. 'Yes. If you touch a lit match to it, it burns very quickly, with a loud bang. I once saw an engineer whose right hand had been blown clean off by a badly-timed explosion. It's very dangerous, and I wasn't allowed to go near it.'

'And it can propel iron balls through the air?'

'Yes.'

'What will we do?' said Abigone.

'Despite what Princess Hygilt said, the outcome is not inevitable, sister. Duke Hector's orders were to block up the gatehouse with rubble. Even if the Wall falls, it doesn't mean that the imperial army will be able to get into Torrent. Still, we must take a few sensible precautions. The safety of Alfie is paramount.' She stood. 'I shall return to my quarters, and start planning a possible evacuation for His Majesty.'

'To where?' said Abigone.

'I don't think information of that nature should be revealed to our imperial guest,' she said. 'Sit tight for now.'

'But you were going to come here tonight,' Abigone said. 'We were going to discuss Hector and Walter.'

'I fully intend to keep that appointment, sister,' she said. 'Expect me around midnight.'

Kilbride walked to the door and let herself out.

'You should surrender,' said Hygilt. 'I will tell my grandfather that you treated me with compassion and kindness.'

'You didn't hear the ultimatum this morning,' said Abigone. 'Even if we had surrendered then, Upper Down would still be occupied and stripped of its property. They were going to merge us into Greater Down, and the kingdom would be abolished. If we surrender now, then who knows what punishments will be devised. Dear spirits, is this the end?'

'If my grandfather's army enters Torrent,' Hygilt said, 'then no matter what happens, stay by my side. I will make sure that you are not personally held responsible for the wicked things done by this realm. As far as I can see, most of that was done by your father. And Hector. If Hector hadn't killed Alfgang the Pius, then I would probably be on my way home by now, and cannon wouldn't be attacking the Kendril Wall.'

'What about Kilbride and Walter?' Abigone said. 'Will you speak up for them?'

'I don't really know either of them, but I will try.'

'Will your grandfather listen to you? Do you get on well with him?'

'Oh yes. He's got lots of grandchildren, but I used to live with him.'

'And the emperor?'

Hygilt shrugged. 'I don't see him as much.'

'You never talk about your parents.'

Hygilt looked away.

'Are they still alive?'

'Yes. Well, I think so. They were exiled from Sanctos years ago. The emperor made them leave their children behind; that's why I became close to my grandfather. My big brother is in the army.'

'Why were your parents exiled?'

'I don't want to talk about it. Shall we go to the library?'

'What, now?'

'Yes, now. Why not? It will help take your mind off things.'

'Maybe we should wait here in case Kilbride comes back.'

'Your sister will be busy, and she has already told you that she will be back just before midnight.'

They stood, and Abigone draped Tulip over her shoulder. She picked up a canvas bag and slipped it over her other shoulder, then they walked to the front door of the apartment. Abigone opened it to find several courtiers standing outside in the corridor.

'We are going to the library,' Abigone said. 'Princess Hygilt will require someone to carry the books she selects.'

A young courtier curtsied, and they set off along the corridor, trailed by several guards. They descended a flight of stairs, and walked to the library, which was open and unguarded. Abigone gestured for the soldiers to remain outside, then she entered the chamber, followed by Hygilt and the young courtier.

'Oh, this is nice,' said Hygilt, as she gazed around.

Abigone smiled. 'I thought you were going to say that it was too small, compared to what you are used to.'

'The library in the Imperial Palace is enormous,' said Hygilt, 'but the old Elestian Empire destroyed most of the books a century ago, and it has never completely recovered. There are whole shelves which are empty; it makes me sad whenever I see them.'

'Did they destroy every book about black powder?'

'Among many other things. Do you remember what I told you about the poets? I don't think the Elestians wanted people to know too much. My grandfather has a theory about why they destroyed so many books – do you want to hear it?'

'All right.'

'Well, he told me that the Elestians relied so much upon Masters and Makers that they deliberately neglected many areas of study. More than that, though, they tried to stop other people from studying subjects that they didn't like, so that no one could become more powerful than them. That was one reason why they disapproved of Sanctos; we allowed people to study whatever they wanted. That's why they came to our island and destroyed most of our books.'

'Does you grandfather remember it happening?'

Hygilt gave her a funny look. 'It took place over a hundred years ago. My grandfather isn't that old.'

Abigone smiled, then she walked further into the library. 'Kilbride spent a large part of her childhood in here. So did Walter. Did you know that they were best friends when they were young? If they weren't in here, they were out in the parkland, playing. I wish I'd had a cousin the same age.'

'Are you glad I persuaded you to write him that note?'

Abigone nodded. 'What type of books are you looking for?'

'The ones you can't find in Sanctos,' Hygilt said. 'Ones about Master and Makers.'

Abigone glanced around, and found a row of shelves containing the books Hygilt wanted. They walked up to them.

'Why can't you find those sorts of books in Sanctos?' she said.

'Because of my great uncle's grandfather.'

'Who?'

'The first emperor of Sanctos,' said Hygilt. 'When the Elestians destroyed the contents of our libraries, they replaced the books with volumes on Masters and Makers. And then, when we regained our independence, the first emperor destroyed all of those books. It was a stupid decision, in my opinion. Even if Masters and Makers are our enemies, why shouldn't we be able to learn about them?'

Abigone eyed the shelves, then she pulled out a thin volume. 'This is a good introduction.'

Hygilt frowned. 'It looks like a children's book. I want something that will take me more than twenty minutes to read.'

Abigone flushed slightly. The book she was holding was one of the very few on the subject she had read. She pushed it back onto the shelf, and Hygilt pointed at a far thicker tome.

'Is that one any good?'

'I don't know,' said Abigone. 'My knowledge in this area is... lacking.'

Hygilt gestured for the young courtier to approach, and then she started passing her large volumes to carry. Abigone wandered off to the far end of the shelves, and eyed the books. She picked out one entitled *Makers of Elestia*, and opened the cover. If the Kendril Wall was threatened, she told herself, then it might be a good idea to learn what she could about her neglected abilities. The volume had a selection of drawings near the beginning, showing some of the basic items that a young Maker could expect to summon – a key, a knife, a wooden toy, a spoon, a glass vase, and a whetstone were represented, among other objects. To Abigone's shame, she had never attempted to summon any of them. The volume was also rich in the invocations to the spirits that needed to be recited, and there were several pages filled with easy-to-remember rhymes about summoning. She skipped to the end of the book, and glanced at the appendix, which depicted a series of objects that only the most experienced and knowledgeable Makers could summon – a working catapult, a stone bridge to span a river, and, for the very best Makers, a live animal. Abigone shuddered at the thought. The text of the book advised Makers never to attempt to summon a living creature, as the difficulties were immense, and the chance of failure overwhelmingly likely. Get even the slightest detail wrong, and the summoned creature would be nothing more than a grisly heap of blood, flesh and bone matter. Worse, other living creatures within the radius of the Maker's powers would be stripped of their own flesh in order to create the summoned animal. It was a nightmarish thought, and Abigone closed the book.

'What have you chosen?' said Hygilt.

Abigone turned, and saw the young princess standing next to the courtier, who was weighed down by over a dozen large volumes. Abigone showed Hygilt the spine.

'*Makers of Elestia*?' said Hygilt. 'I might read that one, too. Why did you pick that?'

'No reason,' said Abigone.

Two soldiers from the Royal Guard burst into the library.

'Your Highnesses,' cried one; 'you must come with us at once.'

Abigone frowned. 'Why?'

'There is a disturbance in the Royal Parkland, ma'am.'

'What kind of disturbance?'

'Westlanders have scaled the walls of the parkland, and are approaching the palace, ma'am. We have orders to evacuate all members of the Royal Court to safety.'

'Have the Royal Guard been sent out to investigate?'

'Most of the Royal Guard have already left the palace to obey Duke Hector's summons, ma'am. They will be at the Kendril Wall by now.'

'But...'

'We don't have time for a debate, ma'am,' said the other soldier. 'We have to leave, now.'

The Guardsmen urged the two princesses and the courtier out into the corridor. It was deserted, and Abigone raised an eyebrow.

'Where are all the...'

'They've gone, ma'am,' said a soldier. 'Everyone is pulling out until reinforcements arrive.'

'Are the Westlanders inside the palace?'

A scream rose up from the corridor to the right, and the two soldiers drew their swords. A Westlander bounded into view, a giant war axe grasped in both hands, but he turned into a separate hallway without noticing the small party by the library door.

'Shit,' muttered one of the soldiers. 'They shouldn't be here by now. They must have circled past us.'

'The Courtyard of the Shrines?' said the other soldier.

'That sounds like our best bet. Your Highnesses, you must follow us. Stay close together, and remain quiet.'

'What about me?' said the courtier.

'Leave the books, and stay right behind the princesses.'

The courtier placed the books onto the floor, and Abigone slipped the volume she had taken into her bag, so that her hands were free. The two Guardsmen set off, and the others followed. They went down several deserted corridors, passing large halls, and wings where servants lived. They reached a junction with a skylight, and the soldiers slowed.

'Where the fuck are the Mountain Rangers?' said one.

'Half were sent on some operation,' said his colleague, 'and the others will be at the damn Wall.'

'This cannot be a coincidence. On the one night the Rangers and the Royal Guards are nowhere to be seen, and this is the time the Westlanders pick to attack the palace?'

'Where is my sister?' said Abigone. 'And the boy-king? Are they safe?'

'Yes, ma'am,' said one of the soldiers. 'They were escorted out of the palace twenty minutes ago. We were sent to your quarters, but you weren't there. Listen; we have a little way to go. As soon as we reach the Courtyard of the Shrines, we will run for the main gates. The soldiers there will see us, and you will be safe.'

'I'm scared,' said Hygilt.

Abigone took the girl's hand.

They rounded a corner, and came across the first body. An old courtier was lying on the floor with his head split open, and his brains were leaking from his broken skull. Hygilt gasped and put a hand to her face, as the soldiers led them around the body. When they turned the next corner, the carnage was far worse. Over a dozen courtiers and men from the Royal Guards were scattered over the length of the corridor. Many had been dismembered, and all had died violent deaths.

'Can we go another way?' said Abigone.

'Sorry, ma'am,' said one of the soldiers. 'This is the fastest route out of the palace.'

The two soldiers cajoled them onwards, and the two princesses stepped their way over and around the bloody remains. Abigone's left shoe went into a pool of sticky blood, and she left dark red footprints along the corridor. She gripped Hygilt's hand, as Tulip hissed at the bodies.

'Be quiet, Tulip,' Abigone whispered.

They passed the last body, and came to a halt as the sound of raised voices echoed through the stillness. One of the soldiers put a finger to his lips, and the small group sheltered by a wall, as the voices grew louder. Abigone listened, but she couldn't understand any of the words. Westlanders, it had to be. Westlanders were invading her home, and killing at will. Fear and anger rose in equal measure as she cowered next to the others by the wall. Her sister would be beside herself with worry. If only they had remained in Abigone's quarters, then they would probably be safely out of danger.

The sound of the voices peaked, and then began to fade again, and the two soldiers exhaled in relief. One of them signalled ahead, and the little party hurried onwards. Ahead of them, Abigone saw the door that led out into the Courtyard of the Shrines, and they almost broke into a run. When they were ten yards from the door, it opened, and a group of armed Westlanders ran inside. The two parties stared at each other, then Hygilt screamed.

The two soldiers raised their swords, but the Westlanders cut them both down within seconds, their long swords and war axes tearing through their flesh. The young courtier tried to pull Abigone away by the arm, and a Westlander crushed her skull with a mace blow. Abigone and Hygilt backed up against a wall as the Westlanders surrounded them.

'This is it, lads,' said one. 'This is what we came for. Grab them, and let's get the fuck out of here.'

One of them reached out for Abigone, and Tulip sprang at the man's face, his claws extended. There was a flash of blood, and the man cried out as Tulip tore his razor-sharp claws across the Westlander's eyes. The other Westlanders took a step back, then one grabbed Tulip by the throat and ripped him from the man's face. He threw him against a wall, and Tulip fell to the floor, motionless. Abigone screamed as two Westlanders took hold of her shoulders and dragged her away. She struggled, desperate to get to Tulip, but her strength was no match for the two huge men. Behind her, Hygilt was also trying to get free, and one of her escorts lifted her off the floor and carried her to the door. At the rear, the Westlander injured by Tulip was being helped along, his left eye a ragged and bloody mess.

They went through the door, and emerged into the lamplit courtyard. The sky was dark and clear, and the stars were shining down upon them, along with the Silver Moon, just three days from full. Over to the West, the Big Red Moon was also visible, sitting above the horizon, and the Westlanders hailed the sight of two of their gods. One of the men pulled a horn from over his shoulder, and gave three short blasts. He took a breath then repeated the signal, and Westlanders began to pour out of every door in the palace. Others took up the same signal, and the Westlanders ran towards the Royal Parkland. They left the lamps behind, and entered the darkness of the gardens, with only the light of the Silver Moon guiding their steps. More Westlanders joined them, and Abigone was dragged along in their midst. Whenever she stumbled or tripped, the two Westlanders flanking her would keep her upright. On Abigone's left, Hygilt had been slung over a man's shoulder, and he was gripping on to her legs as he ran. The parkland seemed to fill with retreating Westlanders, and all were running at full speed towards the wall on the far eastern side of the gardens. Abigone tried to look over her shoulder, but all she saw were more Westlanders.

After running for twenty minutes, the men slowed as they reached the perimeter wall of the parkland. Four Royal Guardsmen were lying dead next to a gate that had been forced open, and the Westlanders funnelled through. On the other side of the gate was open countryside, with the town of Twinbrook a few hundred yards to their left. Several ladders were still leaning against the outside of the wall, but they were ignored as the Westlanders reached two wagons parked by the side of a road. A man was sitting in the back of one of the wagons, watching as the Westlanders streamed out of the gate. His gaze landed on Abigone and Hygilt, and a wide smile spread across his features.

'*Two* princesses,' the man said, 'when I had only asked for one? The gods are with us tonight, boys.'

Abigone and Hygilt were shoved up against the wagon, and the man pulled them up into the back. The young imperial princess cowered against the wagon railings, her eyes distraught, as Abigone was shoved down next to her.

'Welcome back, Princess Hygilt,' said the man. 'And you must be Princess Abigone. Let me introduce myself, Abigone – my name is Chief Dravid, and I am here to claim what is mine. I captured Hygilt, and she belongs to me. You are just an unexpected bonus.' He laughed. 'Hey, lads, shall we let Stefan know that I've taken his bride?'

The Westlanders cheered and laughed.

'That's everyone back, Chief,' said one.

'Any casualties?' said Dravid.

'Three dead, Chief,' said the Westlander, 'and seven injured.'

'Get the injured up into the back of the other wagon,' said Dravid. 'It's time to get out of this shithole.'

The Westlanders helped their wounded comrades board the other wagon, then the drivers pulled on the reins to get both underway. Most of the Westlanders remained on foot, and they flanked the two wagons as they were pulled along the road.

Dravid sat down next to Abigone and Hygilt. He leered at them.

'What a rich prize this night,' he said. 'Whatever shall I do with two princesses?'

CHAPTER 21
RETURN

South of Torrent, Upper Down – 15th Day of Lamenta 107

The long column of men halted by the side of a steep valley, as the order came down from the front to extinguish all lamps. Light was growing in the east, signalling the approach of dawn, and after a long night trekking through the darkness, the mountains were emerging from the gloom.

Walter crouched by the others. He had no lamp, but the all-night march had sapped his energy, and the cold air had penetrated his bones. He glanced around at the sides of the valley, but had no idea where he was. He had allowed the scouts of the Mountain Rangers to lead the way, and had asked no questions about the route they had taken. Walter looked up, to see if rain was likely. The cloud cover had appeared not long after dusk, obscuring the light from the three moons, but it had remained dry.

A lieutenant was edging his way down the column. He saw Walter, and stopped by his side.

'Good morning, sir,' the officer said, as he knelt by the King's Champion. 'We are close to the main ravine. Once we ascend out of this valley, we shall be able to see a sizable stretch of the pass.'

'Is it time for me to move up to the front of the column?' said Walter.

'We think that would be a good idea, sir.'

The two men got to their feet, and began to walk up the rough path towards the head of the valley, passing the Rangers, who remained crouching by the side of the track. Several eyed Walter as he went past, and he wondered what they thought of his leadership. Any decision to attack the imperial army would be his to take – did they trust him to make the right choice? He had been on many training expeditions with the Rangers since he had been appointed as their formal commander, but he had never led them into battle. With one wrong decision, they could all die that day, and Walter felt the responsibility weigh upon him.

One of the Rangers glanced up at him, then he averted his eyes, and Walter did the same. He had allowed Lothar to join the operation when he had turned up at the assembly point in the Royal Parklands on the afternoon of the previous day, but that didn't mean he wished to speak to the man. As far as Walter knew, Lothar was still on his brother's payroll, and was probably spying on him. The betrayal hurt, and Walter attempted to push it from his mind. He had two hundred Rangers to look after, and didn't wish to obsess about only one of them.

He tried to think of something else, and an image of Kilbride entered his thoughts. She was holding up the towel to his chin to stop the bleeding, and, for the briefest of moments, she had looked at him in a way that had awoken some old feelings. The look she had given him had been out of character, but so too were the words she had spoken. It had been Walter she had wanted when she had returned from Greater Down, not Hector; and if he hadn't acted like an idiot, the previous few years might have developed very differently. It was pointless to dwell on it. He *had* acted like an idiot, and Kilbride had ended up in Hector's bed. The past was unchangeable, and he should be grateful that he and Kilbride had somehow emerged from it as friends. His feelings towards Abigone were becoming clearer to him – she was his cousin, but she also felt like a younger sister; and he loved her, even though she frequently annoyed him. With Kilbride, though, nothing but confusion reigned. She, too, was his second cousin, but he didn't regard her as a sister, for that would imply an absence of other feelings, feelings he was desperate to suppress. No one had blinked an eye when Alfgang the Pius had married Frida, even though they shared Alfgang the First as a great grandfather, and Walter knew that marriage between second cousins, especially among the nobility, was accepted by most people in Upper Down. All the same, he felt guilt whenever his thoughts of Kilbride were less than pure. Perhaps being with Hector had tainted her in his eyes. No, it wasn't that. He was revolted by the thought of them together, but he didn't blame Kilbride. Her marriage to Roderick might have been arranged, but the trauma she had endured in the aftermath of his murder had been real enough. It was Hector he blamed. His brother had known what Kilbride was going through, and he had taken advantage of her vulnerability. Hatred for Hector bubbled up within Walter's mind, and an urge to survive the coming day arose with him, if only to spite his brother.

The lieutenant came to a halt by the opening of a narrow gorge, where four Ranger scouts were waiting.

'Good morning, sir,' said one.

'Good morning,' said Walter. He gestured towards the gorge. 'Does that lead down into the pass?'

'No, sir, it leads up to the top of the cliffs. We thought it might be wise to survey the terrain before coming to any decision about today's attack.'

Walter glanced over his shoulder at the long column of Rangers crouching by the side of the track.

'I recommend that we leave the rest of the Rangers here for now, sir,' said the lieutenant. 'With only six of us, we should be able to remain hidden from the imperial army, but if we bring all two hundred up onto the cliffs, then it is likely that someone will notice us.'

'All right,' said Walter; 'take me to the cliffs.'

The lieutenant gave a few orders to the Rangers at the head of the column, then he and Walter set off after the four scouts. They entered the narrow gorge, and followed a stream as it tumbled down from the higher slopes to their right. At the end of the gorge, they had to climb, and Walter scrambled over the moss-covered rocks. His stomach began to churn and ache, and the pain in his chin re-appeared. If he and Lothar had still been friends, then he had no doubt that the Ranger would have given him a few sips of whisky from the hip flask he carried everywhere. The alcohol would have soothed his pains and steadied his nerves, and he felt exposed without any. His hands had trembled a few times during the night, but no one had noticed in the darkness. With the light of dawn growing, the Rangers would be able to see everything, and Walter was starting to doubt his abilities. It wasn't right that the most elite force in Upper Down was led by a drunken fool who had continually disgraced himself in every tavern and beer hall. Walter had got away with it during the long years of peace, but with the realm facing its worst crisis in a century, he was expected to lead the Rangers into a confrontation with thousands of imperial soldiers.

Walter almost slipped, his left foot missing the narrow ledge as he climbed the side of the cliff. He righted himself, and carried on, giving his full attention to what he was doing. If he focussed on the possibility of failure, then he would make it more likely. Sweat appeared on his brow as he lifted himself up onto a shallow platform of rock.

'Keep low, sir,' whispered a scout. 'The edge of the cliff is just a few yards away.'

Walter nodded, then he crawled along the rock after the scouts, the lieutenant on his right. A low murmur of sound reached his ears – the sound of hundreds of soldiers eating breakfast. Walter reached the edge of the cliff, and crept into position between two scouts, who were lying on their fronts. The sun was beginning to rise behind them, but the ravine remained shrouded in shadow. Walter gazed down at the endless rows of tents spread out over the floor of the ravine. Men were scooping buckets of water from the stream, and several small campfires were dotted around, where soldiers were heating their morning rations. Over to the right, the sight of the Kendril Wall was cut off by a rocky escarpment, but a large section of the imperial army was visible. Walter's gaze went to a cluster of enormous tents, from which a dozen flags and banners were fluttering in the autumnal breeze. The largest tent presumably housed Prince Valentino, who had marched his army for hundreds of miles across the patchwork of tiny realms that had once formed the Central Provinces of the Elestian Empire. Many of those realms were no doubt destined to be swallowed up by the new Sanctian Empire as it spread and expanded. If Greater Down succumbed, then even if Upper Down was successful in retaining its independence, they would have the new empire as their neighbour to the south.

One of the scouts patted Walter on the shoulder, then he pointed to the north, where the front of the imperial camp was located. Walter squinted his eyes in the light, but what he saw made no immediate sense to him. The imperial army had set up several rows of strange-looking wagons behind their palisade defences. Each wagon consisted of a long cylinder of some kind, and they were sitting up at an angle, all pointed towards the Kendril Wall. Around them was a flurry of activity, as dozens of soldiers and engineers busied themselves.

'What are they?' Walter whispered.

'I'm not sure, sir. I would guess that they are a new type of offensive weapon from the south.'

'They could be defensive,' said another scout. 'Perhaps they issue flames that would destroy any counter-attack.'

'There are too many of them for that,' said Walter.

The scouts and the lieutenant glanced at him.

'What are your orders, sir?' said the officer.

'I need more information before I can decide our next step,' said Walter. 'I haven't asked any questions about the route we took over the mountains, but now I need you to be a little more honest with me. How many ways are there into the ravine from here, and where do they lead?'

The scouts eyed each other.

The most senior among them pointed to their left. 'The main way down emerges through a tight gorge about eight miles to our south, sir. That is the way we took when we retreated after the death of King Alfgang the Pius, but it would take us until sunset to get there, and we would be far south of the imperial army. A second way into the ravine lies just a hundred yards to our left. Its entrance is almost invisible to anyone in the pass, but if we enter the ravine from there, we shall be seen immediately.'

Walter looked down into the ravine, and his eyes scanned the likely place where the hidden track began. Opposite it were dozens of tents, and a large supply depot that was being guarded by at least a company of imperial soldiers.

Walter shook his head. 'If we go that way, we will be dead within thirty minutes, and the imperial soldiers will discover the entrance to the gorge. What are our other options?'

'The cliffs can be scaled with ropes in two other locations close to here, sir.'

'Forget it,' said Walter. 'We would be seen before we are halfway down, and the enemy's crossbows would pick us off one by one. Is there no other way?'

'There is one other way, sir,' said the scout, 'but it leads to the north, and emerges from the cliffs via a waterfall.'

'That sounds more promising.'

'Yes, sir, but the waterfall is only a hundred yards from the Kendril Wall, and we would appear directly in front of the imperial army's palisade. If we were planning to get back to Torrent as quickly as possible, then that would be the route to take; but we wouldn't be able to attack the enemy from that position.'

Walter frowned. 'So, our four options are death, death, death, or run away? Shit.'

'We could always split our forces, sir,' said the lieutenant. 'We could send some Rangers down the cliffs, while others attempt to engage those... machines, or whatever they are.'

'I refuse to sacrifice the lives of the Rangers for the sake of a diversion,' said Walter. 'Whoever we pick to go down the cliffs would be slaughtered; and, in any case, how would the others get past the palisade wall?'

'I don't know, sir,' said the officer. 'What were the exact orders given to us?'

'Assault the enemy,' said Walter. 'My brother wasn't any clearer than that.'

'Then, shouldn't we do that, sir?'

'I have differing priorities. We cannot allow the imperial army to discover how we got here; if they do, they could bypass the Kendril Wall and invade Upper Down via the Royal Parkland. And, I am not going to throw away the lives of two hundred Rangers just because my brother said so. You might think I'm being paranoid, but Hector hopes that I will not be returning to Torrent alive; and he doesn't give a shit how many Rangers die.'

The officer said nothing, while the four scouts glanced away. Walter gazed down at the imperial army. If a Master or a Maker had been with them, they might be able to induce a massive rockslide; at least Walter thought so – he had barely any idea how the abilities worked in practice. He considered ordering the rest of the Rangers up onto cliffs, from where they could loose every one of their arrows from the longbows each carried. That would inflict casualties upon the enemy, but it would also reveal their location, and the hunt would begin. The waterfall seemed the only option that would keep the Rangers alive, and protect the secret route over the mountains, but the thought of scurrying back to the Kendril Wall empty-handed depressed him.

'All right,' he said; 'this is what we'll do. I want a detachment of thirty Rangers sent north to secure the entrance to the ravine that passes through the waterfall, to ensure that our way out of here isn't blocked, and then I want the rest of the Rangers brought up onto the cliffs. We'll rain arrows down onto the imperial army, then run for the waterfall when we have nothing left to loose.'

The officer saluted. 'Yes, sir. I will head back down to the track, and get the men organised.'

The lieutenant crawled back the way they had come, and disappeared from sight.

. . .

The sun had cleared the horizon to the east by the time the Rangers had moved into position. Each was lying on the ground by the edge of the cliff, preparing their longbows; while a small detachment was making their way north to the waterfall. Walter had told everyone to wait in silence until word arrived to confirm that the route to the waterfall was clear, and several Rangers had taken the opportunity to catch some sleep. After an hour had passed, two scouts appeared from the direction of the stream, and they crawled along the cliff until they reached Walter's position. Walter glanced at the scouts, then he cursed under his breath when he realised that one of them was Lothar.

'We have scouted the way north, sir,' said the other Ranger, as Lothar lowered his gaze.

'Is it clear?' said Walter.

'The path there is clear,' said the scout, 'but a small party of imperial soldiers is sitting in the cave behind the waterfall, as though they were sheltering from something. Should the detachment engage them, sir?'

Walter chewed his lip, then he gestured for the lieutenant.

'Yes, sir?' said the officer.

'I am going down to lead the detachment stationed by the waterfall,' said Walter. 'A group of imperial soldiers is blocking the way into the ravine, and I will take care of them. Wait ten minutes, and then order the Rangers to loose on the army below. The moment they use the last of the arrows, order them all to fall back to the waterfall. I should have cleared the obstruction by then. Have you got all that?'

'Yes, sir.'

Walter gestured to the two scouts, then he followed them off the cliff. They climbed down to where the stream tumbled along its rocky course, and then they began to make their way north along the edge of a steep ridge. They descended again, scrambling over boulders until they reached another stream, which they followed. The ground levelled off a little, and the men were able to walk side by side along a wide ledge, with a precipice to their left. Walter caught Lothar's gaze for a moment, then both looked away.

'Thank you for allowing me to come along on the operation, sir,' said Lothar.

'You are a commander of the scouts,' said Walter. 'Why would I have left you behind?'

'You might have had your reasons, sir.'

'Are you carrying your hip flask?'

'No, sir.'

Walter shook his head. 'Did you only drink in my company, Lothar?'

'To be honest, sir, I feel a little sickened by the thought of alcohol just now.'

'Why?'

Lothar eyed the other scout. 'Go on ahead. I want to speak to the King's Champion alone for a moment.'

'Yes, sir,' said the scout, who quickened his pace until he was lost amid the thick undergrowth flanking the stream.

'Do you have something to say to me, Lothar?' said Walter.

'Duke Hector ordered me to accompany you on this operation, sir.'

'Did you speak to him?'

'Yes, sir. I went to see the duke after I resigned as your aide.'

'Then he knows that I discovered the truth about you?'

'Yes, sir.'

'What else did he say?'

Lothar fell into silence.

'I'm not stupid, Lothar,' said Walter. 'You sent the other scout away for a reason. Either you want to tell me something, or you're planning to push me off this ledge. Did my brother order you to make sure I didn't get home alive?'

Lothar remained silent.

'I see,' said Walter. He came to a halt, and turned to face the Ranger. 'Get it over with, Lothar. If you intend to kill me, you may as well do it here. You can tell everyone that I slipped.'

Lothar stared at him, then his shoulders sagged. 'Sir, I... I'm sorry. The duke threatened to burn down my parents' house if you made it back to Torrent in one piece. But I can't do it. I am already living with the guilt of what I did to you, and I couldn't bear it if I added murder to the list. I wish I had said no to Duke Hector all those years ago, but I was greedy, and I wanted the money. Perhaps you should push me off the damn ledge.'

Walter started to laugh, his nervous exhaustion overwhelming any restraint he felt. Lothar raised an eyebrow, but remained silent. Walter wheezed, then he put his hands on his knees to steady himself.

'Where do we go from here, Lothar?' he said.

Lothar smiled, and pointed at the path, 'Down there, sir.'

'That wasn't what I meant.'

'I know, sir.'

Walter straightened his back, and they set off again.

'If we make it out of here alive,' Walter said, 'take forty Rangers straight to your parents' house. Hector's men will shit themselves at the sight.'

'Thank you, sir.'

They walked on for another few minutes, then they reached the detachment of Rangers, who were waiting by the narrow entrance to a cave, from where the stream issued.

'The imperial soldiers are forty yards from here, sir,' Lothar whispered. 'The cave widens at that point, and there is enough room to fit an entire battalion.'

'How many soldiers did you see?'

'Not many, sir.'

'I counted five, sir,' said another. 'One officer, and four others.'

Walter frowned. 'What the fuck are they doing out of their camp?'

'We don't know, sir,' said Lothar. 'When we saw them, they were sitting by a pool.'

'All right; we're moving in,' said Walter. 'Our aim is to arrest them, but defend yourselves if they attack.' Lothar signalled to the others, and the Rangers began to enter the cave. Walter was the third to crawl through the opening. The cave was narrow for a few yards, then it opened out into a large cavern. Light was filtering through from the waterfall that dominated the left side of the cavern, and the interior glistened with stalactites and stalagmites. In the centre of the cavern was a pool, and a man wearing an officer's uniform was sitting on a rocky formation by its side, while four others were standing close by.

Walter nodded to the Rangers, and they rushed out into the cavern. Four Rangers raised their longbows, their arrows nocked, and Walter drew his sword, as more Rangers piled through behind him.

'Nobody move!' Walter cried, as the five men turned to see the Rangers streaming into the cavern.

One of the men hurried forwards, as though he was trying to protect the seated officer, and three Rangers aimed their bows at his chest.

'Stop, or we shall loose!' Walter cried.

He led a dozen Rangers down the left-hand side of the cavern, cutting off the escape route of the five men.

'You are surrounded,' Walter said. 'Drop your weapons; you are now prisoners of Upper Down.'

The officer got to his feet, a look of calm bemusement on his features. 'How did you get here?'

Walter smiled. 'You look important, but I don't recognise your insignia. Who are you?'

'I am Count Sebastian,' said the officer.

'There is no way out, Count Sebastian. You cannot win this fight. Order your men to drop their weapons.'

'And if I do so?'

'Then you will be escorted through the Kendril Wall.'

'So that we can be hanged from the battlements?'

'Upper Down does not hang prisoners of war.'

'No? You execute emissaries, or so I am told.'

'That was Alfgang the Great,' said Walter. 'Upper Down is no longer ruled by that king. If you surrender yourselves into my custody, then I will ensure that you and your men are well treated.'

'If I am to surrender myself to you,' said the count, 'I shall need to know to whom I am submitting.'

'My name is Walter, and I am the King's Champion.'

'Very well. I can surrender to the King's Champion.' He gestured to his men. 'Place your weapons on the ground.'

The four men did so, then the count drew his sword, and held its hilt out towards Walter, his head bowed.

'We surrender,' he said.

Walter sheathed his own sword, and took the count's. 'This is a fine blade,' he said.

'It was given to me by my wife's uncle.'

'And who might that be?'

'His Imperial Majesty Emperor Antonio of Sanctos.'

Several of the Rangers stared at the count.

'What was someone of your rank doing hiding in a cave?' said Walter.

'We were not hiding,' said the count; 'we mistimed our trip, and we were taking shelter.'

'From what?'

The count smiled. 'From the imminent bombardment. In a few moments, our entire force of cannon will open fire upon the Kendril Wall. You say that you will lead us through that wall, but I fear you may be mistaken.'

Walter gestured to a scout. 'Get your arse back up the hill. The rest of the Rangers will be coming down from the cliff by now; tell them to get here as quickly as they can. Go.'

The scout ran off, then Walter walked over to the waterfall. He clung to the left of the opening, where the flow of water was at its lightest, and stepped through to the other side. To his left was the palisade wall the imperial army had constructed when they had first arrived, and the cylindrical machines, or cannon, as the count had called them, were out of sight, hidden by the tall timber beams. Walter turned to gaze to his right, and his mouth fell open. The front of the Kendril Wall was pocked and cracked, and a large pile of rubble had accumulated at its base. Several turrets had disappeared from the battlements, and one of the gatehouse towers had been wrecked. The left half of the main gates was still standing, but the right had been blown to pieces, and rubble was blocking the ruined entrance.

The count appeared by his shoulder, flanked by four Rangers.

'We ventured here to inspect the damage, Lord Walter,' said Sebastian. 'It is quite impressive from this distance, is it not? And to think that all of that was caused by a mere handful of preliminary firings, to test the range and accuracy of the cannon. Can you imagine what the Kendril Wall will look like when all sixty commence today's bombardment?' He pointed at the gate. 'And do you see? The entrance is blocked. If I may, I wish to extend to you the same courtesy you offered me, King's Champion. If you surrender yourself and your men into my custody, I will ensure that your lives are preserved.'

Another scout emerged through the waterfall. 'The rest of the Rangers are arriving at the cave, sir; what are our orders?'

'Tell them to keep coming,' said Walter. 'We're going to run up the path by the side of the cliffs, and make for the postern gate. Tell them to stop for nothing.'

'Yes, sir.'

'There is a postern gate?' said the count. 'I cannot see it.'

'It's sheltered under the eaves of the cliff,' said Walter.

'It may also be blocked.'

'It might.' He gestured to the others. 'Let's go. Guard the prisoners and get moving. Stay as close to the cliff as possible, and run as though your arses were on fire.'

The Rangers set off, sprinting up the steep slope towards the Kendril Wall. Walter waited for a moment, the count by his side, as he made sure the Rangers were all underway, then they started to run, keeping the sheer cliff face to their right as they ascended. The Wall was barely a hundred yards in front of them, and Walter saw several militia soldiers up on the battlements.

They were halfway to the postern gate when the ground rumbled. A deafening crack echoed off the cliffs, then, an instant later, the Kendril Wall was struck by dozens of projectiles. Fragments of stone showered the ground as the Wall was pounded. Turrets crumbled and fell, and the left-hand gate under the gatehouse exploded into a thousand pieces.

'Keep moving!' Walter cried, but his voice was lost to the cacophony. Six Rangers were hit by an enormous piece of falling masonry as it tumbled down the slope, and others were struck by a hailstorm of flying fragments. By Walter's feet, a smoking ball of iron rolled down the hill. The count slipped, and Walter grabbed his arm and pulled him to his feet, then he pushed the aristocrat up the slope.

Ten yards from the postern gate, a second roar sounded, and the valley shook again as the Kendril Wall bore the brunt of sixty more cannon balls. Rangers were falling all around Walter, struck by red hot fragments of disintegrating stone, or crushed by falling blocks. Walter dragged the count to the far right of the Wall, and pounded on the intact postern gate.

'Open the fucking door!' he yelled, as his fist battered off the gate.

The postern slid open a few feet, and several soldiers from the Wall Militia peered out. Walter shoved his way past them, and pulled the count through after him. They ran into the forecourt between the Wall and the edge of Torrent, and were immediately surrounded by dozens of militia.

'Let the Rangers pass,' Walter cried. 'Leave that fucking gate open until every one is through.'

'My lord?' said a militia officer, as Walter panted.

Walter ignored him. He turned, and watched as more of the Rangers made it through the postern safely, along with the four other captives. He glanced at the count, who inclined his head.

'I underestimated your courage, King's Champion,' Sebastian said, as the pounding from the cannon continued behind them. 'I am now at your mercy.'

CHAPTER 22
RENOWN

Torrent, Upper Down – 15th Day of Lamenta 107

Kilbride's gaze went to a commotion by the left-hand side of the forecourt.

'Who ordered the postern gate to be opened?' she cried.

The soldiers around her stared in confusion, and none answered her question. The ground shook under her boots as the intense bombardment continued, and rubble fell from the gatehouse, smashing against the cobbles of the forecourt. Kilbride hurried towards the postern gate, the only gate still intact along the entire length of the Kendril Wall. She came to a halt as she saw dozens of Mountain Rangers funnelling through the gate and into the forecourt. Some were supporting their wounded colleagues, while others were guarding a small number of captives. Her eyes scanned the growing crowd. She saw Lothar, who was limping from a leg injury, then her gaze alighted on Walter. She pushed her way through the mob of Rangers and militia, and reached the gate just as it was being closed. Many of the Rangers looked exhausted, and fewer had returned than had set off the previous afternoon. She reached Walter, who was speaking to a man dressed in the fine uniform of the imperial nobility.

'Walter,' she said.

He turned, and gazed at her.

'I wasn't expecting you to return this way,' she said. 'How did you make it through the bombardment?'

'With exceptional courage, my lady,' said the imperial aristocrat, inclining his head.

'This is Count Sebastian,' said Walter, 'and he's exaggerating. All we did was run as fast as we could.'

'The King's Champion is being modest,' said Sebastian.

'And this is Princess Kilbride,' Walter went on; 'a member of the regency council governing Upper Down.'

'My humble apologies, Your Highness,' said Sebastian. He took her hand and kissed it. 'Had I known I was speaking to royalty, I would have acted accordingly.'

The bombardment ceased, and the air stilled. Several soldiers slumped in relief, but officers got them back to work. Carts appeared, and soldiers loaded them with rubble to be used to block the breached gates.

Walter glanced at the gatehouse. 'We should go somewhere quieter.'

'What is the count doing here?' said Kilbride.

'I am his prisoner,' said Sebastian. 'I surrendered myself to the King's Champion, and gave him my sword. In return, he pledged that my men and I would be treated fairly.'

'You captured a count, Walter?'

'He's not only a count,' said Walter. 'He's married to the emperor's niece.'

'The ground floor at the rear of the gatehouse is the most secure place here,' said Kilbride. 'Or should we take him to the Royal Palace? There is something I need to tell you, Walter.'

'Can it wait a minute?' said Walter. 'Stay here.'

Kilbride frowned as Walter strode away. He crouched down by Lothar, who was resting his injured leg, and the two men shook hands. Walter stood, and ordered a small formation of Rangers to gather in front of him, and then the soldiers marched off towards Torrent, with an officer in the lead.

'How goes the defence of Upper Down, Your Highness?' said the count.

Kilbride eyed him. The count appeared to be the calmest person in the forecourt, his demeanour unruffled, as the bewildered militia scrambled amid the debris and rubble.

'I imagine that you are able to guess that for yourself,' said Kilbride. 'The Wall of Kendril... may not be as impregnable as was once believed.'

'Nothing lasts forever, Your Highness,' said the count. 'There is still time for an honourable surrender. If you wish, I can begin negotiations for your submission. My rank entitles me to treat with the enemy.'

Walter rejoined them, leading a dozen Rangers and the four other captives. Kilbride gestured towards the back of the gatehouse, then she led the way, with Walter by her side.

'Something happened while you were away,' Kilbride whispered.

'Tell me as soon as we've dealt with the count,' Walter said.

'What do you mean? What do you wish to do with him?'

'I have an idea.'

They entered the rear of the gatehouse, and Kilbride cleared a small chamber. Walter led the count inside, while the Rangers guarded the four other prisoners in the hallway. Kilbride entered last, and closed the door behind her.

'I have a proposal to make,' said Walter.

'And I would like to hear it,' said the count, as Kilbride narrowed her eyes.

Walter turned to Kilbride. 'We should release the count and his four companions, and allow them to to return to the imperial camp.'

'Why?'

'So that the count can request a temporary truce. He's married to the emperor's niece, Killie, which means he is probably close to Prince Valentino. If the count can secure a truce, it will give us time to regroup.'

'I would be most grateful if you choose to allow this, Your Highness,' said the count. 'In fact, I am a little humbled by the suggestion. Rest assured that I will bring all of my authority to bear when I approach the Illustrious Prince Valentino.'

'But you cannot guarantee that he will agree?' said Kilbride.

'No, I cannot,' said the count. 'However, the illustrious prince is a man of great honour, and I feel sure that he will allow a short truce, if you were to release me and my four companions unharmed.'

'How long a truce will you be able to secure?'

'That will be up to the illustrious prince, Your Highness. I would suggest that I request a cessation of hostilities until this time tomorrow. Would that be acceptable to you?'

Kilbride walked over to a table and sat down.

'I have one further request, Your Highness,' said the count. 'I would very much like to have a short conversation with Princess Hygilt, so that I can assure her grandfather that she is well. If you can do this, then I am convinced that the illustrious prince might agree to a longer truce.'

Walter turned to Kilbride. 'That sounds reasonable.'

'Unfortunately,' said Kilbride, 'that will not be possible. Princess Hygilt was evacuated from Torrent yesterday.'

'I see,' said the count. 'That is probably for the best, bearing in mind the unequal nature of this struggle. You did well to remove the princess from danger, Your Highness.'

Kilbride lowered her gaze. She was desperate to tell Walter what had happened in the palace overnight, but she couldn't while the count was present. If he took word back to Prince Valentino that his granddaughter had been abducted by Westlanders, Upper Down would be held responsible.

'I acquiesce in this request, Walter,' she said, 'and I sanction the release of the five prisoners, on the condition that they attempt to negotiate a temporary truce with the illustrious prince.'

The count bowed low before her. 'You have earned my deepest gratitude, Your Highness. If I return safely to the imperial camp, I will be sure to tell Prince Valentino that you, Princess Kilbride, and you, Walter, the King's Champion, behaved with honour and a great generosity of spirit. I had been told that the rulers of Upper Down were naught but corrupt savages, murderers, and bullies who preyed upon the weak, and I am pleased to have been proved wrong. I solemnly pledge to you both that I will beg the illustrious prince to agree to this truce. If His Highness refuses, then I shall return here, and hand myself back into your custody.'

Walter opened the door, and faced the dozen Rangers.

'Escort the prisoners to the postern gate and let them go. Fetch a white sheet from the barracks that they can hold in front of them, then bar the gate when they have safely departed.'

The Rangers eyed each other, then the officer saluted.

The four lower-ranked captives were led back to the forecourt, while the count turned and extended his hand. Walter shook it, then Kilbride offered her own hand. Sebastian smiled at her, and kissed it again.

Walter held out the count's sword. 'I have something that belongs to you.'

The count smiled again as he glanced at the weapon. 'Will you hold on to that for me, Walter? Perhaps we shall meet again, and you can return it to me if we do.'

Walter unstrapped his own sword from his belt. 'In that case, I insist that you take this, then we can return both blades at the same time.'

The count took the sword, and attached it to his belt. 'It has been an honour to meet you both,' he said, 'and I will not forget this.'

Walter and Kilbride escorted the count out into the forecourt, and they followed the Rangers to the postern gate. They waited there for a few minutes, until a Ranger returned from the closest barracks, carrying a white bed sheet. He handed it to one of the captives, and Walter signalled for the gate to be opened.

'Hold that out in front of you, sergeant,' the count said to the man with the sheet, 'and let us pray to the spirits that the bombardment holds off for a few more minutes.'

The sergeant moved into the lead position, the sheet held up in both arms, then the other freed captives followed him through the gate. Kilbride and Walter walked up to the postern, and Walter closed it most of the way, leaving only a small gap, through which they could watch the count and his men edge their way back down the steep slope.

Kilbride's eyes went to the bodies lying crushed and bloody on the track. 'How many Rangers did you lose, Walter?'

'Perhaps two dozen,' Walter said. 'I have yet to perform a roll call. We got caught up in the bombardment.'

'Two dozen Rangers, so that you could capture a count that you immediately release? Some will struggle to understand this.'

'If it buys us a day's truce, many more lives will be spared. And if we hadn't released them, my men would still be dead.'

The cannon remained silent as the count and his men made their way down the slope. A few imperial soldiers rushed out from behind the palisade wall and approached the small group, then the count was ushered to safety. Walter closed the postern gate, and gestured to the militia for it to be barred.

'Come with me, Walter,' Kilbride said.

'Do I not get five minutes to rest, Killie? I've been up all night.'

'So have I,' she said.

She set off for the gatehouse, and heard Walter follow her. She re-entered the building, and they walked into the same chamber where they had spoken to the count. Kilbride closed the door.

'The first cannon began firing yesterday evening,' she said, 'a few hours after you had departed. There was panic, as you can imagine, and Hector ordered all militia here, to pile up rubble to block the gates.'

'All militia?' said Walter.

'Yes, all of them. Even the Mountain Rangers you left behind were summoned. Also, the garrison defending the Royal Palace was stripped to its bare bones. A mere two hundred were left to protect the Royal Court.' She looked into his eyes. 'It wasn't enough, Walter.'

His face paled. 'What happened?'

'Over a hundred Westlanders invaded the palace from the direction of the Royal Parkland. We have found the ladders they used to scale the walls. Around fifty Guardsmen were killed, along with forty palace staff.'

'The boy-king? Please tell me Alfie is safe.'

'He is safe. He is back in the palace now, and we have sent all of the Royal Guard there to protect him. His mother, too, is safe, and I was with them when we were evacuated.' She looked away. 'Unfortunately, Abigone and Hygilt weren't in their quarters when the soldiers arrived to evacuate them. It appears they decided that it was the perfect moment to visit the library, and we had trouble finding them. Then we discovered Tulip. He was lying on the floor next to two dead militia soldiers, and the courtier who had escorted Abigone and Hygilt to the library. There is only one conclusion – the Westlanders have taken both princesses.'

Walter fell into a seat and put his head in his hands.

'We also found the bodies of three slain Westlanders,' Kilbride went on. 'One of them was recognised as a close associate of Dravid. Therefore, we should assume that Dravid was behind the attack.'

'He must have known that the palace was practically undefended.'

'Perhaps. Maybe he got lucky. In any event, Chief Stefan has set off in pursuit, in order to reclaim his bride-to-be.'

'And Hector?'

'Your brother was in the ducal palace during the attack.'

'Could he have leaked this information to Dravid?'

'I cannot see how that could possibly have been in Hector's interests. You and I both believe that he wants Abigone to marry Stefan, and he knew Hygilt's value in any negotiations. No; in this case, I deem him to be innocent.' She paused for a moment. 'Walter, I know that you have only just returned, and I know how tired you must be, but I cannot bear the thought of Abbie suffering at the hands of Dravid; and is Stefan much better? My sister needs someone she can trust; someone who will put her interests first. Will you go after them?'

Walter said nothing for a long moment, then he nodded. 'When did Stefan leave?'

'An hour ago. If you go on horseback, and take a spare mount, you should be able to catch up with them before nightfall.'

'Do we know where Dravid is taking the princesses?'

'Their most likely route is due north, to get out of Upper Down as soon as possible. The militia found wagon tracks by the parkland walls, but most of Dravid's men appear to be travelling on foot.'

Walter stood and walked to the door. He opened it a crack.

'Fetch me two good, long-distance horses, both saddled, and carrying enough water and provisions for six days,' he said to the Rangers standing outside. 'And get me some breakfast, please.'

He closed the door.

'Thank you, Walter,' Kilbride said.

'If I find Abigone,' he said, 'she will want to know about Tulip. What should I tell her? I assume the creature is dead?'

'We thought he was dead at first,' she said, 'but the little animal is hardier than it looks. He was limping, and his breathing was hoarse; but other than that, he seemed fine. He was hissing at everyone, as though he was angry, and then... well, I'm not sure where he went, but I didn't see him in the palace again.'

'He's probably hiding somewhere. Check under the floorboards, and lure him out with some bacon.'

'I will suggest that to the staff.'

Walter's expression darkened a little. 'Hector will soon discover that I have returned.'

'Is that a problem?'

'Hector told Lothar to ensure I was killed today, but he couldn't go through with it.'

'Hector ordered Lothar to kill you?'

'Yes. Does that surprise you?'

'No. It should, but it doesn't.'

Walter gazed at the floor. 'I will have to kill him when I get back.'

'Are you capable of such a thing, Walter?'

'I don't know.'

'Have you ever taken another's life?'

'No.'

'Yet you believe you would be able to strike your own brother down?'

'What choice do we have, Killie? It's him or us. If we don't get rid of Hector, then we may as well hand him the realm. That's what he wants. We are just obstructions in his path.'

The door was knocked, then it opened, and a Ranger walked in carrying a tray of food. He set it down onto the table, then inclined his head.

'The horses are being prepared for you, sir.'

'Thank you,' said Walter.

The Ranger left the chamber, and the door was closed. Kilbride sat down opposite Walter, and watched as he began to eat.

'You could always leave Hector to me,' she said.

Walter eyed her, but said nothing.

'If we are serious about this,' she went on, 'then we need to do it properly.'

'Have you ever killed anyone before?' he said.

'Not with my bare hands, but there are other means.'

'Who have you killed?'

'I think that, perhaps, deep down, you already know the answer to that question.'

Walter frowned, then his eyes widened a little.

'Are you disappointed in me, Walter?' she said.

'And Captain Joachim?'

'I had nothing to do with that. He really did kill himself.'

'But you used him to get to Alfgang the Great?'

'I did. My father was a cruel and vindictive man. A tyrant. Maybe you didn't see all of the evil things he did, but...'

'I know what kind of man he was.'

'And?'

'I did not mourn his death.'

'Then should I proceed? Do you want me to proceed with this?'

'Shit, is this a fucking conspiracy – is that what we're doing? We're seriously discussing murdering someone?'

'It was your idea, Walter. Look at how Count Sebastian reacted when we told him he was going to be released. To say he was surprised would be a gross understatement. I was unsure when you first suggested it, but you were right. If he speaks to Prince Valentino about us, then we might have laid the foundations to negotiate a peaceful agreement with the Sanctian Empire. However, two things have to occur before that becomes a possibility – we need to rescue Princess Hygilt; and we have to rid the kingdom of Hector. If you take care of the first task, I will take care of the second. Do we have a deal?'

'I wouldn't want you to put yourself into any danger.'

'We are all in danger, Walter. Doing nothing will not change that. The truce, if agreed, will give us a short interval in which to act.'

'All right. Don't give me any details about what you are planning to do.'

Kilbride smiled. 'I wasn't going to.'

Walter pushed his plate to the side and got to his feet. 'My priority remains Abigone,' he said, 'but I will do what I can to bring Hygilt back.'

Kilbride stood, and they walked out of the chamber. The Rangers escorted them back into the forecourt, where three Rangers were preparing Walter's two horses for departure.

'Are you travelling alone, sir?' said one of the Rangers.

'I am,' said Walter. 'If Princess Kilbride requires any assistance while I am away, place yourselves at her service.'

'Yes, sir.'

Kilbride reached out and took hold of Walter's arm. 'Be careful.'

'You, too,' he said.

She kissed him on the cheek, then he pulled himself up into the saddle. He looped the reins of the other horse around his left wrist, then he dug his ankles in and rode away, the hooves of both horses clattering off the cobbles. Kilbride watched as he disappeared to the left, in the direction of the western gates of Torrent, then she turned to gaze at the Rangers who were still in the forecourt. The wounded were lying or sitting close to the cliffside, and she walked towards them. A few broken bones were being attended to, and several men were covered in bandages. Kilbride halted by Lothar, who was sitting a little way from from the others, his left shin streaked in blood. The Ranger looked up at her, then he glanced away, his expression mired in guilt.

Kilbride crouched down beside him. 'Are you badly wounded, Commander?'

'No, Your Highness,' he said, keeping his gaze averted. 'My leg is not broken.'

Kilbride lowered her voice. 'I know what you did. Walter told me everything.'

'Are you going to have me arrested, ma'am?'

'Why would I do that? How would you be able to help with the defence of Upper Down if you were in prison? I am here to find out what kind of man you are. For three years, you took the Duke of Ridden's money, and yet you were unable to carry out his final orders. Why?'

'I... Lord Walter is the King's Champion, ma'am. It seemed different when we were at peace. But now? I couldn't do it anymore, not when our enemies are so close. As for the duke's final order, I... I agreed to it at the time, but only because the duke was threatening to evict my parents from their home. I knew even then that I wasn't going to go through with it. I hate what I did to Lord Walter. He trusted me, and I betrayed him.'

Kilbride kept her eyes on him. 'And what are your current thoughts regarding the Duke of Ridden?'

Lothar turned his gaze to her, his eyes narrow, as though he suspected a trap.

'I am far closer to Lord Walter than I am to Lord Hector,' Kilbride went on. 'I, too, believe that Upper Down needs its Champion. If you had harmed Walter when you were south of the Wall, I would have killed you myself.'

'What are you saying, ma'am?'

'I merely wish to know if you are willing to right some of your wrongs. Lord Hector will be angry that his brother has returned unscathed. He will be angry at Walter, naturally; but he will also be angry with you, Commander. I can offer you protection. In return, I want to know where your true loyalties lie.'

He stared at her.

'Are you loyal to the Duke of Ridden, or are you loyal to Lord Walter? You don't need to answer me right away. Think about it. If you are interested in redeeming yourself, come to the Royal Palace tomorrow, and ask for me. If, however, I discover that you have gone running to Duke Hector about this, I will be displeased. It is time to choose a side, Commander; you cannot serve two masters.'

She stood. 'I hope you recover quickly, Commander Lothar.'

'Thank you, ma'am,' he said.

Kilbride strode away. She made for a set of stairs cut into the side of the Kendril Wall, and several Rangers escorted her as she ascended to the battlements. The steps were cracked, and a few blocks were loose, but they made it to the top of the Wall. Kilbride stared at the damage caused by that morning's cannon fire. The parapets were ragged, and whole sections of the walkway were missing. She glanced over the side of the battlements. Great piles of pulverised rock were lying at the base of the Wall, and the cracks had grown and spread; while the upper floor of the gatehouse had gone, along with both of its towers.

'It is not safe to go any further, ma'am,' said one of the Rangers. 'The stairs we climbed are the only ones left, and the rest of the battlements are now out of our reach.'

Kilbride nodded, but kept her mouth closed. She turned her gaze to the imperial camp. The rows of cannon were being worked on by a swarm of engineers, and the forge was issuing thick tendrils of black smoke into the sky. Platforms were being reinforced, and the sound of hammers rang out. Several cannon looked as though they were being repaired, while others were being loaded with iron balls, ready for another bombardment.

'I suggest that we make our way back down to the forecourt, ma'am,' said the Ranger. 'If the cannon start firing again, we might get stranded up here.'

'In a moment,' she said.

The minutes passed, and Kilbride sent a silent prayer to the spirits. A whistle blasted somewhere in the imperial camp, and a large group of officers approached the rows of cannon. They summoned the engineers, who left what they were doing to walk downhill to where the officers had gathered. Kilbride couldn't hear what anyone was saying, and the discussion ended after a few moments. The officers withdrew, and the engineers followed them, leaving the cannon guarded, but without any crews to load or fire them. As the engineers vanished from view, another imperial party emerged from among the tents – four men, one of whom was holding a white sheet aloft in his arms. They strode past the palisade wall, and began to climb the slope towards the postern gate.

'What are they doing?' said one of the Rangers.

Kilbride smiled. 'I think the truce might have begun, gentlemen.'

She led the Rangers back down the stairs, and strode to the postern. A handful of Wall Militia were on duty by the intact gate, and Kilbride ordered them to open it.

The four men approached, keeping close to the sheer edge of the cliff, then they halted a few yards from the postern gate. Kilbride stepped forward, until she was standing in the open doorway.

One of the men bowed. 'I bear a message for Princess Kilbride and Lord Walter, the King's Champion,' he said.

'I am Princess Kilbride.'

'Greetings, your Highness. The message is from His Illustrious Highness Prince Valentino, commander of the imperial army. His Illustrious Highness has agreed to your proposed truce, and he wishes to thank you and Lord Walter for the swift mercy you showed to his niece's husband Count Sebastian, following his capture. The truce is in force from this moment, and shall expire at noon tomorrow. His Illustrious Highness also wished to reiterate that you can end this war at any time of your choosing, by accepting the terms offered by the imperial emissaries.'

'Thank you,' said Kilbride. 'Please advise His Illustrious Highness that we accept the terms of the truce, and that we shall not initiate any hostilities until it elapses. Please also tell him that Lord Walter and I shall use this time to discuss the offered terms. It remains my hope that we can resolve this situation without the need for any further bloodshed. However, His Illustrious Highness should be aware that Lord Walter and I are not the only members of the regency council.'

The delegate bowed again. 'I shall deliver your words to the illustrious prince, Your Highness.'

Kilbride inclined her head slightly, and the four men departed, making their way back down the steep slope. Kilbride stepped back from the doorway.

'Close and bar the postern gate,' she said, then she turned to the masses of militia soldiers and Rangers filling the forecourt, many of whom were staring at her.

'We have a truce until tomorrow at noon,' she said; 'a truce which has been earned by the courageous actions of the Mountain Rangers under the command of Lord Walter, the King's Champion.'

She smiled, as the soldiers eyed each other with relief. 'Let us use our time wisely.'

CHAPTER 23
RESPITE

Torrent, Upper Down – 15th Day of Lamenta 107

Hector strode into the busy forecourt, as Amery trailed along by his side. The area between the Kendril Wall and the edge of Torrent was packed with soldiers from every militia in Upper Down, and they were hard at work, wheeling barrows of rubble into the gatehouse, and clearing fragments of fallen masonry from the cobbles.

Kilbride was directing operations from the left-hand side of the Wall, and, Hector noticed, she appeared to have several Rangers standing close by, as though they had been assigned to protect her.

'Damn Rangers,' he muttered. 'So, the rumours are true?'

'That would seem to be the case, my lord,' said Amery, 'although I see no sign of your noble brother.'

Hector and Amery made their way through the crowds towards the princess, and the militia cleared a path for them. Kilbride saw the two men approach, and a faint smile passed over her lips.

'What is the current situation, Your Highness?' Hector said. 'And why have the cannon stopped?'

'We have secured a short truce,' said Kilbride. 'Prince Valentino has agreed to cease hostilities until tomorrow at noon.'

Hector blinked. 'Was this your doing?'

'As much as I would like to take credit for it,' said Kilbride, 'it was the actions of Lord Walter that forced the illustrious prince into agreeing to the truce. He captured Count Sebastian, a member of the imperial royal family, and used him to secure this respite.'

'My brother did what? And where is this Count Sebastian?'

'He has been released.'

Blind fury rose up within Hector, and he struggled to preserve his composure. 'You released him – for a mere handful of hours? You stupid girl.'

Many of the militia within hearing distance paused in their work, and several turned to watch the exchange.

'And you did this without consulting me first?' Hector went on, his voice rising.

'Lord Walter and I are both members of the regency council,' said Kilbride, her expression unruffled. 'We were well within our rights to act as we did.'

'She is quite correct, my lord,' said Amery; 'from a legal point of view.'

'Shut up,' said Hector. 'Tell me this, Your Highness – what will the imperial army be doing during this truce? They will be repairing their blasted cannon, to ensure that the next bombardment shall be the last. You should have informed Valentino that we would slit the count's throat in front of his army, unless he agreed to withdraw. You threw away a decent tactical advantage with your naivety. Count Sebastian will be laughing at us, and so will Valentino. All you did was show him our weakness.'

'Is that all you came here to say?' said Kilbride. 'Do you think that losing your temper in front of our soldiers is anything other than weakness? Perhaps you should return to the ducal palace, Hector; the strains of the conflict seem to have unmanned you.'

'How dare you?' he cried. He glanced at the faces of the Rangers. 'Where is Walter? Where is my idiot brother?'

'You just missed him,' said Kilbride. 'He will have left Torrent by now.'

'Walter has abandoned Torrent?'

'He has set off in pursuit of those who took Abigone and Hygilt.'

'Duke Stefan is already leading that search.'

'Forgive me, Hector, but whereas you would place your trust in a Westlander, I would rather rely on the King's Champion to rescue my sister.'

Hector calmed a little. 'Walter has gone? Then you and I remain the only regents still in Torrent, and my vote outweighs yours by two to one. Perhaps you should have thought things through before sending Walter off after Abigone, Your Highness. I order you to return to the Royal Palace, where you will remain until further notice. This is no place for a woman.'

'And if I object?'

Hector leaned in closer. 'You know what I could do to you if I wished, Kilbride. You know the powers I possess.'

'Then why haven't you used those powers against the enemy?'

'Had those cannon been but twenty yards closer, then we wouldn't have required a truce.'

'Twenty yards? Here's a suggestion – why don't you walk through the postern gate, so that you can get a little nearer to the enemy lines? After all, if your brother was able to brave cannon fire to reach the gate, what is stopping you?'

'Are you calling me a coward?'

'Yes, Hector – that is exactly what I am calling you. Prove me wrong. If you truly love Upper Down, and wish to defend it, then walk through the postern gate and reveal your Master abilities. Turn the cannon into wood, or whatever else takes your fancy. Go on. I dare you.'

Hector stared at the princess and, at that moment, he knew he had lost her.

'Go to the palace, Your Highness,' he said, 'and await further orders. You are dismissed.'

Kilbride inclined her head, then she strode away. The Rangers moved off after her, and formed a tight circle around Kilbride.

'Remain at your posts, Rangers,' said Hector.

One of their officers turned. 'Apologies, my lord,' he said, 'but Lord Walter is the commander of the Mountain Rangers, and it is from him, and no one else, that we take our orders.'

Hector said nothing as the Rangers escorted Kilbride towards a line of waiting carriages. The soldiers from the militias were still staring in his direction, and many of the glances he was receiving were far from friendly.

'Carry on with your work,' Hector said to them. 'There is no time to waste.'

He walked through the crowds, as Amery hurried to keep up. They reached the carriage that had brought them from the ducal palace, and both men climbed inside. The door was closed by one of the Ducal Guard, and the carriage set off, its wheels trundling over the uneven cobbles.

'That could have gone better,' Hector muttered.

'Quite, my lord,' said Amery. 'Should I continue with the preparations to evacuate to Castle Ridden?'

'What the fuck do you think? Yes. Press ahead with our plans. Truce or no truce, the Kendril Wall is doomed.' He shook his head. 'And damn Kilbride. That stupid little bitch thinks she can take Walter's side, does she? She has no idea of the fate I have in store for her. Oh, and instruct my Guardsmen to go ahead with the orders I gave them regarding the house where Commander Lothar's parents dwell. I want it set alight by the end of the day.'

'Yes, my lord.'

'Don't look at me like that. Are your morals troubling you again?'

'I was under the impression, my lord, that I was hired for my legal expertise. I did not think I would be ordering soldiers to burn down the house of an elderly couple. Nor, for that matter, did I ever wish to be involved in a conspiracy to kill a king.'

'It is too late for regrets, Amery – you are complicit in the death of Alfgang the Pius. It was you who told Chief Dravid where the king would be that fateful morning, not I.'

'I was following your orders, my lord.'

'I know that, but who do you think the people will believe, if you ever try to speak to anyone about this? You are a foreigner in Upper Down; worse, you are a lawyer, and you know what the common folk in these parts think of people in your profession. No, Amery, for better or worse, you are tied to me. If I rise, you will benefit; if I fall, then you will be swinging from the gallows next to me.'

'Might I ask, my lord – what did you whisper into the ear of Princess Kilbride?'

'That is none of your concern.'

'If I am tied to you, my lord, then should you be keeping secrets from me? If the only way to survive this crisis is to see you flourish, then perhaps I would be able to help you, if I had more information to work with.'

Hector studied the young lawyer. Nobody but Kilbride knew his secret, and she had only learned the truth about him being a Master when he had slipped up one day, while they had been conducting their affair. He had forgotten that she was in the other room, and had been oblivious when she had walked in on him transforming a heap of scrap metal into gold coins. He had been terrified that she would tell everyone but, as far as he knew, she had kept her promise to remain silent. If everyone knew, then more would be expected of him, and he had found it far more beneficial to conceal his abilities. They were his own secret weapon.

'My lord?' said Amery.

'My answer remains no,' said Hector. 'What passed between me and Princess Kilbride was not for your ears.'

He looked out of the carriage window as they passed through the streets of Torrent. The marketplaces were still open, but many citizens looked fearful, and some stalls were running low on goods. People were beginning to hoard, he realised, and the thought made him almost as angry as he had been when speaking to Kilbride. Hoarding would lead to a rise in the cost of basic goods, which would lead to shortages and instability. With hundreds of Westlanders having died in the troubles, and hundreds more having fled north, Hector's income from the beer halls, brothels and casinos of Twinbrook was already starting to fall. Stefan was his last hope, but would the chief remain loyal if he was unable to pluck Abigone from the clutches of Dravid's men?

An unfamiliar feeling wormed its way into Hector's mind as the carriage drew closer to the ducal palace.

It was despair. Hector had gambled everything on the assumption that the Kendril Wall was impregnable, and his beliefs had been shown to be nothing but folly. He tried to think how the knowledge of the imperial army's cannon would have affected his earlier decisions. Would he have gone ahead with the assassination of Alfgang the Pius? Would he have recommended to Alfgang the Great that Upper Down should ignore Prince Valentino's demand to have his granddaughter returned to him unharmed?

None of it mattered. What was done was done, and he needed to think only of the future.

The carriage pulled through the open gates of the ducal palace, and halted close to the front entrance. A Guardsman opened the side door, and Duke Hector stepped down onto the gravel. Most of his men-at-arms were at the Kendril Wall, helping out with emergency repairs, but Hector had kept his small group of knights in the palace. None of them knew about his plan to evacuate north to Castle Ridden, and he started to consider how he would word it. He was keen to leave Torrent, but if he departed too soon, while the Kendril Wall was still standing, then he would look like a coward. However, if he left it too late, the roads north would be congested by fleeing civilians.

Amery joined him on the gravel driveway, and they strode up the steps and into the compact palace.

'Work on the plan,' Hector said. 'I do not wish to be disturbed.'

'Yes, my lord,' said the lawyer, then he bowed and walked away. Hector continued on to his private rooms, passing members of his staff, who bowed or curtsied before him. He reached his office, entered, and closed the door behind him. He went to his favourite armchair and sat down, his gaze on the manicured gardens on the other side of the window. He opened a drawer in his desk and withdrew a bottle of brandy, an expensive import from the renowned distilleries of Greater Down. He poured himself a large measure and sipped from the glass as he watched a bird sitting on the branch of a tree.

He began to sort through his priorities, as he always did during moments of stress. Survival came first, of course, followed by his desire to remain rich and powerful. The plan he had concocted for the future of Upper Down still seemed the best course to take, despite the imminent destruction of the Kendril Wall. If he could get to Castle Ridden, taking the Royal Court with him, then there was always the chance that Prince Valentino would be satisfied with the pillage of Torrent and Twinbrook. Valentino would only move north if he knew that Hector still had Princess Hygilt in his possession, but Dravid had ruined that aspect of his plan. If he ever saw Dravid again, he would kill him on sight; and the same went for Walter. He had lost Kilbride's trust thanks to his brother, and only the Champion's death would cow the princess into complete submission. Perhaps Stefan would do the job for him. His thoughts turned to Alfie, the boy-king. Under the guise of protecting him, Hector would lure the child to Castle Ridden, far from the gaze of the public. Hector would make it look like an accident. He would use Master powers against the young king that were too subtle to be detected by anyone else. Perhaps he would weaken the boy's knees as he was descending a staircase, or perhaps he would cause the boy to choke on his food.

And then? Then he would be free to take full control of Upper Down, with Kilbride by his side, whether she was willing or not. He would rule from Ridden, and Stefan would be welcome to the ruins of Torrent left behind by Valentino's army.

It would work, he told himself; he just needed patience and resolve. There was one last thing he had to do before leaving the ducal palace in the coming days and, in many ways, it was the hardest task of all.

A knock sounded at the door.

'Enter,' said Hector.

The door opened, and an old servant walked in. 'My lord,' she said, 'your wife Perpetua the Duchess of Ridden has arrived.'

Hector smiled. 'Thank you. Please show her in.'

'Yes, my lord.'

The servant departed, and Hector sipped some more of the brandy. A few moments later, his wife appeared at the door.

'Husband,' she said, 'I see you couldn't be bothered to greet me by the front door. Too busy, were you?'

'Terribly busy,' he said.

Perpetua strode into the room. 'Pour one of those brandies for me; I endured an exceptionally long and uncomfortable journey to get here, and I will need a stiff drink before I hear your reasons for summoning me all the way to Torrent.'

Hector picked up the bottle and filled a second glass.

Perpetua took it, and drained most of it in one mouthful. 'I half expected you to be in here with that little whore – what was her name? Ireni, was it? Where is she? Did you have the good manners to send her away before my arrival, or is she pretending to work in the kitchens again?'

'I sold her to a Westlander.'

Perpetua narrowed her eyes. 'I presume you are joking?'

'Do I ever joke with you, my dear wife? You sapped any humour out of me years ago. How are our sons?'

'They are well. Should I wait for you to invite me to sit?'

Hector gestured to a chair, and Perpetua sat down, her long dress reaching the carpeted floor.

'Rupert is doing very well with his lessons,' Perpertua went on, 'and he is currently learning how to ride a horse.' She smiled. 'He fell off a young gelding a few days ago, but he got right back up again. Artur, on the other hand, is turning out to be a most sensitive little boy. He cries at the mildest admonishment. He received the back of my hand for drawing all over a new tablecloth, and I thought his screams were going to bring the castle walls tumbling down. Both boys wanted to accompany me here; they wished to see their father, but I noticed the summons was for me alone.'

Hector said nothing.

'Is there something going on that I should know about?' she said. 'You haven't summoned me to Torrent in several years. You have invited me, but you have never summoned me. I almost tore up the letter you sent; the sheer presumption of it, that I, as your wife, was being commanded to obey you, as if I were one of your men-at-arms. I was a landowner in my own right before King Alfgang the Great arranged our marriage. I think you forget that sometimes.'

'How could I forget it, when you are always so keen to remind me?'

'You still have a propensity to exaggerate, I see. I haven't seen you in five months, husband, so how is it possible that I am always reminding you? I think I know what your problem is – everyone in this horrible little town worships the ground you walk on; whereas, I saw through your façade many years ago, and that irritates you intensely. Am I close?'

'The Kendril Wall is not impregnable,' he said.

Perpetua raised an eyebrow. 'Excuse me?'

'An imperial army, under the command of the emperor's brother, is currently encamped just south of the Wall.'

'I know. I heard about it on the way here.'

'But did you hear what Valentino brought with him? I would doubt that, seeing as the machines were only unveiled yesterday afternoon.'

'What machines?'

'I believe they are called cannon, and they have been smashing the Kendril Wall to pieces. It is still standing, but its demise is inevitable.'

The colour drained from Perpetua's face, and Hector almost laughed at her stricken expression.

'When the Wall has been thoroughly reduced to rubble,' he went on, 'there will be nothing to prevent Valentino's forces from entering Torrent.'

'And you summoned me here?'

'I sent the summons long before the cannon arrived. I have instructed Amery to start planning the evacuation to Castle Ridden. Had I known of these events in advance, I would not have dragged you all the way here.'

'Should I return north?'

'Not yet. You only just got here, and it would be unwise to let the people of Torrent see you rush off so soon. Keeping the people calm is one of my primary objectives.'

'You still haven't told me why you summoned me.'

He gazed at her. 'I wondered if you would be amenable to a divorce.'

Perpetua seemed at a loss for a few seconds. 'Did I hear you correctly? After ten years of marriage, you want a divorce? And what would I get out of it?'

'I would pay you a sizeable sum,' he said, 'but I would keep the boys, and all of the property and titles. You would no longer be able to style yourself as a duchess.'

'Are you out of your mind?' she cried. 'Do you honestly believe I would give up the boys? I don't care about the castles and estates, or about my damn title, but you are not getting the boys. If we divorce, then I will be taking them back to my father's realm.'

'That is never going to happen, Perpetua. The boys belong with me. Rupert is destined to become the next Duke of Ridden.'

'You dare speak about the boys as if you know them? You don't know them, Hector. How many days have you spent in their company? When was the last time you took them on a trip, or even just sat down and had dinner with them? Have you ever played with them, or helped them with their lessons? For years, I have been doing your job as well as my own – raising those boys single-handedly.'

'Who is exaggerating now? You have had dozens of servants and staff to assist you.'

'They needed their father, not a few servants. What they got was me, and I will never give them up. Do you hear me?'

Hector nodded. 'Very well. I felt it was worth asking, but you have made your point. Consider the matter closed.'

'There is something else going on, isn't there? Have you found another woman? Someone younger, no doubt. Is that it? Do you wish to remarry? You should know by now that I couldn't care less about any of the little whores you take to your bed. Just leave me alone to live my life with the boys in Castle Ridden, and I will never disturb your life in Torrent. I thought that was the deal; why do you wish to break it now?'

'I said that the matter was closed.'

Perpetua eyed him. 'You could have put all that in a letter.'

'I thought it would be more polite to ask you in person. However, as I have stated, things have changed since I sent the summons. Castle Ridden is likely to become a far busier place in the near future. War is going to consume much of Upper Down. Farms and villages will be plundered, and Castle Ridden may even come under siege. If you had agreed to a quick divorce, I would have loaded your carriage with gold. You could have travelled all the way around the mountains to reach your father's kingdom, and you would have been spared the horrors that will surely come when the Kendril Wall is breached. Alas, it is not to be. Shall I have someone show you to where you will be sleeping?'

'You can show me yourself,' she said. 'It is the least you could do.'

Hector and Perpetua got to their feet, and the two unfinished glasses of brandy were set down onto the desk. Hector opened the door, and led his wife out into the hallway.

Hector caught the glance of a servant. 'Are the rooms in the eastern wing ready, as I requested?'

The servant bowed. 'Yes, my lord. The duchess's luggage is currently being taken there.'

Hector smiled at Perpetua. 'This way,' he said.

They strode along the hallway, and passed an open atrium in the centre of the palace, where a fountain was sending water into the air. They walked into the eastern wing, and entered a well-furnished suite of rooms, with long windows that overlooked the palace gardens. Sitting in the middle of the living room floor was a large pile of trunks and suitcases.

'Is this to your satisfaction?' Hector said.

Perpetua glanced around. 'This is where I always stay when I visit,' she said. 'Have I ever once complained about these rooms?'

'You complain about many things, but no, you have never voiced any displeasure about these quarters. The drinks cabinet is well-stocked, so please help yourself to whatever you find. Dinner will be served at sunset.'

'Be honest with me for once in your life, Hector,' she said. 'Did you really expect me to agree to a divorce that would keep me separated from the boys?'

'I admit I thought it was unlikely.'

'You have just wasted eight days of my life – four to get here, and four for the return journey. And for what – to get an answer you already expected?'

'It was a courtesy, nothing more.'

'The next time you get a foolish notion into your head, do me a favour and travel up to Castle Ridden to deliver the news.'

'I fear we will all be in Castle Ridden soon enough.'

'You may go now, husband. I wish to take a long bath, to clean four days of travel from my skin. And before you ask, no, you cannot stay. I am not one of your little whores, and I grew tired of you pawing at me many years ago. I did my duty and bore you two strong boys; you will be getting nothing more from me.'

Hector said nothing, then he inclined his head and strode from the rooms. He closed the front door behind him, and leaned against the wall.

He had known she would say no to his request for a divorce, and yet he was glad he had asked.

Her refusal would make things easier; after all, he had given her a choice, and she had thrown it back in his face. Whatever happened next would therefore be her fault.

His conscience eased, he straightened his shoulders, and walked back to his office.

CHAPTER 24
RESEARCH

North of Torrent, Upper Down – 16th Day of Lamenta 107

If Abigone lay flat against the bottom of the wagon, she could see a thin sliver of the outside world. The rear of the wagon had been draped in a thick canvas covering, held aloft by a wooden frame, and the two princesses were wreathed within its thick shadows.

'What can you see?' said Hygilt.

'Fields,' said Abigone. 'The sun is coming up on our left, and I can see the mountains.'

'Could we run for it? What if we jump down and run?'

'There are a dozen Westlanders walking just behind the wagon,' Abigone said. 'We wouldn't get ten yards.'

'It's my turn to take a look.'

Abigone pulled herself up into a sitting position. 'Do you not believe me?'

'I believe you,' said Hygilt, as she lay down on the floor of the wagon. 'I just wanted to see the sunlight.'

Abigone picked up one of the blankets they had been given, and wrapped it round her shoulders to keep out the chill air. It had been a long, cold night, their second since being snatched from the Royal Palace.

'You forgot to mention the frost,' said Hygilt, as she peered out of the narrow gap between the canvas and the wagon. 'No wonder we were freezing last night. We need to think of a plan to escape.'

Abigone rolled her eyes. 'Let me know if you get any ideas.'

'They haven't tied us up,' the girl went on. 'Our arms are free; our legs are free. We need some sort of distraction, and then we could run away.'

'The wagon is completely surrounded.'

'I'm not giving up. There must be something we can do.'

'Do you think Tulip is dead?'

'I don't know.'

'The poor little baby. I will never forget what they did to him.'

'And that man whose eye was scratched will probably never forget Tulip, either. I had no idea cats could be so vicious.'

'He was trying to protect us.'

Hygilt got to her knees and sat down, leaning her back against the side of the wagon. 'What are we going to do?'

Abigone glanced at the girl.

'If we don't try to escape,' Hygilt went on, 'then Dravid will take us both somewhere far away, and we'll never be found. Or they might just kill us and leave our bodies by the side of the road.'

'Don't say that,' said Abigone.

'But it's true.'

'I don't want to think about it. People will be looking for us.'

'But there's no guarantee they'll find us. I don't want to stay here and hope to be rescued. My grandfather told me that the world is ruled by people who take what they want, and not by people who sit around waiting for things to happen.'

'That sounds like something my father used to say.'

'My grandfather is nothing like Alfgang the Great. Did your father really turn three men into salt?'

Abigone frowned. 'No.'

'That's what I heard. He killed the two emissaries sent to ask for my release.'

'He turned the water in their bodies to salt. That's what Masters do. They cannot change an entire body into anything, because a body is made up of lots of different things.'

'Oh. I wish I'd had a chance to read those books I picked out from the library. I feel quite ignorant about Masters.'

'It's quite simple. Masters can change one thing into something else, if they are close enough. They can say something like *change the wood in that tree to gold*, or *change the water in that cup to lead*.'

'They can turn a tree into gold; they can make a golden tree?'

'No. Trees are less... dense, and the amount you get at the end depends upon, um... the...'

'The mass of the object?'

'Yes. So, the gold you get looks smaller than the tree, as though it's been squashed together.'

'Can I ask you more questions?'

'If you want, but I probably won't know the answers. I didn't like learning about Masters and Makers; the lessons used to bore me.'

'I wish I had been taught about them. All right; I know that only men can be Masters, and only women can be Makers, but why?'

'I don't know. It's like asking *why can only women have babies*. It's just the way it is.'

'And Masters change things, and Makers... make things?'

'Makers summon objects out of thin air.'

'Like what?'

'Anything they can see in their mind.'

'So a Maker could summon a dragon?'

Abigone smiled. 'I suppose, if dragons were real, and if the Maker could see every single part of the dragon in her mind. They would have to know exactly what a dragon's brain looks like, for example. If they get any parts wrong, it won't work, and they will end up with a... giant dragon-shaped mess.'

'That doesn't seem very fair.'

Abigone raised an eyebrow.

'Masters have an easy life, it seems,' Hygilt went on. 'If they can see something, they can change it into something else; but Makers must have to study hard if they want to summon anything remotely complicated.'

'Yes. It is unfair. To be a good Maker, you need to travel, to see lots of different things, and read, and study.' She glanced at her pile of blankets, then delved beneath them and retrieved the bag that had been slung over her shoulder when they had been captured.

'What's in there?' said Hygilt.

'The book I took from the library.'

'You had a book with you all this time and you didn't tell me?' said Hygilt. 'Can I see it?'

Abigone slipped *Makers of Elestia* from the bag and handed it to the girl. 'You will learn more from that than you will from me.'

Hygilt laid the book down on the floor of the wagon, in a patch where some sunlight was coming in through the narrow gap, and then she started to leaf through the pages. She came to the part where the book depicted several illustrations of simple objects.

'Oh,' she said. 'These are for Makers who are beginning their studies. It says that they should practise making these before moving on to more complicated things. That key looks easy; it's just a small piece of metal.' She frowned. 'But where does the metal come from?'

'The local environment,' said Abigone. 'Imagine an area in front of a Maker – their range. If the key is made of iron, then the Maker will summon any iron from within that range to build it. The more you practise, the bigger your range gets. Or, at least, that's how I think it works. The book will know.'

'What happens if there isn't a lot of iron in the Maker's range?'

'Then I suppose there wouldn't be enough to make the key.'

'It sounds as though you know quite a lot.'

'I have already reached the limits of my knowledge,' said Abigone.

'Have you ever known any Makers?'

'My father's aunt was one, but she died before I was born.'

'You have two sisters, don't you? Kilbride and...'

'Nolan.'

'Yes, Nolan. Three sisters, all descended from a family of Masters and Makers, and none of them have any abilities?'

Abigone said nothing.

'That sounds a little unlikely,' said Hygilt. 'Imagine what we could do if we had a Maker with us. We could summon something to help us escape.'

'I thought you hated Masters and Makers. You told me their existence was blasphemous.'

'That's what the emperor believes. What do the people of Upper Down think?'

'They think Masters and Makers are blessed by the spirits. If they weren't, then why would the spirits allow them to change and summon things? There are spirits inhabiting everything – yes? The trees, the mountains, the rivers; and they allow Masters and Makers to use their abilities. Turn a few pages in that book, and you will see some of the common prayers used by Makers. I was always told that a Maker has to use the right words, but I don't know if that's actually true.'

Hygilt leafed through the book until she reached the common invocations. She quietened for a few minutes as she read, her finger following the lines on the page.

'You have to ask the spirits' permission first,' the girl said, 'and you have to remember to give thanks at the end. It says here that being a Maker is a great privilege, and one must never forget that. One should always thank the spirits for the great blessings they have bestowed.'

'That's right. Giving thanks afterwards is the most important part. You could get in trouble if you forgot that step.'

Hygilt looked up at Abigone. 'Why did you pick this particular book?'

'No reason.'

The girl narrowed her eyes. 'Are you a Maker, Abigone?'

'Of course not.'

'What about your sisters?'

Abigone shook her head.

'I think you're lying. Your brother was a Master, but not one of his three sisters is a Maker? It can't be Kilbride. If she was a Maker, then everyone would know about it. I won't tell anyone, Abigone; I can keep a secret.'

Abigone remained silent.

'We might die soon,' said Hygilt, 'or we might be chained up somewhere horrible. If we had a Maker with us, then we might have a chance to prevent that. One thing bothers me, though – why would you keep it a secret? Are you embarrassed?'

'Shut up,' said Abigone.

'I see that you are no longer denying it.'

'There's no point. You have already called me a liar.'

'Did your father tell you to keep it a secret? I know – was it so he could arrange a marriage for you? You were betrothed to someone else, weren't you? A prince. Did your father think that the prince would say no if he knew you were a Maker?'

'You don't know what you're talking about,' Abigone said, her irritation growing. 'Even if I were a Maker, I wouldn't be able to help us escape. Do you have any idea how much training Makers need before they can summon anything useful? It's all right for Masters; they don't have to spend half their lives studying. And there is no one around to teach young Makers – no one. In the old days, there were schools and academies all over the Elestian Empire, and old Makers would train the next generation. All of that has gone, thanks to your family. The Sanctians think we're evil; they think...'

Abigone paused before she could say anything else, but from the look on Hygilt's face, it was too late.

'Try to summon a key,' said the girl. 'Please.' She turned the pages of the book back to the illustrations. 'Or what about a wooden spoon? That looks simple, and there's plenty of wood in the wagon. Please, Abigone; please try.'

'You are an extremely annoying girl.'

'Yes, but I'm right though, aren't I? What are you scared of?'

'Say we get out of this alive, and say your grandfather's army smashes through the Kendril Wall. The Sanctian Empire wants to hunt down and kill every Master and Maker. You have already told me how much the emperor hates us, and you wonder why I might be scared? You were right before – no prince in the Central Provinces would want to marry a Maker. The folk down there are terrified of people like me. The kingdom of Campsie burned two Makers just a few years ago, and thousands of people watched. Upper Down was the last place where we were safe. Do you see why I have to keep it a secret?'

Hygilt lowered her gaze. 'Sorry. I hadn't thought about it like that. I was just thinking how to get out of our current situation. If my grandfather invades Upper Down, I promise I won't tell him about you. But, right now, Abigone, your powers might be the only way we can escape from the Westlanders. If you summoned something enormous, it might scare them away. They are very superstitious, you know; they believe that the moons are gods.'

'I know what the Westlanders believe.'

'Will you try it?'

'No.'

'Why not?'

'Because I don't know how! I have never summoned anything in my life; not once. What if the spirits refuse to grant their permission? What if I summon the wrong thing? I could kill you by accident.'

'Not if you try to make a wooden spoon. I am pretty sure there is no wood in my body. The first step is to visualise the object,' she went on, her gaze on the book; 'then you invoke the spirits. You say, *Blessed spirits, with your permission, summon...*'

'I am aware of the correct wording.'

'Then try it.'

Abigone lowered her head. 'All right, if it will shut you up for a while. Let me see the book.'

Hygilt moved the book over the floor of the wagon to where Abigone was sitting.

Abigone stared down at the diagram of a wooden spoon. It seemed simple enough, so she closed her eyes and tried to picture it in her mind. She took a breath.

'Blessed spirits, with your permission, summon for me a wooden spoon.'

A strange rustling or scratching sound arose for the briefest of moments, then something fell onto the floor of the wagon. Abigone opened her eyes. Sitting on the pages of the book was a shapeless lump of wood.

Hygilt picked it up. 'Well, it's a start, I suppose; though I wouldn't be able to eat any soup from it.'

'See?' said Abigone. 'I can't even get that right.'

'It appeared in front of you,' Hygilt said, 'and then it fell onto the book. Are you supposed to put your hands out to catch it? Oh, and you haven't thanked the spirits.'

Abigone closed her eyes again. 'Blessed spirits, I give thanks to you for the honour of being a Maker.'

'That's better,' said Hygilt. She gazed at the oddly-formed lump of wood in her hand. 'This wood came from the planks of the wagon, yes? If you summoned a much larger spoon, would the wagon fall apart?'

'I suppose so.'

'Should we try that?'

'If I did, then the Westlanders would make us walk.'

'They might get scared and run away. The wagon would disintegrate before their eyes, and a huge spoon would appear in its place. Seeing that could be quite unsettling.'

Abigone raised her head. 'The wagon is slowing down.'

Hygilt lay on the floor of the wagon, her face pressed up against the narrow gap below the canvas covering.

'We're next to a river,' the girl said. 'Maybe we're stopping to get water.'

Abigone closed the book and slid it under the blankets. Her stomach rumbled at the thought of breakfast, and she wondered if they would be fed that day.

The wagon came to a halt, and Abigone listened to the sound of the Westlanders speaking in their own language.

'Do you know what they're saying?' she whispered.

'No,' said Hygilt.

'I thought you knew four languages.'

'I do, but Westlander isn't one of them. I had the choice to study it at school but, funnily enough, I didn't think it would ever come in useful.' She pulled herself back from the opening, and sat. 'Someone's coming.'

The canvas covering was lifted, and Abigone blinked in the daylight as three huge Westlanders peered into the back of the wagon.

'Good morning,' said Hygilt.

A Westlander eyed her, then he threw a sack and a water skin into the wagon. One of the other Westlanders smiled at Abigone, but she read his expression as sleazy rather than friendly, and she shuddered.

The three men backed away, and the canvas was pulled back into place. Abigone remained where she was, as Hygilt rummaged around in the sack.

'Did you see the look that man gave me?' Abigone said.

'I saw it,' said Hygilt. 'Try not to think about it.' She pulled two apples from the sack. 'Are you hungry?'

'I've lost my appetite.'

'Don't be silly. You should eat something.'

'I'm frightened, Hygilt. Those men could do anything to us. I'd rather die than let them touch me.'

'You should still eat,' said Hygilt. 'And you should have some water.'

'No. Do you remember when we stopped yesterday? The Westlanders wouldn't even let us pee in private. They were watching us when we were in the bushes.'

'They were making sure we didn't try to run away.'

The canvas covering was pulled away, and Abigone saw Chief Dravid staring into the rear of the wagon.

'How are you today, girls?' he said. 'Enjoying the trip?'

'I would enjoy it much more if you took us back to Torrent,' said Hygilt.

Dravid laughed. 'That's the Hygilt I remember.' He glanced at Abigone. 'This is what she was like the last time I took her. No matter what happened, she always had a smart comment to make.'

'The last time you kidnapped her,' said Abigone, 'was when you murdered my brother.'

'That's right,' said Dravid. 'Did you know that he refused to fight back? He just stood there, and let us kill him. No man like that should ever be king.'

'Why don't you tell Abigone how you knew where Alfgang the Pius would be?' said Hygilt.

'I think I will,' he said, 'seeing as how we'll never be going back to Torrent again.' He turned his gaze back to Abigone. 'I paid a little visit to Hector's home, and his lawyer told me where your brother could be found. What was his name? Amery, was it? That little reptile was terrified of me; I could see his hands shaking. He told me that Pius was going to surrender to Valentino, and that it was in my interests to stop him.'

'So, it wasn't Hector?' said Abigone.

'Are you an idiot, girl?' said Dravid. 'Of course Hector was behind it. It was the duke who asked me to speak to Amery in the first place. Hector loathed your brother. He thought Pius was weak, and he wasn't wrong. I was doing Upper Down a favour, and what happens when I get back? Hector turns against me! That fucking dog betrayed me. You are not the only one to lose a brother, girl. If I ever see that bastard again...' Dravid fell into silence for a moment. 'Do you know Hector well?'

'I suppose so, or at least I thought I did.'

'Something... uncanny happened the night Stefan's men attacked my beer hall.'

'What?' said Hygilt.

'I was up on the balcony, and I had barricaded the stairs. Stefan's men were trying to get at me, but we were keeping them back. I saw Hector; he was down on the ground floor, sitting in an alcove. Can you imagine? There were swords swinging and blood everywhere, and Hector's just sitting in a fucking alcove, as if he's enjoying the show. Anyway, a few seconds after that... well, my armour, it...'

'Yes?' said Hygilt.

'This is going to sound fucking stupid, but...'

'Must you swear all the time?' said Hygilt.

Dravid blinked, then he laughed again. 'May I please continue with my story, Your High-and-Mighty-ness? Thank you. As I was saying, my armour disappeared, or it exploded into flames. The metal vanished, and my underclothes were on fire. Then, just as I was trying to get the flames off me, tons of rock fell from the sky. Rock. There was no fucking rock in the roof of the beer hall, so how did it get there? Can you explain any of that?'

Abigone shook her head.

'Is Hector a Master?' said Dravid. 'Only a Master could have done all that.'

'Is it possible that you got confused in all the chaos?' said Hygilt.

'I know what I saw. Armour doesn't vanish. Stone doesn't appear from nowhere.'

'I have never heard anyone say that Hector was a Master,' said Abigone. 'Did he really kill my brother?'

'Hector provided the information, but I killed him.'

'And then you mutilated his body.'

'The lads wanted a few souvenirs. It was me who cut off the bastard's head, though. I was going to take it back to Twinbrook, but we got drunk on the ride home, and I fucking left it sitting in the town square of Torrent.'

Abigone started to cry.

'That's right, girl,' said Dravid. 'Is reality finally sinking in?'

'What are you going to do to us?' said Hygilt.

Dravid grinned. 'Let me see. You, Hygilt, I am going to marry. I already have a wife, somewhere, but who gives a fuck about that, eh? I want an imperial princess as my bride. As for Abigone's fate, well, I think I might keep that a secret for now.'

'I am not going to marry you,' said Hygilt.

'You have no say in the matter,' said Dravid. 'Your opinion means nothing. You are going to bear a whole litter of children for me, whether you like it or not. I won't touch you until then, though, and none of the lads would dare – they know what I'd do to them. You are for me, and me alone.'

'I will kill you while you sleep.'

Dravid laughed again. 'You could try, but it wouldn't end well for you. Do you think I wouldn't give you a good beating just because you're a girl? But, if you are obedient, and quiet, then I will treat you well enough. This probably wasn't the future you were expecting; try to make your peace with it. If you respect me, and do as I say, then your life will be tolerable.'

'Leave us alone,' sobbed Abigone.

Dravid raised his palms. 'Behave yourselves, girls, and there will be no trouble.'

He dropped the canvas covering, and the back of the wagon was plunged into shadow. Abigone felt Hygilt take her hand.

'I know I sounded brave,' the girl whispered, 'but I'm just as frightened as you are.'

'Pass me the damn book,' said Abigone.

Hygilt reached under the blankets and placed the book in front of them. Abigone wiped her eyes and opened it. She returned to the pages with the illustrations, and stared at them.

'How long does it take to get to the Westlands?' said Hygilt.

'Is that where he's taking us?'

'I don't know.'

'It will be another four or five days before we leave Upper Down,' Abigone said. 'If I start practising now, then…' She started to cry again. 'It's pointless. It takes years to train a Maker.'

'Don't give up,' said Hygilt. 'All we can do is use the time we have.'

Abigone stared at the book. Her gaze fell onto a small wooden doll, similar to one she had owned as a child. She closed her eyes, and found that she could picture it with ease, despite the dread Dravid's visit had engendered within her. She visualised every aspect of the doll, from its carved face and hair, and the tiny buttons down the front of its dress.

'Blessed spirits,' she said, 'with your permission, summon for me a wooden doll.'

She heard the same strange scratching noise, and reached out with a hand. Something wooden fell into her palm, and she smiled.

'Thank you spirits,' she said, then she opened her eyes.

Hygilt frowned. 'What is it?'

Abigone stared at the misshapen lump of wood in her hand. 'It was supposed to be a doll.'

'A doll?' said Hygilt. 'I'm glad I didn't have a toy that looked like that when I was growing up. It would have given me nightmares.'

'I don't understand,' said Abigone. 'I knew what it was supposed to look like. I used to have a doll just like it, and I could see it in my mind – so why didn't it work?'

Hygilt's eyes went back to the book, her finger tracing over the columns of text. 'Seeing an image of it isn't enough,' she said. 'It says here that you also have to understand how it was made, and you need to know everything about the materials that went into its construction. What type of wood is it made from, and did the person who crafted it use a knife or a chisel – that sort of thing.' She glanced at Abigone. 'Don't give up.' She passed Abigone an apple. 'And please eat something.'

Abigone bit back her despair. 'All right,' she said. 'I'm going to read this stupid book, and I'm going to keep practising. It might end up being for nothing, but it's better than sitting here crying.'

Hygilt smiled. 'Let's read the stupid book together.'

CHAPTER 25
HARD WON

North of Torrent, Upper Down – 16th Day of Lamenta 107

Walter forded the river, his left hand gripping the reins of the two horses, as his boots splashed through the shallow water. On the opposite bank, the fresh ruts left by wagon wheels were visible in the mud, along with dozens of footprints. Walter climbed the bank and took his bearings. The sun was halfway down the western sky, and he had been trailing Dravid for over a day, travelling through the night in an attempt to catch up with them.

Of Stefan's force, he had seen no sign, and Walter wondered what he should make of that. Had Stefan gone by a different route, or had he lied about his intentions? Perhaps the events at the Kendril Wall had caused him to panic, and he had fled north with his men to escape before Valentino's army entered Torrent. Walter tried not to get his hopes up. If Stefan had abandoned Hector, then his brother's position would have been weakened, and the flight of Westlanders from Twinbrook would intensify. Besides, Stefan was the last person he wanted to meet out in the open countryside. The chief had vowed to kill him after Walter had punched him, and Walter had little desire to see him face to face.

He unbuckled the heavy saddle packs from one of the horses, and moved them to the other. He had been driving the two mounts hard, but not hard enough to exhaust them. Every hour or so, he would lead them on foot, to give them a rest, just as he had been trained to do by the Mountain Rangers. It was frustrating, but they had made steady progress, and Walter was sure that he couldn't be too far behind Dravid.

He mounted the fresher of the two horses, and looped the reins of the other horse round his wrist. They took off at a slow trot, their hooves digging into the soft turf. On either side, the mountains that almost completely encircled Upper Down were radiant in the afternoon sunshine, and the first snow of the year had appeared on a few high summits.

Walter rode onwards for an hour, keeping the pace even and steady. He descended into a grassy dell, and saw more footprints. Ahead, the dell narrowed into a valley, with thick copses of trees on either side. Walter brought the horses to a stop, and dismounted. If he couldn't see the way ahead clearly, he would have to take his time. He walked the horses down the slope to a small stream, then they entered the woods. The ground was carpeted in brown leaves, and Walter led his two mounts silently down the valley.

Walter heard something, and froze, his eyes scanning the area in front of him. He remained completely still, and heard the sound again. Voices. Someone was speaking further down the valley, hidden by the trees. Walter turned to his left, and led the horses behind a thick row of conifers. He tied the reins to a branch, and then crept back down the slope again. He padded through the fallen leaves, going from tree to tree as he descended deeper into the valley. The sound of the voices grew louder as he crept along, and Walter realised that a large number of men were talking. He dropped to the ground, and crawled under the branches of a large spruce, edging his way forwards over the dry ground. He entered a patch of thick undergrowth, and gazed down into another dell. It was clear of trees, and large groups of Westlanders were sitting or standing, while others were eating close to the banks of the stream. Parked off to the right were two wagons. Several wounded men were lying on the back of one, while the other was covered, and had several Westlanders posted around it as guards.

Walter crawled forward for another yard, then lay still again. There was no sign of Abigone or Hygilt, and he guessed they were in the covered wagon. He listened, but the men were using their own language to converse, and none of it meant anything to Walter. He had picked up a few words from his time drinking in the beer halls of Twinbrook, but not enough to understand a conversation.

He began to count the Westlanders, but lost his place when he neared two hundred. He couldn't understand it – how could Dravid have gathered so many men together? He had been told that the Westlander chief had attacked the Royal Palace with a hundred men, and yet twice that number were in the dell. He caught sight of Dravid himself. The tall chief was talking to another man, who had his back to Walter. Dravid laughed at something, and the two men embraced. Then the other man turned, and Walter swore softly.

It was Stefan.

The Westlander chief had indeed betrayed Hector, but not in the way Walter had been expecting. Had Stefan informed Dravid that the palace was under-defended? Had the two men arranged to meet in the dell? The two chiefs were supposed to hate each other, so why were they chatting amicably, and laughing at each other's jokes?

And, more importantly, how was Walter supposed to reach Abigone and Hygilt when two hundred Westlanders were in the way? When Kilbride had asked him to go after the princesses, they had assumed that he would reach Stefan's force long before they found Dravid; and they had assumed that Stefan's men would assist in the freeing of the two captives. Both assumptions had been wrong, and Walter was alone. He closed his eyes for a moment, as tiredness seeped through him. Just as he had done in the aftermath of Alfgang the Great's death, he had spent two nights awake, and his head was groggy from lack of sleep. Worse, he was craving a drink. He wished he was back in his tower apartment, with the door safely closed, and with a glass of whisky in his hand. Life had been easier when he had spent most of it drunk. With sobriety had come responsibility, and responsibility had led him to a dell where he had to get past two hundred Westlanders in order to rescue Abigone and Hygilt.

He opened his eyes again, determined not to fall asleep, and gazed down at the resting Westlanders. Two choices seemed to crystallise in his mind. He could attack the Westlanders, or he could creep back to where he had tied the horses, and ride south to Torrent. He could tell Kilbride that Stefan had beaten him to it, and that the princesses were now in his custody. A direct assault on the makeshift camp had only one positive aspect – it would be over quickly. Death or shame, which was worse? A third choice emerged – he could take the horses and flee north. He could put a thousand miles between himself and Upper Down, and start a new life somewhere no one would know him. He would be forever missing, presumed dead. He would still feel shame, but he would never have to endure Kilbride's disappointment.

He heard a rustle through the trees, followed by the clank of steel armour. Walter slowly turned his head, and saw a Westlander making his way through the woods. The man stood seven yards from where Walter was lying, placed his helmet and sword on the ground, and began loosening his belt. Moments later, the sound of him urinating against a tree reached Walter's ears.

Without thinking, Walter crawled backwards out of the undergrowth. Some part of his mind was screaming at him to stop what he was doing, but he ignored it. He eased himself out of the bushes, and got to his feet. His hand went to Count Sebastian's sword, and he drew it. Then it struck him – what exactly was he intending to do with the weapon? The Westlander was covered in a full set of plate armour. He pushed the sword back into its scabbard, and looked around. He saw a heavy branch and picked it up. He must have made a noise, because the Westlander turned to see who was there, his hands still down by his crotch.

Walter swung the branch with both hands, and it cracked against the Westlander's face. The man flinched, as blood trickled down from his nose, but he remained standing. He shook his head at Walter, then buckled his belt.

'Did you hit me with a stick, little man?' the Westlander said.

Walter drew his sword.

The Westlander nodded, then he pointed at it. 'Nice blade. It will be mine soon.'

Both men glanced at the Westlander's own sword, which was still lying on the ground next to his helmet.

'I am going to reach for my weapon now,' said the Westlander. 'I advise you to start running.'

He extended his arm, his gaze still on Walter, then he stooped down. Walter lunged out with Sebastian's sword, aiming for the Westlander's neck. The man shrugged away at the last moment, and the blade sliced through the top of his ear. The Westlander staggered, then he reached out with both gauntleted hands and pushed Walter to the ground. Walter landed on his back, and the Westlander placed a knee onto his chest. He pulled Sebastian's sword from Walter's grasp, while blood dripped down from the wound in his ear.

'Where did you get this beauty?' the man said, gazing at the count's blade.

Walter's right arm reached out, scrabbling around in the dirt for anything to use against the Westlander, as the breath was squeezed from his chest. His fingers found the hilt of the man's sword, but it was too heavy to lift from that angle; then his fingers grabbed hold of the Westlander's steel helmet.

'If you beg, little man,' said the Westlander, 'I will give you a quick death.'

Walter swung the helmet, and it battered off the man's head. The Westlander dropped the sword, and Walter swung his arm again, cracking the steel helmet against the Westlander's skull a second time. The man stared down at him, then his eyes closed and he rolled over, collapsing on the ground next to Walter. Walter scrambled free, and almost broke into a run, his only thought to get back to the horses before the Westlander regained consciousness.

He stopped himself, and picked up Sebastian's sword. He gazed down at the prone Westlander, trying to summon some ruthlessness. The man had been about to kill him, and he had likely been part of the war band that had attacked the Royal Palace. It was justice, he told himself, and he knelt by the body. He raised the sword. What would he do with it? Stab the man in the eye? Slit his throat? None of the options seemed appealing, and his hand remained where it was.

The Westlander groaned, his eyes opening, and Walter's instincts took over. He lifted the sword higher, then brought his arm down in a chopping motion. The steel blade struck the Westlander by the bridge of his nose, and bit deep. Walter tried to pull the blade free, but it had embedded itself in the man's skull. He let go of the hilt and moved back as the Westlander writhed on the ground. His mouth opened and closed a few times, but only blood came from his lips. He gargled, and then lay still.

Walter remained where he was, his gaze never leaving the enormous, steel-clad body lying on the ground in front of him. Was he really dead? Despite the sword that was lodged in his head, Walter wasn't completely sure. He picked up a small branch and poked the warrior with it, then he pulled himself up onto his knees and took a closer look. The Westlander wasn't breathing. Walter placed a boot against the side of the man's head, placed both hands onto the hilt of Sebastian's sword, and pulled. The blade came free, along with a spray of blood that hit Walter's arms. It was still warm, and Walter almost threw up.

He had killed someone – and not just anyone. He had killed a huge Westlander. True, the man had been unconscious when Walter was preparing to deliver the death blow, but no one else needed to know about that detail. Walter tried to think about what to do next, but his mind was still replaying the entire incident. He recalled his training, but nothing he had done in the Mountain Rangers had prepared him for the situation in which he found himself. He listened to the sounds coming from the dell for a moment. If he fled, then the body would be discovered. With all that shiny steel, it would be hard to hide.

Or, he thought, he could use the slight advantage his actions had given him. The Westlanders in the dell would be expecting their colleague to return, so perhaps he should oblige them. He tried to gauge the man's height. He had been much broader than Walter, but only an inch or two taller; would the others notice the difference? He knelt down, and got to work, unbuckling the dead man's armour, and stripping it from his body. Within a few minutes, the pieces of armour were lying on the ground next to the corpse. Walter stood again, and dragged the body into the thick undergrowth, then he returned to the armour and began to strap it over his clothes. The greaves were a little too long for his shins, and the breastplate was heavier than any armour Walter had ever worn before. He staggered around for a moment, trying to get used to the weight, then he picked up the Westlander's sword with both hands, and threw it into the bushes. He strapped Sebastian's blade to his belt, then leaned over and placed the helmet over his head. It was too large for him, and Walter could barely see through the grille in the visor. He stood up straight, raised his chin, and began walking through the woods in the direction of the dell, his heart pounding.

He knew it was easily the most stupid thing he had ever done in his life. He listed everything that could go wrong. Someone might call out the Westlander's name; or say something to him in their own language. The difference in height and bulk might be noticed, or perhaps Sebastian's fancy sword might give him away. He reached a track leading down the slope into the dell, and tried to project an air of confidence. A few Westlanders glanced up at his approach, but none commented. Walter strode down the hill without falling over, then he made his way through the crowds until he was a few yards from the wagon. He eyed the eight warriors posted around it, then he sat down, his back against a tree.

Stefan's forces had brought a few horses with them, and bottles of whisky and brandy were removed from several saddle bags and passed round the men. Dravid was talking in a loud voice, as though he was telling everyone what they were going to do next, and Stefan interjected a few times. From the various hand signals, Walter intuited that the two groups were planning to go their separate ways. What did that mean? Dravid would presumably be fleeing north, to get out of Upper Down, but where was Stefan going? Back to Torrent? If so, then they were probably going to divide the spoils. Dravid would get Hygilt, and Stefan would be taking his bride-to-be with him.

Someone offered a bottle to Walter, but he feigned snoring, and the warrior passed it to someone else. He sat still for several minutes, his eyes taking in the Westlanders as they drank and talked. The eight men around the wagon were given a bottle of something, and they began to swig from it. Time was slipping away from Walter, and he still had no idea what to do next.

As the eight men guarding the wagon passed the bottle around, Walter heard a strange sound, as though fingers were scratching the rough ground. At that moment, three of the trees surrounding the wagon began to creak, and two toppled without warning, crashing down into the dell, and sending the Westlanders into a wild panic. The wagon then fell apart, it chassis splitting, though no tree had hit it. A massive chunk of wood three yards wide appeared in the dell as if from nowhere, and it rolled down the slope, adding to the mayhem breaking out in the dell. Five of the wagon's eight guards had been among those struck by the falling trees, and Walter got to his feet. Westlanders were rushing around, looking for an ambush, while others were staring at the huge mass of wood that had appeared in the middle of the dell. Some fell to their knees and began praying, while Dravid was gesturing for his men to pull back. Walter hurried to the rear of the ruined wagon. He reached out, pulled up the canvas covering, and saw Abigone and Hygilt huddled beneath it. The two princesses stared up at him, and Walter lifted his visor.

'Run,' Walter whispered. 'Circle back to the south; I have horses behind the tall conifers. Go.'

For a moment, neither moved, then Abigone grabbed Hygilt's hand and they raced off into the woods. Walter set off after them, but the steel armour was weighing him down, and he lumbered along. He was twenty yards from the dell when more cries broke out from the vicinity of the broken wagon. Walter pulled his helmet off and dropped it to the ground, then he began unbuckling the armour as he ran. He crashed through some undergrowth, then realised he couldn't see either princess ahead of him. He shed the breastplate, and his pace quickened. He began to turn back for the south, hoping that the princesses had understood his words by the wagon. As he circled back on himself, he saw over a dozen Westlanders off to his right, searching through the woods for the missing prisoners.

Walter pulled the last of his armour off, and broke into a sprint, weaving through the trees, the scabbard containing Sebastian's sword clutched in his left hand. With no steel encumbering him, he knew he was moving faster than any of the Westlanders. They would find the armour scattered through the forest, but that would slow them down a bit. He reached the track where he had first dismounted, and raced across it, heading for the row of conifers. He ran behind them, and almost wept with relief when he saw Abigone and Hygilt standing next to the two horses, the reins held in their hands.

Abigone ran to him and threw her arms round his shoulder. 'Thank you, Walter.'

'Get on the fucking horse, Abbie,' he hissed. 'Thank me later.'

Abigone pulled herself up on to the grey gelding, and Walter helped Hygilt get onto the saddle in front of her. He went to the other horse, put his foot in the stirrups, and swung his other leg over. He gripped the reins, and dug his heels in, just as two Westlanders raced past. They skidded to a halt as they saw Walter and the princesses, and drew their weapons. Walter urged his horse into a gallop, and barged right past them, his right boot catching one in the chest and sending him flying to the ground. Walter raced away, with the gelding a yard behind him, as the two horses ran at full speed up the track.

An hour later, Walter and the others dismounted in the middle of another patch of woods, around eighteen miles from the dell. The two horses were exhausted, and they were led down to the bank of a river so they could drink, as Walter, Abigone and Hygilt glanced back at the way they had come.

They sat by the banks of the river as the horses drank.

'Our mounts will be out of action for a while,' Walter said, 'though we can walk them for another few miles before it gets dark. Now, uh... about what happened in the dell. What the fuck was that thing? The trees fell, and then... something appeared.'

'Abigone is a Maker,' said Hygilt. 'Didn't you know? And you are Walter, the King's Champion. You were accompanying King Alfgang the Pius when he tried to take me to my uncle.' She smiled. 'Thank you for rescuing us.'

'I think you mostly rescued yourselves,' said Walter. 'Abbie, is it true – are you a Maker?'

'Not a very good one,' said Abigone.

'And the giant chunk of wood?'

'That was supposed to be a dragon,' she said. 'I was trying to summon a wooden dragon to frighten the Westlanders.'

'It didn't look much like a dragon, but it certainly scared the shit out of the Westlanders,' said Walter. 'Some of them were praying to it. And Stefan was there; did you know that? Stefan and Dravid dreamed this up together.'

'Stefan came to the wagon,' said Abigone, 'but he didn't say anything to us. When we first saw him, we thought that maybe he had defeated Dravid's men, but then we saw them all talking together as though they were friends.'

'Are you both unharmed?' said Walter.

'Yes,' said Hygilt. 'How did you know where we were?'

'I have been chasing you since yesterday morning,' he said.

'I heard that you were a useless drunk,' she said, 'but that doesn't appear to be the case.'

Walter smiled. 'Who told you that about me?'

'Abigone did.'

'Wait,' said Abigone; 'that was before you punched Stefan, and before you rode halfway across Upper Down to find us.'

'I'm not offended,' he said. 'I am a useless drunk.'

Hygilt squinted at Walter's waist.

'What are you looking at?' he said.

'The hilt of your sword,' said the girl. 'Might I see it?'

Walter nodded. He slid it out of the scabbard, realising at the same time that he had neglected to wipe the Westlander's blood from the blade.

'Where did you get that?' Hygilt whispered.

'From a man named Count Sebastian.'

Hygilt's eyes widened. 'Did you kill him?'

'No. I captured him, and then I released him in exchange for a day-long truce. He gave me his sword to borrow, and I gave him mine.'

'When was this?' said Abigone.

'Yesterday morning,' said Walter.

'You captured him, and then released him?' said Hygilt.

'That's right.'

'Why?'

'I told you that – to get a truce. The Kendril Wall was being battered by cannon fire, and I thought it was a fair exchange. Do you know of him?'

'Of course I do – he's my uncle. He's married to my Aunty Carmen, and I used to have school lessons with their two children. I didn't know he had come with the army. He is renowned as one of the bravest knights in the empire – and you captured him?'

'He was sheltering from the bombardment in a cave with a handful of men, and the Rangers surrounded them. He knew there was no point in fighting; the Rangers had a dozen longbows aimed in their direction. He surrendered to me with honour, and so I released him, after he pledged to ask Prince Valentino for a truce.'

Abigone smiled. 'This all sounds suspiciously like you are actually behaving like a real King's Champion, Walter. And to top if off, you also saved us from Dravid and Stefan.'

Walter grimaced. 'Don't say that. It was your Maker powers that freed you from the Westlanders. I had very little to do with it. I was sitting around like an idiot before you made your wooden dragon appear.'

'He's modest, too,' said Hygilt. 'I like him.' She gazed at Walter. 'That sword is worth a fortune. You should clean it before the blood tarnishes the surface.'

Walter leaned forward, and plunged the blade into the water of the river. Hygilt passed him a handkerchief, and he began wiping the blood away.

'Whose blood is that?' said Abigone.

'A Westlander's.'

'You killed one of those brutes? On your own?'

'Try not to sound too surprised, Abbie. I've trained with the Mountain Rangers for over six years.'

'Yes, but you have spent the last three of those completely drunk. Why now, Walter? Why have you woken up after so long asleep?'

Walter shrugged. 'I don't know. You're my cousin, Abbie; you're family. How could I have lived with myself if I had done nothing to help you? It was Kilbride's idea. She asked me to go after you.'

'How is my sister?'

'She was fine when I left her.'

'And... Tulip? Is my little Tulip all right?'

'Yes. He's fine.'

Abigone exhaled. 'Praise the spirits.'

Walter smiled. 'I thought that might cheer you up.'

'Listen, Walter; there's something we have to tell you.'

He lifted the sword out of the river, and started to dry the blade with his sleeve.

'Hygilt and I know who killed Alfgang the Pius,' Abigone went on.

'I was there, Abbie. It was Dravid.'

'Yes, I know that. Dravid was the one who carried out the murder; but who told him where the king would be?'

Walter turned to her.

'It was Hector,' Abigone said. 'Hector betrayed my brother to the Westlanders. Hector killed the king.'

'What? Not even Hector is that bad.'

'Are you sure about that? Dravid told us all about it. It was Amery who passed on the information about my brother's route that day, but it was Hector who ordered him to do it.'

A memory of that awful morning in the ravine passed through Walter's mind, and he recalled the moment King Alfgang's body had been pierced with a lance. He lowered his gaze.

'Do you believe me?' said Abigone.

'Yes.'

'What are we going to do?' said Hygilt.

'We are going back to Torrent,' he said.

'Won't the Westlanders be chasing us?'

Walter gave her a wry smile. 'Every damn step of the way.'

CHAPTER 26
HARD NOSED

Torrent, Upper Down – 16th Day of Lamenta 107

Frida stood as Kilbride entered the living room.

'What's happening at the Wall?' Frida said. 'We could hear the cannon all afternoon. Why have they stopped? Has the Wall been breached?'

'The Kendril Wall is still standing,' said Kilbride. 'Today's bombardment has damaged it further, but it hasn't fallen.'

'Then why have the cannon stopped?'

'I'm not sure. Maybe they overheated. Perhaps they can only fire for a few hours each day.'

Frida sat on the couch next to Alfie, who was fidgeting nervously.

'What happened to the truce?' said Frida, taking the boy's hand. 'I thought there was a truce.'

'It elapsed at noon,' said Kilbride. 'Prince Valentino gave us a day, and Hector wasted it.'

'My brother has his faults,' said Frida, 'but you can't blame him for this catastrophe. Shouldn't we be thinking about evacuating? Will the Wall last another day?'

'I don't know.'

'Then why don't you find out?' Frida cried. 'You are a regent,

Kilbride; shouldn't you be rallying the defences at the Wall? Why have you been sitting around the palace all day?'

Kilbride said nothing.

'Well?' said Frida.

'Hector ordered me to stay here,' Kilbride said.

'He... ordered you? What is that supposed to mean?'

'Hector and I are the only regents in Torrent, Frida, and my vote is worth half of his.'

'That doesn't make any sense. Hector can't tell you what to do. Why don't you call for a carriage?'

'Because every militia in Upper Down takes its orders from Hector,' she said, 'and they have been commanded to make sure I stay in the palace. It is for my own protection, apparently. Your brother is effectively in sole control of Upper Down.'

Frida stared at her. 'And your vote is only worth half of his?'

'Yes. That's what was in the agreement.'

'Then why did you sign it, Kilbride?'

'Because Abigone and Walter were here at the time. Our three votes together could defeat Hector's two. With both of the other regents out of Torrent, I have no legal authority to do anything without Hector's permission.'

'Where is Hector? I want to see him.'

'I think he is in the ducal palace with his wife.'

'Perpetua is in Torrent? Why would she come here at a time like this?'

'I don't know. I am not only physically isolated in the palace; I have very little means of finding out what is going on elsewhere. If I order one of the militia to do something for me, they send a message to the ducal palace asking for Hector's permission before they will act. And, so far, Hector hasn't replied to a single request.'

Frida lowered her gaze. 'Why is my brother behaving like this? He must be planning something. Is there any word about Abigone?'

'No. There has been no news.'

'I can't bear this,' said Frida. 'Should we surrender to Valentino? You are the clever one, Kilbride; everyone says that – what should we do?'

'If it were up to me, I would be negotiating with the imperial army, Frida. But it's not up to me; Hector has made sure of that.' She took a step forward, and crouched by Alfie. 'How are you feeling, Your Majesty?'

'I don't want to stay in the palace,' the boy said. 'The Westlanders might come back.'

'We have over a thousand Royal Guardsmen defending us here, Your Majesty,' said Kilbride. 'An entire regiment is patrolling the Royal Parkland. The Westlanders won't be able to break in again.'

'What if they do?'

'Hundreds of Westlanders have already run away,' said Kilbride, 'and more are leaving Twinbrook with every hour that passes.'

'Shouldn't we be doing the same?' said Frida. 'The cannon have stopped; we should leave Torrent before they start again.'

'That's not up to me,' said Kilbride. 'My hands are tied until Walter and Abigone get back.'

'I will write to Hector,' Frida said, 'and demand to know what he is planning to do.'

Kilbride stood. 'That's a good idea. Now, if you will please excuse me, I need to return to my study.'

Frida frowned, then Kilbride turned and strode away. She left the chamber, and four Mountain Rangers began to flank her as she walked along the palace corridors. Of all the things she had told Frida, one hadn't been completely true. The Rangers answered to Walter, not Hector, and Walter had ordered them to place themselves at Kilbride's service. Alone among the armed forces of Upper Down, the Mountain Rangers did not go to Hector to seek his permission; they obeyed Kilbride without question. They were too few in number to stand up to the thousand Royal Guardsmen in the palace, but they shadowed Kilbride wherever she went, and she felt safe in their presence.

She reached her quarters and entered, the four Rangers remaining by the front door. She walked into her study, and saw Lothar standing by her desk, a young woman next to him. Kilbride frowned.

'Apologies for entering your apartment, ma'am,' said Lothar; 'but you requested discretion, and I did not wish to be seen waiting outside your front door.'

Kilbride eyed the young woman, who was staring at the floor. 'Who is this? Who have you brought here, Commander?'

'Might we speak candidly first, ma'am?' said Lothar. 'I need some assurances that I am doing the right thing.'

Kilbride walked round her desk and sat down. 'What kind of assurances?'

'I have been pondering the words you spoke to me yesterday, ma'am. If they meant what I think they meant, then I believe that this woman may be able to help us. But first, I need to hear you say it plainly.'

Kilbride rubbed her face with a hand. 'I would like you to speak first, Commander. Does your loyalty lie with the King's Champion or the Duke of Ridden?'

'With the King's Champion, ma'am.'

'Despite the fact that you betrayed the King's Champion?'

'Yes, ma'am. I accept responsibility for my actions, and I would like to make amends. Now it is your turn, ma'am. Are you conspiring with the King's Champion against the Duke of Ridden?'

Kilbride kept her gaze on the Ranger. With one word, she would either find an ally, or expose herself to charges of treason.

'Yes,' she said.

Lothar nodded, then he gestured towards the young woman. 'As commander of the scouts, I have several intelligence contacts within the Mountain Rangers, ma'am. One of them brought this woman to my attention not long after dawn this morning. She had been held in Twinbrook by one of Dravid's allies, and she escaped when the house was raided by Stefan's men four days ago. She made her way to Torrent, where she was recognised and debriefed. I think you might be interested in what she has to say, ma'am.'

'Does she have a name?'

'Yes, ma'am. Her name is Ireni.'

'Tell me your story, Ireni,' said Kilbride.

'Yes, ma'am,' said the young woman. 'I used to work for Duke Hector.'

'In what capacity?'

'I... I was his mistress, ma'am.'

'I see. How did you end up in Twinbrook?'

'Duke Hector sold me to Chief Dravid, ma'am, and then Dravid passed me on to one of his friends.'

Kilbride lowered her gaze. 'He sold you?'

'Yes, ma'am.'

'Tell Her Highness what you told me, Ireni,' said Lothar.

'Yes, sir,' said the young woman. 'I was in the ducal palace on the day King Alfgang the Great died. Chief Dravid arrived, and spoke to Mister Amery. I heard everything. They were plotting to assassinate Alfgang the Pius. Mister Amery told Dravid that the new king would be travelling south the next morning, to hand over Princess Hygilt to the imperial army. Mister Amery also told him that the soldiers on the Kendril Wall had been bribed to allow Dravid's forces through. Then Dravid took me to Twinbrook. After Alfgang the Pius was murdered, I heard Dravid boast about it many times, but he was angry with Hector. Dravid had expected to be rewarded for carrying out the duke's orders; instead, Hector attacked his forces.'

Kilbride stared at the woman, unable to form any words.

'I thought you needed to hear this, ma'am,' said Lothar. 'I admit that I was still undecided about the correct course of action before I heard what Ireni had to say. Her testimony is damning. If Hector arranged the murder of King Alfgang the Pius, then he is a traitor to Upper Down.'

Kilbride raised her eyes. 'Did you actually hear Amery say that Hector was behind the orders, Ireni?'

'Yes, ma'am. Dravid stated that the Duke of Ridden had told him to speak to Mister Amery, and Mister Amery had been expecting him to arrive.'

'And why did they allow you to hear this conversation?'

'Because I was part of the bargain they struck, ma'am. Dravid wished to see what he was being given. You have to understand something, ma'am – every Westlander in Twinbrook knew that Hector was behind the king's murder; they discussed it openly. They celebrated the king's death.'

'Who else in Torrent knows of this?' said Kilbride.

'As far as I know, ma'am,' said Lothar, 'only the two Mountain Rangers who brought Ireni to my attention this morning. They can both be trusted to keep quiet, but perhaps we should allow this information to leak out. If the people of Upper Down knew what Hector had done, they would turn on him.'

'Perhaps, but it would also alert Hector. If we are going to move against him, it would be better if he wasn't pre-warned. Before we go any further, I require you both to swear an oath of secrecy. If we three are to conspire against the most powerful man in Upper Down, then we will need to trust one another. I will go first. By all the spirits, I swear to keep our deliberations a secret from all but the King's Champion, were he to return from the north.'

'I swear the same, Your Highness,' said Lothar.

'Ireni,' said Kilbride; 'do you wish to be a part of this? Do you seek justice for the wrongs Duke Hector has done, not only to you personally, but to the realm of Upper Down?'

'I do, ma'am, and I swear the same oath. Your brother was a good man, and he did not deserve what Hector did to him.'

'Then we are agreed. Please sit.'

Lothar and Ireni sat down on the other side of the desk from Kilbride.

'What I am about to say will complicate matters,' Kilbride said; 'and it will demonstrate the difficulty of the challenges we face. Duke Hector is a Master.'

Neither Lothar or Ireni spoke, but Kilbride could see the fear and surprise glimmer in their eyes.

'With a wave of his hand and a few muttered invocations,' Kilbride went on, 'Hector could kill the three of us in the blink of an eye. Were he brave enough to approach the cannon, the Kendril Wall would not be on the verge of collapse; however, Hector does not wish to place his life in danger to save us. He is a coward, as well as a murderer. In order to eliminate him, we shall have to think very carefully. We cannot simply send the Mountain Rangers to arrest him, and no prison cell would be able to hold him. We need to act swiftly, and we need the element of surprise. A crossbow bolt in the back of his head when his attention is elsewhere, for example. Or poison placed into his food. There are myriad possibilities, and I need you both to start thinking about how we can get close enough to the duke to implement some of them. Ireni, your presence at the ducal palace would certainly surprise the duke, but it would also put him on his guard. As for you, Commander Lothar, it is likely that you have lost the duke's trust.'

'I agree, ma'am,' said Lothar. 'I would add that Duke Hector will now distrust every member of the Mountain Rangers. When his own ducal soldiers attempted to evict my parents from their home last night, it was the Mountain Rangers who chased them away.'

'Hector also mistrusts me,' said Kilbride, 'which is why he has ordered me to remain in the palace. We need someone else; someone the duke still trusts. If Walter returns to Torrent, we must warn him immediately not to confront his brother. The King's Champion does not know about Hector's Master abilities.'

'I have a suggestion, ma'am,' said Ireni.

'Yes?'

'Mister Amery might help us, ma'am. It seemed clear to me that he did not wish to get involved in the plot to kill Alfgang the Pius, and he was terrified of Chief Dravid. He even attempted to exclude me from the bargain. He said it was against the law to sell a free citizen of Upper Down.'

'Did he? How did Dravid respond to that?'

'He threatened to rip off Mister Amery's head, ma'am. After that, he cooperated.'

'I fear Amery might be too timid to be of much use to us,' said Kilbride. 'We may need to look elsewhere.'

'If we are successful, ma'am,' said Lothar, 'what happens next?'

'That depends upon which regents are in Torrent at the time,' said Kilbride. 'If I am the sole regent present, then I would signal our willingness to negotiate with the imperial army. However, I would like us to focus on the task at hand. If we cannot get close to the duke, then we shall have no chance of success. Can either of you suggest any other potential allies?'

'I know a few people who work in the ducal palace, ma'am,' said Lothar. 'I could sound them out, but it would take time.'

'I can do the same, ma'am,' said Ireni.

'You must both be very discreet,' said Kilbride. 'If any word of this reaches Hector's ears, then he will move swiftly against us. Do you have a place to stay, Ireni?'

'I could go to my parents' house,' she said.

'I would prefer that you stayed in the Royal Palace,' Kilbride said. 'Commander, ensure that a few trusted Rangers guard her. I will have Marie find her an apartment.'

'Yes, ma'am,' said Lothar.

'That will be all for now,' said Kilbride. 'We do not have much time in which to act, and so I will need you both to contribute to our plan. Access to the duke is key – once we have that in place, we can move forward.'

Lothar and Ireni got to their feet. They bowed their heads before Kilbride, then left the room. Kilbride stood, and walked out on to her balcony. A warm wind was blowing from the south, and the sun had almost set over the mountains. She thought back to the plot that had ended with the death of Alfgang the Great. He had also been a Master, and it had taken time to find someone willing to loose a crossbow bolt at him. With Hector, they did not have the luxury of time. If he remained sealed up within the ducal palace, then he was almost untouchable.

Even after all that had happened, she still did not understand

Hector's purpose. What did he want? Did he wish to become the sole regent, or were his ambitions aimed higher than that? And what would he do if and when Valentino broke through the Kendril Wall? Would his resolve crumble, or would he try to fight on? She cursed him. Thanks to his orders, she was stranded in the palace under a form of house arrest, unable to leave, and unable to have her wishes carried out.

An hour later, Kilbride was lighting the lamps in her study when Marie entered her quarters. The lady-in-waiting bowed low before Kilbride, her eyes anxious.

'I was hoping to see you,' said Kilbride. 'I need you to look out a small apartment, somewhere close to the barracks where the Mountain Rangers are stationed. I also need...'

'Duke Hector is here, my lady,' she said.

Kilbride put down the lamp she had been carrying. 'Is he in the Royal Palace?'

'Yes, ma'am. He arrived ten minutes ago, and made his way to the quarters where the Queen Mother and King Alfgang the Sixth have recently moved.'

Kilbride strode towards the front door.

'My lady, please wait,' said Marie, clutching her hands together.

Kilbride opened the door. Outside were her four guards from the Mountain Rangers, along with over a dozen soldiers from Royal Guards, who were blocking the corridor.

'Please move aside,' said Kilbride. 'I wish to speak to the Duke of Ridden.'

'Sorry, Your Highness,' said one of the Royal Guards. 'We are under orders not to allow you to leave your quarters. It is for your own protection.'

'And who gave those orders?'

'The Duke of Ridden, ma'am.'

The four Rangers gazed at her. If she ordered them to clear the way, then she had no doubt that they would obey, but what chance did they have against a dozen Guardsmen?

She smiled through her anger. 'Very well.'

She closed the door.

'That's what I was trying to tell you, my lady,' said Marie. 'I heard the soldiers saying that you wouldn't be allowed to leave. Are you in trouble, my lady?'

'I'm sure everything is fine. Return to your own quarters, Marie.'

'But, my lady, perhaps I shouldn't leave you alone.'

'That was an order, Marie. Go.'

The lady-in-waiting curtsied. 'Yes, my lady.'

Kilbride watched her leave, then she sat down on her long couch. If Hector had come to arrest or kill her, then she just wanted it over with. It crossed her mind that Lothar and Ireni might have lured her into a trap, but their loathing of the duke had seemed genuine, and she had believed their tale about Hector being responsible for the murder of her brother.

Thirty minutes elapsed before the expected knock came at the door.

'Enter,' said Kilbride, as she got to her feet.

Hector strode into the apartment, followed by Frida and the boy-king.

'Why was I told I could not leave this apartment?' said Kilbride.

'Sorry about that,' said Hector. 'I needed to know where I could find you, Your Highness. How long will it take you to pack some things?'

'And why would I pack?'

'Hector has it all worked out,' said Frida, a look of relief on her face. 'He's going to take us to Castle Ridden.'

Kilbride narrowed her eyes.

'My sister is quite correct, Your Highness,' said Hector. 'For the last day or so, I have been planning the evacuation of the entire Royal Court to the safety of my family castle. But first, however, we shall be travelling to the ducal palace. My wife awaits us there, along with a sizeable quantity of ducal men-at-arms and knights loyal to my service. They shall act as escorts for the journey north.'

'I was just talking about all this to Kilbride earlier,' said Frida. 'I told her that we should evacuate, and here you are, brother, with the perfect plan to do so.'

'What about Walter and Abigone?' said Kilbride.

'With any luck, Your Highness,' Hector said, 'Duke Stefan will have located your sister by now, and she will be safely in his custody. Duke Stefan was aware that I was planning to fall back to Castle Ridden, and I have no doubt that he will catch up with us there.'

'You told Stefan you were going to evacuate, and you didn't tell us?'

'Apologies, Your Highness. I have been exceptionally busy. Until now, I have had no time to visit the Royal Palace.'

'Do I have any say in this, or am I being ordered to go?'

Frida frowned at her. 'Why are you being so difficult, Killie? Do you want to be in Torrent when the Wall is breached? That might be as soon as tomorrow.'

'I believe we have a little longer than that,' said Hector. 'But, when it does happen, every road north will be blocked by fleeing citizens. We must seize this opportunity to reach Castle Ridden before it is too late. With the Royal Court based out of my ancestral home, the government of Upper Down will be able to function. There is every chance, is there not, that Prince Valentino will be satisfied with the pillage of Torrent and Twinbrook, and that he will not continue his pursuit all the way to the Duchy of Ridden.'

'That depends upon the whereabouts of Princess Hygilt,' Kilbride said.

'Indeed. If Duke Stefan has saved Abigone from the clutches of Dravid, then he will also have Hygilt with him.'

'And will you instruct Stefan to release her into the custody of her grandfather?'

'That depends upon the attitude of the illustrious prince. If he is willing to leave the realm of Upper Down intact, then I would be delighted to hand the little princess over to him.'

'You see?' said Frida. 'Hector has thought of everything.'

'He has neglected to mention Walter.'

'My brother is a grown man,' said Hector. 'He can look after himself.'

Kilbride struggled to keep her composure in front of the duke. A hundred accusations were forming on the tip of her tongue, but if she allowed her temper to get the better of her, then Hector would know what she knew. She tried to see the ultimatum as an opportunity to get close enough to Hector to kill him. She had been looking for a way to gain access to him, and Hector had handed it to her on a plate.

'Very well,' she said. 'How long will we be staying in the ducal palace?'

'For as long as it takes to organise the carriages, Your Highness,' said Hector, a faint smile on his lips. 'Understandably, there is much we need to move to Castle Ridden, if we are to run the entire government from there. We must also save the archives of the realm from the depredations of the imperial army, along with countless courtiers and guards. However, I do not wish for the Royal Court to linger here for any longer than necessary. I aim to be ready to depart Torrent the dawn after tomorrow.'

'And if the Wall is breached before then?'

'Then we shall take to horseback and ride north,' said Hector. 'However, as I stated, I believe that the Kendril Wall will continue to protect us for a few more days. Three cannon exploded during today's assault, and a dozen others overheated and were damaged. Tomorrow's bombardment will not be as severe as this afternoon's, and it is likely that even more cannon will become inoperable.'

'How long do I have to pack?'

'Twenty minutes, Your Highness. I have carriages awaiting us in the palace forecourt.'

'Then I will show you out, so that I can get ready to leave.'

Hector smiled at her, then he inclined his head. 'Thank you for being so reasonable about it, Your Highness. I will see you down in the forecourt.'

Kilbride walked them to the door, then she watched as Hector, Frida and the boy-king were escorted along the corridor by armed Guardsmen. Kilbride gestured to the four Mountain Rangers.

'Step inside my quarters for a moment, gentlemen.'

The four Rangers walked into her apartment, and she closed the door.

She glanced at two of them. 'Please find Commander Lothar, and inform him that I am being taken to the ducal palace by Lord Hector. In fact, by the time you reach him, I will probably be on my way.'

'Yes, ma'am,' said one.

She turned to the other two. 'I would be obliged if you escorted me to the ducal palace. I need good soldiers around me that I can trust.'

'What should the rest of the Rangers do, ma'am?' said one.

'Hold tight, and wait for Walter to return. If he gets back to Torrent in one piece, then he will likely make for the Royal Palace. Ensure that you are here to protect him.'

'Yes, ma'am.'

She opened the door, and two of the Rangers left. She closed the door again, and smiled at the remaining two.

'Would you like to help me pack?

CHAPTER 27
HARD LUCK

Torrent, Upper Down – 17th Day of Lamenta 107

Hector awoke with a smile on his lips. The soft light of dawn was creeping through the slats in the wooden shutters, and Hector stretched his arms.

It was going to be a good day. Frida, Kilbride and the boy-king were safely ensconced in rooms within the northern wing of the palace, guarded by forty ducal men-at-arms, while his wife would most likely still be sleeping in her comfortable apartment in the eastern wing. Hector swept the blanket aside and got to his feet. He listened for a moment, but could hear no trace of the rumbling sound that accompanied a cannon bombardment. He wondered when that day's assault upon the Kendril Wall would begin. It was hard to believe that, only a few short days before, he had been utterly convinced that the Wall could never be breached; and yet, there he was, preparing to evacuate the entire Royal Court to the safety of Castle Ridden.

There were just a couple of things he needed to take care of first.

He walked into his bathroom and opened the narrow shutters. He filled the washbasin with cold water from a covered jug, rubbed soap onto his face, and began to shave. He caught his reflection in the mirror, and smiled. People often told him that he was the most handsome man in the realm, and he had lost count of the young women who had thrown themselves at him over the years. At thirty-four, he had shed much of his boyish looks, but he was evolving into something altogether more distinguished. Even better, he had retained all of his hair. He had been paranoid throughout his late twenties whenever he had spied a stray hair on his pillow, but the worry had been for nothing.

He finished shaving, and dabbed his face with a towel. He reached over to a small bottle of cologne, then he stopped himself. Everyone recognised the scent, and he did not wish to leave any traces of himself where he was going. He returned to the bedroom, and got dressed; then he reached under the bed and withdrew a length of cord that he had removed from a woman's dressing gown. He stuffed it into a pocket, and strode from his room.

Two men-at-arms sprang to attention in the hallway outside.

'I am going for a walk in the gardens,' Hector said, 'and I wish to do so alone. Remain here.'

The two soldiers saluted, and Hector walked away. He descended a flight of stairs, and opened a door that led to the gardens. It was his favourite place in Torrent. He remembered when he had first seen the walled garden of the ducal palace, when his father had taken him to Torrent for the first time as a boy. He had loved living in Castle Ridden, but the gardens had seemed like a vision to his young eyes. It had been spring, and the air had been filled with the heady aroma of the flowers blooming everywhere he had looked. Even in autumn, it was still a beautiful place, and Hector took his time as he strolled along the paths. He walked past the northern wing of the palace, and came to a halt by a window on the eastern wing. He knew which shutter had a loose latch, and he reached up with a hand and slid it open. He gazed into the darkness of the interior, then climbed in silently, and closed the shutter behind him. He waited for his eyes to adjust to the gloom, then he crept over the rug to a door. He placed his ear against it, but heard nothing. He opened the door as quietly as he was able, and padded into the large bedroom.

As he had expected, his wife was still sleeping. She had stayed up late the previous night with Frida, and Hector had noticed how many bottles of wine the two women had consumed. He crept over to the bed, and gazed down at Perpetua. There had been little love between them, but she had been a decent-enough wife, at least in public, and she had never humiliated or embarrassed him. More than that, though, he was grateful to her for the two sons she had given him. Still, he wouldn't miss her.

He placed his left hand firmly over her mouth, and grasped her neck with his right hand. He had large, strong hands, and her throat felt weak under his tight grip, as he began to strangle her. Her eyes flashed open, and she gazed up at him in panic. Her hands went to his, and tried to peel his fingers from her, but Hector held on, and increased the pressure round her neck. He stared into her eyes.

'Hush, my darling,' he whispered. 'It will be over soon.'

She punched his arm, but the blows were feeble, and he shook his head at her.

'Die with a little dignity, my dear,' he whispered. 'There is no escape.'

The panic on her face grew as he continued to choke the life from her, then, finally, she lay still, her eyes blank. Hector removed both hands from her, and her head lolled to the side. He checked for a pulse, but there was none. He glanced up at the ceiling, then moved a chair to a position directly under a lamp fitting. He climbed up onto the chair, removed the cord from his pocket, and secured one end to the lamp, tying it around a thick metal pinion. He fashioned a noose at the dangling end of the cord, then he stepped off the chair, and picked up Perpetua's body in his arms. He hoisted her up, and placed the noose around her neck. He let go of her, and kicked the chair over. The cord held, and he watched her body sway back and forth for a few minutes, the taut cord creaking under the strain. He glanced back down at the bed, and made sure that he had left nothing behind, then he retraced his steps. He closed the bedroom door, crept to the window with the loose shutter, and peered outside. The gardens were deserted, and he climbed out of the room, his boots landing on the gravel of a path. He closed the shutter, smiled, and went on with his walk.

Hector glanced up as Frida entered the dining room. 'How is your head this morning, sister?' he said.

Frida said nothing as she sat down at the long dining table.

'That bad, is it?' Hector said.

'My head is pounding,' she said. 'I shouldn't have drunk so much last night. Have you seen Perpetua this morning?'

'No. I imagine she is still in bed. Where is Alfie?'

'With Kilbride,' she said. 'They will be down in a minute. Do you want to tell me why Kilbride is so angry with you?'

Hector raised an eyebrow. 'I wasn't aware that she was angry with me. Did she say something?'

'No, and that is why I'm asking you, brother. She said practically nothing yesterday evening, and she didn't want to sit and talk with me and Perpetua. And why did she bring two Mountain Rangers with her?'

'Perhaps she is worried about Abigone.'

Frida gave him a look. 'We are all worried about Abigone. But what can we do, except hope that Stefan and Walter find her before it is too late? This family has suffered enough.'

'It certainly has,' said Hector. 'Where did we go wrong, do you think?'

'It's obvious,' said Frida. 'Alfgang the Great should have handed Princess Hygilt over the moment he found out that she was related to the emperor of Sanctos. If only my husband had survived. He knew what to do. He would have resolved this awful situation.'

'Indeed. His loss was a terrible tragedy for the realm, and I mourn him deeply.'

Kilbride and the boy-king entered the dining room, and took their seats next to Hector and Frida.

'My home is your home,' said Hector. 'Please help yourselves to food and beverages. I could call in some staff to serve us, but I thought it would be nice if the family ate breakfast together, without any distractions. Should we wait for my wife to join us?'

Frida smiled. 'Perpetua is likely nursing a slight hangover, brother. Let her sleep in. We don't need to wait.'

'As you wish, sister.' He glanced at Alfie as he uncovered a few dishes. 'Did you sleep well, Your Majesty?'

The boy nodded. 'Yes, but I want to go to Castle Ridden now. Why do we have to wait another day?'

'It takes an awful lot of work to prepare all the carriages we need to move everything to Castle Ridden, Your Majesty, and we also need to think about what we shall eat and drink along the way. It will take us four days of travel to reach my old castle. Are you looking forward to the journey?'

'Not really,' said the boy. 'Four days in a carriage sounds boring.'

'Yes, I see your point. It will be rather boring, I'm afraid. However, it is better than remaining in Torrent, Your Majesty. Would you agree?'

Alfie nodded, then he turned his full attention to the food Frida was piling onto his plate.

'And how about you, Your Highness?' Hector said to Kilbride. 'Tell me – when was the last time you were in Castle Ridden?'

'Over ten years ago,' Kilbride said.

Hector smiled again as he gazed at the princess. She was doing a fine job of keeping her emotions shielded from him, and he wished he knew what she was thinking. Did she loathe him, or was she merely a little suspicious of his motives? She was hoping that Walter would make his return, that seemed clear to him, but what were the two of them planning?

A servant opened a door and glanced in Hector's direction.

Hector frowned. 'I explicitly asked not to be interrupted.'

'I'm sorry, my lord,' said the servant. 'May I speak to you in private?'

'Whatever is it now?' Hector muttered, as he got to his feet. He strode to the door. 'Yes?'

The servant leaned in closer. 'My lord, something terrible has happened. Your wife... she...'

Hector narrowed his eyes. 'Yes?'

'Lady Perpetua is dead, my lord. She hanged herself.'

Hector staggered back a few steps, then he fell to his knees and gripped the sides of his head. 'No,' he cried, his voice wavering. 'This cannot be true!' He burst into tears, and lowered his head, sobbing.

Frida ran to his side. 'What has happened?'

Hector wept uncontrollably, and his sister put an arm over his shoulder. She stared at the servant.

'Lady Perpetua is dead, ma'am,' the servant said. 'We found her this morning, in her bedroom. She hanged herself.'

Frida's eyes widened, then she also started to cry. Hector embraced his sister, as Kilbride and Alfie went over to the door.

'Show me,' said Kilbride.

The servant led Kilbride from the room, then others entered, ready to await the duke's orders.

'Leave us!' Frida cried.

The servants bowed, then filed back out of the dining room.

'Why would she do this?' Hector wailed. 'Tell me, sister – did my wife give you any indication that she was thinking of doing this to herself?'

'No, brother; I swear it,' said Frida. 'She seemed... normal.'

'This is all my fault!' Hector cried.

'Why would you say such a thing, brother?'

'When Perpetua arrived two days ago,' Hector went on, 'I asked her if she wanted a divorce.'

'A divorce? I don't understand. What did she say?'

'She refused, and I told her the matter was closed. Perhaps she thought I would divorce her anyway. What have I done?'

'Why did you want to divorce her, brother?'

'I thought she was unhappy with the marriage, and I wanted to offer her a chance to escape it. She told me that I was wrong, and that she still loved me. How I wish I had never mentioned it!'

Kilbride returned to the dining room, her face ashen.

'Did you see my beautiful wife?' Hector sobbed.

'Yes. I am sorry, Hector, but what the servant told us was true. Perpetua appears to have hanged herself. Her body has been brought down from the noose, and she is lying on her bed if you want to see her.'

'I don't think I could bear it,' he said.

'You should go, brother,' Frida said. She took her arm from Hector's shoulder, and took hold of the boy-king's hand. 'I will stay here with Alfie.'

Hector slowly got to his feet. 'Will you come with me, Kilbride?' he said. 'I cannot do this alone.'

The princess looked torn for a moment, then she nodded, and they left the dining room together.

Feigning grief was tiring, and Hector was exhausted after a few hours of weeping and bewailing the loss of his wife. Kilbride had stood next to him in silence as he had clung on to the body of Perpetua, refusing to let go of his wife's hand as the servants tried to remove her from the bedroom. Eventually, of course, he had acceded to their wishes, but not before most of the palace staff had seen how devastated he was. Afterwards, Kilbride led him up the stairs to his private rooms, the two Rangers and over a dozen ducal men-at-arms trailing behind them. They reached the door leading to his bedroom, and he turned to face her.

'Don't leave me alone,' he said, as the tears streamed down his face. 'I fear what I might do if there is no one with me.'

Kilbride narrowed her eyes.

'I am begging you,' said Hector.

Kilbride nodded, and they entered the bedroom, leaving the soldiers outside. Hector remained by the door, and locked it, but Kilbride was halfway to the window, and didn't notice. Hector wiped the tears from his face, then he strode over to a cabinet and filled two glasses with brandy, as Kilbride opened the shutters to let in some light.

'We need to talk,' he said.

Kilbride glanced at him, and he wondered if she knew his grief had been a pretence. He offered her a brandy, but she shook her head.

'I have a proposal to make,' he went on.

'Will this take long?' she said. 'Your wife's funeral needs to be organised.'

'Amery can take care of that. I need you to listen very carefully to what I have to say.' He gestured to a seat.

Kilbride eyed him, then they both sat.

'From the moment Alfgang the Pius passed away,' he said, 'something occurred to me. I am sure that it will have also occurred to you.'

Kilbride said nothing, her expression neutral, and he smiled at the ease with which she was able to mask her feelings.

'You are next in line to the throne of Upper Down,' he said. 'If something terrible were to happen to little Alfie, then you would automatically be elevated to queen. This state of affairs leaves the realm vulnerable.'

'How so?' she said.

'Is it not obvious? There are dozens of princes and dukes all over the old Central Provinces who would snatch at the opportunity to seize the crown of Upper Down. Little Alfie is at risk, but so, too, are you, Your Highness. You are unmarried, and that status will attract an unseemly host of suitors, all vying for your hand. Some will be opportunists, hoping that Alfie might expire of natural causes, while others might try to bend fate to their will. Any husband you marry would be but one step from the throne, and their desire to be king might tempt them into murder. If we do not act, then Upper Down will be inundated with such unscrupulous men. They will bring their own armed retinues to this realm, and turn it into a battlefield as they each fight to win you.'

'This is a curious subject to bring up,' said Kilbride, 'when an imperial army is pounding at the Kendril Wall. Shouldn't our priority be to ensure that King Alfgang the Sixth has a long and fruitful reign?'

'Of course, yes; I am in full agreement. However, the risks I have outlined should not be ignored. Word will soon spread that a seven-year-old boy sits upon the throne of Upper Down, and that his successor is an unmarried princess. You must be able to see how weak this will make us appear to others, Your Highness.'

'Your wife has just died, Hector.'

'I know. Her end was tragic, and my heart may never recover. Even so, we two are the most senior regents of the realm, and its future is our responsibility. Might not my wife's death have opened up a way to safeguard that future? There is one simple step we could take that would prevent a flood of suitors from squabbling over your hand.'

Kilbride eyed him. 'You cannot possibly be serious. Were anything to happen to Alfie, then I would reign as queen. I would not require a husband in order to rule.'

'Are you that naïve? How many realms are there across the old Central Provinces – two dozen? More? And how many of the kings currently ruling those realms have second or third sons, with no hope of ever inheriting their father's kingdom? Would they not race to Upper Down to compete for the prize of becoming king? Even if you were to refuse every one of their advances, they could band together, and force you to choose. They could lay siege to Castle Ridden, and compel you to marry one of their number. And then, a foreigner would rule Upper Down. Would it not be far better for the realm if you married now? I could have Amery conduct a short ceremony this very day.'

Kilbride gave him a cold smile. 'And who do you suggest would be my husband?'

'Oh, come now; I think you can guess the answer to that.'

'Yes, but I wish to hear you say it.'

'Very well. I would be your husband, Your Highness. If we wed, then we would bring our two families back together – the royal line and the Duchy of Ridden. It would be a political marriage, naturally, designed to deter outsiders from seeking the throne.'

'It would be a marriage that would place you one step away from that throne.'

'What are you saying? Surely you cannot imagine that I would ever harm our nephew?'

'You are discussing marriage on the morning of your wife's suicide,

Hector. I wouldn't like to hazard a guess at what goes through your mind.'

Hector glanced away, as though hurt by what she had said. 'Your cruel words cut deep, Your Highness. I am merely trying to secure the safety of the realm. Where is your sense of duty? Can you not place your personal feelings aside for the good of Upper Down?'

'I have been doing exactly that for many long years,' she said. 'What I will not do is facilitate your ambitions. How long have you been planning this?'

'The idea did not come to me until I had seen the body of Alfgang the Pius,' he said. 'Were you aware that I had brought up the notion of divorce with the fair Perpetua? I fear that this is what may have driven her to suicide. To save this realm, I am prepared to sacrifice my own happiness by marrying you; and yet you accuse me of being ambitious?'

Kilbride got to her feet. 'I think this little conversation is over. Before I go, I would like to make sure that you understand my feelings on this – I will never marry you, Hector. Never.'

'Do you think I am stupid?' he cried. 'Is this what you and Walter have been discussing behind my back? Do you intend to make my brother king of Upper Down?'

'You are delusional,' she said. 'Walter and I have never even broached the subject. Alfie is the king of Upper Down, and it is our job to ensure that his reign succeeds. Good day, Hector.'

He watched as she walked to the door. She gripped the handle, but it wouldn't open.

'Do you think I would just let you walk away?' he said.

'Unlock the door, Hector.'

'No. Not until you agree.'

A flicker of fear passed over her face, and he smiled.

'I will scream,' she said.

He shrugged. 'Feel free to bellow at the top of your lungs, my dear. Nothing will happen. I could murder you in this room, and no one would come to your assistance.'

'But if you murdered me, then how would you ever become king?'

'Oh, I am sure I would think of something. Let me put it this way, if you continue to refuse my offer, then I will kill you in the most gruesome manner imaginable. Do you know how much iron is held within an average human body? More than you might think. If I were to replace it with lead, or silver, or even gold, then you would suffer the most exquisite agony. It would only take a minute for you to die, but it would feel a lot longer. For every second, you would be begging me to end it.'

'Is that supposed to scare me, Hector?'

'Think of it more as a promise. If you reject my proposal, then this will be the outcome. Would you like to sit down again?'

Kilbride banged on the door with her fist. 'Let me out!' she cried.

Hector got to his feet. He strode to the door and struck Kilbride in the face with the back of his hand. She stumbled backwards, tripped, and fell to the floor. Hector crouched down next to her, and gripped a handful of her hair. He turned her face towards him.

'One word,' he said to her. 'One little word; that's all it will take. Say yes, and you will be my wife by the end of the day.'

'I would rather die,' she said.

'I will kill you,' he said, 'but not yet. Perhaps when you have borne me a son, and after you have helped me dispose of poor little Alfie, I will give you the death you crave. Make no mistake, Kilbride; by sunset, you will be mine. Through you, the royal line will once again fall to the House of Ridden, from whom it was stolen.'

Kilbride stared up at him. 'I will never consent to this.'

'Do you think I need your consent? I tried persuasion, as a courtesy to you, but I will take what I want regardless of your desires. Rest assured that our marriage certificate will state that you were a most willing bride.'

He drove her head against the floorboards, and she grimaced in pain. He released her hair and got to his feet. He took the key from his pocket, and unlocked the door. Outside, the dozen ducal soldiers and the two Mountain Rangers turned to stare at him.

Hector nodded to an officer. 'Kill the two Rangers.'

A struggle broke out in the hallway as the men-at-arms drew their swords. The two Rangers tried to reach Kilbride, who was still lying on the floor inside the apartment, but they were cut down from behind. One of them fell by Hector's feet, and he glanced down.

'Princess Kilbride is not to leave this room,' he said. 'Summon more men-at-arms, and clear away the bodies. Bury them in the garden. Right now, I need two men to bind, gag and hood the princess.'

The officer gestured to two men-at-arms. 'Get to it.'

The two men entered the apartment. One pulled Kilbride's arms behind her back, and the other bound her wrists together with cord. They made a makeshift gag from a handkerchief, and tied it round her face.

'We have no hood, my lord,' said one.

Hector frowned. 'Tie her to a chair; the hood can wait.'

The two men lifted Kilbride, and sat her down onto a chair. Her ankles were bound to its wooden legs, and another cord was secured round her waist, pinning her to the back of the seat.

'That will be all,' said Hector. 'Wait outside.'

The two soldiers saluted, then they retreated from the room and closed the door. Hector walked over to Kilbride, and examined the knots.

'Such a shame about the two Rangers,' he said. 'You really shouldn't have brought them here, Your Highness; their deaths are your fault.' He crouched down and met her glance. 'I shall be king of Upper Down, Kilbride, and you have two choices; either you can decide to cooperate, or you will be destined to live out your life not only as my wife, but as my prisoner. Castle Ridden has a dozen towers, and several would be suitable places for you to dwell in solitude. I wouldn't be the first king whose wife is seldom seen in public. And do not worry about little Alfie; I shall make his end a painless one.' He smiled. 'I may even make it look like suicide.'

He got to his feet and strode from the apartment.

'Ensure that this door is guarded at all times,' he said to the soldiers in the hallway. 'With the sole exception of Amery, no one is to enter. If anyone asks, tell them that the princess is feeling poorly and has had to lie down for a while.'

The officer bowed. 'Yes, my lord.'

Hector paused as the bodies of the two Rangers were carried away, then he strode across the hallway. His expression changed as he walked down a staircase, as he donned his mask of grief. His wife was dead, but he would not remain unmarried for long.

He suppressed a smile. His intuition upon awakening that morning had been correct – it had been a good day.

CHAPTER 28
HARD PRESSED

Torrent, Upper Down – 17th Day of Lamenta 107

One benefit of never having left the grounds of the Royal Palace was that Abigone was not recognised by the people her family ruled. Hygilt's features also remained unknown to them, but the same could not be said about Walter. From the moment they had entered the town of Torrent that afternoon, countless people had noticed the King's Champion as he had accompanied the two princesses. Many of the glances were scornful, and a few looked disappointed that Walter appeared to be sober.

Walter didn't seem to notice, or care. He left the two exhausted horses by a sentry post next to the western gates of Torrent, then they walked along a busy thoroughfare in the direction of a line of carriages for hire.

'So this is Torrent?' Abigone said, as she glanced at the wooden houses on either side of the street. 'It's very pretty.'

'I imagine it's even nicer in spring,' said Hygilt. 'Look at all the empty flower boxes by each window. Is it beautiful in spring, Walter?'

The man frowned as he turned his head. 'What?'

'Never mind,' said Hygilt. She smiled at Abigone. 'I think he's a little preoccupied.'

A dull rumble began, and many citizens cast anxious glances towards the south-east, where the Kendril Wall lay.

'That will be the cannon starting again,' said Hygilt.

A small crowd gathered round Walter and the two princesses.

'What's happening, my lord?' one asked Walter. 'Are you going to the Wall to fight?'

Walter said nothing as he eased his way past.

'You are the King's Champion,' cried another. 'Are you going to do something about the damn cannon?'

'He doesn't give a shit,' said another. 'All he cares about is getting drunk.'

Walter pushed his way closer to the line of carriages, as Abigone and Hygilt stayed close behind.

'Coward!' someone shouted.

Walter opened the side door of a carriage, and gestured for Abigone and Hygilt to get inside. He spoke to the driver, then he climbed up and sat down opposite the two princesses as the door was closed. The crowd shouted abuse as the carriage pulled away from the side of the street, its wheels rolling over the cobbles.

'Why didn't you talk to them?' said Hygilt.

Walter eyed her. 'And what would I have said? Bear in mind that I did not wish anyone to know your identities. Besides, most of their accusations are true.' He turned to Abigone. 'So, you are a Maker?'

'I told you this yesterday,' Abigone said.

'I know, but we have been riding hard for an entire day and night. I was too busy keeping us alive to stop for a nice chat. How long have you known?'

'A few years,' said Abigone.

'Who else knows?'

'Only the people inside this carriage.'

Walter narrowed his eyes.

'My father knew,' Abigone went on, 'but no one else; not even Kilbride.'

'Why was it kept secret?'

'It was to make sure she found a suitable husband,' said Hygilt.

'I can speak for myself,' said Abigone.

'This changes everything,' said Walter. 'Are you willing to use your abilities to help defeat the imperial army?'

Abigone's eyes widened. 'I... What? How would I do that?'

'I don't know,' said Walter. 'I have little idea how your abilities work in practice. Couldn't you make some cannon for us? That would certainly surprise Prince Valentino.'

'I don't know how to do anything like that. I have only ever summoned a few pieces of wood. I haven't been trained, and I didn't study. You saw how my dragon turned out, and you think I could make a cannon?'

'It takes years and years to become a good Maker,' said Hygilt, 'and I don't like the idea of firing a cannon at the imperial army. My grandfather might get hurt.'

Walter narrowed his eyes. 'Your grandfather has been attacking Torrent for days.'

'No, he has been attacking a giant wall.'

'Ah,' said Walter, 'then we needn't worry – is that what you're saying? Does Valentino intend to greet us with flowers when he breaks through the Kendril Gap?'

'The empire didn't start this,' said Hygilt. 'Upper Down has been given numerous opportunities to do the right thing.'

'If I were to hand you over to your grandfather right now,' said Walter, 'can you guarantee that he would turn around and take his army home?'

'I don't know. I certainly can't guarantee it. Is that what you are planning to do with me?'

'We can't do it right now, not while sixty cannon are pounding the Wall.'

'Then where are we going?' said Abigone.

'To the Royal Palace.'

'But Hector might be there.'

'Kilbride told me that Hector was staying in the ducal palace.'

'That was two days ago. A lot might have changed since then.'

Walter raised his palms. 'I'm open to suggestions.'

'Well, we should start spreading the news that Duke Hector arranged the murder of my brother,' Abigone said. 'If the people of Upper Down knew his true character, they would turn against him.'

'We would need evidence before we could go down that path. The word of a treacherous Westlander chief doesn't hold much weight. We would need Amery to confess, as my brother would never admit it. And, you have to realise that, even if we had iron-clad proof of his guilt, many would still refuse to believe it. The people of Upper Down, for whatever reason, have chosen to adore that arrogant bastard. He could commit open murder without upsetting his followers. Perhaps, if I could arrange the Mountain Rangers to get close to him, they could arrest him, but there would be an uproar.'

'The Rangers wouldn't be able to arrest him, even if they were surrounding him,' said Hygilt.

'Why not?'

'Because Hector is a Master.'

Walter started to laugh. 'Really? My brother is a Master? Abigone is a Maker, and Hector is a Master?'

'I *am* a Maker,' said Abigone.

'And Hector?'

Abigone shrugged. 'I don't know. That's what Dravid told us. He says he saw some strange things happen when he was captured.'

'Things that only a Master could do,' said Hygilt.

'And you believed him?' said Walter.

'She does,' said Abigone; 'I'm not convinced.'

'If Hector was secretly a Master,' said Walter, 'then...'

'Then what?' said Hygilt. 'He might have positioned himself as the most powerful man in the kingdom? He was close to King Alfgang the Great, was he not? And then he assassinated King Alfgang the Pius, only to become the senior member of the regency council. Tell me, Walter – you believe your brother to be a worthless fraud, so how could he have achieved so much if he wasn't a Master?'

Walter smiled and shook his head. 'All right; if he was a Master, then why hasn't he destroyed the cannon?'

'That is a good question,' said Hygilt. 'Let's explore the possibilities. Perhaps the distance is too great. How close to an object must a Master be for his abilities to work? Perhaps he is a coward. Perhaps he would rather keep his ability a secret, even at the cost of the Kendril Wall. You know him better than I do, Walter; what do you think?'

Walter chewed his lip for a moment, as though lost in thought. Abigone glanced out of the south-facing side window, but her view of the Wall was blocked by the wood-framed houses. The rumbling was getting louder, and she could hear the impact of the cannon balls striking stone.

'I hate that noise,' she said.

'Yes,' said Hygilt, 'and I admit that I would prefer to be on the other side of the cannon when they are firing. All the same, we are not in any immediate danger. If we can get word to my grandfather that I am in the custody of the King's Champion, and that the King's Champion is willing to negotiate, then there still might be a peaceful resolution.' She smiled at Walter. 'You are willing to negotiate, aren't you?'

'Yes,' he said. 'Right now, I would give Valentino pretty much all that he asked for, with one exception – Upper Down remains a free kingdom. I'm not going to compromise on that.'

'That is good to know. Have you finished thinking about Hector?'

'I have.'

'And what did you conclude?'

'I don't know. Some things would make more sense if he were a Master. His unending supply of gold, for example. I used to marvel at how much he was able to spend without plunging the duchy into bankruptcy; in fact, the account books showed that we were richer than ever. A lot of the love and affection he has earned has been through lining other people's pockets. All the same, I find it hard to believe that he contrived to keep it a secret from me all these years.'

'Why? Abigone managed her secret well.'

'Yes, but I didn't grow up next to Abigone.'

Abigone smiled. 'No, you grew up next to Kilbride. Hector was never around in those days. He was always away training with his knights and men-at-arms.' Her smile vanished. 'Walter, why are your hands trembling?'

Walter folded his arms over his chest. 'They're not.'

'Don't lie. I saw them. You didn't seem very scared when we were fleeing the Westlanders; has the sound of the cannon unnerved you?'

'It's not that,' said Hygilt.

'Then what is it?'

Hygilt eyed Walter. 'Will you tell her, or shall I?'

Walter turned to look out of the window.

'His body is craving alcohol,' Hygilt said. 'It has been a few days since he drank any, and he is probably feeling a little unwell. I have seen these signs before, in certain members of my family who persistently over-indulge.'

Abigone's eyes widened. 'Is that true, cousin?'

Walter kept his gaze on the street. 'Yes.'

'If he keeps this up, he will kill himself,' Hygilt said.

'Oh, Walter,' said Abigone; 'I feel both angry and sorry for you.'

'It's not too late for him,' said Hygilt. 'He needs self-discipline, and he will recover in time.'

'How much time do you think we have?' said Walter. 'If I don't have anything to drink, then I might be sick for... I don't know how long, because I've never tried to give up. It's not exactly perfect timing, is it? Not when the fucking Wall is being blown to pieces.'

Hygilt raised a finger. 'I have spoken to you before about your use of profanities.'

'Am I being scolded by a fucking fourteen-year-old?' he said. 'Look; the trembling will stop if I have a drink.'

'You can't be thinking of getting drunk at a time like this,' said Abigone.

'Did I say anything about getting drunk? Besides, it takes a lot to get me drunk these days; I could hold my own in any beer hall in Twinbrook. No, I just need a few sips to sort me out. Maybe, once this is all over, then I'll think about cutting down.'

'How long have you been drinking?' said Hygilt.

'About ten years. The last three have been... a blur.'

'He's done other things besides drinking,' said Abigone. 'My father told me that he frequented every brothel in Twinbrook, and there are lots of those.'

'I don't care if you judge me,' said Walter. 'I am unmarriable. After I refused to wed one of Alfgang the Great's captives, he made sure that no eligible woman would ever be allowed to court me.'

'What are you talking about?' said Abigone.

'Did you think Princess Hygilt was the only young aristocratic woman your father had the Westlanders abduct, Abbie? A few years ago, I was supposed to marry one of them – a gift from your father. I refused, and he told me that I would remain unmarried for the rest of my life.'

'What happened to her?' said Hygilt.

'Her family paid a ransom, and she was sent home.'

Abigone frowned. 'No. You're making it up. My father would never have done such a thing.'

Both Walter and Hygilt rolled their eyes.

'It's still just an excuse,' Abigone went on. 'So, you weren't allowed to marry? That didn't mean you had to pay prostitutes. No one forced you to do that.'

'I know,' he said. 'I just... like being in the company of women, I guess.'

Abigone pulled a face.

'You don't have to do it any more,' said Hygilt. 'King Alfgang the Great is dead. You might find someone you love.'

'Don't you sometimes hate having noble blood, Hygilt?' he said. 'Your marriage will probably be arranged, just as Abbie was supposed to marry Prince Henry; and Kilbride had to marry Duke Roderick. Nolan is also married to a prince, and even Hector's marriage to Perpetua was arranged by the old king. We don't get to decide whom we wed; those choices are made by others. So please, spare me your talk of love.'

'We do these things to keep the royal houses intact,' Hygilt said. 'Maintaining our status comes with certain sacrifices.'

'By that logic, Abbie should marry Stefan.'

'Can we please change the subject?' said Abigone. 'I don't want to think about that again.'

'But Stefan will be on his way here,' said Walter. 'He was chasing us all the way south. Could you not use your Maker abilities to kill him?'

'I daren't try,' she said. 'I can't control where the pieces come from. Does that make sense? When I summon something made from wood, I don't know what wood will be chosen to build whatever it is that I have summoned. I didn't mean for the wagon to fall apart, for instance. If I summoned something made from flesh and blood, then it might kill Stefan, but it might also kill any others who happened to be close by.'

'Could you summon something like poison?'

'I would need to know the exact ingredients first, and I would need to remember them perfectly. Do you see the problem? To be a good Maker, I will have to study, and train hard. When will I be able to do that?'

'I don't know. We need to talk to Kilbride; she's read countless books on the subject. She might know some things you can do that will make a difference.'

Abigone sagged in her seat. 'But that would mean telling her.'

'Of course we should tell her,' said Walter.

'The news will make her angry. She'll say things like: *Why didn't you tell me, you stupid girl?*'

Walter smiled. 'That was quite a good impression of your sister, but we should tell her, all the same. She's the cleverest person in Upper Down.'

Abigone snorted. 'Or so she likes to believe. She hasn't exactly achieved much with all of her legendary intelligence.'

Walter glanced out of the window, then he knocked on the little window separating the interior of the carriage from the driver's bench.

The driver turned his head, and Walter signalled for him to stop the carriage. The wheels slowed on the cobbles, then they came to a juddering halt.

'This isn't the palace,' said Abigone.

'We'll walk the rest of the way,' said Walter, as he opened the door.

He stepped down to the ground, then he helped Abigone and Hygilt descend from the carriage. He paid the driver, and they set off along the quiet street. The cannon were still roaring away over to their right, and Abigone could feel the vibrations through the soles of her boots as they walked.

'Why didn't we drive to the main entrance?' Abigone said.

'We're being careful,' said Walter. 'We don't know the situation in the palace. It's unlikely, but Stefan may have already returned by now, and he might have decided to go straight to the palace. Or, Hector could be there.'

They reached the end of the street, and Walter raised his hand for them to stop. The southernmost gate leading into the grounds of the Royal Palace lay ahead of them, guarded by several men from the Royal Guards. Abigone, Walter and Hygilt remained close to the side of a building as they watched the soldiers by the gate for a few minutes.

'The Mountain Rangers are barracked close by,' Walter said, 'which is why I chose this gate.'

'Why don't we just approach the Royal Guardsmen?' said Abigone.

'Because I don't trust them. They take their orders from Hector.'

'I'm starting to get cold,' said Hygilt, 'and the sun is setting. It will be nice and warm in the palace.'

Walter cupped his hands to his mouth, and emitted a strange squawking sound that made Abigone laugh. He eyed her, then did it again. The soldiers by the gate peered out into the early evening gloom, then a few Rangers emerged from a nearby building behind them.

Walter made the noise again, then he gestured to Abigone and Hygilt. 'Let's go.'

They walked out into the street opposite the gate, and the Guardsmen tensed when they saw who it was. Behind them, more

Rangers emerged from the building, and began to gather next to the gate. Walter raised his hands into the air, and strode forwards, keeping the princesses behind him.

'Open the gate,' called out a Guardsman. 'Quickly.'

The gate was pushed open, and a few Guardsmen ventured out into the street, their crossbows trained on Walter.

'You are under arrest!' cried an officer. 'Detain Lord Walter.'

'I don't think that would be a good idea,' said Walter. 'It might upset the Mountain Rangers standing behind you.'

The Guardsmen turned. The crowd of Rangers had grown, and they were outnumbering the Guardsmen ten-to-one.

'We are going to enter the palace grounds,' Walter said. 'Rangers, I would be obliged if you gave us an escort.'

Several dozen Rangers piled through the gate, pushing the Guardsmen aside. They formed up around Walter, Abigone and Hygilt, while the Guardsmen looked on.

'It's good to see you, sir,' said one of the Rangers.

'Thank you, Commander Lothar,' said Walter. 'Arrest the Guardsmen, and have a squad of Rangers take up their positions by the gate.'

The twelve men from the Royal Guards surrendered without a fight, and the Rangers led them into their barracks, along with Walter and the two princesses. The captives were taken away to a secure wing, and the others entered a large mess hall, where more Rangers were sitting. They sprang to their feet at the sight of Walter, and saluted.

'At ease,' said Walter, 'and please find some food and drink for the two princesses. We have had a long journey, and the Westlanders pursued us all the way.' He sat down in an armchair, then he nodded to Abigone and Hygilt. 'Sit. We're safe with the Rangers. Now, would someone like to tell me why the Royal Guards tried to have me arrested?'

'It could only have been Duke Hector, sir,' said a lieutenant; 'the Rangers certainly didn't receive any such orders.'

'Is my brother in his own palace?'

'Yes, sir. As are King Alfgang the Sixth, the Queen Mother, and Princess Kilbride. They travelled there yesterday evening.'

'What are they all doing in the ducal palace?' said Abigone, as she and Hygilt took seats close to Walter.

'We believe that the Royal Court is intending to flee north to Castle Ridden, Your Highness,' said the lieutenant. 'Again, though, the Rangers were given no orders to that effect. We have seen a few companies of Royal Guards begin to pack up their things, so we suspect that they have been told.'

Walter nodded. 'I also have orders that I don't wish to spread around. I need four Rangers to travel over the secret pass as soon as possible. They are to raise a white flag when they reach the ravine, and then they are to attempt to send word to Prince Valentino, stating that I am more than willing to hand over his granddaughter without any preconditions. In return, I hope that he will pause hostilities long enough for us to begin negotiations. However, that is not why I am handing her back; I shall do it because it's the right thing to do. It's what we should have done months ago. If you have trouble reaching the prince, ask for Count Sebastian. If anyone will talk to us, he will.'

'Yes, sir,' said the lieutenant. 'I shall find four volunteers and have them begin the trek this evening.'

'Is there a secret route over the mountains?' said Hygilt.

'There is,' said Walter.

'Can I go with the four Rangers?' the girl went on. 'If you want me sent back to my grandfather, that would be the quickest way to do it.'

'It's too dangerous for a girl of your age.'

Hygilt narrowed her eyes. 'I have trekked over mountains before, Mister King's Champion. I have received all manner of training in how to survive being out in the wilderness.'

'All right; you are forcing me to be honest. The reason you're not going is because the route is a damn secret, and I don't want anyone outwith the Rangers to gain that information. Sorry, but there it is.'

'You don't trust me.'

'Your grandfather is currently doing his level best to break into

Torrent, and I have no doubt that he would use the secret pass to send soldiers to outflank us.'

Hygilt glared at Walter, who shrugged.

'Sorry to interrupt,' said Abigone, 'but has anyone seen Tulip?'

'Your... creature was last seen on the night you were abducted, ma'am,' said the lieutenant. 'He seemed badly injured when we first encountered him, but he made a fast recovery, before disappearing. None of the Rangers have seen him since.'

'Can I go to the palace to look for him? The poor baby is probably terrified.'

'Not yet,' said Walter. 'I want to speak to every Ranger in the building first.' He glanced at Lothar. 'Can they all be summoned here?'

'With the exception of the squad guarding the southern gate, sir,' said Lothar, 'almost every fit Ranger is inside the barracks.'

'Almost?'

'Yes, sir. Princess Kilbride took two with her when she went to the ducal palace.' He nodded to a group of sergeants. 'Fetch everyone.'

The sergeants hurried away, just as other Rangers entered the mess hall with trays. They placed them onto a long dining table.

'Dinner is served, Your Highnesses,' said Lothar.

'Thank you,' said Abigone, as she and Hygilt stood. They walked to the table and sat down. She turned her head to see if Walter was joining them, and watched as he was handed a small flask by another Ranger. Walter lifted it to his lips and took a long drink, then he passed the flask back to the man. Abigone frowned, then she noticed that Lothar had also been watching the exchange. The Rangers commander had an odd look on his face – part guilt, part anger.

'What type of cheese is this?' Hygilt said, as she poked a white substance with a fork.

'It's goat's cheese, ma'am,' said a Ranger.

'I didn't know goats had any use.'

Abigone pulled her eyes away from Lothar and turned to gaze at the food. She smiled at Hygilt, and they began to eat, as more Rangers entered the mess hall. Walter got up onto a low table when the hall was full, and raised a hand for silence.

'Rangers,' he said; 'as you can see, I have returned with Princess Abigone and Princess Hygilt. They were with Dravid, as we had suspected, but someone else was there – Stefan, Hector's new friend. Now, we all know that Stefan was sent north to rescue the princesses, but when I got there, Stefan and Dravid were behaving like old friends. It is my assumption that the two bastards were working together. Hector may not know it yet, but his agreement with Stefan is fucking worthless.' He turned to Hygilt. 'Apologies for the language, Your Highness.'

'I am starting to get used to it,' said the princess.

'Something else happened while I was north,' Walter went on. 'Princess Abigone and Princess Hygilt told me a little story – regarding something that Dravid had told them. At this stage, it is merely conjecture, but I wanted to let you all know. Dravid claims that it was Duke Hector who told him where King Alfgang the Pius would be on the morning he was murdered. Dravid also claimed that it was Duke Hector who ordered him to assassinate the king. Without evidence, however, we cannot repeat this in public. Instead, we need to investigate the truth of Dravid's claims. If anyone here knows of anything that could...'

'I know, sir,' said Lothar.

Walter turned to him. 'Tell us.'

The hall hushed as the commander stepped forward. 'I have information that confirms the truth of it. I have spoken to someone who was present in the ducal palace on the day Dravid was told the whereabouts of Alfgang the Pius. Dravid's claims are true. Duke Hector murdered our king. He is a traitor.'

The crowd of Rangers broke out into a raucous chorus of questions and shouts.

'Shut up!' Walter shouted. 'Thank you. Dravid had another claim,' he went on. 'He said that he thinks Hector is a Master.'

'I can confirm the truth of that, too, sir,' said Lothar.

'Who told you this?' said Walter, as the noise levels in the hall increased again.

'I can tell you in private, sir,' said Lothar, 'but I was sworn to secrecy.'

'Quiet!' Walter shouted. 'Right. Now you know the truth about what we're up against. Hector is a Master, and a traitor. He is also in control of every militia in Upper Down, with the exception of the Mountain Rangers. If you see him, and have a clear shot, take it. Forget about honour, and forget about what you think you know about my brother. Hector is a grave danger to the future of this realm, and he must be punished for what he did to Alfgang the Pius. Show the bastard no mercy, for he will certainly show us none. Get ready to leave the barracks in thirty minutes.'

'Where are we going, sir?' said the lieutenant.

'The Kendril Wall; where else?'

Walter stepped down onto the floor, and then he and Lothar had a quiet conversation. The two men disappeared through a doorway, and Abigone put down her fork, her appetite gone. She got to her feet.

'I need some fresh air,' she said.

The lieutenant clicked his fingers, and four Rangers followed Abigone to the front door of the barracks. The sun had set behind the mountains, and a few lamps were being lit in the streets of Torrent. Abigone listened to the rumbling of the cannon for a few moments, as her four escorts flanked her. Dravid had been right about everything. Hector, a man she had idolised for most of her life, was a Master and a traitor. The knowledge that he had slain her brother had seemed unreal and vague until Walter had announced it openly in front of the Rangers, only to have it confirmed by Commander Lothar.

She turned towards the palace. Many of its windows were dark, as few lights had been lit within; and the building seemed almost deserted. If Hector was allowed to flee north to his bastion at Castle Ridden, then he would have moved beyond the reach of justice. And if he had Alfie and Kilbride with him, he could use them as hostages. How could she have been so blind to Hector's true intentions? Of course he had planned for her to marry Stefan; the talk of it being a ruse was simply to lull her into complacency. Had her sister joined him? Why else would Kilbride be in the ducal palace?

'Oh, Tulip,' she whispered. 'If you are out there, please take care, little one. I miss you.'

Something small darted across the dark courtyard, racing towards them. The Rangers peered into the shadows, then Abigone felt tears come to her eyes. The small shape reached her and she scooped it up into her arms.

'Tulip,' she cried, as she held the animal close to her chest. 'You waited for me. Clever boy.'

She held him up to her face to kiss him, and he licked her nose. She laughed.

'I will never let you go again.'

CHAPTER 29
THREE MOONS

Torrent, Upper Down – 17th Day of Lamenta 107

Walter leaned against the wall of the dark room within the Rangers' barracks.

'I remember Ireni,' he said. 'I saw her a few times in the ducal palace. Are you saying that my brother sold her to Dravid?'

'He gave her away, sir,' said Lothar. 'No money changed hands. She told me that she was part of the deal to get Dravid to agree to kill King Alfgang the Pius, not that he needed much persuasion.'

'And you took her to see Kilbride?'

'Yes, sir. Not long after our meeting with the princess had concluded, we heard that Her Highness was moving out of the Royal Palace, along with King Alfgang and the Queen Mother. As far as I can gather, Duke Hector is planning to leave Torrent tomorrow morning, to begin the journey north to Castle Ridden.'

Walter nodded.

'There is one more rumour that I have heard, sir,' said Lothar.

'Yes?'

'Apparently, Lady Perpetua was found hanged in her rooms at dawn this morning.'

'Perpetua is dead?'

'That's what my contacts in the ducal palace told me, sir. Her death is being attributed to suicide.'

'Do we have any reason to doubt that version of events?'

'I don't know, sir. I cannot see how Duke Hector would benefit from the death of his wife.'

'Me, neither. I barely knew Perpetua; she spent all of her time up in the duchy. Maybe she found out about my brother's affairs.'

'I am told that she already knew about them, sir. She has been turning a blind eye to your brother's indiscretions for many years.'

'What about Kilbride? Did she go to the ducal palace willingly?'

'She was ordered to go by Duke Hector, sir. Something about his vote as a regent being worth more than hers. She had no choice in the matter. However, she may use the opportunity to get close enough to Hector to kill him. That was what we were planning to do.'

'You should know that I have my concerns about you,' said Walter. 'It wasn't so long ago that you were on my brother's payroll.'

'Yes, sir. I told Princess Kilbride that I want to make amends for what I did to you, and I meant it. To think that I was taking money from a fucking traitor; my mother would slap me if she found out. I, uh... I saw you take a drink from that Ranger in the mess hall, sir.'

'So?'

'I blame myself. I did this to you, sir. I'm sorry.'

'I am responsible for my actions, not you.' Walter froze. 'The cannon have stopped.'

The two men remained still for a moment.

'They ceased firing about the same time yesterday evening, sir,' Lothar said. 'It might not signify anything important.'

'Round up the Rangers,' said Walter. 'Make sure they are ready to leave. We'll release the twelve Guardsmen at the same time, and they can resume their old position by the gates.'

'Yes, sir.'

Lothar walked from the room, but Walter remained where he was. He rubbed his eyes, as tiredness seeped through every part of his body. The whisky had calmed his nerves and sorted out his trembling hands, but it had also awoken a fierce desire to consume more. He missed the days when he had little to worry about except which beer hall or tavern he was going to visit, and he cursed Alfgang the Great for bestowing upon him the title of King's Champion. For the briefest of moments, he was tempted to slip out of the barracks unseen, and head to his cramped tower apartment. He would lock the door, drink whatever he could get his hands on, and fade into oblivion. He smiled to himself. If only. That world had gone, and he had a job to do.

He walked back into the mess hall, and found the Rangers preparing to leave. Hygilt and Abigone were sitting on a couch, and Walter saw Tulip asleep on Abigone's lap. He walked over, but kept his distance from the creature.

'It's all right, Walter,' said Abigone. 'I told Tulip that you helped rescue us from the Westlanders. Do you want to stroke him?'

'Are you sure he won't bite my fingers off?'

'Well, fairly sure.'

'Hey, Tulip,' he said.

The creature opened his eyes to stare at Walter, but didn't hiss at him. Walter reached out with a hand, and the animal allowed him to scratch him behind the ears.

Abigone laughed. 'See? He likes you now.'

A Ranger ran into the hall. 'The Wall has fallen!' he cried. 'The Kendril Wall has collapsed!'

Walter pushed his way through the crowd towards him.

'Someone from the Wall Militia ran all the way to tell the soldiers on duty at the palace gates,' the Ranger went on. 'The imperial army is preparing to advance.''

'Everybody outside,' Walter shouted. 'Form up in front of the barracks.'

The Rangers grabbed their equipment and filed out of the doors. Abigone and Hygilt made their way over to Walter.

'What will we do?' said Abigone.

'You should stay here,' said Walter. 'I will leave a couple of squads of

Rangers to protect you. If things become catastrophic, I will send word, and then the Rangers will lead you north, out of Torrent.'

'No,' said Hygilt. 'Only I can save Torrent. Take me to the remains of the Kendril Wall, and I will speak to the officers from the imperial army.'

'The Kendril Gap is about to turn into a battlefield,' said Walter. 'The one thing I will not do is put your life in danger. That goes for you, too, Abigone.'

'You can't order me around,' said Abigone. 'I am a member of the regency council. If you are going to the Wall, then so am I.'

'What was the point of me saving you from Dravid, if you are going to throw your lives away?'

'As you pointed out, cousin, we practically saved ourselves,' said Abigone. 'I am a Maker, and Hygilt can negotiate with the imperial army. If you don't take us with you, your Rangers will die for nothing.'

Walter felt his temper surge, then he strode from the hall and out into the chill autumnal evening. The Rangers had lined up in their squads, with the officers and sergeants at the front of each column, while Lothar and the other commanders were waiting for Walter.

'How many do we have?' Walter said.

'Two hundred and eighty-one, sir,' said a lieutenant.

'Is that all that's left of us?'

'Over forty Rangers are currently in the infirmary, sir; two are with Princess Kilbride, a dozen are guarding the palace gate, and four have been sent over the pass as ordered.'

Walter gazed at the ranks of Rangers standing in front of him.

'The day has come,' he said; 'a day none of us thought we'd live to see. For five centuries, that damn Wall has protected Upper Down from any invasion coming from the south, and we grew rich and lazy, believing it could never be breached. We were wrong, and now we are in the fight of our lives. We will be escorting Princess Abigone and Princess Hygilt to the front line, but we shall be keeping them back from the fighting. When we get to the Kendril Gap, we will join forces with the other militias to defend this realm, and to protect the tens of thousands of civilians who live in Torrent and Twinbrook. We might die, but we will not flee, or surrender; not this night; not ever. Follow me.'

Walter set off, and he heard the sound of nearly three hundred Rangers marching behind him. They reached the southern gates of the palace grounds, and picked up the dozen Rangers who had been stationed there, leaving in place the Guardsmen they had arrested earlier. Abigone and Hygilt walked next to Walter, with Tulip draped over Abigone's right shoulder.

They took the road that led directly to the Kendril Wall. Civilians were already starting to stream north, while others stood by the side of the street, watching as the Rangers marched past. When they were halfway to the Wall, a small group of Town Militia ran across the road, fleeing north in disarray.

Walter raced forward to meet them.

'Has the imperial army entered Torrent?' he cried.

The soldiers from the militia stared at Walter and the Rangers, and kept running. Walter cursed under his breath, and continued onwards. They reached the large forecourt that lay between the Wall of Kendril and the edge of the town. Much of its expanse was filled with huge blocks of rubble. Soldiers from the Wall Militia had gathered in groups – some were carrying wounded soldiers towards the streets of the town; some were building barricades; while others were staggering around in the lamplight as though they were in a daze. Walter stared up at the Kendril Gap, as the Rangers followed him into the forecourt.

The mighty Kendril Wall had fallen. A huge pile of rubble in the centre marked out where the large gatehouse had stood, while a wide breach had been created on either side of it by the cannon fire. Each gap was filled with a great mound of rubble, but Walter knew that soldiers would be able to climb over either of them. A captain from the Wall Militia was trying to rally his men, ordering them to load their crossbows and take cover behind their makeshift barricades, but several soldiers were arguing with him, telling him that the cause was lost.

The officer and the soldiers fell silent as Walter and the Rangers approached.

'My lord,' said the captain, bowing.

'Are you the senior officer present?' said Walter.

'At the moment, yes, sir. I don't know where the major is.'

'Where is the rest of the Wall Militia?'

The captain gestured to the giant heap of ruins where the gatehouse had been. 'Many were inside when the building collapsed, sir. Others have... fled. They wouldn't listen to my orders, and they panicked.' He glanced at the Rangers. 'Are more reinforcements on their way, sir?'

'Let's hope the answer to that question is yes,' said Walter.

'One hundred and fifty yards!' cried a voice from somewhere in the rubble.

Walter turned.

'I have a scout up on what's left of the Wall, sir,' the captain said. 'He's pointing out the location of the imperial army. I have been trying to get two barricades built, one in front of each of the main breaches.'

'Good man,' said Walter. 'The Rangers shall support your crossbow teams.' He jumped up onto a large fragment of masonry, and the soldiers in the forecourt gazed up at him.

'I am assuming command of the defences,' Walter said. 'We will take shelter behind the barricades, and shoot anything that comes over the rubble. Crossbow teams will take up their positions in front of the Rangers, who will ready their longbows.' He gestured at the soldiers. 'This half will take the western breach; and this half the eastern. Loose only when you have a clear target, and wait for the imperial soldiers to appear. Do not advance, and do not cross the field of rubble. We will draw the enemy into the forecourt and pick them off. Look at what they will have to cross to engage with us. Hold the line and do not retreat. Officers, get your men into position.'

The soldiers and Rangers began to rush off – half going west, and the others east. They took shelter behind the huge blocks of rubble littering the forecourt, and readied their bows. Walter jumped down.

'Send a few of the walking wounded into the town,' he said to the captain. 'Go door to door, and ask the civilians for help. We need weapons, bolts, arrows, bandages, water, oil lamps – anything they might have in their homes that could help. And if they see any fleeing militia, order them to get their cowardly arses back here.'

'Should we not order a general evacuation, my lord?' said the captain.

'No. This is where we stand and fight. Any civilian who wishes to help us is welcome; they can sit behind the barricades and reload the crossbows.'

'One hundred yards and closing!' cried the scout up on the rubble.

The captain stared at the ruins of the Wall for a moment, then he rushed off. Walter approached Abigone and Hygilt, who were being guarded by six Rangers.

'I'm going to ask you both to step away from the Wall,' he said to them. 'Shelter in one of the houses that borders the forecourt.'

'Shouldn't I try to talk to the imperial soldiers?' said Hygilt.

'It's too dark for that,' Walter said. 'If you poke your head over the rubble, all the imperial army will see is a silhouette, and you're likely to get an arrow loosed your way.'

'The moons will be coming out soon,' said Abigone; 'all three of them.'

'Three full moons,' said Hygilt.

'Shit,' said Walter; 'is that tonight?'

Abigone nodded.

Walter glanced up. The sky was clear, and thousands of stars were shining down upon Torrent. In the east, the Silver Moon was starting to rise. Its light would bathe the forecourt in silver hues as soon as it was high enough, and the red glow from the other two moons would turn that light into the colour of blood.

'Fifty yards!' cried the scout.

'Go,' Walter said to the princesses. 'Abigone, if you work out how to be a Maker in the next few hours, let me know. Hygilt, stay safe, and keep your fucking head down.'

The six Rangers led Abigone and Hygilt away, and Walter turned back to the defences. He strode to the barricade facing the breach in the eastern half of the Kendril Wall, and a Ranger handed him a stringed longbow. Walter got into position by the right of the barricade, from where he could also see the defences guarding the western breach, and practised his aim, straightening his left arm and pulling on the bowstring. A few civilians were joining the lines of soldiers, and each was led to a pile of crossbows abandoned by the fleeing militia. The civilians crouched on the ground, and began to load them.

A figure appeared on the rubble.

'Do not loose!' shouted a sergeant. 'That's our scout!'

The figure scrambled down from the ruins of the gatehouse and sprinted across the forecourt.

'Ten yards,' he gasped, as he took shelter behind a massive block of rubble.

'Conserve your bolts and arrows,' Walter shouted. 'Loose only when you have a clear target.'

An anxious silence descended over the forecourt, as every soldier gazed at the enormous heap of rubble spread across the Kendril Gap. Walter flexed his fingers, then reached down to pluck an arrow from the bucket that sat on the ground in front of him. He nocked it as the first imperial soldier raised his head over the rubble. A Ranger loosed, and the arrow struck the soldier in the throat, sending him toppling backwards out of sight.

A cheer rose up from the defenders, then dozens more soldiers from the imperial army appeared, crowding the two breaches as they scrambled over the wreckage.

'Loose at will!' Walter shouted, then he released his arrow into the densely-packed group attacking the eastern breach.

The imperial soldiers were carrying large shields, but their lines broke up amid the mounds of rubble, and the defenders shot down the first wave before they had reached the forecourt. A second wave appeared, and a hail of bolts and arrows rained down upon them. The bolts began to peter out as more crossbows needed to be reloaded, and the second wave made it halfway across the forecourt before the last of them was felled by an arrow to the head. Other imperial soldiers had remained in the rubble, taking shelter behind the largest fragments of masonry, and from there they began to loose back at the defenders.

A third wave appeared over the top of the rubble as the arrows began to run low. Civilians were still emerging from the town to lend their assistance, and a few were carrying sheaves of arrows with them, which were snatched up by the Rangers. Behind the barricades, every crossbow reloaded by the civilians was put back into action immediately, and the third wave faltered. Bodies were starting to block the eastern breach, and wounded imperial soldiers were crying out in torment amid the blood-slicked rubble. The third wave began to retreat, taking shelter behind the ruins of the gatehouse.

A crossbow bolt flew past Walter's head as he reached for another arrow, but the bucket was empty. He placed his longbow down against the barricade, and drew Count Sebastian's sword. He gestured to a few squads of Wall Militia, who were waiting for their crossbows to be reloaded.

'With me,' Walter said. 'Stay left, and we'll go along the edge of the cliff face, and engage the soldiers hiding among the rubble. Move.'

Walter raced off, running to the east towards the far edge of the forecourt, where the postern gate had been located. He slowed when he reached the sheer cliff rising up to his left, and crept into the field of rubble. Most of those hidden amid the ruins were in the process of reloading their bows, and they were set upon by Walter and the militia, as they scrambled over the rubble. Walter kept as low as he could, as arrows passed over his head, and the militia went from shelter to shelter killing any imperial soldier they could find, and ending the suffering of the wounded. Walter crawled up to a huge fragment, and peered over the summit of rubble. Below, the entire imperial army seemed to be trying to ascend the steep slope. The cannon were sitting idle behind the palisade wall, and the ravine was full of soldiers. Many were carrying lit brands, and the little dots of flame were bobbing around in the confusion. The advance had stalled, and dozens of imperial soldiers were taking shelter just behind the ruins.

At that moment, the two red moons rose over Torrent, joining the Silver Moon in the cloudless sky, and the soldiers of the imperial army gazed up in awe at the sight. Each moon was full on the same night, and their combined light made the entire encampment in the ravine visible in shades of red and silver.

Walter glanced back. His squads of Wall Militia were still scrambling around the ruins, collecting every arrow and bolt they could find, and ripping some from the multitude of bodies that lay scattered around in heaps. Walter signalled the retreat, and they scrambled back to the barricades. Every crossbow had been reloaded, including the piles of spares, and civilians were bringing more arrows and bolts to the front lines. By the barricades, several groups of militia had returned to their posts, shamed into doing their duty by the other defenders of the Gap.

'Get ready for another wave,' Walter shouted, as he reached his position by a barricade.

'Here they come!' cried a Ranger, and the first crossbows spat out their bolts.

Walter took an arrow from the replenished bucket, nocked, and loosed. The fourth wave was the largest yet, and more imperial soldiers kept appearing, driven on by their officers further down the slope. Several made it onto the forecourt, and hand-to-hand fighting broke out by the western breach. The crossbow teams would loose, then hand their bows to the civilians, who would pass them another loaded bow, and the stream of bolts hitting the imperial army continued without cessation. A company of Town Militia joined the melee by the western breach, their swords drawn, and the imperial soldiers were pushed back amid the storm of arrows and bolts.

The loosing stopped as the last of the fourth wave retreated in disarray, and the defenders slumped against the barricades.

'I'm out of arrows again,' said a Ranger.

Walter stared at the eastern breach, then he turned and walked to where the houses began. Civilians were tending several wounded, while others were still carrying supplies for the front, and Walter could see the grim defiance in their eyes.

'Hail the King's Champion!' cried an old man, and a cheer rose up from the crowd.

Walter paused, then realised that everyone was staring at him.

An old woman held out a flask. 'Do you want a drink, son?' she said.

Walter took the flask and drank. The crowd cheered again, and Walter was slapped on the back by many in the crowd.

'Who'd have thought it, eh?' said the old woman. 'Who'd have guessed it'd be Lord Walter leading the defence? I heard your brother is fleeing to Castle Ridden.'

'I couldn't give a shit what Hector does,' said Walter. 'We're not running,' he went on, raising his voice. 'This is our fucking town, and we'll fight for it.'

The crowd roared. Walter eased his way through them, and reached the house where the two princesses had taken shelter. He entered, and saw Abigone and Hygilt in the front room, from where they had been watching the battle.

'Well done,' said Abigone. 'Have they gone?'

Walter shook his head. 'They're regrouping. There are thousands of the bastards on the other side of the ruins. I just wanted to check that you two were all right.'

'We're fine,' said Hygilt. 'Is it safe for me to speak to the imperial army?'

'It's chaos out there,' he said. 'Stay in the house. If the imperials break through our lines, run north as fast as you can.'

'I heard you say that we wouldn't be running away,' said Abigone.

'I'm not going anywhere,' he said, 'but you don't need to die tonight.'

A Ranger burst into the room. 'Sir; there's something you have to see.'

Walter followed the man outside. Over to the left, taking up half of the forecourt, were hundreds of Westlanders. Each man was kneeling on the cobbles with their heads bowed and their arms raised, their weapons laid out in front of them, and their steel armour shimmering in the light of the three moons.

Chief Stefan made his way to the front of the crowd. 'The gods are with us!' he cried. 'Do you see them watching over Torrent? King Aloth is sitting in judgement, a witness to the glory this night shall bring us; while Queen Ninia's heart is bursting with pride as she bestows her blessings and love upon her people. Prince Logar, too, is here, waiting to see which of us will be honoured enough to join his eternal feast. This is our night! With our gods by our side, we cannot lose! Pick up your weapons and stand.'

The Westlanders rose as one, their long swords, maces and battle axes gripped in their hands.

Stefan pointed at Walter. 'Do you see that craven wretch – the so-called King's Champion? While he and his men cower behind barricades, we will take the fight to the enemy. Will you join us, Lord Walter – will you join the charge that will win this battle?'

'Go fuck yourself,' Walter shouted back. 'We're already winning this battle – our way.'

The Westlanders tensed and cried out in anger, as the Rangers and militiamen watched in silence.

'Did you hear that?' said Stefan. 'We Westlanders will save Upper Down. We shall destroy the imperial army this night, while the gods watch us from the heavens; and when we return, Upper Down shall be ours!' He pointed his sword at the breach. 'Charge!'

Six hundred Westlanders set off. They ran through the rubble, clambering over the stones and the bodies. They reached the summit of the ruins and kept going, and the sounds of a violent struggle rose through the air. Walter and the defenders watched from the barricades, as the last of the Westlanders disappeared from view.

'Should we go after them, sir?' said an officer from the Wall Militia.

'No,' said Walter. 'Every soldier under my command will stay here. Reload the bows and replenish the supply of bolts and arrows. We're not going to throw our lives away just because the three fucking moons are out. We will, however, observe.'

He nodded to a few officers, and then they ran towards the ruins, keeping to the left-hand cliff face. They scrambled over the carnage and the ruined masonry, until they reached a point from where they could see down into the ravine. The noise coming from the battle below them was tremendous. Six hundred steel-clad Westlanders were cutting their way through the advance companies of the imperial army, delivering a slaughter that made the deaths by the Kendril Gap pale in comparison. Huge battle axes were slicing through the leather armour and grey uniforms worn by the imperial soldiers, and they were retreating headlong back to their camp, as the Westlanders pressed on in a bloody frenzy.

'They're going to win the damn battle on their own,' murmured an officer to Walter's left. 'If they reach the cannon, it's over.'

'We should have gone after them,' said another. 'They will never let us forget that we refused to join their charge.'

Walter ignored them, his gaze fixed on the slaughter down in the valley. The last of the imperial soldiers fled the scene, and the jubilant Westlanders took a moment to regroup and form up their lines into a solid wall of steel. A hundred yards down the slope from them, there was a flurry of activity by the palisade wall. Imperial soldiers were still fleeing, but others had remained at their posts, and were hard at work.

A horn blasted out from the ranks of the Westlanders, and they resumed their charge down the hill, their voices roaring out as they approached the front of the imperial camp. At that moment, engineers pulled at the wooden posts by the palisade, and the wall toppled over, each wooden beam falling forwards. Behind, thirty cannon had been arrayed in a long line, all pointing up the slope at the charging Westlanders.

A red flag was raised, and the cannon fired. The front ranks of the Westlanders were only sixty yards away, and the thirty cannon balls ripped through their lines, blasting steel armour and flesh apart. The cannon were reloaded, their crews synchronised and disciplined, and a second barrage was unleashed. More Westlanders fell, their ranks torn apart. Behind the thirty cannon, another row of two dozen had been prepared, their muzzles aiming slightly higher. They fired, and the iron balls rained down onto the Westlanders from above. The two rows started to work together, alternating their barrages, and churning up the slope into a sea of mud, iron and flesh. The Westlanders were being cut to pieces, but still they charged, as though the idea of retreat was unthinkable.

One of the cannon smouldered, its barrel overheating, then several others were also rendered inoperable, but the others kept up the bombardment, until nothing was moving on the slope. The cannon fell silent, then steam hissed as buckets of water from the stream were poured over the red hot metal. The steam rose up like mist and drifted over the ravine, obscuring the view of the slaughter that had taken place.

One of the officers glanced at Walter. 'I take back my earlier words, sir. Praise the spirits that you didn't order us down there.'

A few scattered survivors among the Westlanders arose from the mud and devastation, and began to retreat back up the slope, their armour caked in blood. A few wounded men tried to crawl, but soon lay still on the ground, while a handful of others managed to make it back to the shelter of the ruins of the Kendril Wall. In the midst of one small group, a man was struggling, as though he didn't want to be saved.

'Let me die with my men!' he cried out, as the Westlanders dragged him past the place where Walter and the others were hiding.

'It's Stefan,' whispered one of the militia officers.

'The lucky bastard's alive,' said Walter.

'He doesn't sound as though he thinks he's one of the lucky ones, sir.'

They watched as the chief was hauled across the ruins and set down by the base of the cliff. The other survivors surrounded Stefan, to protect him, and to prevent him from running back down the slope to meet his end.

'Let's get back to the barricades,' said Walter, 'and prepare for the next wave. This is going to be a long night.'

CHAPTER 30
ONE HOUR BEFORE DAWN

Torrent, Upper Down – 18th Day of Lamenta 107

Anger kept Kilbride awake. No one had lit any lamps in Hector's quarters, and she had been sitting alone in the darkness for hours, her face sore, and her wrists and ankles aching from the tight cords. Her back was stiff, and the rope round her waist had been digging into her skin. Next to her anger, her pain and discomfort were insignificant. Hector had struck her and threatened the boy-king, and she would make him pay if it was the last thing she ever did.

She kept her gaze on the door, willing it to open. A narrow sliver of light was spilling into the room from under the entrance, and Kilbride could sometimes see shadows moving in the hallway beyond. She tensed every time that happened, hoping that someone would enter the room, but she had received no visitors since being tied to the chair.

She had listened to the pounding of the cannon during the previous afternoon and evening, and then they had fallen silent, leaving her even more angry that she didn't know what was happening by the Kendril Wall. She tried to guess the time. She was sure that midnight had come and gone several hours before, but she could see no signs of the approaching dawn, when the members of the Royal Court were scheduled to board their carriages and begin the journey north to the Duchy of

Ridden. Kilbride wondered how Hector would deal with her transfer to the carriage. Would she be carried out kicking and screaming, or would she be bundled quietly into a waiting carriage with a hood over her head? What would Frida and little Alfie think? What would Hector tell them?

The shadows under the door moved again. A key sounded in the lock, and the door opened. Four men walked in, three of whom were armed.

'Light some lamps,' said a voice. 'I can't see a thing in here.'

'Yes, sir,' said another voice.

A match ignited, and a wall lamp by the door was the first to be lit. Kilbride blinked and narrowed her eyes. Amery was the unarmed man who had entered the room. He had a sheaf of documents under his left arm, and a bag was slung over his shoulder. He gazed at Kilbride, as the three soldiers who had also entered walked round the room lighting more lamps.

'That's better,' said Amery, his gaze never leaving Kilbride. 'Remove the princess's gag. I need her to be able to speak.'

One of the soldiers moved behind Kilbride, and unfastened the knot holding the handkerchief round her face. She gasped as she inhaled.

'I need some water,' she said.

Amery nodded. 'Give her some,' he said, as he fetched a chair. He set it down a few yards in front of Kilbride, but remained standing as a soldier filled a mug with water. He took it to Kilbride, and placed it by her lips. She drank, letting half of it spill down her chin as she satisfied her thirst.

'Now, everyone leave,' said Amery.

'We were instructed to remain in the room, sir,' said one of the soldiers.

'I'm afraid that's out of the question,' said Amery. 'At this precise moment, I am acting as this woman's lawyer, and I require confidentiality with my client.'

The soldiers remained where they were.

'If you don't leave,' Amery went on, 'then I will be unable to complete the marriage contract, as its terms would be invalidated. Tell me – who will Duke Hector blame?'

A soldier frowned. 'But…'

'Come now,' said Amery. 'Do you think it likely that she will escape and overpower me? She is tied to a chair, gentlemen. She is going nowhere.'

The three soldiers frowned, then they walked towards the door.

'We'll be right outside if you need us, sir,' said one, then they left the room and closed the door.

'Was that true?' said Kilbride.

Amery glanced away, then he sat down in the chair he had positioned in front of her.

'Answer me,' she said.

'Was what true, ma'am?' he said, as he placed the sheaf of papers onto his knee.

'That excuse you gave to the soldiers to make them leave – was it true?'

Amery shrugged. 'I suppose that depends upon your interpretation of the law.' He looked her in the eye. 'I don't particularly like soldiers hovering by my shoulder as I work. I'm sure you understand. Now, shall we begin?'

'Why are you here?'

'To fill out the marriage contract, ma'am,' he said, as his gaze went to the papers on his lap. He sorted through a few. 'Duke Hector has informed me that he wants a quick and simple service to take place. Did you know that I am empowered to join two people together in matrimony?'

'I do not give my consent to any marriage.'

Amery smiled as he set up his quill and ink pot on a nearby side table. 'The duke mentioned that you might say that. He requested that I invoke an old law that does not require the explicit consent of both parties.'

'That law was superseded by the statutes of the Elestian Empire several centuries ago.'

'Oh, so you are an expert on law, are you?'

'Did I say that? I am not claiming to be an expert, but I know the law you are talking about. It no longer applies in Upper Down.'

'Yes, well, the duke has taken the liberty of changing the law, to reinstate this old formula. As you and he are the only regents known to be in Torrent, and as his vote is worth twice yours, from a legal point of view I have no grounds upon which I can make an objection. Effectively, Duke Hector's word is the law. I need a few details from you – place and date of birth, your mother's maiden name, and so on and so forth. Will you cooperate?'

'No.'

Amery nodded, then he scribbled a few notes on the paper in front of him with the quill.

'I know what you did,' said Kilbride.

Amery ignored her.

'I know it was you who gave Chief Dravid the location of King Alfgang the Pius.'

Amery's hand juddered, and the tip of the quill snapped. He glared at Kilbride, then he fished in his bag for another quill.

'I am not the only person who knows this,' Kilbride went on. 'You are complicit in the murder of our king, my brother. You should have had Ireni killed – that was your mistake. Did you know that she has returned to Torrent? Right now, she is being protected in a secret location. It was rather foolish, was it not, to have allowed her to hear the entire conversation you held with Dravid? That was your other mistake.'

Amery cleared his throat. 'The law regarding marriage that the duke wishes to invoke…'

'You dare talk to me about law?' said Kilbride. 'You, whose hands are red from the blood of our slain king? You hypocrite. What would the famed law institutes of the Central Provinces say if they knew the laws you had broken?'

Amery set down the quill. 'I signed a contract with the duke, ma'am. A legally binding contract. Said contract contains a clause requiring me to do whatever the duke asks. I knew the clause was there when I signed it.'

'And did you expect the clause to be used to force you into assassinating a king?'

'I did not, ma'am; however, the fact remains that I signed my name at the bottom of the contract, just as you signed the document establishing the regency council, even though you knew the duke's vote was worth twice yours. We are human, and humans err.'

'Do you repeat that to yourself each night when your conscience does not allow you to sleep?'

Amery laughed. 'Ah, you believe that I am in possession of a conscience. That, ma'am, is your mistake.'

'I know you have a conscience, Amery. Ireni told me that you tried to prevent her from being sold to Dravid. That is not the mark of a man without a conscience. You knew it was wrong, and you tried to stop it.'

'I failed to stop it.'

'Only because Dravid threatened your life. People may do terrible things when they are afraid, but that does not necessarily make them evil. Are you now ashamed that you yielded to Hector and Dravid's commands?'

Amery sighed. 'This line of discussion is fruitless. My shame, or fear, or whatever other emotion you wish to ascribe to me makes no difference to what I must do this day. With or without your active cooperation, I am obliged to complete this marriage contract.' He glanced at the window. 'The sun is due to rise in an hour, and the Duke of Ridden requires this business to be concluded by then, so that we can all travel to Castle Ridden.'

'I will not flee Torrent while the Wall stands.'

He gave her a wry smile. 'The Kendril Wall has fallen, ma'am. I apologise for breaking this news to you, but it collapsed yesterday evening. It seems that heavy and sustained cannon fire can get through just about anything.'

Kilbride stared at him as he got back to work, the fresh quill in his hand as he wrote on the paper.

'Has the imperial army entered Torrent?' she said.

'Not yet,' Amery said, his gaze still lowered. 'The King's Champion has rallied the defences, and they are still holding the Kendril Gap.'

'Walter is commanding the defences?'

'It certainly appears that way; although I wouldn't repeat that claim in front of the duke. He got quite upset with an officer who mentioned it a little while ago.' He glanced up, a faint smile on the edge of his lips. 'It seems that the King's Champion's name is being cheered throughout Torrent. A dozen times the imperial army has charged up the slope, and a dozen times they have been repelled. Or, at least that's what the gossips are saying. Having not been to the front in person, I am unaware of the exactitude of these claims.'

Kilbride smiled, and her eyes welled a little. 'Walter is there.'

'And, most surprisingly of all, he appears to be sober.'

'Do you know the whereabouts of Abigone and Hygilt?'

'I know only what the rumours tell me, ma'am – that both princesses are with Walter by the Kendril Gap. I cannot confirm nor deny this information.'

'And Hector is angry?'

'Exceedingly so. That I can confirm. Nothing seems to annoy the duke more than hearing pleasant things being said about his brother.'

'Why are you smiling, Amery?' said Kilbride. 'You hate him, don't you? I can see it written on your face. You loathe Hector.'

'My personal feelings are irrelevant, ma'am. I am a professional lawyer, and I act with all the objectivity I can muster.'

'You are breaking the laws you profess to serve.'

'I am upholding my end of the contract I signed.'

'You are breaking the law, Amery, and you know it. Release me, and I will draw up a new contract for you; one that will not require you to act illegally.'

'I wondered how long it would take,' he said.

'What?'

'I suspected you might plead for my assistance, ma'am. Duke Hector also foresaw it. He told me that you would beg me to help you escape. And then he promised me a thousand gold sovereigns if I completed the marriage contract by sunrise.'

'So you can be bought? I see. How noble. How honourable.'

Amery smiled again. 'How rich. Don't leave that part out.'

'Are you proud of all you have achieved in Upper Down?'

'No. I will be happy if I make it out of this wretched kingdom alive. My contract with Duke Hector expires a few months from now. I shall not be renewing it. State your date of birth, if you please.'

'No.'

'I can get the information from the public records.'

'Then do so.'

'Trawling through the records would be rather time-consuming, ma'am. They are in a somewhat disorganised state since being transferred from the Royal Palace, and I fear that the marriage certificate would not be finished by sunrise.'

'That sounds like your problem.'

Amery laid his quill to the side. 'Is there any possibility of a deal? If you cooperate with the completion of this certificate, then I might split the gold with you.'

'You want me to marry Hector for five hundred sovereigns?'

'You will be wed to him this morning, whether you assist me or not. This way, at least you will come out of it a little richer.'

'Tell me about Ireni,' she said. 'What was it about her that made you attempt to save her from Dravid?'

'There was nothing about her in particular,' he said. 'I merely knew that she was a free citizen of Upper Down, and I pointed this out to the Westlander chief. He declined to take my legal advice.'

'Help me kill Hector.'

Amery raised an eyebrow. 'You seem to have escalated your requests to an alarming degree. You have gone from *release me* to *help me kill Hector* in one small step.'

'If you help me, I will pardon all of the offences you committed while working for the duke – all of them. Your part in the murder of Alfgang the Pius; your complicity in the sale of a free citizen – all of it will be wiped away. You could then return south, or remain here and work for me; you would be rich either way. More importantly, your conscience would be clean, and your honour redeemed.'

'I have noticed that the inhabitants of Upper Down often refer to honour,' he said. 'I always found that to be more than a little ironic, considering how badly Upper Down has behaved over the past few decades. Harbouring raiding parties of Westlanders was never going to endear you to the other realms of this world, but kidnapping relatives of the Sanctian emperor?' He shook his head. 'How did you think this would end?'

'I did what I could to correct the course we were taking.'

'Did you, now? I mean no offence, but you don't seem to have been particularly successful in this endeavour.'

'No? Others would disagree. Captain Joachim, for instance, would surely disagree, were he still alive.'

Amery stared at her.

'If you hadn't conspired to kill my brother,' Kilbride went on, 'this crisis would already be over. Princess Hygilt would be back with her grandfather, and the Westlanders would have been expelled from Upper Down. But Hector didn't want that to happen, did he? He used the crisis to solidify his own authority, and you, Amery, helped him do it.'

'It... it was an accidental discharge. That's what killed Alfgang the Great.'

Kilbride smiled. 'Are you sure about that? If so, it was a shot in a million. Of all the places a stray crossbow bolt could have gone, and it struck the king in the eye. I was surprised anyone believed it to be an accident. You see, contrary to your beliefs, I did what I could to save Upper Down from the fate it now faces. What have you done, Amery, except make it worse?'

'You're lying.'

'Will you help Hector kill Alfie? Will you help him murder the boy king?'

Amery snorted. 'The duke has no intention of doing any such thing.'

'That's not what he told me. Once I am his wife, only little Alfie will stand between Hector and the throne of Upper Down. He intends to rule as king, not as a regent. The boy is the only obstacle in his path. Will you help him murder a seven-year-old child? Was that in your contract?'

Amery stared at the floor.

'What will you tell Frida?' Kilbride went on. 'Will you explain to her that you had no choice, because Hector inserted a clause into your contract? That you murdered her son because of a fucking clause? Answer me, Amery.'

His mask of composure slipped, and Kilbride could see the anguish spread over Amery's features.

'How much gold will Hector pay you to keep your silence?' said Kilbride. 'How much gold is Alfie's life worth to you? I know that you feel nothing for me. I know that you don't care if Hector keeps me chained up in Castle Ridden for the rest of my life, but...'

'I do care,' he whispered. 'I have no choice. Hector... Hector is a Master.'

'I know.'

Amery's gaze went back to her. 'You know? You knew about this? Then why can't you understand? He will kill me if I refuse to help him. He will turn my blood into salt, just as your father did to those emissaries. I cannot fight against that! No one can.'

'Masters are not invincible,' said Kilbride. 'Have you learned nothing from the deaths of Alfgang the Great and Alfgang the Pius? Both were Masters, and both are dead. Help me, Amery. I have friends who will protect you. Just get me out of this damn palace, and I will take care of Hector. There's a knife up on the dresser, over to your right. Use it to free me from this chair.'

'And then?'

Kilbride glanced around. 'The window. We can jump down into the garden.'

'I would be dead within the hour.'

'I would rather die than remain here.'

'Yes, but you won't die, will you? Hector needs you alive if he is ever to be king; just as you said. You would survive being caught, but I? Hector would strike me down in an instant.' He gathered up his papers and stood. He placed the quill and the sealed pot of ink into his bag, and began to walk towards the door.

'Where are you going?' said Kilbride.

'To visit the public records,' he said, without breaking his stride. 'I still have to complete this certificate before the sun rises.'

Amery opened the door, and stepped out into the hallway. A soldier eyed Kilbride from the entrance, then closed and locked the door. Kilbride felt like screaming. She had given all she had to persuade Amery to help her, even hinting at her role in the murder of Alfgang the Great, but her initial instincts had been correct – he was too timid to be of any use. His fear of Hector was greater than his desire to do the right thing.

A minute passed, and Kilbride continued to stare at the door. If Amery told Hector about Alfgang the Great, what would the duke do with that information? Part of her wanted the duke to know what she had done, that she had removed her own father from power, just to see the look on his face.

The door opened again, and Kilbride braced herself.

'I just need a few more answers from her,' Amery was telling the soldiers in the hallway. 'Wait outside.'

Amery walked into the room and closed the door. Without a word, he walked over to the dresser, picked up the knife, then strode over to the chair where Kilbride was bound. He moved behind her, out of her sight.

'Swear you will protect me,' he whispered in her ear.

'I swear it. I know a safe house in Torrent where you can stay until the crisis is over – a house that Hector has no idea exists.'

The knife sliced through the rope round Kilbride's waist, then the knot of cords by her hands was cut away. Kilbride stretched her arms, then she rubbed the raw skin by her wrists, as Amery cut the ropes tying her ankles to the legs of the chair.

Kilbride got to her feet, unsteady at first, then she straightened her back, and grimaced.

Amery's eyes darted at the door. 'You said something about the window?'

Kilbride's right hand shot out, and she ripped the knife from Amery's grasp. The lawyer took a step backwards, and Kilbride held the blade to his throat.

'I did as you asked,' he whispered, his hands trembling with fear.

'Why did you return?'

'Because I can't do this any more,' he said. 'I'm supposed to be a fucking lawyer, and Hector treats me like a servant. A few days ago, he asked me to burn down the house of an old man and woman, but that's nothing compared to what he made me do to your brother. Hector hated Pius; he loathed him so much that he couldn't stand the thought of him being king. And, I think he killed Perpetua.'

Kilbride narrowed her eyes. 'Go on.'

'The abrasions on her face matched a handprint,' Amery went on, 'and the cord used to hang her did not belong with any of the dressing gowns in Perpetua's apartment. Both of these details were missed by the palace courtiers, but I noticed them. I do not believe that she hanged herself.'

Kilbride lowered the knife. 'The window; but first, extinguish most of the lamps.'

Amery ran off to the wall, and began turning down the wall lamps. Kilbride waited until the room was thick with shadow, then she walked to the window, pulled it open, and gazed down. Below were the gardens of the ducal palace, a narrow ribbon of plants, trees and flowers that encircled the building on three sides. She placed the knife into her left hand, while her right lifted the window latch. She pulled it open as Amery rejoined her.

'It's a long way down,' he said. 'We could easily break our legs.

Twisting our ankles would be enough to get us caught.'

'Aim for the large bush,' she said.

'That's a thorn bush,' said Amery. 'Our skin will be torn to shreds.'

Kilbride glanced at him. 'Then stay here, if you would prefer that. Though, I might find it difficult to protect you if you remain in the ducal palace.'

She eased one leg out of the window, then shoved the knife into her boot, jabbing her ankle. She swung her other leg out, and hung from the window frame with both hands. She looked down, and let go. She fell fifteen feet, and landed in the thorn bush. She pulled herself clear, ripping her dress in several places, and scratching her arms and legs. The knife had fallen out of her boot, so she stooped down and picked it up from the ground. She looked up. Amery was dangling from the window, a look of panic on his face.

Kilbride stood back as Amery let go. He missed the bush, and landed in a heap onto the solid ground by the path, then lay there, silently writhing in agony.

'My leg,' he groaned.

Kilbride helped him stand, then she eyed her surroundings. Amery leaned into her, and she struggled to carry his weight as they set off, staggering over the grass. Kilbride clung on to him, his arm over her shoulder, as he whimpered and groaned all the way to the exterior wall. They turned by a beech tree, and sheltered between its thick trunk and the tall brick wall. Kilbride gazed up at the window from where they had dropped. The lights were still low, and there was no sign of anyone in the room. Overhead, all three moons were out, while, to the east, the sky was starting to lighten. Kilbride stared at the sight and, for a moment, she forgot where she was.

The sound of boots on the gravel path approached from the left.

'Stay here,' Kilbride whispered, then she moved round to the other side of the beech and hid in some undergrowth.

A man-at-arms from the ducal militia was striding past. He saw Amery lying by the trunk of the beech, and hurried over.

'Are you all right, sir?' the soldier said. 'How did you get here?'

'My leg,' the lawyer gasped.

Kilbride slipped out the undergrowth, padded across the grass, and drove the blade of the knife deep into the soldier's back. He made a strange exhaling noise, then fell to his knees. Kilbride ripped the blade out, and cut his throat.

The body fell to the ground, and Amery stared at it.

'You killed him. I thought you had abandoned me.'

Kilbride glanced at the branches of the beech, then she dropped the knife and crouched down next to Amery.

'Stand on my back,' she said, 'then pull yourself up and over the wall.'

'I don't know if I can do it,' he said. 'My left leg is in agony.'

'If you don't try, then I will have to abandon you.'

Amery cursed, then he pulled himself up, his hands on the trunk. He clambered onto Kilbride's back, and she smothered a cry as his boot dug into her neck for a moment.

'Sorry,' he whispered. He reached up, and grabbed hold of a branch. Kilbride raised herself up a foot, helping him climb into the branches of the beech. She followed him, jumping up and then pulling herself onto the wide branch where Amery was perched. They edged along it, and Kilbride peered over the brick wall. A quiet backstreet lay beyond.

'I'll go first,' she said, 'and then I will try to catch you.'

Amery said nothing, so she crawled along the branch, lowered herself by her arms, and dropped to the cobbled backstreet. She held her arms out, and Amery fell into them, knocking them both to the ground. They lay there for a moment, Kilbride winded, and Amery sobbing in pain. She struggled to her feet, her dress torn, and blood coming from a dozen scratches on her arms and legs. She helped Amery stand, then they turned, and staggered down the street.

'Is the safe house far?' Amery whispered.

'In five minutes,' she said, 'you will be sitting in a comfortable armchair with a glass of fine wine.'

'And you? What will you be doing?'

'Me?' she said. 'I'll be taking care of Hector.'

CHAPTER 31
BROTHERS

Torrent, Upper Down – 18th Day of Lamenta 107

Hector kept his gaze respectfully lowered as he led the procession of knights across the forecourt towards the waiting carriages. Six knights were carrying the coffin containing the body of Perpetua, and Hector had made sure that the watching staff had seen him weep silent tears. He halted by the first carriage, and waited as the knights loaded the coffin into the interior.

Overhead, the three full moons were still visible, but their light would soon be all but blotted out by the sunrise. Frida and Alfie walked down the steps of the ducal palace, and joined Hector by the carriages.

'How are you feeling, brother?' Frida said. 'I know the shock must be awful.'

'Only you understand how I feel, my beloved sister,' Hector said. 'You lost your husband, and now I have lost my dear wife.'

The two siblings embraced, their black outfits reflecting their grief.

Hector crouched down by Alfie. 'And you have been so brave, Your Majesty. Are you ready to begin the journey to Castle Ridden?'

The boy nodded.

'I shall ride with Perpetua,' said Hector, as he got back to his feet. 'You, sister, shall ride with His Majesty in the second carriage.'

Frida glanced back at the palace entrance. 'Where is Killie? I haven't seen her since yesterday morning. Is she still unwell?'

'I will check on her, but I do not wish to delay our departure. Perhaps she is still getting ready, and just needs a little reminder.'

He helped Frida and Alfie climb aboard their carriage, then he closed the side door and strode back to the palace. He went up the steps and entered the building. Courtiers and soldiers were bustling around, packing up valuables and preparing to leave. Hector saw an officer, and walked up to him.

'My lord?' said the officer, bowing.

'The Queen Mother and His Majesty have boarded their carriage,' Hector said. 'It is time to escort Princess Kilbride downstairs. A hood would prevent gossip from spreading, don't you think? Also, use the side door when you escort Her Highness to her carriage.'

'Yes, my lord.'

The officer hurried away, and Hector strode to Amery's office on the ground floor. He knocked and entered, but the room was empty. Hector's temper flurried a little. If that stupid lawyer had made a mess of the marriage contract, he would see not a single coin of the thousand Hector had promised him. He walked out of the room, and grabbed a young courtier by the arm.

'Send out a search party for my missing lawyer,' he said. 'Find him, and bring him to me.'

'Yes, my lord,' said the courtier.

Hector released her, and she ran away. He walked back to the main entrance hall, and waited by the front doors of the palace. Twenty-two carriages and eight wagons were filling the forecourt, each with four horses harnessed to their yokes. Hector's fingers drummed with impatience against the doorframe. At any moment, the imperial army would sweep aside the defensive line being commanded by Walter in the Kendril Gap, and when that happened, every road north would be clogged by the fleeing lower classes. He glanced towards the east. The sky was brightening, and the sun was about to rise.

Hector hurried down the stairs. 'Get the convoy moving,' he said to a group of knights and officers. 'Order the immediate departure for Castle Ridden.'

'Yes, my lord,' said one.

'But, my lord,' said another, 'some have yet to board their carriages.'

'Send out the ones that are ready to go,' Hector said. 'And tell everyone else to hurry up or they will be left behind.'

Orders were issued, and the palace gates opened. Several carriages began to move towards the entrance, among them the one containing Frida and Alfie, while men-at-arms marched alongside. As soon as the first carriages were underway, Hector hurried back to the emptying palace. He glanced along the hallway, but there was no sign of Amery or Kilbride.

A soldier ran down a set of stairs and almost collided with the duke.

'Watch where you're going,' Hector snapped.

'Sorry, my lord,' said the soldier. 'Your quarters are empty – has Princess Kilbride already been taken to the carriages?'

'What are you talking about? The princess should be in my rooms.'

'But she isn't, sir. There's no one there.'

Hector rushed up the stairs, and strode to his quarters. The front door was lying open, and several soldiers were clustered around the entrance.

'Where is Kilbride?' Hector said.

The soldiers turned.

'She has gone, my lord,' said one. 'Amery, too. They were both inside, and Amery was asking her some questions, and...'

'How could she have gone?' said Hector. 'Weren't there guards watching her at all times?'

The soldiers averted their eyes.

'Well?' said Hector. 'I gave orders that soldiers must be in the room whenever Amery was inside.'

'Amery told us to leave, my lord,' said one.

Hector felt his stomach churn. He pushed past the soldiers and entered his main living room. The seat where Kilbride had been tied was still in position, and a few cut pieces of cord and rope were lying on the rug next to it. He ran to the open window, and glanced down. To the right of a thorn bush, the imprint of someone landing on the ground was clearly visible.

'Search the gardens!' Hector cried.

'I have already sent men to begin the search, my lord,' said a soldier.

Hector turned, his fury building. 'How could you let this happen?'

'Sir, Amery told us that the marriage certificate would be invalid if he wasn't allowed to speak to Princess Kilbride in private.'

'And you believed him?'

A voice cried out from the gardens, and Hector returned to the window. A few soldiers were standing next to a beech tree, and Hector watched as a dead man-at-arms was dragged out of the undergrowth and set down next to the gravel path. Hector reeled backwards, then he stared at the soldiers in the living room. A desire to kill them all swept over his mind, then he calmed himself.

What were his priorities?

Retrieving Kilbride was at the top of the list, but he also had to ensure that the rest of the convoy got underway. Where would Kilbride have gone? If he had been in her place, he would have looked for allies.

Walter.

Hector raced out of the room and ran downstairs. He hurried towards the main entrance of the palace, and emerged into the forecourt as the first rays of the sun appeared on the horizon behind him. Around half of the carriages and wagons had already departed, and the rest were manoeuvring into position to leave through the open gates. Beyond the gates, a crowd of civilians were gathering, and they were watching the carriages roll down the street towards the north.

'Cowards!' shouted someone in the crowd.

A few civilians noticed Hector standing by the palace entrance, and the jeers intensified.

'Shame on you!' cried an old woman. 'The duke is running away, while his brother fights for Torrent!'

Hector turned to an officer from the ducal militia. 'Gather sixty men-at-arms.'

'Should we break up the crowd, sir?' said the officer.

'No. I am taking the men-at-arms to the Kendril Wall. Ensure that every carriage leaves on time, then lock up the palace and seal the gates.'

'Yes, sir.'

The officer ran down the stairs, and began to summon soldiers from the men-at-arms in the courtyard. Hector walked back into the palace, and went to the guard post by the main doors, where his armour was kept. A sergeant who was there helped him don his steel breastplate, and a sword was strapped to his belt.

'My brother is not the only defender of Torrent,' Hector said, as a helmet was placed into his hands.

'Yes, sir,' said the sergeant, keeping his gaze lowered.

'I had to put the safety of our new king first,' Hector went on. 'That is why I wasn't at the Kendril Wall last night.'

'Of course, sir.'

Hector strode from the room, and left the palace. The sixty men-at-arms he had requested were waiting for him in the courtyard, as more carriages passed through the gates. The crowd of civilians had grown, and many were hurling abuse at the ducal soldiers flanking the convoy.

Hector joined the sixty men-at-arms.

'Good morning,' he said to them over the sound of the jeering crowd. 'In a few moments, we shall be departing for the Kendril Wall.'

Several soldiers looked almost relieved by his words.

'When we get there,' Hector went on, 'our primary objective is to find and secure Princess Kilbride. Her Highness has foolishly placed herself in danger, and we shall be ensuring that she joins the convoy travelling to Castle Ridden.'

'Shall we not be staying to assist the defence of the Kendril Gap, my lord?' said a junior officer.

'No, we shall not. What many of you don't realise is that this was all arranged beforehand by me and my brother. He was to hold the Gap long enough for the evacuation of the Royal Court to take place. The King's Champion is simply following my orders.'

Few of the men-at-arms seemed convinced.

Hector gestured to his left. 'We shall leave by the side gates, to avoid the crowds. Lieutenant, order the departure.'

The junior officer saluted, then he led the sixty men-at-arms across the courtyard. Hector fell in with them, and walked by the officer's right. They passed through a small gate in the perimeter wall, and entered a quiet street.

They made good time to the main square of Torrent, where more civilians had gathered. Fletchers, carpenters and blacksmiths had set up makeshift working areas out in the open, and lines of injured militia soldiers were being cared for under a large awning. Buckets of arrows and crossbow bolts were being distributed to a group of young men and women, who rushed off with them in the direction of the Kendril Gap. Dozens of civilians turned and stared as Hector's sixty men-at-arms crossed the square.

'Better late than never, Duke!' someone shouted.

'Hector needs his beauty sleep!' cried another, to the sound of laughter.

Hector's cheeks flushed, but he controlled his fury. The laughter died away as the sound of more boots echoed off the cobbles. Civilians began to move away from one of the other roads leading to the square, as several hundred Westlanders appeared. Hector halted his men-at-arms, and they waited for the Westlanders to enter the square.

Their leader hailed Hector. 'Are you going to the Wall, Duke?'

'We are, Gorgan,' said Hector.

'Stefan will already be there,' the Westlander chief said. 'He went ahead with six hundred men during the night. This lot behind me are the last of the reinforcements he ordered me to bring out of Twinbrook – another three hundred, all told.'

'Stefan has six hundred Westlanders at the Wall?'

Gorgan nodded. 'That's right, Duke. Let's hope he's saved a few imperial soldiers for us, eh?'

'I have not heard any news about Stefan's forces,' said Hector. 'All I keep hearing about is my idiot brother. Does Stefan have Princess Abigone and Princess Hygilt with him?'

Gorgan frowned. 'That would be a no, Duke. The two princesses evaded Stefan's forces in the north.'

'Then does Dravid still have them?'

'They escaped from Dravid, too. We suspect they had help. They were last seen riding south in the presence of a man.'

'Did you see this man?'

'I didn't accompany Stefan north,' said the chief. 'I stayed in Twinbrook, so I can only tell you what Stefan told me. He arrived back yesterday, collected whatever men were ready to leave, and hurried onward towards the Wall. I've spent the night gathering up every last Westlander from the beer halls and brothels.' He laughed. 'Half of them are still drunk. They were celebrating the three full moons.'

Hector eyed the ranks of Westlanders. They looked more like an armed mob than an army, and a few were unsteady on their feet.

'Will you march with us to the Wall, Gorgan?'

The chief gestured towards the south. 'Lead on, Duke.'

The men-at-arms got underway again. They left the town square by the southern road, the Westlanders following. They marched for fifteen minutes, and the streets grew busier as they approached the Kendril Gap. Civilians were pushing carts south, laden with food and barrels of water, while others were carrying buckets of arrows and bolts.

Hector reached the enormous forecourt and gazed at the ruins of the Kendril Wall. The rubble of the gatehouse rose up in the centre of the Gap, creating two large breaches through the pass. In front of the ruined Wall, a long barricade put together from fragments of rock spread out in a semi-circle, and over a thousand militia were standing guard behind it, their eyes on the two breaches. Piles of loaded crossbows sat next to huge baskets of bolts and arrows, while hundreds of other soldiers were resting or eating behind the front line. A few glanced over in Hector's direction, and the duke watched as the men whispered among themselves.

Gorgan appeared by Hector's shoulder, and pointed to the left. Under the shadows of the cliff face, Stefan was sitting on the ground, his head in his hands. Around him stood around twenty other Westlanders, while others were lying on the cobbles, wounded.

'Where are the rest of Stefan's men, I wonder?' said Gorgan.

'Let's find out,' said Hector.

He led the way to the left of the militia soldiers, following the curve of the defensive line towards Stefan and the cliffs. Someone tapped Stefan on the shoulder, and the chief glanced up. He got to his feet, and waited for Hector to approach. The three hundred Westlanders brought by Gorgan filed into the forecourt, following their chief over to where Stefan stood.

'Greetings, Duke of Torrent,' said Hector.

Stefan said nothing.

'I have brought the last of the reinforcements, Chief,' said Gorgan. 'Some of them are a little worse for wear, but they're eager to get stuck into the imperial army. Where do you want them? And, uh, where are the others?'

'My men have joined Prince Logar's eternal feast,' said Stefan.

Gorgan's features paled. 'All of them?'

'All except those you see before you. Walter betrayed us. He sent us out to be annihilated by the imperial cannon. Five hundred and fifty of our kinsmen met their ends in the ravine, and not one of the town's soldiers came to our aid. They left our wounded out in the mud to die.'

A wave of outrage passed through the three hundred Westlanders crowding the eastern part of the courtyard.

'Where is my brother?' said Hector.

Stefan raised a hand and pointed towards the centre of the militia's barricade. 'Walter is preparing to send Princess Hygilt south, to join her grandfather.'

'Has he agreed another truce, or has peace been declared?'

'Neither. He intends to give her away for nothing. Where were you last night, Duke? Why did you leave Walter in charge?'

'I had no idea that you had returned,' said Hector. 'How did Walter come to be in possession of the imperial princess?'

'He has Abigone, too; that bastard has the bride you promised me.'

Hector turned and gazed over at the thick lines of militia soldiers protecting the barricade.

'What are you going to do, Duke?' said Stefan. 'Who runs Upper Down – you, or your brother?'

'Move the reinforcements,' Hector said. 'Place the three hundred Westlanders in a semi-circle just behind the militia.'

'Are we going to attack our allies?'

'Only if Walter refuses to see sense. Do it.'

Stefan nodded to Gorgan, and the other chief began issuing orders to the three hundred Westlanders. They began to retrace their steps, and the militia turned to watch as the Westlanders formed a thin cordon between them and the edge of the town. Hector led his sixty men-at-arms through a small gap in the barricade and out into the centre of the courtyard. He saw Walter and a group of Mountain Rangers standing next to the two princesses, and strode forwards, Stefan and his men from the ducal palace flanking him.

Silence fell over the forecourt as Hector walked towards Walter.

'What are you doing, brother?' Hector called out.

'I am defending this town,' said Walter. 'What the fuck are you doing?'

'I am here to stop you making a dreadful mistake. I hear that you are planning to send Princess Hygilt into the arms of our enemy.'

Walter eyed the young princess for a moment, then he nodded. 'That's right. It is time to let her go. Her presence here was the reason Valentino brought the imperial army to our doors. If we send her back, then the prince might be willing to negotiate.'

Hector laughed. 'You naïve fool. All you are doing is proving how little you understand about how the world works. If you hand Hygilt over for nothing, then Prince Valentino will merely smile, before resuming his assault upon us. You may have done a... decent job of defending the Gap, but I think I shall be giving the orders from now on, little brother.'

'I do not take commands from you,' said Walter.

'You dog!' Stefan cried. 'You allowed my men to be slaughtered by cannon! If you weren't a coward, you would face me here – man to man, without the protection of your soldiers.'

Walter shook his head. 'It wasn't I who ordered your men to charge down the slope, Stefan. And how is your friend Dravid doing? Have you told the Duke of Ridden that you have been working with him? Have you told him that you met Dravid north of here, to discuss how to divide the spoils of war? Abigone and Hygilt are safe, no thanks to you.'

'He is lying,' Stefan spat. 'Every word that comes from his mouth is poison.'

Hector gazed at the faces of the militia in front of him. Many were staring at him in a way that he had never experienced before – with contempt. Among the Rangers, their glances were closer to outright hostility, and even Abigone was looking at him with a mixture of fear and disgust. For a moment, with a long arc of accusing glances cast in his direction, Hector felt as though he were on trial.

'We all know what you did, Duke Hector,' Hygilt said. 'Thanks to a young woman called Ireni, everyone knows.'

Hector narrowed his eyes. 'Ireni? What lies have Ireni and Walter been spreading? I know the truth, though my heart aches with the knowledge.' He raised a finger and pointed at Walter. 'My brother killed Alfgang the Pius! It was Walter! He conspired with Chief Dravid to slay our noble and compassionate king! How else could he have escaped the slaughter with his life? Arrest him, men of Upper Down – arrest this traitor.'

The stony silence resumed as soon as Hector had stopped speaking, and he took a step back. How could this have happened? Overnight, he had lost the love and adoration of the common folk of Torrent. His anger started to build, along with a tide of frustration. Those ungrateful wretches. How many had enjoyed the gold he had lavished on them, and the favours he had bestowed?

'Have you forgotten how to tell the truth, brother?' said Walter. 'Perhaps you never knew how.'

'Hold your tongue, king-killer,' Hector cried.

'Are you still saying that?' said Walter. 'I agreed with every one of Pius's policies – why would I kill him? He wanted the Westlanders out of Upper Down – so do I. He wanted to open the Kendril Gap to merchants again – so do I. He wanted to release Princess Hygilt – what the fuck do you think I've been trying to do? The only problem I had with Alfgang the Pius was that he used to nag me to stop drinking.' He lowered his gaze. 'He was a good man. We did not always see eye to eye, but he would have made a fine king. If you hadn't killed him, Hector, Upper Down would be at peace.'

'Just say the word, Duke,' whispered Stefan, 'and my men will have this forecourt cleared in a few minutes.'

'Wait for my signal,' Hector said. He glanced at his men-at-arms. 'Soldiers of Ridden, as your lord and duke, I command you to arrest Lord Walter, for the crime of assassinating King Alfgang the Fifth.'

'Form up, men,' cried the lieutenant. 'Wedge formation; shields to the front.'

The men-at-arms began to move into position, and a spear-head of shields formed to the right of where Hector was standing. At the same time, dozens of Rangers readied their longbows from behind the barricades.

'Do not do this, brother,' said Walter. 'Do not add to your crimes by killing your own folk. The imperial army are resting, but if we do not return Princess Hygilt to them, they will renew their assaults upon us.'

'The fault lies with you alone,' said Hector. 'Give yourself up, Walter. This is your last chance.'

Walter gazed back at him. He looked exhausted, and he had blood smeared down the front of his Rangers surcoat. For the briefest of moments, hope flared within Hector, then Walter slowly shook his head.

'Do your worst, Duke of Ridden,' Walter called out. 'I am not afraid.'

'As you will it, brother,' said Hector.

He nodded to the lieutenant, and the sixty men-at-arms charged the centre of the barricades. Arrows flew out from the bows of the Rangers, striking shields and armour. Three men-at-arms went down, then the militia loosed their crossbows, and more began to fall before the men-at-arms were halfway to Walter. Hector gestured to Stefan, and one of his comrades raised a horn to his lips, and its harsh note sounded over the forecourt. At once, the long, thin line of Westlanders charged into the rear of the men guarding the barricade, and the forecourt descended into mayhem. Armed only with crossbows, and attacked from behind, the lines of Wall and Town Militia broke within seconds, many leaping over the barricades before the war axes and long swords of the Westlanders could cleave them in two. An arrow whistled past Hector's face, and he ran. More militia crossed the barricades, and several sprinted in Hector's direction, their crossbows raised. An arrow nicked the back of Hector's left knee, and he tripped and fell, sprawling over the blood-slicked cobbles. Eight militia reached him, and aimed down at his chest.

'You are under arrest, sir,' one cried. 'Stay where you are.'

Hector lifted his hand.

'Take the water from these men, and in its place put fire.'

The eight men burst into flames, but no screams came from their lips as they fell to the ground. Hector got to his feet, as blood trickled down his left leg. The militia soldiers in the forecourt stared at him in terror, and began to back away.

'I am a Master!' Hector cried. 'Surrender or die.'

The militia in front of him threw down their crossbows and raised their hands in the air. Over to the left, the Rangers were battling the ducal men-at-arms by the centre of the barricade, unaware of what had taken place. Hector selected a Ranger at random.

'Take the iron from that man, and in its place put gold.'

The Ranger dropped his bow and fell to the cobbles, his scream cut short as he writhed in agony. The other Rangers glanced over, and Hector raised his hand again.

'Lay down your weapons, or I will fill this courtyard with the slain.'

Walter shoved his way forward, his hands in the air. 'Do as he says. My brother is a Master.'

'No,' cried Abigone. 'Do not surrender, Walter; Hector will kill us all.'

'He could kill everyone standing here in an instant,' Walter said.

'You are quite right, brother,' said Hector, as the violence ceased. Hundreds of militia were throwing down their weapons, and the Rangers started to do the same. The Westlanders took up their positions on the barricade, and the ducal men-at-arms dragged Walter, Abigone and Hygilt to where Hector was standing.

'I have won, brother,' said Hector, as Walter was pushed to his knees. 'Duke Stefan, you may take your betrothed back into your custody.'

A Westlander grabbed Abigone by the arm, and pulled her towards Stefan, then a small furry animal leapt from her shoulder. Its claws slashed across the Westlander's face, sending a spray of blood through the air.

'What was that?' cried another Westlander. 'Does anyone see the little bastard?'

The Westlanders looked around, but the animal had vanished from sight.

'It has gone,' said Hector. 'If it returns, kill it.'

'I hate you!' cried Abigone, as two Westlanders gripped her arms. 'For my brother, for Stefan, for everything!'

Hector smiled. 'You look quite fierce when you are angry, Your Highness. Let's bring your marriage forward a little. Duke Stefan, you and the princess will be wed by the end of the day.' He turned to Hygilt, who was standing next to Walter with a defiant look on her face. 'And what shall we do with you, little princess?'

'I can think of a few suggestions,' said Hygilt. 'Would you like to hear them?'

Hector laughed. 'While others scream and panic, how is it that a fourteen-year-old girl has managed to keep her composure?' He snapped his fingers. 'I have the perfect idea. We shall use you to deter any further attacks from your grandfather's army.' He turned to Stefan. 'Have your men lead Princess Hygilt to the highest part of the ruins of the Kendril Wall; up on the rubble of the gatehouse, and then secure her there. Make sure she is facing the ravine, and tie her so that she cannot escape. Let us see if the imperial army is willing to attack if their precious princess is in the way.'

'That is a stupid idea,' said Hygilt, as three Westlanders approached her. 'The imperial army will never see me from that distance.'

The three men reached her, and Hygilt was dragged off towards the huge heap of rubble where the gatehouse had stood.

'Have the militia and Rangers been disarmed?' Hector said.

'They have, my lord,' said the lieutenant from the men-at-arms. 'What shall we do with the prisoners?'

'Move them to the town square, and ensure they are guarded.'

The junior officer frowned. 'By whom, sir?'

'By the soldiers we brought from the ducal militia.'

'But, sir, a dozen were killed or injured when we tried to arrest Lord Walter; we will be out-numbered twenty-to-one.'

'Yes, but you are armed, while they are not. If any show signs of resistance, kill them.'

The junior officer saluted. 'Yes, sir.'

Hector watched as the fifty men-at-arms began to escort the two thousand men of the militias away from the forecourt, then he turned to Stefan.

'Duke of Torrent,' he said, 'I am placing you in charge of the defences.'

Stefan inclined his head, but remained silent.

Hector gazed down at Walter. 'That leaves only you, brother.'

Walter said nothing.

'I would ask if you had any last words,' Hector went on, 'but I know that I would be met with a string of profanities. I hope defeat tastes bitter, Walter; you should have remained drunk in your little apartment.'

'Shame on you!' cried Abigone. 'Walter has done more for us in ten days than you have in your entire life.'

'Duke Stefan,' said Hector, 'please control your betrothed, or I shall.'

'You will not touch her, Duke,' said Stefan. 'She is mine now.'

Hector smiled to conceal his anger. 'Fetch a few carpenters from among the civilians, and find some rope. It is time to hang my brother.'

CHAPTER 32
SISTERS

Torrent, Upper Down – 18th Day of Lamenta 107

Abigone sat on the cobbles with her back resting against the cliff face. A row of badly-injured Westlanders was lying on the cobbles to her left, while six others were standing close by, forming an arc of steel around the princess. Ahead, in the centre of the forecourt, a primitive gallows was being constructed, while up on the heap of rubble, Abigone could just make out where Hygilt had been tied to a stone post that jutted upwards from the ruins. On her right, the three hundred Westlanders who had arrived with Hector had taken up position by the long barricade. Most were sitting or talking, and only a few were paying any attention to the huge breaches in the Kendril Wall. Westlanders found the use of bows to be cowardly, and they had discarded the tactics that had seen Walter's defenders fend off countless attacks during the night. The crossbows and longbows that had been taken from the militia and the Rangers were lying in discarded piles, scattered over the road behind the barricade. Part of Abigone longed for the imperial army to resume its assault, if only to show the Westlanders their mistake.

She caught sight of Stefan talking to Hector by the base of the gallows, but there was no sign of Walter. Or Tulip, for that matter. The moment his claws had slashed the face of the Westlander, the animal had disappeared. Perhaps he had remained close by, and was watching Abigone. He couldn't have abandoned her, she told herself.

Abigone shifted on the cold cobbles, her discomfort matched only by the tiredness she felt coming from every part of her body. The previous few days had been a whirlwind, and somehow she had ended up back with Stefan. The chief had smiled when Hector had told him that they would be wed by the end of the day, and Abigone dreaded the coming night. That was another reason she wanted the imperial army to attack.

The Westlanders cheered as Walter was led out from a house on the street facing the forecourt. His hands had been bound, and four Westlanders hauled him through a gap in the barricades, and towards the gallows. Despair clouded Abigone's mind, and she saw a few of her Westlander guards smirk down at her.

'Two coins says the King's Champion pisses himself,' one of them said.

Walter was led to the base of the gallows, and Hector raised a hand.

'I charge you, Walter of Ridden, with the murder of King Alfgang the Fifth, known as Pius,' Hector said, his clear voice carrying over the forecourt. 'You have been found guilty, and I sentence you to death.'

Abigone glanced down the road in the direction of the town square, but no one was coming to help. Then it occurred to her – if no one was coming, it was up to her. Only she could make a difference; the days of depending upon others to ride to her rescue were over. She took a breath, and steeled her heart.

'Does the condemned have anything to say?' said Hector.

Walter ignored him.

'Very well,' said Hector. 'This act gives me no pleasure, but justice must be done.'

The four Westlanders pulled Walter up onto the low wooden platform. A noose was dangling from a tall wooden beam, and Walter was pushed next to it.

Abigone closed her eyes, and pictured an enormous dragon.

'Blessed spirits,' she whispered, 'with your permission, summon for me a stone dragon.'

The cliffs behind and above her creaked and groaned as huge chunks of rock began to fall, then cobbles were ripped up from the forecourt. An enormous, misshapen lump of rock appeared in the air above the centre of the forecourt, and the Westlanders cried out in terror. The summoned object fell a few feet, and smashed onto the forecourt, rolling and cracking. A huge chunk obliterated the side of the gallows platform, and the tall beam snapped and fell. By the cliff, rocks rained down from the disturbed cliff, showering the wounded Westlanders in rubble. A large piece struck one of Abigone's guards, crushing his skull. Some Westlanders fell to their knees, and began to invoke their gods. The main fragment of the summoned dragon rolled towards the barricade, then it slowly ground to a halt.

Hector was the first to react. He gazed at the destruction of the gallows, where Walter was lying amid the debris, his hands still bound behind his back, then he took a few paces towards the stone dragon. He stared at it, then he turned towards Abigone.

'Bind her hands!' he cried. 'Bind the hands of the princess!'

Stefan shoved Hector to the side. 'What did I tell you, Duke? Abigone is mine.'

'She is a Maker!' Hector shouted. 'Do you understand what that means? She did this – she summoned this... thing.'

'She did the same up north,' shouted another Westlander. 'She created something from wood; that's how she escaped.'

Hector raced over to where Abigone was sitting.

'Blessed spirits,' she began, then Hector punched her in the face.

Abigone slammed back against the cliff, as Westlanders wrestled Hector to the cobbles.

'You dare strike my bride, Duke?' said Stefan.

'She will kill us all, you fool,' said Hector, as three men pinned him to the ground. 'She has to die.'

Abigone put a hand to her lips, and her fingers came away with blood on them. Stefan stared at her.

'I will find you another bride,' Hector went on. 'Nolan! We can summon Nolan home, and you can have her.'

'Why not Kilbride?' said Stefan. 'If what you are saying about Abigone is true, then give me Kilbride.'

'Tell these men to get their fucking hands off me,' cried Hector.

Stefan nodded. 'Release him.'

Hector pulled himself back to his feet as the three Westlanders stepped back a pace.

'If we kill her,' Stefan went on, 'I want Kilbride as compensation.'

'Out of the question,' said Hector.

'Why?'

Hector wiped the dirt from his breastplate. 'Because Kilbride is mine.'

Stefan narrowed his eyes. 'What is this? You and Kilbride? I thought you had a wife, Duke.'

'I did. Perpetua is dead. Tragic. I have chosen Kilbride as her replacement.'

'You devious bastard,' said Stefan. 'I know what you're up to. Is the boy king still alive?'

'Of course he is.'

'But not for long, eh? Will you end his life as soon as you are wed to Kilbride?'

'Oh, I might wait a few days. Perhaps once we have settled into Castle Ridden.'

'And then you shall be king?'

'And then I shall be king.'

Abigone stared at the two men, then her lips began to move.

'Blessed spirits, with your permission...'

A hand went over her mouth, and her arms were pulled behind her back. She was rolled onto her front, and a Westlander placed his knee on her back.

'Did you hear that?' said Hector. 'What more proof do you need, Stefan? Abigone is indeed a Maker. If we allow her to live, she could kill us at any time of her choosing. I am sorry, my friend, but we have no choice. You can be the one to do it.'

Stefan edged closer to Abigone. 'How does it work? Can she summon rock and wood with a hand over her mouth?'

'Perhaps if she was experienced enough,' said Hector, 'but she is clearly a beginner. We are lucky; we have exposed her secret in time. One thrust of a knife, and she will no longer be a threat.'

'What if we cut her tongue out?' said Stefan.

'It wouldn't be enough,' said Hector. 'She could learn how to control her powers silently. You would need to remove her hands and her eyes to be sure. Is that what you want?'

Stefan shook his head. 'No.' He lowered his gaze, then drew a knife from his belt. 'What a waste,' he said.

'Indeed,' said Hector. 'A terrible waste. We shall tell the Royal Family that she was killed by the imperial army.'

'Tell them what you like,' said Stefan. 'Abigone, this pains me. I had dreamt of the strong children you were going to give me, but Hector is right. If you had but waited until tonight to reveal your wicked powers, you could have killed me as I slept. I shall make it quick.'

He leaned forward with the knife.

Hector smiled, then an arrow pierced the left side of his face, driving through his jaws until the steel tip burst through his right cheek. Stefan and the Westlanders jumped up, their eyes searching for the source of the arrow as Hector sank to his knees. The duke was trying to scream, but the arrow was keeping his mouth closed, as blood fell to the cobbles.

Another arrow shot past, striking a Westlander in the stomach, just under his steel breastplate.

'They're coming from one of the houses on the street!' Chief Gorgan shouted. 'Find whoever is loosing arrows at us, and kill them!'

The hand came free from Abigone's mouth as the Westlanders tried to shield Stefan from the arrows. She curled up into a ball by the base of the cliffs.

'Blessed spirits,' she said, mouthing the words silently, 'with your permission, summon for me a stone dragon.'

The cliffside cracked again, and another enormous formation of rock appeared in the air above the forecourt. Cobbles were ripped out, acting like missiles as they flew through the crowd of Westlanders surrounding Abigone. Rubble fell, as the weakened cliff groaned and fractured. A slab of rock crushed three Westlanders just a few feet from where Abigone was lying, and she huddled against the cliff. She opened her eyes, and saw the devastation she had caused. A second monstrous stone object was in the middle of the forecourt. Part of it had shattered upon impact with the cobbles, and bodies were lying scattered around it. The air stilled, and the panicked voices of the Westlanders quietened again.

'Abigone is a witch,' someone muttered.

'Kill her, Stefan,' said Gorgan, 'before she summons another stone creature.'

Another noise arose over the forecourt – the sound of voices.

'The militia!' someone cried. 'The militia are coming.'

Abigone looked up, and saw hundreds of soldiers running down the street towards the barricade. Most were unarmed, and they made for the piles of longbows and crossbows by the edge of the road. They reached them moments before the Westlanders charged into their ranks, and loosed. Within moments, the forecourt was a battlefield. Rangers picked up their discarded longbows and rained arrows down onto the Westlanders; and civilians in their hundreds joined the fight, picking up any weapon they could find. One on one, the Westlanders were stronger and better armed, but the masses of militia and civilians entered the forecourt like a river in spate.

'Hold your lines!' Stefan cried, then he turned back to Abigone. 'You little bitch; you can forget about a quick end; this is going to be painful.'

He stepped towards her, then Abigone heard a noise coming from the breach in the Wall twenty yards to her left. A man in a full coat of burnished steel armour was scrambling over the rubble, a dozen knights by his side.

The man raised a pike in his right hand. 'Charge!'

The six Westlanders around Stefan turned to gaze at the new threat, and then the imperial knights were upon them, their long swords and pikes striking them down. Stefan stood over Abigone, and drew his sword. He fended off a blow from a knight's blade, then the tip of a pike was thrust through his throat. Stefan staggered back, then he fell onto the princess. Hands rolled the dead chief onto the cobbles, and the man in armour opened his visor to gaze down at Abigone.

Abigone edged back, her eyes wide with fright.

The man glanced up at his knights. 'Remain on the offensive,' he said, 'but kill only Westlanders.'

The twelve knights saluted. They formed a line and charged into the Westlanders by the barricade. The man turned his gaze back to Abigone.

'Do you know where I might find Princess Kilbride or Lord Walter, young lady?'

'Who are you?' she said.

'My name is Count Sebastian,' he said. 'I was leading a scouting patrol prior to the launching of a fresh bombardment, and we saw the struggle in the forecourt. Perhaps we share a common enemy. Will you tell me your name?'

'It's Abigone. Princess Abigone. I'm Kilbride's sister.'

The man inclined his head. 'It is an honour to meet you, Your Highness. Have you seen your noble sister, or Lord Walter?'

Abigone pointed at the crushed gallows. 'Walter is over there, somewhere. They were going to hang him.'

'Who was going to hang him – the Westlanders?'

'Yes; them and Duke Hector.'

'Can you stand, Your Highness?'

Abigone nodded, then the count extended a hand and helped her to her feet.

'And where is Duke Hector?' he said.

Abigone glanced at the corpse-strewn ground. Hector was lying on the cobbles, a pool of blood under his head. 'He's there.'

Sebastian and Abigone walked over to the duke.

'He is still alive,' said the count.

Abigone knelt by Hector, and his eyes went to her. She glanced around, and picked up a knife from the cobbles. Hector's eyes widened, but his jaws were clamped together by the arrow. He began to lift his right hand from the ground, and Abigone brought a boot down, pinning it to the cobbles.

'This is for my brother,' she said, then she stabbed the duke in the eye. She pushed down on the hilt of the knife, and the blade sank deeper into Hector's skull. She stared at the motionless body, then got to her feet.

Sebastian eyed her. 'Your brother, you say?'

'My brother was King Alfgang the Pius. Hector murdered him.'

'I am sure you had your reasons, Your Highness.'

A mass of militia broke through to where Abigone was standing next to the count. Among them was a woman in black with a longbow over her shoulder. She ran to Abigone and threw her arms round her.

'Sister,' said Kilbride.

'I killed him, Killie,' said Abigone. 'I killed Hector.'

'I know. I saw.'

'Your Highness,' said Count Sebastian, bowing. 'It is a pleasure to see you once again.'

Kilbride smiled at him, then she released Abigone.

'I had hoped,' the count went on, 'that after our last meeting, we would have reached a peaceful resolution by now; one that would have avoided all this destruction.'

'That is still my hope,' said Kilbride. 'Hector, the fourth regent, took control of Upper Down, and resisted our attempts to negotiate.'

'Hector was allied to the Westlanders,' said Abigone.

Sebastian glanced at the body of the duke. 'I see.'

'It's not too late, is it?' said Abigone. 'Can we start another truce? With Hector dead, we can stop the fighting.'

Sebastian glanced over his shoulder. 'I fear it might be too late for that, Your Highness. If the imperial army saw my knights cross the rubble and enter the town, they will likely assume that I am dead. Where is Lord Walter?'

Abigone ran over to the gallows. The last of the Westlanders were starting to flee north, driven out of the forecourt by thousands of militia and armed civilians, and the barricades were being re-occupied by soldiers. Abigone reached the wreckage of the gallows. A Westlander was lying on his back, his head caved in by a fragment of the stone dragon, and she could see part of Walter's leg beneath him. Soldiers moved the body, and Walter was dragged free of the splintered wooden beams. The cords around his wrists were cut, and then Abigone, Kilbride and Sebastian knelt by him.

Kilbride took his hand. 'Can you hear me, Walter?'

Walter opened his eyes and gazed up at her.

'Are you all right?'

'I think so. I guess being hit by a giant rock is slightly better than being hanged.'

'Hector is dead,' she said.

Walter said nothing, his eyes never leaving Kilbride.

'I am glad that you are alive, Champion,' said Sebastian.

Walter frowned. 'Count Sebastian? What are you doing here? Is the war over? Who won?'

'Unfortunately,' said the count, 'the war goes on. My knights and I were observing what was happening up here, and we saw the soldiers of Upper Down fighting the Westlanders. I thought I would lend a hand. Now, I believe you know the whereabouts of Princess Hygilt.'

'Shit!' Abigone cried. She jumped to her feet, and gazed at the ruins of the gatehouse. 'She's up there! Hector tied her to the rubble.'

A low rumble echoed off the cliffside, followed by a loud crack. Huge chunks of masonry exploded, sending fragments all over the forecourt.

'Pull back!' Kilbride cried, as soldiers retreated from the forecourt.

'I will not be pulling back, Your Highness,' said Sebastian. 'My duty is to the granddaughter of Prince Valentino.'

'I will help you,' said Walter, as he got to his feet.

Kilbride turned to Abigone. 'You are coming with me, sister.'

'Wait,' said Walter. 'Should we raise a white flag?'

'Not yet,' said Kilbride. 'Wait for me to return with Abbie.'

'But Hygilt might get hit.'

'Then go up there and rescue her, Walter. Abbie and I won't be long. Trust me.'

She grabbed Abigone by the arm, and started to run. Abigone pulled her arm free as they crossed the line of the barricades, and kept pace with her sister. They took the road that led to the Royal Palace, but Kilbride veered down a tiny lane that branched off to the right.

'Where are we going?' said Abigone.

'You'll see,' said Kilbride. 'Keep up.'

Five minutes later, Abigone and Kilbride were ascending a steep flight of stairs cut into the side of the cliff face. The steps wound their way up above the rooftops of Torrent, then passed over a high ridge. They descended down a narrow track, and appeared on the edge of the cliffs overlooking the ravine. Abigone heard a mewing sound, and she turned to see Tulip trotting along the path after her.

'What are you doing here?' she cried, as she picked him up.

'He must have followed us up here,' said Kilbride. 'I found him hiding in a house across from the forecourt – the house from where I shot Hector.'

Abigone stared at her sister. 'That was you?'

'Yes. I was aiming for the bastard's eye. My second shot missed him altogether, and I had to run. I made it as far as the town square, where the militia soldiers were fighting Hector's men-at-arms.' Kilbride paused, her gaze never leaving Abigone's face. 'I saw what you did.'

'What?'

'I know what you are, Abbie – why didn't you tell me? All these years, and I had no idea. If you had told me, I could have helped you. You could have been a highly-trained Maker by now; you have wasted so many years.'

'Did you drag me all the way up here to give me a lecture?'

'No,' said Kilbride. She pointed down into the ravine. 'I brought you up here to destroy the cannon.'

Abigone walked to the edge of the cliff and peered down. The front of the imperial camp was visible, and she could see the lines of cannon firing at the remains of the Kendril Wall.

'Why are they still bombarding us?' she said. 'The Wall has fallen.'

'They must be trying to clear the rubble before they make another assault. With those cannon, Prince Valentino can force us to agree to any demand he makes. He could take our realm from us, and merge us into Greater Down. He could strip Upper Down bare. We would become his prisoners. We might even be taken all the way to the island of Sanctos, to be presented as captives to the emperor. But, Abbie, without those cannon? Without them, the cost of defeating us becomes that much greater. If we are to negotiate, then let us do so from a position of strength.'

'What about Hygilt? She's tied to a post in the middle of the rubble.'

'I know,' said Kilbride. 'We shall have to hope that Walter and Sebastian are successful. If Hygilt survives, we hand her over, just as we agreed. Quickly, Abbie; we don't have much time. Summon your stone spheres, and drop them onto the cannon.'

'They weren't spheres; they were dragons.'

'Whatever you say, sister.'

Abigone glanced at the creature in her arms. 'What do you think, Tulip?'

The animal licked her face.

Abigone took a breath, then she placed Tulip over her left shoulder. She reached out with her arms, then hesitated.

'You should know, Killie, there's a chance this entire part of the cliff will collapse. Maybe you should stand back a bit.'

'I'm going nowhere,' Kilbride said. She moved behind Abigone, and gripped the back of her belt. 'I will pull you back if the ground begins to move.'

Abigone nodded.

'Blessed spirits,' she said, 'first of all, sorry for forgetting to thank you for the last two times. I hope you can forgive me. With your permission, summon for me as many stone dragons as you will allow me to make.'

The ground roared as if the ravine was being struck by an earthquake, and thousands of tons of rock was dislodged from the side of the cliff. Half crashed down the slope, while the other half began to reassemble in the air above the ravine, until dozens of huge conglomerations of rock were hovering level with the top of the cliff. They began to fall, plummeting through the air. The soldiers down in the imperial camp gazed up. The crews working the cannon started to flee, abandoning their posts as the first rocks from the landslide battered their right flank, followed moments later by the stone dragons. Abigone's feet slipped as the ground under her bucked and rippled, and Kilbride pulled her back from the edge as it fell away. Abigone landed in a heap, then Kilbride dragged her clear, pulling her twenty yards across the grass, as Tulip clung on to her shoulder.

The noise from the ravine made it impossible to think, and Abigone raised her hands to her ears to blot it out, as Kilbride stood over her, her gaze fixed on the view of the destruction.

A last landslide slipped away down the slope, and its final rumble echoed off the sides of the cliff.

Kilbride crept forward, her feet moving gingerly over the loose rocks, then she gazed down.

'Did I do it?' said Abigone. 'Did I hit the cannon?'

'Come and see for yourself.'

Abigone got to her feet and edged forward. She glanced down into the ravine.

'I can't see any cannon,' she said.

'Exactly,' said Kilbride. 'You buried them under six feet of rubble.'

'I can still see the tents, though. I didn't hit them.'

Kilbride smiled. 'Our objective was the cannon, not the people. Well done, Abbie. With a few years of hard work, you might yet become a fine Maker.'

'What if I don't want to study?'

'You knew Hector was a Master, didn't you? I heard the soldiers in the town square say that he had revealed his powers to everyone.'

'Yes, I knew that.'

'Well, he's dead. Alfgang the Great and Alfgang the Pius are also dead. Upper Down's three Masters – all dead.'

'I presume you have a point?'

'You are now the defender of Upper Down, Abbie. You. What you did today will be talked about all over the Central Provinces, and beyond. Everyone will know that we have a Maker on our side. There's no escaping it. You have a long, hard road ahead of you. When this is over, I shall compile a list of books for you to read, and set up a study schedule. Two hours practice each day will suffice, at least to begin with. Come on; Walter will be waiting for us. It's time for the three regents of Upper Down to decide the realm's future.'

Abigone shook her head. 'And you wonder why I never told you I was a Maker?'

Kilbride smiled, then she strode towards the path. Abigone watched her for a moment, sighed, then followed her sister.

CHAPTER 33
THE SANCTIANS

Torrent, Upper Down – 18th Day of Lamenta 107

Walking into the middle of a Westlander camp in stolen armour was not, Walter decided, the most stupid thing he had ever done. Compared to climbing over the rubble of the Kendril Wall while it was being bombarded by sixty cannon, his earlier recklessness seemed trivial.

'What a day to be alive,' he said, as a cannon ball blasted into a section of fallen tower, spraying the forecourt with fragments of rock. 'While everyone else is running away from the cannon fire, we idiots are crawling towards it.'

'When I relate this story to my wife,' said Sebastian, as they sheltered behind the remains of a gatehouse wall, 'I will leave out the part about the cannon fire, since I don't particularly enjoy being slapped in the face.'

Walter crawled to the ragged edge of the wall, and glanced up. They had climbed more than half the height of the ruined gatehouse, and the remains of the first floor of the building stood above them. He couldn't see Hygilt from where he was lying, and he tried not to think about what might have happened to her. Sebastian joined him. Another cannon ball flew over their heads as they gazed upwards. It struck the cobbles behind them, gouging out a deep furrow along the forecourt.

'Shall we?' said Walter.

Sebastian nodded, then the two men launched themselves forward, scrambling over the debris and clambering up onto the next level of the ruins. Walter crawled forward, and his eyes widened at the sight from the top of the rubble. The cannon were arrayed in their usual rows in the ravine below them, their crews toiling as they maintained the bombardment. Smoke from the metal barrels was drifting upwards, obscuring the view of the rest of the imperial camp.

'I never thought I would ever be on this side of the cannon,' said Sebastian. 'Do you see Hygilt?'

Walter looked around. There was another wall blocking the view to their right, and they crawled towards it. Beyond was a tall chimney block, the only part of the old second floor still standing. Hygilt was sitting at the base of the chimney, her arms bound to metal bars that ran down the side of the old hearth. The girl looked calm, then Walter noticed that she was keeping her eyes closed.

Sebastian drew a knife, then he crawled forward. A cannon ball struck the wall above them, and fragments of stone rained down on the count's armour, denting the steel encasing his body. Walter hurried after him, and the two men ran the last few yards. Sebastian sliced through the ropes securing Hygilt to the chimney, and the girl opened her eyes.

'Uncle?' she said. 'This is a surprise.'

Sebastian smiled. 'You have certainly grown since I last saw you, Hygilt.'

'Can we save the small talk for later?' said Walter.

The lower floors of the gatehouse shook as more rubble was blasted away. Sebastian took Hygilt's hand, and Walter followed them as they climbed and jumped back down to the remains of the wall on the first floor. They sheltered behind it as the cannon fire intensified.

'Why are you here, Uncle?' said Hygilt. 'Shouldn't you be down in the ravine? Was Hector right? Could you see me from all the way down there?'

'No, we couldn't see you,' said Sebastian.

'Hector's dead,' said Walter.

'And we shall be sharing his fate if we linger here much longer,' said Sebastian. 'We will retrace our steps, I think, and...'

The count's voice cut off as a huge portion of the gatehouse collapsed with a thunderous roar. The floor next to the wall fell away, leaving a narrow strip of rock, upon which the three of them huddled.

Sebastian frowned. 'We may need a new plan.'

Walter peered over the edge, but the rising clouds of dust made it impossible to see what lay beneath them. He glanced to their right.

'We could work our way along that ledge,' he said, 'and climb down from there.'

'Lead on, Walter,' said Sebastian. 'We shall be right behind you.'

Walter crawled along the narrow strip of remaining floor, and he came back to a place from where he could see the ravine. A cannon ball struck the ledge in front of him, and it shattered. Walter put his hands over his head.

'What now?' said Hygilt.

'We shall have to find another way down,' said Sebastian.

'I'm terribly frightened, Uncle.'

'As am I, Hygilt,' said Sebastian.

Walter glanced at them both. Neither appeared to be remotely frightened, but maybe that was how the imperial family faced the world.

'Tell me the truth, Uncle,' said Hygilt. 'Why are you here?'

'Lord Walter sent four men to speak to Prince Valentino,' the count said. 'They informed us that you were in Walter's care, and that he was willing to hand you over. I volunteered to lead a small patrol, but when we got here, the folk of Upper Down were fighting the Westlanders. I decided to intervene.' He gave the girl a wry smile. 'I may have gone a little way beyond my original remit; I was only supposed to observe.'

'If this is the end, Uncle,' she said, 'then I am glad you are here with me.'

A roar of noise louder than the cannon erupted from the ravine, then the left-hand side of the cliff exploded. Rocks slid down the slopes, and Sebastian gasped as more rock began to form in the air high above the cannon. The huge formations of stone rained down into the ravine, and the cannon fell silent as they were buried under tons of rubble. The noise echoed against the cliffs, then an eerie quiet fell over the ravine, as a great cloud of dust thickened the air.

'What have we just witnessed?' whispered Sebastian.

'Abigone,' Hygilt whispered back. 'Abigone made stone dragons.'

'She is a Master?'

'No, Uncle; only men can be Masters. Abigone is a Maker.'

'I deem that Prince Valentino may be a little upset by what Princess Abigone has done this day,' said the count. 'Those cannon were his pride and joy; and the emperor will not be pleased to learn that he has lost them.'

'Valentino will be getting his granddaughter back instead,' said Walter.

'This was Princess Kilbride's plan, was it not? This is why she told us to wait for her return before sending up a white flag.'

Walter said nothing. His gaze went to the top of the cliffs, but he could see no signs of any movement. He turned his gaze back to the bottom of the ravine. The dust was starting to clear, but the cannon remained invisible, buried beneath a thick layer of rock. A few imperial soldiers and engineers were emerging from the untouched camp to the rear of the cannon, and were clambering over the wreckage.

'You appear to have us at a severe disadvantage, Walter,' said Sebastian. 'Does this alter matters? Do you now intend to keep both myself and Hygilt as hostages?'

Walter frowned. 'I guess that's a decision for the regency council. I have one vote among three – the others belong to Kilbride and Abigone. However, I will argue in favour of allowing you to go free. This crisis began because King Alfgang the Great refused to hand Hygilt over, and I don't want to make the same mistake.'

'In that case,' said Hygilt, 'we will be fine, Uncle. Abigone would never vote to make us hostages.'

'And Princess Kilbride?' said Sebastian. 'It strikes me that she might be the most ruthless of the three regents. Instead of asking for negotiations while the cannon were firing, she made sure of their destruction.'

Walter glanced over his shoulder. With the bombardment over, soldiers were entering the forecourt. A small group of imperial knights was among them, and they began to make their way towards the heap of rubble in the centre of the Kendril Gap.

Sebastian climbed down to meet them, and Hygilt and Walter followed, crawling over the ruins until they were back on the cobbles of the forecourt. The knights rushed forward, and took up positions around the count and the princess. Walter left them, and walked over the ruined forecourt. Half of the cobbles had been ripped up, and hundreds of fragments of rubble were strewn from one end of the forecourt to the other. Walter scanned the ground as he walked, passing numerous bodies. Westlanders lay in pools of their own blood, along with soldiers from the Town and Wall militias, men from the Mountain Rangers, and grey-uniformed soldiers from the imperial army. Scattered among them were the bodies of civilians – men and women who had joined the last, desperate fight against the Westlanders for possession of the Gap.

Walter found the body he had been looking for, and knelt. It was Hector, but his features were almost unrecognisable. An arrow was piercing both cheeks of his face, and a knife had been buried into his left eye as far as the hilt, while his features were coated in a thick layer of fine dust.

'No crown for you, Hector,' Walter whispered. 'I hated you, but now I see you, I pity you. Sleep with the spirits, and sleep well, my brother.'

He got back to his feet. A few yards away, Walter saw the body of Stefan lying on the cobbles with his throat ripped out. Next to him, a dead Westlander had a familiar sword strapped to his waist. Walter smiled, then he stooped down, and removed the blade that Count Sebastian had loaned him after his capture. He attached it to his belt.

'Walter!' cried a voice.

He glanced up, and saw Kilbride and Abigone hurrying through the ruined forecourt towards him.

'Did you find Hygilt?' said Abigone, as Tulip clung on to her left shoulder.

Walter gestured towards the tight knot of imperial knights surrounding Sebastian and the girl.

'Is she safe?'

'She's fine,' he said. 'Of the three of us up on the ruins of the gate-house, I think she might have been the least concerned. All the same, I doubt we would have made it back down if the cannon hadn't stopped.'

'Were you watching?' said Kilbride.

'We were. Sebastian is a little worried that we might decide to keep them as hostages.'

'It crossed my mind,' said Kilbride, 'but I think we should do what we promised to do. We should escort the imperial princess down to the camp, and see if Valentino wishes to talk to us. Are we agreed?'

'Do you think all three of us should go?' said Abigone. 'What if Prince Valentino arrests us, or executes us? Who would govern Upper Down?'

'That is a risk we need to take,' said Kilbride. 'We can leave the commanders of the militias in charge, in case the worst happens. We will also need to send a message to Frida and Alfie, to tell them what has occurred. They are probably on their way to Castle Ridden by now.'

'Don't tell Frida that I killed Hector,' said Abigone. 'She wouldn't understand.'

'We both killed him,' said Kilbride.

'The arrow injured him,' said Abigone, 'but he was alive until I drove a knife into his eye.'

Walter gazed at the two princesses. 'Does it matter? He's dead. We'll tell Frida and the boy-king that Hector fell in the battle; we don't need to give them any details.'

'If Valentino decides to negotiate,' said Kilbride, 'what is our position?'

'I say we give him everything he wants,' said Walter, 'as long as Upper Down remains a free kingdom. I won't compromise on that.'

'I agree,' said Kilbride. 'Abbie?'

'Yes. By the spirits, is this what power feels like?'

'You had better get used to it,' said Kilbride. 'Let us inform Princess Hygilt and Count Sebastian of our decision, and then we shall need to find a large bed sheet.'

'I have one prepared,' said Walter.

They walked over to where the knights were protecting the two members of the imperial family.

Sebastian inclined his head. 'Well played, Your Highnesses; we are at your mercy.'

Kilbride smiled. 'Are you ready to see your grandfather, Hygilt?'

The girl smiled. 'I am.'

An hour later, the small party climbed over the rubble of the eastern breach, and began to descend the slope towards the imperial camp. Walter had brought a few Rangers to escort the three regents, and Sebastian had his knights to escort Princess Hygilt. They passed a scene of carnage, the churned-up ground mingling with the blasted remains of hundreds of Westlanders and imperial soldiers.

Sebastian pointed towards the middle of the devastation. 'It was there, Lord Walter,' he said, 'where I lost the sword you lent me. It snapped at the hilt when I struck the steel armour of a Westlander. You have my apologies.'

'It wasn't a particularly good sword,' said Walter. 'The one you lent me was far better.' He unfastened it from his belt and offered it to the count.

Sebastian smiled. 'Keep it, Walter, until I find another to replace the one I broke.'

'Did six hundred Westlanders really charge at the cannon?' said Kilbride. 'Even with three full moons, I find it hard to believe.'

'They were unaware that we were re-positioning the cannon as they made their way down the ravine, Your Highness,' said Sebastian. 'We lured them into a trap from which there was no escape.'

'You should know,' said Abigone, 'that the Westlander you killed in the forecourt was their chief. You rammed a pike through his throat.'

'He was their chief?' said Sebastian.

'He was the most powerful Westlander chief in Upper Down,' Abigone went on. 'His name was Stefan. He was Hector's ally, and... and I was being forced to marry him. You saved me from that fate, and for that I thank you.'

Sebastian inclined his head. 'You are most welcome, Your Highness.'

'I will make sure grandfather knows about this,' said Hygilt.

'There is no need,' said Sebastian. 'I do not crave congratulations.'

Walter laughed. 'Are all members of the imperial family as modest?'

'No,' said Hygilt. 'Uncle Sebastian is an exception. He is the bravest knight in the entire empire.'

'Please, Hygilt,' said the count, 'do not embarrass me. I am nothing of the sort. I am unusually reckless and often lucky. That is not the same as courage.'

'You can have the best intentions,' said Abigone, 'but if you are unlucky, then it makes no difference. If you fight for what is right, then sometimes, if you are lucky, you will prevail.'

Walter and Kilbride trailed the others as they continued down the slope.

'What happened to the side of your face?' Walter said.

'Hector hit me,' said Kilbride. 'There's a lot you still don't know, Walter. Hector was planning to marry me, and then he was going to kill Alfie.'

'Was he so desperate to be king?'

'He was content enough when my father ruled.'

'That was because Hector agreed with everything Alfgang the Great did. He wasn't as impressed with Pius, or with the other regents.'

'You were right about Hector all along,' said Kilbride; 'although, perhaps for the wrong reasons. Have you forgiven Lothar?'

'Yes. Are you going to start paying him to keep me sober?'

Kilbride smiled. 'I might.'

They reached the area where the cannon lay buried under heaps of rubble. Several imperial engineers stopped what they were doing to glance up at the small party, then a squad of soldiers rushed forwards, and several fell to their knees before Sebastian and Hygilt.

'Will you take us to His Illustrious Highness Prince Valentino?' said Sebastian. 'His granddaughter is eager to see him.'

The soldiers escorted the party through the imperial camp, where neat rows of tents stretched down the valley as far as the eye could see. The largest tent was heavily guarded by knights in armour, but they moved aside for the count and Princess Hygilt, and the party began to enter. The knights raised their weapons as the Mountain Rangers approached.

'The soldiers must wait outside,' said a knight.

Walter nodded. 'Remain here,' he said to the Rangers.

The knight gestured towards him. 'This man must remove his sword before being allowed into the presence of the illustrious prince,' he said.

'That is my sword he carries,' said the count. 'Lord Walter is an honourable man, and he will not breach the hospitality of the illustrious prince. If he does, I shall be the first to strike him down.'

The knight bowed his head before Sebastian, and the party was led into the largest part of the tent. Warm rugs covered the canvas floor of the tent, and long couches sat around low tables. One couch had been raised onto a foot-high platform, and upon it an old man was sitting. He was tall and lean, and his dark eyes were flashing with anger and impatience.

'Grandfather!' Hygilt cried.

She ran towards him, and the old man's expression transformed as he saw her. He got to his feet, then crouched as Hygilt ran into his arms. A tear trickled down the old man's cheek.

'My Hygilt,' he whispered. 'My girl.'

Walter, Kilbride and Abigone stood in silence before Hygilt and Valentino, and the old man did not seem to notice their presence for a long time.

'Your Imperial Highness,' said Sebastian, 'the regents of Upper Down wish to begin negotiations.'

Valentino raised his gaze towards the count. 'You crossed the line of the Kendril Wall.'

'I did, Your Highness.'

'You told me you were going up the slope only to observe.'

'I did, Your Highness.'

'Why did you mislead me, nephew?'

'It was not intentional, Your Highness. I saw the citizens of Upper Down at war with the Westlanders, and I decided to intervene.'

'I am grateful that he acted as he did, Your Highness,' said Abigone. 'Count Sebastian saved me from a Westlander chief.'

Valentino got to his feet. 'You will speak when spoken to, girl, and not before.'

'You will not talk to my sister in that manner,' said Kilbride. 'We are here to negotiate, not to be insulted. We three are the sole regents of Upper Down, and we wish to bring this conflict to an end. If, however, we do not receive the respect to which we are entitled, we shall return to Torrent.'

Valentino's eyes glimmered with rage. 'You dare address me thus? Where is the respect that I am due?'

'I am more than willing to treat you with respect, Your Highness,' said Kilbride, 'if you afford us the same dignity.'

'Very well; here are my terms. You will surrender unconditionally. If you do so, I will order an end to the violence.'

'We reject those terms,' said Kilbride. 'We have conditions.'

'This audience is at an end,' said Valentino. 'You may return to

Torrent with your lives. Unlike Upper Down, the Sanctian Empire does not execute emissaries.'

'The old regime that ruled Upper Down has fallen,' said Kilbride, 'and we three have inherited all authority, in the name of King Alfgang the Sixth.'

'You set three conditions when you sent those emissaries to us,' said Walter. 'You wanted the Westlanders expelled from Upper Down; you wanted the Kendril Wall opened, and you wanted the safe return of Princess Hygilt. We have fulfilled those conditions. The last Westlanders are fleeing north, and your cannon have ensured that the Kendril Wall is no longer blocking the pass. What else do you want from us, Prince?'

'I want the complete dissolution of the realm of Upper Down,' said Valentino. 'Your kingdom has been a thorn in the flesh of the Central Provinces for decades, and it is time that came to an end. Upper Down shall be incorporated into Greater Down, just as it was in the days of the Elestian Empire.'

'Or what?' said Kilbride.

'If you refuse, then my army will break through the Kendril Gap and seize control of your realm.'

Kilbride smiled. 'May we please sit?'

'That would be the polite thing to do, Grandfather,' said Hygilt. 'We shouldn't argue while standing up. We are not savages.'

Valentino smiled at the girl, then his stern expression returned as he gestured to the couches.

'Be seated,' he said.

The three regents sat down on one couch, as Valentino resumed his place where he had been sitting before, with Hygilt by his side. Sebastian took a seat on a separate couch between the two groups.

'I would like to hear your conditions before I reject them,' said Valentino.

Kilbride leaned forward a little. 'The Mountain Rangers reported that you brought twenty thousand men with you. If this was a normal army, that might allow for around ten to twelve thousand combat soldiers among the cooks, carpenters and every other worker an army needs. However, this is far from a normal army. How many engineers and workers did the cannon require? How many blacksmiths and labourers were needed to keep sixty cannon operational? I would guess that you likely brought around eight thousand combat soldiers. Would that be an accurate estimate?'

Valentino said nothing.

'How many soldiers have you lost so far, Your Highness?' Kilbride went on. 'Half of that total? Do you intend to place swords into the hands of your engineers, and order them up the ravine? If you attack, Upper Down will defend itself. We regents are united in rejecting both the Westlanders and the Sanctians, and we shall fight to the end to preserve the freedom of our realm. Are you willing to return south, your soldiers dead, and your cannon lost, without any semblance of an agreement?'

Again, Valentino remained silent.

'Here is our condition,' Kilbride said. 'Upper Down shall remain an independent realm, free of any outside interference. We are willing to sign a peace treaty with the Sanctian Empire, and we will abide by the original conditions as Lord Walter has laid out for us; but we will not be subsumed into Greater Down, nor will we become a province of the Sanctian Empire.'

Hygilt glanced up at Valentino. 'What do you think, Grandfather?'

'I believe the three regents to be honourable people, Your Highness,' said Sebastian. 'We can trust them to keep their word.'

'Can we?' said Valentino. 'Tell me, regents – would any peace treaty include a defensive alliance between Upper Down and the Sanctian Empire?'

'That would depend upon its terms,' said Kilbride. 'We will not tolerate a garrison of imperial soldiers stationed on our territory.'

'And if your realm is invaded by Westlanders? The Sanctian Empire will never again allow Upper Down to be used as a refuge by raiders from the wild lands to the far north-west. We have promised the many kingdoms of the Central Provinces that we would protect them from any such threat. If you are invaded, we will send forces to... assist in your defence.'

'That is acceptable,' said Kilbride. 'We would be grateful for any such assistance.'

Valentino exhaled, then he put a hand to his forehead. 'You have placed me into an impossible position. I was ordered by the Most Exalted Emperor Antonio to seize control of Upper Down; were I to return south with anything less than that, I would likely incur His Majesty's wrath.'

'We are prepared to be your friends,' said Walter, 'but not your subjects.'

'And so the myriad crimes your realm committed should go unpunished?'

'Do you think we haven't suffered?' said Abigone. 'Your cannon and your soldiers have killed many of our people; and the Westlanders have brought nothing but misery to our citizens. We have been punished enough.'

'That is a matter of opinion,' said Valentino. 'There was one further task allotted to me by the Most Exalted Emperor Antonio. I was ordered to seek out and kill any Masters or Makers within the bounds of Upper Down. I am aware that the two deceased kings were both Masters, but today has shown that there must be others dwelling among you with these dark powers. Who else could have wreaked such devastation upon the cannon?'

'I am a Maker,' said Abigone, 'and I acted to protect the realm and the people who live there.'

Valentino's gaze turned cold. 'I see. Am I to assume that you could end my life with a few muttered curses?'

'They are prayers, not curses,' said Abigone. 'Would the spirits have given me such power if they did not grant their permission?'

'Blasphemers such as yourself abuse the gifts of the spirits,' said Valentino. 'The world would be a better place without Masters and Makers; that is a simple fact.'

'The world would also be a better place without cannon,' said Abigone, 'but that did not stop you bringing them to our front door.'

'You do not understand. I cannot return to the imperial court with the news that I have allowed a Maker to remain in a position of authority within Upper Down. I have no choice but to ask you all to leave. Return to Torrent. I shall grant you the grace of two hours before hostilities resume.'

'I sensed we were close to an agreement,' said Kilbride, 'but if that is your final word on the matter, we shall take our leave.'

'No,' said Hygilt. 'This is stupid. Sorry, Grandfather, but Kilbride was right – you don't have enough men to conquer Upper Down, not without the cannon. If you kill all their soldiers, and they kill yours, then who will stop the Westlanders from invading?'

'My dear Hygilt,' said Valentino, 'you know my brother's feeling regarding Masters and Makers.'

'The choice seems simple, Your Highness,' said Kilbride. 'Allow Abigone to remain in her position and accept the treaty we are offering you, or gift Upper Down to the Westlanders. Which would displease the emperor more?'

'I can guess the answer to that, Your Highness,' said Sebastian. 'If the Westlanders seize control of Upper Down, the Central Provinces will erupt in fury. We marched here to retrieve your noble granddaughter, but do we not have treaty obligations with those kingdoms? They are depending upon us to defend them from the threat the Westlanders pose.'

'Then you think I should choose the lesser of two evils, nephew?'

Sebastian turned to the regents. 'Could I make a suggestion? What if I were to volunteer to remain in Upper Down with a small number of my knights? As a guest, not as an occupying force. If you are willing to accept this, it could be presented to the imperial court as a victory.'

'Do you want me to lie to the emperor?' said Valentino.

'No, Your Highness; that was not my intention. The truth will suffice. If it is known that a count of the imperial household is resident within Upper Down, might not the Most Exalted Emperor Antonio perceive that as a success?'

'Perhaps, were I to elevate you to the status of imperial ambassador,' said Valentino. 'The Sanctian Empire would have an official diplomatic presence within Upper Down.'

The three Sanctians turned to gaze at the three regents.

'I can accept that,' said Walter.

'And I,' said Abigone.

Kilbride nodded. 'Very well. Do we have an agreement, Your Highness?'

Valentino's stern features softened slightly. 'In principle.'

Hygilt grinned. 'Praise the spirits. That was a good idea, Uncle; thank you.'

Sebastian smiled at his niece. 'It was my pleasure; though I am not altogether sure how my wife and children will take the news that I am to live in Upper Down.' He glanced at the regents. 'Might I invite them north to stay with me?'

'Your family is very welcome to stay in Upper Down,' said Abigone. 'We will find you a nice home in Torrent.'

'Let us not assume too much too soon,' said Valentino. 'We have a treaty to write before we abandon ourselves to giddy joy. And why is there a large brute of a cat sitting upon your shoulder? It is looking at me in a hostile manner.'

'His name is Tulip,' Abigone said, 'and he takes a while to get to know people.'

'Shall we reconvene this meeting tomorrow?' said Kilbride. 'We would like to extend an invitation to you, to join us in the Royal Palace of Torrent. I will have our lawyer begin the process of drafting a treaty.'

'And I shall instruct mine to do the same,' said Valentino.

They got to their feet.

'Shall we say midday?' said Kilbride. 'We shall await you by the Kendril Gap.'

'It would be my pleasure,' said Valentino.

'It may take several days to complete the details,' said Kilbride. 'If your army requires anything in the way of provisions during that time, we will be happy to assist.'

'Thank you. My quartermaster will no doubt be in touch. A prolonged negotiation would suit us well, as my army will need a few days to salvage what is left of the cannon from the rubble.' He shook his head at Abigone. 'A real Maker, in the flesh. I had half-expected you to have horns and a tail. Nephew, please escort the regents back to Torrent. You will need some time to settle into your new home.'

Sebastian bowed low, then the three regents inclined their heads. The count led them from the interior of the tent, and they met up with the Mountain Rangers who had been waiting outside. Among them, Walter saw the four men he had sent over the mountains pass the day before.

'How did it go, sir?' said the Rangers' officer.

Walter smiled at Kilbride and Abigone.

'We did it,' he said. 'The war is over.'

CHAPTER 34
THE REGENTS OF UPPER DOWN

Torrent, Upper Down – 24th Day of Lamenta 107

Kilbride gazed at her reflection in the full-length mirror. For the first time in over three years, she wasn't wearing black. She had taken it upon herself to declare her mourning period to be officially over, despite her father having insisted that it would last until the day she died. She looked different, it was undeniable. She had got so used to seeing herself in black, that she had forgotten what she looked like in other colours. She wondered what others would think, but then she realised that she didn't care. She was doing it for herself.

'Do you like it, Marie?'

The lady-in-waiting wiped a tear from her eye. 'Yes, my lady. You look like a different person. Regal, and beautiful. Is it just for today?'

'No. I don't want to ever wear black again.'

'Should I let Lord Walter in, my lady? He has been waiting outside in the corridor for several minutes.'

Kilbride nodded, then she walked away from the mirror so Walter wouldn't think she had been admiring her own reflection. She went to the centre of the room and faced the door of her quarters as Marie opened it. Walter walked in, wearing a smart dress uniform, with

Sebastian's bejewelled sword hanging from his belt. He looked up, and his eyes widened a little.

'Killie,' he said, 'you look like... how you used to, before... That colour suits you.'

'Thank you, Walter.'

'I was wondering if I might accompany you to the throne room.'

'I would like that,' she said. 'Are you ready to carry out your duty?'

'I think so. I have been practising with Lothar and a hat.'

'And did Lothar find this amusing?'

'He did the first twenty times.'

'I am glad you and he have remained friends.'

Walter shrugged. 'Who else have I got?'

'You have me, Walter. Am I not your friend?'

'You will always be more to me than just a friend, Killie. Does this change of clothing mean that you are now open to receiving offers of courtship?'

Kilbride smiled. 'Were those two statements in any way related?'

Walter's cheeks flushed. 'I was just imagining all the dukes and princes who will be knocking on the front door of the palace.'

'I will not be entertaining any suitors, not while I remain next in line to the throne of the realm.'

'Ah. Of course.'

'I would have to completely trust someone, before I allowed them to get that close to the crown, Walter.'

'I understand.'

Kilbride shook her head. Walter, despite his words, had clearly not understood.

She extended her left arm, and Walter linked his right with hers. They walked out from her quarters and into the corridor, which was flanked by dozens of courtiers and soldiers from the Royal Guard. A few of the Guardsmen eyed the King's Champion warily, but Kilbride knew that they hadn't been at the Kendril Wall when Walter had led the defence. Among the Wall and Town Militia, and among many of the inhabitants of Torrent, Walter was now beloved and admired, taking the place of his brother in their affections. Abigone had also undergone a radical change-of-mind about him. When once she had seen Walter as nothing but a useless drunk, she had begun to treat him as a slightly annoying older brother. The love she felt for him was genuine, but it wasn't the same kind of love that Kilbride felt.

They descended the stairs to the ground level, and made their way along the palace corridors to the grand throne room. They entered through a door in the rear of the hall, and stepped up onto the platform that bore the throne of Upper Down. Kilbride smiled at the crowds packing the hall. The front doors were wide open, and another crowd was standing outside, all trying to get a glimpse of what was about to occur.

Abigone put a gloved hand to her mouth and laughed when she saw Kilbride.

'I almost didn't recognise you,' she said. 'You remind me of the old days.'

'That's what Walter said.'

Count Sebastian was standing to Abigone's left. He bowed, and kissed Kilbride's hand.

'You look stunning, Your Highness,' he said.

'Thank you. I am so pleased that you and your illustrious uncle could be here today.'

'As am I. The prince should be arriving soon, with Lady Hygilt.' He glanced at Walter. 'I understand that you have a rather important role to play in the proceedings. Is that a duty of the King's Champion?'

'It should be carried out by the Duke of Ridden,' said Walter, 'but Hector's sons are too young. As the late duke's brother, the responsibility has fallen to me.'

The crowd in the hall hushed as Prince Valentino strode through the main doors with Princess Hygilt by his side. Ahead of them were four heralds, while behind walked two dozen imperial knights, their polished steel breastplates shining in the sunlight coming in through the gaps in the long colonnade. Valentino and Hygilt ascended the steps to the platform, and took their positions alongside Sebastian, while the knights spread out to flank the side walls.

'May I offer a formal apology for the lateness of our arrival?' said Valentino. 'My granddaughter took an age to get ready.'

Hygilt pulled a face. 'I did not.'

'You made it in time, Your Highness,' said Kilbride; 'there is nothing to apologise for.'

Valentino inclined his head a fraction. 'Might we have a few moments together after the ceremony? It appears that the paperwork for the treaty has been completed.'

Kilbride glanced at Walter.

'We are ready to sign if you are, Your Highness,' he said.

'Excellent,' said Valentino. 'With the treaty sealed, our business in Upper Down shall be at an end.'

The crowd hushed again as another door opened. Courtiers strode into the hall, followed by soldiers from the Royal Guard. In their midst was a boy and his mother, and they were escorted up onto the platform at the end of the hall. Alfie looked nervous as Frida led him to the century-old gilt throne. He sat upon it, and Frida joined Kilbride and the others.

Walter nodded to a young courtier, who was carrying a red cushion, upon which lay the crown of the realm. Walter stepped forward, and the courtier followed him towards the throne. Kilbride watched as they came to a halt in front of Alfie, and Walter smiled at the seven-year-old king.

'Alfgang of House Shiel,' Walter said, his voice ringing through the hall, 'do you solemnly swear to govern the citizens of the realm of Upper Down to the best of your ability and according to the law? Do you swear to temper your judgements with mercy and justice, and to rule and defend the lands of this realm with fairness, strength and wisdom, from this moment, until you join the spirits in death?'

Alfie looked out at the crowd as though awestruck. 'I do,' he said.

Frida stepped forward. She took a set of crimson robes from a courtier, and draped them over the young king's shoulders.

'You are doing well, son,' she whispered. 'I couldn't be prouder.'

Frida retreated to her place next to Kilbride, and the commander of the Royal Guards stepped forward. He bowed before the throne, then extended his arms, holding out King Alfgang the Great's sword of state. Alfie took it in both hands, and laid it across his lap. Walter then took the crown from the red cushion, and approached the throne.

He smiled down at Alfie again, then placed the crown on to the boy's brow.

Walter moved aside, and turned to face the crowd. 'Long live King Alfgang the Sixth!' he cried.

'Long live the king!' the crowd responded, their voices lifted to fill the hall.

A fanfare of trumpets sounded, and the crowd erupted in cheers.

'Mind you look after my boy,' Frida whispered to Kilbride, as a tear slid down her cheek.

Amid the cacophony of noise, Kilbride watched as Walter knelt before the throne, as the first to take the oath to their new monarch.

'We will, Frida,' she whispered.

Two hours later, after the nobility of Upper Down had each pledged their allegiance to the boy king, the Royal Court sat down with Valentino and his retinue in a smaller meeting hall. King Alfgang was sitting upon another throne at the head of a long table, and the three regents took their seats to his right, while the representatives of the Sanctian Empire sat down opposite them. At the far end of the hall, Amery was talking in hushed tones to the two lawyers that Valentino had brought up from the encampment in the ravine, then a few last minute alterations were made to two sheets of starched parchment. The twin documents were carried to the table, and Amery set them down between Kilbride and Valentino, along with a quill, a pot of ink, and a silver sand shaker.

Amery bowed to the boy king. 'Your Majesty,' he said, 'the treaty is ready for your regents to sign on your behalf. The treaty shall bind the realm of Upper Down to the Sanctian Empire in eternal friendship, and each will pledge to assist the other in times of trouble. Your Majesty, do you give assent for your regents to proceed?

'I do,' said Alfie.

Amery bowed, then he turned to the three regents. Kilbride picked up the quill, dipped it into the pot of ink, and signed her name at the bottom of the two copies of the treaty, followed by Walter and Abigone. Amery took the documents, and set them down in front of Valentino. The prince glanced over the words of the identical parchments, then he wrote his name next to the signatures of the three regents. Count Sebastian was the last to sign both documents, his name scrawled under that of the imperial prince.

Amery spread sand over the ink, then one of the copies was given to Valentino's lawyers, who rolled it up and placed it inside a pewter canister.

Valentino smiled, though his eyes remained distant, as though he had found the ceremony a little distasteful.

'I shall present our copy of the treaty to my most exalted brother upon my return to Sanctos,' he said, 'and then we shall see if it costs me my head. Count Sebastian, I now appoint you as imperial ambassador to the realm of Upper Down. Serve the Sanctian Empire as you have always done, with integrity and honour.'

'I shall, Your Highness,' said Sebastian.

Valentino turned back to the regents. 'When you are ready to do so, send an ambassador of your own to the imperial court in Sanctos, to represent the interests of Upper Down before the Most Exalted Emperor Antonio.' He paused. 'If I were you, I would wait a few months, so you can learn how this treaty is received in the imperial capital. When Sebastian's family arrive here, I will have them bear a letter from myself, to let you know how things stand.'

Valentino got to his feet, and the rest of his retinue, bar Sebastian, did the same.

'I will now return to the camp in the ravine, to prepare for our departure.' He gazed at the regents with his steely eyes. 'It has been a pleasure conducting business with you.' He turned to the throne, and inclined his head a fraction. 'Good day, Your Majesty.'

The prince swept from the hall, his courtiers, lawyers and guards escorting him out.

Sebastian turned his gaze to the regents sitting opposite him. 'I am not sure if any of you realise how painful this has been for the illustrious prince,' he said. 'He came here to conquer, and he is returning home with a piece of paper. But that's not the half of it. When the emperor understands that a Maker has been left here as one of the realm's three regents, there is no saying what His Imperial Majesty might do. Prince Valentino has taken a tremendous risk by signing a treaty with a nation that, only a few days ago, was a mortal enemy of the empire and its allies in the Central Provinces.'

Walter smiled. 'We will behave ourselves, if that's what you're getting at, Count.'

'We will adhere to the treaty in every regard,' said Kilbride. 'And you, Sebastian, will be here to witness.'

'The prince has recovered most of the cannon,' said Abigone. 'That will please the emperor.'

Sebastian shook his head. 'The illustrious prince will return with forty bashed and broken lumps of metal, Your Highness; and I can assure you that the emperor will not be pleased by the sight. However, what is done is done, and all three of you have played your roles in this turn of affairs. Princess Abigone, were it not for your Maker powers, it is likely that the realm of Upper Down would no longer exist. Similarly, if Lord Walter had not conducted the defence of Torrent with such vigour, the outcome would have been the same. And behind you both, the wisdom of Princess Kilbride has brought us to this juncture. Together, you have achieved much, but your troubles are only just beginning – you have saved your realm, and now you will have to rule it. I look forward to offering my counsel and guidance, but for now I would be satisfied with a drink, to toast our success.'

'You took the words out of my mouth, Ambassador,' said Walter.

They stood, and courtiers opened a few bottles of wine that had been placed onto a table at the rear of the hall. Frida escorted the boy king back to his rooms, as the others filled their glasses.

'To the new king,' said Walter, raising his glass.

'And to peace,' said Sebastian.

'And prosperity,' said Kilbride.

Abigone frowned. 'You took all the good ones,' she said. She lifted her glass. 'To a life without fear.'

Two days later, the three regents stood on a spot where the Kendril Wall had once crossed the ravine. Much of the rubble had been cleared away, and dozens of workers were repairing the cobbles of the large forecourt. The ruins of the gatehouse were the last reminder of what had once been, and teams of labourers had begun the job of dismantling it. A new tollbooth was being planned for the site, so that merchants and travellers could pay their way to enter Upper Down. Down in the ravine, the imperial army was marching south. The tents had been uprooted, and the mangled remains of the salvaged cannon had been loaded onto the back of a long line of wagons, and were being led down the road towards the frontier with Greater Down.

'They certainly made a mess of our valley,' said Abigone.

'I think a lot of the mess was caused by you,' said Walter. 'It will take months to remove all of the rubble you poured down onto the cannon.'

'Oh, I'm sorry,' said Abigone. 'Would you rather I hadn't done it?'

'Your eighteenth birthday isn't until tomorrow, Abbie,' he said. 'There's still time to remove your vote.'

Abigone laughed. 'You wouldn't dare. Tulip would never allow it.'

'Something else is happening tomorrow,' said Kilbride.

'And what's that?' said her sister.

'Your Maker lessons are due to begin.'

'On my birthday?'

'The sooner we start, the better.'

'But there is no one around to teach me,' Abigone said. 'Where are you going to find someone?'

'We have plenty of books.'

'Books? I'll never become a decent Maker if all I have are books. I need an old Maker to show me what to do.'

'Then I will begin the search for one. Until then, you will be reading for two hours each day in the palace library, followed by one hour of practice, and I will be there to make sure you do it.'

'Come on, Killie,' said Walter; 'could you let her enjoy her birthday first?'

'I shall consider it,' said Kilbride.

'You might not wear black any more,' said Abigone, 'but you're as mean as ever.'

Kilbride smiled. 'You have the rest of today to enjoy yourself before the work begins. I thought I was being generous.'

'Is there anything you want for your birthday?' said Walter.

'Not having to study would be nice,' she said. 'Maybe you could distract Kilbride for a few days.'

'And how would I do that?'

Abigone laughed at them both. 'Oh, I don't know. Perhaps you could start by telling her how you feel about her; and then maybe she might do the same. You must both think I'm stupid. I see the way you look at each other when you think the other person isn't watching. Right. I think I shall return to the palace, to savour my last day of freedom.'

Abigone smiled as she walked away, and Tulip glanced at Walter and Kilbride from her shoulder.

'What did she mean by that?' said Walter.

'Who knows?' said Kilbride. 'It's just Abigone being Abigone.'

There was an awkward silence for a few moments, then Kilbride gazed down into the ravine. 'Are you working with Count Sebastian again this evening?' she said. 'And by working, I mean drinking.'

'Sebastian is a wine drinker, and I feel it's my duty to educate him in the ways of beer and whisky.'

'Well, if you decide not to do that this evening, I thought it might be pleasant if we talked. We haven't talked in a while, not since the crisis ended. We could, perhaps, get some food. The weather has held up well this year, and we could have dinner out on my balcony. If you wanted to. It's up to you.'

Walter said nothing for a while, then he frowned. 'I have already told the count that I would meet him.'

'That's fine.'

'Sorry.'

'Think nothing of it, Walter. It was merely an idle suggestion. I think my carriage is ready; I can see Marie waiting for me. Goodbye.'

She strode away before the embarrassment could swallow her whole. She had told herself that she would try, and she had. If Walter chose to drink with his new friend rather than be with her, there was nothing she would do to stop him. She wondered if Walter had even realised what she had been suggesting. For an intelligent man, he could be surprisingly stupid at times.

Kilbride reached the line of waiting carriages, and smiled at Marie.

'It's over,' she said, as a soldier opened the side door of her carriage. 'Prince Valentino and his army are marching south. Let's go home.'

That evening, Kilbride decided to work for a few hours. She knew that the other two regents would be relaxing, but that didn't concern her. The crisis had left a mountain of neglected paperwork that needed sorting, and the public records had been muddled up while being moved back and forth from the Royal Palace.

Amery entered the study to deposit another box of documents onto her desk, and then Kilbride was left alone. She settled down in her chair, and was beginning to sift through the papers, when there was a knock at her door.

'If that's you, Amery, you can just come in; you don't need to knock.'

'It's not Amery,' said a voice.

Kilbride arose from her chair and walked to the front door. She opened it, and frowned.

'Walter?'

'Yes. It's me.'

'What do you want? I thought you were with Sebastian.'

'I told him there was something more important I had to do. Can I come in?'

'But I haven't ordered anything for dinner.'

He smiled at her. 'I don't care about the food, Killie. It's you I'm here to see.'

'Why have you changed your mind?'

'So much has happened in the last month,' he said. 'Your father, and brother; and my brother; Upper Down has been pulled inside out. And the responsibility... It's hard, knowing that our decisions affect so many people. Dravid is still on the loose up north somewhere, with his band of Westlanders, and...'

'I know all this, Walter.'

'But one thing hasn't changed,' he said. 'You, Killie. You are the most important person in my life, and I want... Well, I don't exactly know what I want, but if you let me in, then I could try to explain it to you. It could be the start of something. Is that what you want?'

'Let's just talk, and see where it leads.'

'I can do that. So, may I come in?'

Kilbride stood to the side, and Walter entered her apartment.

'Make yourself at home,' she said, then she smiled and closed the door.

AUTHOR'S NOTES

MAY 2024

Thank you for reading ***Fall Seldom Kings***, the first book of the Masters & Makers series. I don't think I have ever enjoyed the process of writing a book as much as I enjoyed drafting ***Fall Seldom Kings***. As a first book in a new series, I had no back stories, histories, or previous character development to worry about; I could just let it all flow out through my fingers and onto the keyboard. It was liberating, and I quickly fell in love with the new characters and the tiny realm of Upper Down. I have big plans for the Masters & Makers series, and ***Fall Seldom Kings*** is just the beginning.

I hope you enjoyed it.

JOIN MY NEWSLETTER

Building a relationship with my readers is very important to me. Join my newsletter for information on new books and deals and to keep up to date on my writing progress.

www.ChristopherMitchellBooks.com/Masters

ABOUT THE AUTHOR

Christopher Mitchell is the author of the Magelands and Masters & Makers fantasy series.

For more information:

www.christophermitchellbooks.com
info@christophermitchellbooks.com

Printed in Dunstable, United Kingdom

64120218R00272